LP FI
Mason,
Lionheart
03/03
W9-BUE-209

Lionheart

Also by Connie Mason in Large Print:

The Outlaws: Jess
The Outlaws: Rafe
The Outlaws: Sam
The Dragon Lord
The Rogue and the Hellion
To Love a Stranger
To Tame a Renegade
To Tempt a Rogue

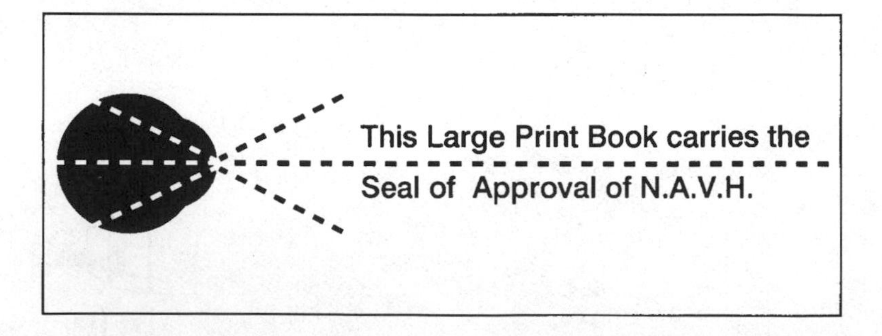

Lionheart

Connie Mason

Thorndike Press • Waterville, Maine

Published in 2003 by arrangement with Leisure Books,
a division of Dorchester Publishing Co., Inc.

Thorndike Press Large Print Basic Series.

The text of this Large Print edition is unabridged.
Other aspects of the book may vary from the original edition.

Set in 16 pt. Plantin by Ramona A. Watson.

Printed in the United States on permanent paper.

Library of Congress Cataloging-in-Publication Data

Mason, Connie.
Lionheart / Connie Mason.
p. cm.
ISBN 0-7862-5136-0 (lg. print : hc : alk. paper)
1. Wales — History — 1063–1284 — Fiction.
2. Knights and knighthood — Fiction.
3. Large type books. I. Title.
PS3563.A78786L5 2003
813′.54—dc21 2002042966

To Diane Stacy, Brooke Bornerman
and Alicia Condon.
I hope you know that your efforts on my behalf and on behalf of all Dorchester authors are very much appreciated.

Chapter One

Northeast Wales, 1258

The battlefield ran red with blood. Fighting under the banner of young Prince Edward of England, Lionel de Coeur, known as Lionheart throughout the realm, wielded his sword with strength and dexterity. The battle had been met near Cragdon Castle, long considered a stronghold of Llewelyn ap Guffydd, the prince of Gwynedd and leader of the rebellion now taking place in Prince Edward's Welsh lands.

The battle was fierce. Hand-to-hand combat was being waged in an all-out effort to decimate Llewelyn's forces. Prince Edward's army and Lionheart's forces had formed a pincer to prevent the Welsh prince's escape.

As abruptly as it had begun, the din died away to occasional groans and the cries of the dying. A blood-drenched sword clutched in his hand, Lionheart gazed across the battlefield and realized that the only men left standing were his own. The bulk of Llewelyn's forces had fled.

"Llewelyn has fled, Lionheart," his friend Giles de Clare reported.

Removing his helm, Lionheart turned his steely silver gaze upon Cragdon Castle, rising above the banks of River Clwyd. "As much as I would like to believe Llewelyn has fled to Snowdonia, I am more inclined to think he is licking his wounds in yon fortress. Lord Rhys of Cragdon has ever been Llewelyn's champion."

"Then we shall take the castle," Giles said with conviction.

"I am all for storming the castle, but we must await orders from Prince Edward. Gather up our dead and wounded and have them transported to Edward's fortress at Grantham." A frown touched his brow. "It angers me that Lord Edward has been offered no help from either the king or the marcher lords."

"Mayhap the power struggle between Simon de Montfort and the king concerns them more than Edward's Welsh lands."

"Aye," Lionheart said, removing his gauntlet and wiping the sweat from his forehead with the back of his hand. "Find my destrier, Alan," he commanded his squire.

Returning his gaze to the fortress,

Lionheart studied the ancient ramparts and battlements, wondering how long it would take to batter down the walls and gain entry. If Edward wanted the castle taken, Lionheart would not hesitate to launch an attack.

"The prince approaches," Giles cried, pointing toward a contingent of horsemen and foot soldiers pouring down from the surrounding hills and forest.

Clad in chain mail and a blue tabard bearing his coat of arms, the golden-haired prince was a handsome and splendid warrior. Taller than any man in England, he was affectionately dubbed Longshanks by those close to him. Edward and Lionheart were a contrast of light and dark. Where Edward was a powerful golden god even at his young age, Lionheart was just as impressive. Handsome in his own rugged way, dark, dangerous and dynamic, and nearly as tall as Edward, Lionheart was ten years older than the nineteen-year-old prince. Edward had been the first to call him Lionheart. During a battle in Gascony, Lionel had displayed uncommon courage, and the name Lionheart had stuck.

Mounted on his black destrier, Lionheart rode forth to meet Edward, aware that the prince's famous temper would explode when he learned Llewelyn had slipped through their trap.

"Tell me Llewelyn is lying dead on the field," Edward said without preamble.

"I wish I could," Lionheart replied. "I suspect he has taken refuge in Cragdon Castle with Lord Rhys."

"Blood of Christ, Lionheart! I refuse to be defeated by the prince of Gwynedd."

"I suggest we storm the castle and rout Llewelyn from his safe haven. Once Lord Rhys surrenders both Cragdon and Llewelyn, the rebellion will lose its teeth."

"Your advice, as always, is sound," Edward said. "Unfortunately, I cannot remain in Wales to lend support. You will be on your own. I am to meet with Simon de Montfort, my uncle by marriage, in ten days."

"Simon de Montfort is a man in search of power. He will try to woo you to his cause against your own father," Lionheart warned.

"I am well aware of that," Edward replied. "The barons are enraged at the king for appointing Frenchmen to high offices while neglecting his own English barons. They want him to sign the Provisions of Oxford, which sets up a council of barons to advise the king. So far their powers of persuasion have failed."

"Where do you stand?" Lionheart asked. "At first you favored Simon. Will you join forces with him and turn against your own father?"

"I will make no pact with Simon until I have studied all the ramifications."

"Simon wants to rule England," Lionheart cautioned.

"Make no mistake, my friend. I will rule England one day, not Simon de Montfort. 'Tis my God-given right. I will not let de Montfort seize power from me."

"I am your man, Lord Edward. No matter what you decide, I am with you."

The fury in Edward's eyes waned as he regarded his friend and staunch defender. "I know, Lionheart. If anyone can bring Llewelyn to heel, 'tis you. Dead or alive, it matters not. If he is not put down now, he will become a powerful enemy once I ascend the throne."

Weary from the fierce battle he had just fought, Lionheart squared his broad shoulders and gazed at the fortress, whose walls sheltered Edward's enemy. "Go meet with Simon, Edward. I have sufficient men at my command to storm the castle and seize Llewelyn."

"What do you know of Lord Rhys of Cragdon?" Edward asked.

"Little beyond the fact that he is a respected and powerful Welsh baron and a supporter of Llewelyn. I had heard he was ill, but have received no report of his death."

"The wily bastard is probably holed up in his stronghold, laughing at us and thinking he and Llewelyn are safe. I will leave you half my foot soldiers and knights to bolster your own forces, Lionheart. I must leave immediately, but I will not accept this defeat easily. Send word to me at Simon's demesne at Shrewsbury when the fortress falls. Should you succeed, I will be most grateful."

With the departure of young Edward Plantagenet, Lionheart returned his attention to the ramparts rising above Cragdon's walls. Sir Brandon, another of Edward's principal knights, broke away from a group of warriors and strode up to Lionheart.

"Did Edward leave orders?"

"Aye. We are to lay siege to Cragdon and capture Llewelyn. Pass the word. Instruct the men to make camp on the hillsides above the castle and post guards along the perimeter. We will begin our assault tomorrow."

"Aye, Lionheart," Brandon said, hurrying off to follow the orders. Suddenly he stopped and whipped around.

"Lionheart! Look! The castle's defenders are spilling through the portcullis."

"Muster our forces. If Lord Rhys wants to fight, we shall accommodate him."

Surprise etched Lionheart's features when he noted the large number of mounted knights and foot soldiers pouring forth from Cragdon. Obviously, Lord Rhys was a man of means, for his substantial forces appeared to be well armed. They were also well rested compared to his battle-fatigued forces.

His gaze narrowed on the knight riding at the forefront of Cragdon's men-at-arms, and an uneasy feeling clenched his gut. Wearing a white tabard trimmed in gold over his chain mail and a helm with the visor lowered, the slim knight sat tall and proud atop a pure white steed.

Giles de Clare sidled up beside Lionheart. "Lord Rhys's forces are formidable, but our own numbers are superior."

"Our men are tired and Rhys knows it," Lionheart observed. "He waited until Llewelyn's forces had done their worst before showing his strength, but we shall prevail."

"Think you the white-clad knight is Lord Rhys?" Giles asked.

Lionheart considered the knight in question. "Nay. Lord Rhys is a man with many years upon his shoulders. I have heard he is squat and sturdy, like most Welshmen. Yon white knight is young and slim and probably one of his sons. It matters not. He will be defeated. Give the signal, Giles. We will ride out to meet Cragdon's forces. If fortune favors us, we will find Llewelyn among them."

Raising Lionheart's standard of a rampant red lion on a field of blue, Alan followed as Lionheart charged into yet another battle in England's defense. The battle was met on the broad plain below the castle. Though his men were battle weary they acquitted themselves admirably. At first, Lord Rhys's forces appeared to be winning the day, but as the battle progressed, Lionheart's men began driving the defenders back toward the castle.

Wielding both sword and battle-ax, Lionheart kept his eye on the White Knight, noting that while his sword appeared lighter than Lionheart's broadsword, he lacked naught in skill. With a knowledge that stunned him, Lionheart realized he wanted the White Knight beneath his sword and at his mercy more than he wanted Llewelyn.

There was something about the way the White Knight carried himself that provoked him. His calm arrogance, his skillful handling of his weapons, his ability to lead his forces, all combined to make him a formidable foe. Determined to bring the White Knight down, Lionheart galloped toward the knight, who was handily dispatching one of his foot soldiers.

Suddenly the sun slipped below the hills, transforming the battlefield into a shadowy morass of men, horses and bodies. Lionheart could no longer tell the enemy from his own men. For a moment he lost sight of the White Knight. Then he saw him retreating behind the protective walls of Cragdon. Rage surged through Lionheart when the White Knight stopped, looked directly at him, and raised his sword in mock salute.

"We are not finished yet!" Lionheart roared across the distance. "Beware, for we will meet again!"

Wheeling his destrier, the White Knight galloped through the portcullis and disappeared behind the high walls of Cragdon.

"Bring me a count of our dead and

wounded," Lionheart barked as Giles rode up to join him. "We begin the siege tomorrow."

Aggravated beyond endurance and brimming with impatience, Lionheart stalked through camp, barely taking note of the activity going on around him. Trees had been felled for a battering ram, and stones were being piled up to feed the catapult that had been constructed during the first days of the siege. Newly built ladders were being made ready to scale the walls.

Twenty days had passed since Lord Rhys's warriors had ridden forth to engage Lionheart's forces in fierce battle and then retreated as suddenly as they had appeared. As aggravating as it was to Lionheart to wait out the enemy, he knew time was on his side. With all the people enclosed inside the castle walls, food must be in short supply.

Shading his eyes against the glare of the sun, Lionheart gazed up at the battlements, more than a little annoyed when he saw the White Knight among the warriors raining arrows down upon him and his men.

"The ladders are ready, Lionheart," Sir Brandon reported.

"We shall launch an attack on two fronts," Lionheart declared. "You and Giles take charge of the ladders while I direct the battering ram. I grow weary of this game Rhys is playing. Our siege machines have done considerable damage to the outer wall, but 'tis not enough."

"Their food supply cannot hold out much longer," Giles said.

"That depends on how much they had stored in advance. They should be feeling the pinch by now. Lack of food is a powerful deterrent to war."

Inside the fortress, Vanora of Cragdon sat in her father's carved chair, contemplating Cragdon's future. Without her father to direct the castle's defense, she was on her own. However, she considered herself more than capable of managing. Cragdon's defenders had learned just how capable she was during her father's long absences, and his death six months ago had changed naught. Cragdon still remained faithful to Llewelyn.

Llewelyn and her betrothed, Daffid ap Deverell, had escaped Prince Edward's advancing horde, and it had been due entirely to the diversion she had created.

Vanora prided herself on her ability to

lead Cragdon's warriors, but some things could not be helped. Like the shortage of food, or the fever that was fast spreading among the villeins and freemen who had taken refuge inside the keep.

Sir Ren, the captain of the guards, approached, a worried expression marring his craggy features. "My pardon, Vanora, but Lionheart, Edward's principal knight, is preparing to breach our walls. His men are setting ladders in place as we speak."

Vanora leapt to her feet. "God's bones, will this never end? How long can we survive with warriors such as Edward and Lionheart threatening our gates? How long can Llewelyn stand against such determined men? Llewelyn is our chosen leader and our only hope of remaining free of English oppression."

"The castle walls still hold, but the constant battering of stones have weakened them."

"Prepare the hot oil."

"Aye, but I doubt even that will stop them. They want Llewelyn. Though he has fled to safety, we must pay the price for his flight," Ren said sourly.

Vanora's shoulders stiffened. "Father trusted Llewelyn. He came to our assistance when we needed him. Prince Edward is but a young lad. He will not prevail."

"Young though he may be, he was wise to choose Lionheart to lead his army. Lionheart is a force to be reckoned with," Ren grumbled. "I must go. Should Lionheart break through our defenses, you must follow Llewelyn and Daffid and leave by way of the secret exit."

"I am not leaving," Vanora declared. "I will think of a way to foil Lionheart. No man is invincible."

Later, from atop the battlements, Vanora directed the archers, who used their longbows with typical Welsh skill and dexterity. But Vanora knew that skill alone would not win the day. Cragdon did not command the numbers Lionheart had available to him. The only thing that might save them was a surprise attack.

Closing her ears to the cries of the wounded, Vanora helped push ladders away from the battlements and watched men fall to their death. The constant thud of the battering ram below mingling with the cries of the wounded warned Vanora that she had deluded herself into thinking Cragdon was impregnable. If she did not do something soon, her people were doomed.

Had some of Llewelyn's warriors remained at Cragdon instead of scattering to the winds, the outcome might have been different. Vanora knew Llewelyn was too important to Wales to risk his life for Cragdon, so Father Caddoc had led him and Daffid to safety while she and her warriors kept Lionheart's men occupied. It did not sit well with her, however, that her betrothed had not remained behind to direct the castle's defense. Though Daffid had professed his concern, he had left with Llewelyn.

"Pull the men from the walls," Vanora ordered Sir Ren. "I want every available man in the outer bailey when the portcullis is breached. We will show Lionheart and Prince Edward that Cragdon cannot be taken without a fight."

"The portcullis cannot hold much longer," Lionheart shouted encouragingly. "Do not let up now. Cragdon and Llewelyn shall be ours."

Cheered by Lionheart's words, the warriors put their backs to their task. A great cry went up when the portcullis bent beneath their blows, then gave with a resounding crunch. Men on horses and foot soldiers poured through the opening. Lionheart, followed closely by Giles and his squire, galloped past the advancing horde, then pulled up short, his destrier pawing the air.

"God's nightgown! What is this?" He had expected to find Cragdon's defenders defeated and submissive, but such was not the case. The White Knight, flanked by Cragdon's warriors, looked anything but defeated.

"Surrender to me!" Lionheart shouted. "You are outnumbered."

The White Knight said naught as he stared at Lionheart through the narrow eye slit of his visor. So volatile was the knight's animosity that Lionheart could almost feel the heat of it. The only acknowledgment Lionheart received was a slight dipping of the knight's lance.

"There has been enough bloodshed," Lionheart continued. "Once you surrender Cragdon and deliver Llewelyn to me, the killing will cease."

Obviously, the White Knight was not about to surrender, Lionheart thought as he lowered his visor and prepared for battle. "The White Knight is mine," he growled to Giles. "Spread the word."

Then, drawing his sword, he charged. He slashed and hacked his way toward the arrogant White Knight, grinning at the pleasurable thought of his sword finding a vulnerable place in the knight's armor.

They met in a deafening clash of swords, fighting in quarters so close that their horses had difficulty maneuvering. Lionheart's strength was formidable, and he knew the slender knight must soon yield beneath his brutal onslaught. But even as Lionheart wielded his broadsword with deadly purpose, his wily opponent skillfully dodged his blows.

The White Knight moved with the speed of lightning. Whenever Lionheart aimed a lethal blow, the knight was not where Lionheart expected him to be, or else the blow was deflected by the knight's shield. Frustrated, Lionheart increased the savagery of his thrusts and finally landed a blow that nearly unseated the knight. But the knight recovered quickly and delivered an amazingly agile sword thrust that pierced Lionheart's mail at the shoulder. Blood welled, but Lionheart ignored the pain.

Putting all his strength behind the blow, Lionheart slashed out with his broadsword, and was heartened when he saw the White Knight sway beneath the impact. The savage in Lionheart took control as he pressed his advantage, hacking his way past the knight's defenses.

He is tiring, Lionheart thought jubilantly.

"They're falling back!" Sir Giles called from behind Lionheart.

"I will accept no less than total surrender," Lionheart shouted. "Did you hear that, Sir Knight? Surrender. Your army has been defeated."

A vicious blow to the White Knight's ribcage accompanied Lionheart's words. A grim smile stretched his lips when he saw the knight fall from his destrier and hit the ground. Lionheart would have dismounted and delivered a killing blow had not two of Cragdon's defenders come up behind him, forcing him to divert his attention from the knight in order to protect himself. Giles joined in the melee, and Cragdon's men-at-arms were soon subdued. But when Lionheart returned to the place where the White Knight had fallen, his foe was gone.

Cursing violently, Lionheart vowed vengeance on the devil that had caused him and his men so much trouble. Had Cragdon's men not interfered, Llewelyn would not have escaped. But the tide was turning. Lionheart's army had surrounded Cragdon's knights, and one by one they were surrendering their weapons. The battle was won. Once his victorious army entered Cragdon, both the White Knight and Llewelyn would be his for the taking. He would deliver Llewelyn to Edward, but the White Knight would be Lionheart's to do with as he saw fit.

"To the keep!" Lionheart shouted. "Victory is ours!"

"Foolish girl," the old nursemaid clucked as she lifted the helm from Vanora's head. A wealth of rich sable hair tumbled over Vanora's shoulders, spilling down to her waist. "Had Alun and Moren not risked their lives so you could be carried from the battlefield to safety, you would be dead," Mair continued. "Lionheart was determined to slay you."

Vanora winced when Mair tugged the chain mail over her head. Her ribs ached and every part of her body felt bruised. Tomorrow there would be no place on her that was not black and blue.

Mair's dumpling face creased in concern. "What is the matter, lambie? Where do you hurt?"

"Everywhere," Vanora said with a gasp. "But mostly my ribs. That foul English bastard has the strength of an ox."

"You should have never taken on Lionheart. He is a man without mercy. You could have been killed."

"I had no choice. Had I not intervened, Llewelyn and Daffid would not have escaped. I am as well trained as any of Cragdon's warriors, and capable of holding my own against any man. My men depend upon me to lead them."

"Your father was remiss in his duty toward you, Vanora. He should not have treated you like the son he wanted but did not have."

Vanora gulped back her tears. "Father was proud of my accomplishments. I wanted to be strong for him. He knew I was capable of protecting Cragdon in his absence."

"Your father is dead, Vanora. 'Tis time you acted like the woman you are and not the son your father wanted. Think you Lionheart will take pity on you when he learns your interference allowed Llewelyn to escape? Cragdon has fallen. Lionheart can do what he wants with us and no one will say him nay. He can slay our entire garrison, should he wish it. Thank God he does not know he was fighting a woman. Wounding a man's pride can be dangerous."

Vanora's confidence was unwavering.

"My people will not betray me. They are loyal to Cragdon."

When Vanora lifted her arms so Mair could slip her dress over her head, the pain made her stagger and nearly pass out. Mair helped her to a bench, wagging her head in dismay.

"You may have broken ribs, lambie. Bide here while I find strips of cloth to bind them."

"Hurry, Mair. Lionheart will enter the keep soon, and I must be on hand to greet him. I am not going to hide like a coward. I am the lady of the keep. I need to be in the hall to speak for my people when Lionheart arrives."

"You will be lucky to be standing on your feet," Mair muttered as she hurried from the chamber.

A triumphant Lionheart entered the keep a few steps ahead of Sir Brandon and Sir Giles. He paused just inside the wide oaken doors and glanced around the hall, his steely gaze sweeping over knots of people clinging together with fearful looks on their faces. He saw naught to indicate danger or opposition; nor did he see Lord Rhys, or Llewelyn, or the White Knight.

"Where is your master?" Lionheart asked

in a voice that resounded loudly throughout the large hall. "Where is Lord Rhys?"

His words were met with blank stares. Few could speak or understand English, and those who did were not forthcoming.

"You, there," Lionheart said, pointing to an elderly knight whose clothing proclaimed him a man of some importance. "Come forward."

The man slowly approached Lionheart.

"Can you understand me? Do you know who I am?"

"Aye, Sir Lionheart, we all know who you are."

"Who are you?"

"I am Sir Penryn, Cragdon's steward."

"Where is Lord Rhys? Is he too cowardly to face me?"

"Lord Rhys is dead. He passed to his reward last winter."

Lionheart was stunned. Without Rhys leading them, how could Cragdon's defenders have launched the attack that had cost lives, time and wasted effort? Then it occurred to him that Rhys's sons must have defended the castle.

"How many sons does Lord Rhys have, and where are they?"

"Lord Rhys was not blessed with sons, Sir Lionheart."

"Who was the knight leading your garrison? The one clad in white and gold."

A blank look settled over Penryn's face. "I know not of whom you speak."

"Do you not?" Lionheart asked with deceptive calm. "Forget the knight for a moment. 'Tis Llewelyn I want. Where have you hidden the cowardly Black Wolf of Snowdon?"

"Llewelyn is no coward," Sir Penryn said.

An ominous scowl darkened Lionheart's face. Grasping Penryn's tunic in both hands, he jerked him forward until they stood nose to nose. "Do not play games with me. If Llewelyn does not present himself immediately, your life is forfeit."

"Sir Penryn speaks the truth. Llewelyn is not here."

The female voice rang with authority. Lionheart dropped Penryn and whipped around, his face a mask of fury.

"Who are you?"

The maiden was tall, taller than most women he knew, and pleasingly formed. Her gleaming sable hair, held in place by a jeweled circlet, was parted in the middle and tumbled over her shoulders and down to her waist in glossy waves. Her scarlet wool undertunic with long fitted sleeves that hugged her shapely arms was worn beneath a dark blue gown and girdled at her impossibly tiny waist.

Looking him in the eye, she said, "I am Vanora of Cragdon."

Her voice, while melodious, held a note of confidence. Her stance was confrontational and her gaze unwavering, not at all like the women he was accustomed to dealing with. She lacked the modesty, the downcast eyes, and the submissiveness one expected from an unwed maiden.

"Who is in charge of Cragdon?"

Vanora drew herself up to her full height. "That would be me, Sir Lionheart."

"Are you Lord Rhys's daughter?"

"Aye."

"Your steward informed me that your father is dead. Is that true?"

"Aye."

"Have you brothers?"

"Nay."

"Who is the knight who led your men in battle?"

Vanora shrugged. "Cragdon has many knights."

Lionheart's patience dangled by a slim thread. He was unaccustomed to being thwarted, and never by a mere wench. Apparently, her father had been too lenient and she had assumed a male's authority. He was going to enjoy putting her in her place.

"Do not lie to me, lady. I saw the knight with my own eyes. We crossed swords on the battlefield, and I felled him."

Vanora remained stubbornly silent.

Grinding his teeth in frustration, Lionheart said, "Very well, have it your way. I shall learn his name myself. Produce Llewelyn now and spare yourself my wrath."

Momentarily distracted by her beauty, Lionheart noted her unusual violet eyes, pert nose and lush mouth. Her skin was as finely wrought as porcelain, and her face, while memorable, was set in stubborn lines. His avid gaze followed the generous curve of her breasts and continued over slim hips and downward, imagining her long legs entwined with his as they writhed naked on a bed of furs. He couldn't recall when he had seen a woman as tall or with such a commanding presence as Vanora of Cragdon.

"Did Sir Penryn not tell you? Llewelyn is not here."

Lionheart sent her a look that would have felled a lesser woman. Vanora merely stared back, which served to increase his anger.

Lionheart summoned Giles with a glance. "I want the castle, outbuildings and stables searched from top to bottom." To Sir Brandon, he ordered, "Bring the prisoners into the hall for questioning. Men do not disappear into thin air."

Outwardly composed, Vanora seethed inwardly at Lionheart's arrogance. He might be Prince Edward's principal knight but to the Welsh he was naught but an unwelcome intruder who threatened their land and their people. No Welshman worth his salt liked Englishmen, for they were determined to subdue the Welsh and seize their lands.

While Lionheart issued orders, Vanora silently observed him. Grudgingly she admitted that the man was a handsome brute. Dark and dangerous, he was reputed to be a man without compassion, one who demanded complete obedience. He was tall, broad and powerful, and his visage hinted at dark passions and hidden tempests. What drove this knight called Lionheart? she wondered.

Vanora suffered a moment of anxiety when Lionheart questioned Cragdon's warriors. Much to her relief, they all denied knowledge of the knight he referred to as the White Knight. Nor did they reveal what they knew about Llewelyn's disappearance. Lionheart must have realized he had naught to gain from continuing the questioning and ordered her men taken to the tower and confined under lock and key. Silently Vanora vowed they would not remain there long.

"It seems, wench," Lionheart said after the prisoners were led away, "that you are not the only one determined to defy me. All you Welsh dwelling on Prince Edward's lands are a rebellious lot."

"Cragdon does not belong to Edward. Cragdon and the land upon which it was built belonged to my father and now to me."

"Once you gave sanctuary to Llewelyn, Cragdon became fair game. I claim it for Prince Edward and England, Vanora of Cragdon."

"I am *Lady* Vanora to you," Vanora said calmly but clearly.

"Very well, *my lady,* so be it. Escort me to the solar. Since my squire is occupied elsewhere, you may help me disrobe and bathe."

Vanora's chin rose defiantly. "I am not a servant."

Fixing his steely gaze on her, Lionheart said, "You will be anything I desire you to be."

Chapter Two

"Prepare hot water for a bath and food for my men and me," Lionheart ordered a nearby servant as he nudged Vanora toward the stone staircase.

Her lovely face set in defiant lines, Vanora preceded Lionheart up the stairs and along the gallery to the solar. She could hear his heavy tread behind her and wondered what he would do to her once they were alone. She had heard that Englishmen were brutal beasts who took what they wanted without a care for their victims. Although the English brute had shown no sexual interest in her, she thanked God that she was not a helpless female incapable of defending herself.

Vanora opened the door to the solar and stepped inside. Lionheart followed close on her heels. She watched him warily as his silver gaze roamed over the large chamber and its furnishings. Everything was just the way her father had left it six months before. Vanora had not claimed it for herself, for the chamber held too many memories.

"Your father lived well," Lionheart said with a hint of sarcasm. "Cragdon will make an excellent addition to Edward's Welsh holdings."

"Surely you do not intend to remain long at Cragdon," Vanora returned, aghast at the thought.

"I intend to headquarter here until Llewelyn is brought to heel or I am sent elsewhere by Edward. I am weary. Help me remove my armor."

He held up his arms, his expression harsh with impatience. Vanora moved cautiously, wary of the Englishman who had just claimed her castle and lands for his prince. Grasping his mail shirt, she tugged it upward, but despite her own height, he was so tall she had difficulty pulling it over his head.

Growling in impatience, he pushed her aside and finished the task himself, and as he did so, his hand inadvertently scraped along her rib cage. A jolt of pain shot through her and she bit her tongue to keep from crying out. Unaware of her distress, Lionheart removed his mail shirt and gambeson and tossed them aside.

Then he lowered himself to a bench and held out his right foot. "Remove my boot."

Vanora wanted to tell him to go to the

devil, but caution prevailed. She feared Lionheart would take revenge on her people if she were belligerent. Grasping his foot, she tugged with all her strength, but the boot refused to budge. Then suddenly it gave, and she sprawled on her backside, the boot in her hand and her skirts flying up past her knees.

Vanora was not prepared for the onslaught of pain and she doubled over into a fetal position, clutching her ribs and rocking back and forth.

"God's nightgown!" Lionheart cried. "What is wrong with you? I've never known a woman with such a tender backside."

With a snort of disgust, he pulled off his remaining boot himself. Then he stood and rolled his chausses down his legs.

"Nay!" Vanora cried, turning her face away.

Lionheart paused, his chausses halfway down his muscular legs. "What is wrong now?"

"You cannot disrobe until I am gone."

"Have you never seen an unclothed man before?"

"Nay, never. I am a maiden," Vanora said over the debilitating pain still gripping her.

"You are pale. Are you ill?" She shook

her head. "Have you injured yourself?"

Vanora thought a moment before deciding to placate him with half-truths. "I took a spill recently and may have broken a rib or two."

His silver eyes took on a speculative glow. "Shall I wrap them for you?"

Holding her side, she rose slowly, maintaining a safe distance. "Nay. Mair has seen to it."

"Who is Mair?"

"My tiring woman. She is skilled in the art of healing."

"Then mayhap you should summon her to see to my wound. 'Tis naught but a scratch, but wounds have a tendency to fester and go putrid."

A knock on the door forestalled further conversation. Lionheart gave permission to enter. Two men rolled a large wooden tub inside the chamber and set it before the hearth. A procession of servants followed, bearing buckets of hot water. When the tub was full, Lionheart dismissed everyone. But when Vanora attempted to leave with the servants, he stayed her with a harsh command.

"Nay! You will remain here and bathe me."

Vanora stiffened when he removed his

chausses, fearing to look yet unable not to. Had he no shame? A surreptitious glance showed her that Lionheart was magnificent in his nakedness. Naught in her imagination had prepared her for the darkly chiseled lines of his face or the powerfully cut ridges and planes of his warrior's body. He was hard and strong and sleek, like the lion for which he was named. For a brief, insane moment she wondered what it would feel like to have his arms wrapped tightly around her, to feel the width of his hard chest pressed against her soft breasts, to feel his mouth against hers.

Vanora conquered her madness and regained her wits when Lionheart stepped into the tub and settled down into the water.

"You can start with my back," he said, handing her the washcloth.

Vanora snatched up the cloth, applied soap and moved behind him. Then she began to scrub.

Lionheart was more aware of Vanora than he had led her to believe. The moment she set the cloth to his flesh, he felt his cock harden and his ballocks tighten, and realized it had been a long time since he had tasted a woman's sweet passion.

When Vanora passed the cloth over his

wound, he caught his breath. "Careful, woman!"

"Did you not say it was insignificant?" Vanora asked sweetly.

"Would you like me to show you something that is *not* insignificant?" Lionheart taunted as he caught her hand and brought it down to his groin.

Vanora recoiled in shock. Beneath her hand his flesh was hard as steel yet sleek as velvet. Being a maiden, she had not been required to help bathe her father's guests and had never seen, much less felt, the male organ, but pride would not allow Lionheart's blatant masculinity to intimidate her.

Forcing a smile, she curled her fingers around his erection and announced in a bored voice, "You are overly vain if you think *that* impresses me. What is remarkable to some is less noteworthy to others."

Lionheart's dark brows slanted upward. "Perhaps you would like me to demonstrate what my less-than-remarkable cock can do."

Vanora pulled her hand away and would have fled had he not grabbed a handful of her gown and held her in place.

"You have not finished bathing me."

Vanora opened her mouth to fling back a

scathing retort but was forestalled when the door crashed open and a man, his brown robes flapping around his scrawny ankles, sailed inside, his keen blue eyes ablaze with righteous fury.

"I came as fast as I could, Vanora. When I heard the Englishman had dragged you to the solar, I feared the worst. Take your hands off her, Sir Lionheart."

"Who are you?" Lionheart's tone of voice sent fear racing through Vanora. "Father Caddoc means no harm," she cried, flying to the priest's defense.

"Do not defend me, Vanora," Father Caddoc said, patting Vanora's shoulder. "I am but doing God's work."

"God's work?" Lionheart questioned. "Pray tell what enjoyment of one's bath has to do with God."

Drawing his meager frame up to his less-than-impressive height, Father Caddoc thinned his mouth in disapproval. "You will not dishonor Vanora, sir. She is betrothed to a brave Welsh warrior."

Lionheart's dark gaze searched the far corners of the chamber. Contempt colored his words. "Where was the 'brave Welsh warrior' when Vanora needed him to defend Cragdon?"

Father Caddoc darted a glance at

Vanora, then said, "He is with —"

"Father!" Vanora cried. "Mind your tongue. Do not provide information to the enemy."

With a jolt of insight, Lionheart believed he had uncovered the White Knight's identity. He was Vanora's betrothed. An unexplained fury seized him.

"Where is he?"

Vanora gave him an innocent stare. "Who?"

"Your betrothed. He is the one who led Cragdon's warriors, the one wearing the white and gold tabard, is he not?"

Vanora's smile was far too smug for Lionheart's liking.

"Nay, he is not."

"She speaks the truth," Father Caddoc confirmed.

Lionheart surged to his feet, water dripping from his powerful form as he stepped out of the tub. "May God forgive you your lies, priest, for I will not," he growled. "Men do not disappear into thin air. Fetch the healer to stitch my wound, and send Sir Giles to me."

Father Caddoc stared at Lionheart's naked, scarred body a long, thoughtful moment, then said, "I will not leave Vanora alone with you."

"I said go!" Lionheart roared.

When Father Caddoc hesitated, Vanora said, "Fear not, Father, I shall be fine."

With a compassionate glance at Vanora, he turned and fled. Vanora attempted to follow, but Lionheart stopped her with a single word.

"Stay. I did not give you permission to leave, lady."

Two long steps brought him close enough to touch her. Reaching out, he spun her around to face him. She tried not to look at anything but his chest, but her wayward gaze wanted to stray to more interesting areas of his anatomy, although his chest was certainly memorable. Dark ringlets swirled around his flat male nipples. The sculpted ridges of muscle were marred by numerous scars and nicks. Her gaze took in the extraordinary width of his shoulders, then wandered down his bulging biceps to his large hands.

From there it seemed only natural to drop her gaze to that part of him that proved his masculinity. He was in full arousal, erect and hard and rampant. Her breath caught in her throat, and she returned her startled gaze to his face, where a modicum of safety lay. Their gazes clashed with the force of a volcanic eruption.

"Have you looked your fill?" Lionheart asked. "How do I compare with your betrothed?"

Refusing to be cowed, Vanora swallowed her embarrassment and glared at him. "I was not staring. Besides," she said, forcing her gaze downward to his groin, "you have naught to be proud of."

The taunt must not have set well with Lionheart, for Vanora could almost feel the unrelenting heat of his anger sweep over her. His hands tightened on her shoulders, but she struggled free and backed away.

"I will see what is keeping Mair. Your wound needs tending."

"I am here," Mair said from the doorway. Such was their preoccupation with one another that neither Lionheart nor Vanora had heard the tiring woman enter.

Vanora was the first to react. Putting distance between herself and Lionheart, she retreated to relative safety behind Mair's comfortable bulk. "Sir Lionheart needs your attention, Mair. He has suffered an 'insignificant' wound that is in need of stitching."

Hands on ample hips, Mair let her contemptuous gaze sweep over Lionheart's nude body. "Cover yourself, Sir Lionheart," she rebuked. " 'Tis not right that you should bare yourself before my mistress. Have you no shame?"

Vanora's brows lifted in surprise when Lionheart grabbed the towel from the bench and wrapped it around his loins. "Do you not fear me, woman?"

Mair's gaze slid down his body. "I am an old woman; I fear no man. You may bare your 'weapon' to *me,* but I will not allow you to shame Vanora. I fear not what you may do to me but what you intend to do to my lady. Vanora is an innocent, and not for the likes of you to despoil. Now sit you down and let me get on with my stitching. Fetch the medicine chest from yon cupboard, Vanora."

Vanora acted with alacrity, removing the chest with its precious contents from the cupboard where it was kept and placing it on the bench within Mair's reach. Mair probed Lionheart's wound with a fingertip, then wiped away the blood with a soft cloth.

"Thread the needle, Vanora," Mair ordered.

Vanora opened the chest, found a needle and pushed a fine silk thread through the eye. Then she handed it to Mair.

"Brace yourself, Sir Lionheart," Mair

warned as she took the first stitch.

Vanora observed Lionheart from beneath lowered lids as Mair stitched. His expression did not change, nor did he flinch as the needle slid through his flesh, closing the gaping wound on his shoulder. If he felt pain, she saw no sign of it. The man was not human, she thought with a hint of disgust.

"Finished," Mair said as she tied off the knot. "Smear some of that marigold salve on his wound whilst I prepare a bandage, Vanora."

Vanora dipped a finger into a small pot of salve and applied it to Lionheart's wound. She felt his muscles contract beneath her touch, and a jolt of awareness tingled up her arm. He must have felt it too, for he grasped her wrist to stop the sensual slide of her fingers over his skin.

"Enough," he growled. "My squire will help me dress. I'm sure you have duties elsewhere. My men and I are famished. The meal can be simple, but we will require something more substantial later."

Vanora nearly laughed in his face. There was not enough food in the keep to feed her own men, much less Lionheart's. "Where, pray tell, am I supposed to find the food to feed your army? Our stores were depleted during the siege."

Sir Giles chose that moment to present himself to Lionheart. He rapped once on the door, then entered. Seizing the opportunity, Vanora fled through the opening.

"The priest said you wanted me," Giles said.

"Aye. Has Llewelyn been found?"

"Nay. Doubtless he has fled into the mountains, where we are unfamiliar with the territory. Sir Brandon has taken out a patrol to search the area."

"I need to send a message to Edward immediately. He should be informed that we have taken Cragdon. Meanwhile, I will make my headquarters here. There is a problem, however. The stores on hand are inadequate and cannot feed our numbers. As soon as I dress, I will instruct the villeins as to their duty to supply the keep with food. Gardens and orchards should be at their peak this time of year."

"Good luck," Giles said. "Cragdon's people look like a sullen lot to me, little better than the uncivilized savages that pour down from the hills to harass our marcher barons."

Lionheart mulled over Giles's words as he descended the stairs to the hall. Welshmen did not like the English, but Edward was determined to unite Wales and England once he became king, and when Edward made up his mind to something, he was unstoppable.

A hush followed Lionheart's entrance into the crowded hall; the hostility was palpable. He strode to the dais and waited until he had everyone's attention before speaking in a voice that rang with authority.

"People of Cragdon, heed me. I claim Cragdon and all it encompasses in the name of Prince Edward of England."

A nervous stirring followed his announcement.

"Naught will change. You will be allowed to return to your homes unharmed and you will still belong to Cragdon. Due to the long siege, the keep is in desperate need of food. Go home, harvest your crops, and bring the produce and livestock you owe in tithes to the keep as you have always done. I intend to send out huntsmen, but beef, lamb and pork will be tasty additions to wild game. I pledge that no man, woman or child shall go hungry during the coming winter."

A sea of sullen faces stared back at Lionheart. Then the truth dawned on him. They did not understand his words. His discovery was confirmed when Vanora approached him and said, "Few of my people understand English, Sir Lionheart."

"Translate for me," Lionheart ordered. "Make them understand that no one will be harmed if my orders are obeyed."

Lionheart could understand some Welsh and listened carefully to make sure Vanora was relaying his words correctly. He had decided before entering Cragdon that keeping his limited knowledge of Welsh a secret would serve him better than admitting he could understand what was being said about him.

Vanora finished her translation and turned to Lionheart. "Is that all? Are they free to return to their homes now?"

"Aye, but I shall expect to see food arriving at the castle very soon."

Once Vanora translated his message, the crofters gathered their children and belongings and began to file out of the hall. Vanora would have followed, but Lionheart ordered her to remain.

"My stomach is touching my backbone. When can we expect a meal?"

"There is naught in the larder but oats. Do you fancy gruel, Sir Lionheart?"

Lionheart's stomach clenched. "We need meat to fill our bellies."

He hailed Sir Osgood, one of his knights. "Has Sir Brandon returned?"

"Nay, Lionheart. He is still out with his patrol."

"We need food, but there is naught here for us. Organize a hunting party. Game should be plentiful this time of year. Mayhap you will come across some of the livestock the farmers hid away in the woods when they fled to the keep."

Osgood left immediately to carry out Lionheart's orders.

"What about the warriors imprisoned in the tower?" Vanora asked. "Will they be provided with food and water?"

"Aye. When we eat, they eat."

"What is going to happen to them?"

"They will be given the opportunity to join Edward's army."

Vanora gave an unladylike snort. "That will never happen. My people are loyal to Wales and Llewelyn."

"And to you," Lionheart added.

Vanora bristled. "My father charged them with my protection during his long absences from home. Serving in Edward's army would betray both Father and Cragdon. Do not expect them to deny their heritage."

"Cragdon belongs to England now.

Mayhap they will accept my offer of amnesty for practical reasons."

"We shall see," Vanora replied.

Lionheart watched Vanora walk away. Her head was held high and her shoulders were squared, emphasizing her unusual height. He could not help admiring her indomitable spirit, though he did so against his better judgment.

Vanora's vibrant beauty and curvaceous form pleased him. His mind conjured a vision of her long legs wrapped around him as he thrust into her heated center. That heady thought captured his imagination. Her temperament bespoke a passionate nature, and he wanted to be the first to unleash it.

Vanora was the complete opposite of the leman he kept at the village of Dunsford, near one of Edward's estates where they often stayed. Althea, the village innkeeper's daughter, was small, dainty and submissive, yet passionate and responsive to his needs. Lionheart was more than satisfied with her and visited Dunsford whenever he was able.

He felt no compulsion to wed. His parents' marriage had been disastrous. His mother had produced the required heir and promptly left his father's bed and home. Lionheart had no idea where she was and did not care. His father had told him his mother had taken a lover and abandoned him when he was still in leading strings. He had neither seen nor heard from her since and could not even recall what she looked like. Dimly he remembered a soft voice and comforting arms, but beyond that, memory failed.

Though his father, Lord Robert, was an earl and one of King Henry's courtiers, he drank and gambled to excess and had been forced to sell his poor and badly managed lands to pay his debts. At the age of seven, Lionheart had been fostered; he had seen little of his father since, which was fine with him.

Lionheart had first met young Edward when they were both fostered with Simon de Montfort. Ten years older than the prince, Lionheart had become Edward's protector even then. If not for young Edward's friendship, Lionheart would have been forced to sell his services to the highest bidder after earning his spurs. He had accompanied Edward to France, and when Edward had been given his own household, the young prince had asked Lionheart to remain in his service.

Turning his thoughts in another direction, Lionheart went in search of Cragdon's steward. He was still undecided whether or not he should replace Sir Penryn with one of his own men; nor was he sure Penryn would accept if the position was offered to him. He found the steward in a small chamber that served as the castle office.

"I suppose you intend to replace me with one of your own men," Penryn said, as if reading his mind.

"That depends on whether or not you are willing to serve Prince Edward," Lionheart said.

"Sir Penryn is faithful to Cragdon," Vanora said from the doorway. "He will serve neither Prince Edward nor you."

Lionheart spun on his heel, frowning when he saw the determined look on Vanora's face. "Why not let Penryn speak for himself? If he is faithful to Cragdon, then he will want the estate to prosper. It can only do so with an experienced steward at its helm. What say you, Penryn? Will you remain as Cragdon's steward until Edward decides otherwise?"

"He will not!" Vanora persisted.

"Vanora, you are not thinking clearly," Penryn cautioned. "Lionheart has claimed Cragdon for England, but what if Llewelyn succeeds in winning it back? You want your land returned to you in good condition, do you not?"

"That will not happen," Lionheart said with conviction. "Cragdon is firmly in English hands."

"My father would turn over in his grave if he knew his people were serving England's prince," Vanora said.

"Your father is dead," Penryn reminded her. "We do what we must to survive."

"Listen to Penryn," Lionheart said. "He is older and wiser than you. You can best serve your people by cooperating. Naught will change for them under English rule. They will still till your fields, harvest your crops, care for your livestock and pay their tithes. The only difference is that the tithes now belong to Prince Edward."

"I will continue my duties as steward, if you will have me," Penryn allowed. "I have served Cragdon too long to see it wither and die for lack of direction. I know you are a warrior and cannot remain to see to Cragdon's welfare, so I shall do it because 'tis my home and I love the land upon which Cragdon stands."

"You will not be sorry, Sir Penryn," Lionheart said. "Please prepare a complete inventory of Cragdon's assets, including stores and money. Edward will want to know the value of the great prize I have won for him."

"There is no money," Vanora insisted. "We produce everything we need to survive."

Lionheart's dark brows rose in disbelief. "Surely there are funds to purchase that which the land does not produce. Do you make your own pots and farm tools? Grow your own spices? I think not, yet I am sure you own such items. Do not lie to me, Vanora."

"I told you, there is no coin."

Lionheart stared at her a long moment, then said, "Very well, if that is the way you want it. I can be stubborn, too. One of your men will be executed for each day you refuse to turn over Cragdon's assets, starting with Sir Ren."

Penryn protested vigorously. "Vanora, your stubbornness will gain us naught. If you do not give over Cragdon's monies to Lionheart, I will."

"There is a cache of gold and silver coins in Father's war chest. You'll find it in the solar," Vanora spat. "Sir Penryn is right. The life of a Welshman is more valuable than any possession."

"Leave us, Sir Penryn," Lionheart commanded.

Penryn bowed stiffly and left the chamber. Vanora rounded on Lionheart the moment Penryn was out of hearing.

"Only an animal would execute men in cold blood. Your name alone tells me what you are capable of. You can have the gold and silver, but Cragdon is mine. Once I wed Daffid ap Deverell, he will become lord of the keep."

"Daffid ap Deverell shall not have you," Lionheart bit out. *Now, why had he said that?* "Prince Edward will decide your fate. Mayhap he will wed you to one of his trusted lieutenants. What say you to that, Vanora of Cragdon?"

"I will kill any Englishman who attempts to touch me," Vanora vowed.

Laughter rumbled from Lionheart's chest. "A simple Welsh maiden is no match for an English warrior. Think you your betrothed has the ballocks to fight for you?"

"Daffid will fight for Cragdon; 'tis his right to protect what will be his when we wed."

With the sleek grace of a predator, Lionheart stalked toward Vanora. She retreated, her eyes spitting defiance. He did not stop his pursuit of her until she was backed up against the wall.

"Your defiance does not please me," he said. And because he wanted to put her in her place, or mayhap because her lips looked so tempting and he could not resist a challenge, he raised her chin with the tip of his forefinger and kissed her.

Her lips were sweetly provocative; she tasted of defiance, of unleashed passion, of challenge. Even as her body stiffened, her lips opened beneath his prodding tongue. Grasping her face between his hands, he deepened the kiss, savoring her fully, exploring the warm cavern of her mouth with his tongue. A groan rumbled in his throat. His ballocks were full and aching; he wanted this feisty Welshwoman in his bed for however long he remained at Cragdon.

Vanora's senses were reeling. Lionheart's mouth and tongue were making a shambles of her self-control. Never had she felt anything as earth-shattering as Lionheart's kiss. It was her first kiss and not at all what she had expected. Would it have been the same with Daffid?

Though Vanora knew Lionheart was using his mouth as a tool to subjugate her to his will, she realized he was enjoying himself. Her own pleasure in the unwanted kiss stunned her. His kiss was demanding, yet surprisingly gentle. He could have thrown her skirts over her head and taken her without her consent had he wanted to, and she thanked her Maker that he did not.

When his hands left her face and slid down her back to her waist, she tried to push him away, but he was an immovable force despite her own considerable strength. He adjusted his weight, leaning his chest against hers, making her aware of his erection. With strength born of desperation, she broke off the kiss. "Nay, do not dishonor me."

He gave her a lopsided grin. "Most women do not consider themselves dishonored by my attention."

"This one does."

"It has been a long time since I have had a woman. There is no greater pleasure, except for the thrill of battle, of course. Has your 'brave' Welshman bedded you yet?"

"When I wed Daffid, I intend to go to him as pure as the day I was born," Vanora vowed.

"Do not count on it, my lady," Lionheart mocked. "Should I desire you, you will come to me and no one shall say me nay."

"Then I shall make certain you do not desire me, sir knight. Touch me again and I will run you through with my father's sword. I will not submit willingly."

She scooted away. Laughing, he reached for her and hauled her into his arms. "I am beginning to enjoy this, vixen. 'Tis a game you cannot win, however much you try."

"We shall see," Vanora returned, spinning away.

His laughter followed her as she fled. Was there nowhere in the keep she would be safe from him? She could leave, should she choose to. Escape through the secret exit was always possible. Unfortunately, she had not the heart to desert her people. If she left, there would be no one to protect them from Lionheart.

There was something she could do, however. She could arrange an escape for the warriors imprisoned in the tower. With that thought in mind, Vanora hurried to the kitchen to help prepare a meal for her enemy.

Lionheart shook his head in dismay. Whatever had possessed him to kiss Vanora? He had always taken great pride in his ability to control his sexual urges, but Vanora had broken through his reserve with little effort. His groin still ached and his body was rock hard. One day, he vowed, he would have Vanora on her back, with her legs open for his pleasure and her arms welcoming him.

Chapter Three

The hunting party bagged enough fresh game to feed everyone in the keep. A satisfactory meal was served that evening, and Lionheart went to bed with a full stomach. He had taken the solar for his own use and after securing the keep for the night, he retired with every intention of sleeping well in Lord Rhys's comfortable bed.

The night, however, proved anything but restful. Not only did Vanora haunt his dreams, but also did the mysterious knight whose identity remained a well-guarded secret.

The church bell had just tolled the hour of Prime when Lionheart awoke the following morning, his mood as dark as his thoughts. He washed and dressed and went down to the hall to break his fast. Only a few early risers were about, but Lionheart's spirits lifted when a serving woman appeared from the kitchen and placed a cup of cider, fresh bread and sliced cheese before him and quickly retreated.

Sir Brandon joined him and helped himself to bread and cheese.

"The prisoners are becoming fractious, Lionheart. We cannot keep them in the tower forever."

"I intend to speak to them after I break my fast. Mayhap I will let the mercenaries leave if they pledge fealty to Prince Edward."

"Think you they will agree?"

Lionheart shrugged. "What choice do they have? If they accept my offer of amnesty, they can sell their services elsewhere."

"My warriors will not swear fealty to you," Vanora said from behind Lionheart.

"Lady Vanora," Brandon said, rising. "Will you join us?"

"Nay, I broke my fast in the kitchen. I wish a private word with Sir Lionheart."

Brandon bowed and took himself off.

"Be ready to accompany me to the tower after I have spoken with Vanora," Lionheart called after him.

Vanora blanched. "What are your plans for my guardsmen? What must I do to save them?"

A slow smile stretched Lionheart's lips. How far was Vanora willing to go to save the lives of her men? he wondered. No time like the present to find out.

"Sit you down, my lady, while we discuss terms," he said.

Vanora stiffened. "Terms? I know not what you mean."

"Do you not? I will spare your warriors' lives in return for your cooperation."

"How must I cooperate? You have robbed me of everything I own. I have naught with which to barter."

A lustful gleam lit Lionheart's eyes. "How much of yourself are you willing to give to save the lives of those you claim to care for?"

The violet of Vanora's eyes darkened with understanding. "Speak plainly, sir knight. Tell me what you want of me."

His gaze slid down her body in bold regard. "I think you know what I want. Give yourself to me, and I will spare your men."

"What you are suggesting is sinful and immoral!" Father Caddoc cried from where he stood not two feet away from them. "Do not listen to him, Vanora."

Lionheart sent the priest a disgruntled look. "Every time I turn around, either you, Mair or Vanora is lurking about. Go away, priest. I would speak privately with Vanora."

"Nay. I am Vanora's confessor. 'Tis I

who absolve her of her sins and I who must protect her virtue. She does not need one such as you leading her astray."

Lionheart turned his steely gaze on Vanora. "Does Father Caddoc speak for you, Vanora? You know the consequences of your refusal, do you not?"

"Please leave us, Father. I am old enough to make my own decisions."

"Vanora, listen to reason," the priest pleaded.

Vanora pulled the priest aside and spoke to him in a voice meant for his ears alone. "Many lives depend upon Lionheart's goodwill," she whispered. "I promise not to do anything rash. Think you I want to surrender myself to Lionheart? I have a plan that will save both my virtue and my men."

"Ahhh," Father Caddoc said. "I should have known. Very well, I will leave you to placate Lionheart as best you can."

"What did you tell him?" Lionheart asked when the priest withdrew. "I trust neither of you."

"I told him I am old enough to make my own decisions," Vanora replied.

Lionheart's brows lifted. "Does that mean I will have you in my bed tonight?"

"It means I will think about it. Meanwhile, you must vow to do naught to my men until I reach a decision. In return for your restraint, I promise to give your request serious thought."

Lionheart settled back in his chair and stared at Vanora. He had not thought to gain so great a concession from her. His eyes narrowed. Something was not right. Vanora liked him not. She would never agree to become his leman unless she had some mischief in mind. It suddenly occurred to him that she was bargaining for time to plot against him. Stifling a grin, Lionheart considered himself up to the challenge of curtailing whatever mischief one insignificant Welsh maiden could cause.

"I will give you a sennight to make up your mind. But consider carefully, lady, for many lives depend upon your answer. When I want something, I usually get it."

Vanora's eyes widened. "You would force me?"

His gaze raked over her with lustful intent. "I vow there will be no force involved when I take you to my bed."

Vanora inhaled sharply. "Your arrogance appalls me, sir. Not all women find you irresistible. I, for one, find you presumptuous, overbearing and contemptible. If you will excuse me, duty calls."

Chuckling to himself, Lionheart did not try to stop Vanora as she strode off. The stiffness of her lithe form betrayed her outrage, but Lionheart could not help admiring her spirit. She did not walk with the mincing steps of a woman; nay, her stride was long and confident, as if she knew her strength and took pride in it. She would bear watching closely, he decided, for, given the chance, she would make a fool of him.

While Lionheart hated to admit it, Vanora's defiance was arousing. Women rarely, if ever, defied him, and most men thought twice before doing so. Whether she realized it or not, Vanora's passionate nature was apparent in her every word and deed, in the way she carried herself and in the proud tilt of her chin. That brand of fiery temperament was rare in a woman. He wanted to plumb the depths of her passion.

Sir Brandon interrupted Lionheart's introspection. "Are you ready to speak to the prisoners now?"

"Aye. How many guards have you posted in the tower?"

"Two above and two below."

The conversation halted when Alan appeared, bearing Lionheart's weapons. Lionheart strapped on his broadsword, then nodded to indicate that he was ready to speak to the prisoners. As he followed Brandon up the winding tower staircase, the two sentries at the bottom fell into step behind them.

"Unlock the door," Lionheart ordered when he reached the top landing. One of the sentries produced a key from his belt and fitted it into the lock. The door swung inward, and Lionheart stepped inside.

The prisoners surged forward. Immediately the guardsmen drew their swords and pushed them back. The air was fetid and thick with the stench of unwashed bodies and human waste. Lionheart was willing to bet that after two days of confinement, the prisoners would agree to whatever terms he offered.

"Have you decided our fate, Sir Lionheart?" asked Sir Ren, Vanora's captain of the guard. "Are we to be executed?"

Recalling his promise to Vanora, Lionheart said, "That depends. How many mercenaries serve the castle?"

"Half our numbers are mercenaries, some English, some Welsh, some foreign," Ren replied. "The rest of us are Welshmen pledged to serve Sir Rhys's daughter."

"To the mercenaries I offer amnesty in return for their fealty to Prince Edward," Lionheart said. "They are free to serve another lord if they so desire."

A hush fell over the prisoners as each man considered the offer and what it meant to him in terms of monetary and personal gain. Mercenaries usually cared not to whom they sold their services as long as they were paid. At length, one man stepped forward, dropped to his knee before Lionheart and swore fealty. One by one, others followed, until all the mercenaries had pledged themselves to Lionheart.

"Sir Brandon, give these men their arms and horses and escort them to the portcullis."

"You are deserting Cragdon and Lady Vanora," Ren cried as the warriors filed through the door.

"Knights fight when and where they are paid to do so," Lionheart said. "Cragdon no longer belongs to Lady Vanora, nor does she possess the coin to pay her mercenaries. You judge them too harshly, Sir Ren. Even Penryn has seen the wisdom in serving Edward. He will carry on at Cragdon as Edward's steward.

"As for Cragdon's Welsh defenders,"

Lionheart continued, "I offer no terms. Edward will decide your fate. He may be inclined toward leniency if you decide to swear fealty to him."

"We are sworn to protect our lady," Ren replied.

"So be it. You shall remain prisoners until Prince Edward returns and decides your fate," Lionheart continued. He turned to leave.

"Can you not find more hospitable quarters for us?" Ren asked. "We lack bathing facilities and are not allowed to visit the garderobe. We are forced to make do with buckets."

"Prisoners do not make demands," Lionheart said harshly, "but mayhap I will take your request into consideration if you reveal the identity of the knight who led the battle against my forces."

" 'Twas I," Ren said.

Lionheart raked him with a contemptuous glare. "Think you I am stupid? If you refuse to reveal the knight's identity, mayhap you would be more inclined to tell me if the castle has a secret exit."

Ren's lips remained tightly clamped.

"Very well, so be it. I shall find the knight without your help and search for the exit myself."

So saying, he exited the chamber, leaving the disgruntled Welshmen to mull over his words.

Vanora had no idea that half of Cragdon's defenders had pledged themselves to the enemy, but even if she had known, it would have changed naught. She had but a sennight to find a way to free her loyal warriors. Should she fail, she would have no recourse but to become Lionheart's leman and destroy her hope of marrying Daffid ap Deverell, for she refused to go to her betrothed soiled by an Englishman.

Damn all Englishmen! Damn Lionheart!

The following days were a trial for Vanora. Lionheart's dark, intent gaze seemed to follow her everywhere. Though she tried to avoid him, their paths seemed to cross far too often for her liking. The only peaceful moments she had were when he went hunting or joined his men on patrol, or when she hid from him in her chamber.

Vanora had to admit that the castle was running smoothly, but a good deal of the credit went to Penryn, who had the ability to hold her people together. Though she wished it otherwise, rebellion was not feasible with the castle's defenders imprisoned in the tower. Regrettably, Vanora's plan to free the prisoners had been shot down by Father Caddoc. He had insisted it was too dangerous.

Vanora would not give up, but time was running out for her.

One day Lionheart cornered her in the gallery. A thin beam of waning daylight streaming through the high arched window slanted across half of his face, painting it with harsh strokes, delineating the aggressive thrust of his chin and the gleaming silver of his narrowed gaze. The other half remained in brooding darkness.

"Have you been avoiding me?" he asked harshly.

"I am surprised you noticed," Vanora shot back.

He crowded her against the cold stone wall. "I notice everything about you. Have you come to a decision yet?"

"You gave me a sennight."

"Why do you refuse to accept the inevitable? I will settle for no less than total surrender. Your protectors cannot help you, and your mercenaries have abandoned you."

"You lie!"

"I speak the truth. There are but a

handful of stubborn Welsh knights remaining in the tower. The others were wise enough to accept my terms. They chose life over death."

"Damn you!" She tried to maneuver away, but his hard body blocked her retreat.

"Not so fast," he growled. "Mayhap you need a sample of the pleasure to be had in my bed."

Grabbing her about the waist, he pulled her to him for a hard, thorough kiss. She struggled against him, keeping her mouth firmly closed as he tried to pry it open with his tongue. Then he urged her hips against his, forcing her to feel his arousal, and to her utter shame her hips surged forward against his erection. When she realized what was happening, her resolve grew firmer and she stomped on his foot with her heel.

Laughing, he broke off the kiss. "You cannot hurt me, vixen."

With the supreme confidence of a man accustomed to getting his way, Lionheart's mouth claimed hers again. This time he showed no mercy, forcing her mouth open and stabbing his tongue inside. He kissed her like a lover instead of an enemy, hot and deep, his hands sliding down to cup her buttocks and mold her against the bulge straining his chausses.

Trying a different tactic, Vanora bit down on his lip, hard. It worked. He reared back, roaring in outrage. "Bloodthirsty wench! Yield to me."

"Never!" Her words rang hollow. How could one sound decisive when one's legs had just been reduced to a boneless, quivering mass of jelly by a man bent on seduction?

"We shall see, Vanora," he said with typical male arrogance.

Then the insolent devil continued on his way.

Vanora sagged against the wall, left weak and trembling by the encounter. God help her. What if she failed to find a way to free her men? The alternatives were unpalatable. She would either be forced to abandon them or give herself to the English devil.

But a niggling little voice inside her head whispered of buried feelings that had never been awakened until Lionheart had kissed her and touched her.

Vanora knelt in the chapel, praying for guidance. She had remained on her knees so long that dampness had seeped into her bones and her legs were trembling with fatigue. She was waiting for Father Caddoc to return from the village, where he had gone to pray at the bedside of a woman stricken with childbed fever. She was determined to wait however long it took for the priest to return. Lionheart's assault upon her senses made her realize he was more dangerous to her than she had thought before.

"Vanora, what are you doing up so late?" Father Caddoc said from the doorway. He hurried over to join her, his knees creaking when he knelt beside her. "Are you ill?"

"I had to speak with you, Father," Vanora began. "About the plan we discussed earlier."

"Nay, child, 'tis too dangerous."

"Dangerous or not, I am committed to saving my men." She looked down at her hands, refusing to meet the priest's eyes. "Time is running out. If I do not act soon, I will be forced to yield to Lionheart in order to save the lives of our brave Welsh knights."

"I will pray on it."

" 'Tis not enough."

"What if Lionheart does not take the bait?"

"He wants the warrior he calls the White

Knight almost as much as he wants me. God willing, he will not have either."

The priest's eyes lowered with resignation. "What do you want me to do?"

"Help me don my armor. I intend to leave through the exit behind the altar, fetch my horse from the village, and remain hidden until morning. Then I will present myself outside the castle walls until I attract the attention of the guards on the parapet."

"I fear for your life, child."

"Nay, Father, I shall be fine. Once I draw Lionheart's attention, he will empty the castle of warriors to give chase. They do not know these lands as I do. I shall lead them into the mountains, then disappear into one of the numerous caves. The rest will be up to you and Mair. Think you can release the men from the tower?"

"How do we get past the sentries?"

"Mair will tell them about the appearance of the White Knight at their portal and lure them to the battlements to watch. While she is distracting them, you can lift the key from the guard."

"I like it not, Vanora. Lionheart is not stupid. He will suspect trickery."

"He wants that knight as badly as he wants Llewelyn. Naught will go wrong."

"Pray God you are right," Father Caddoc said fervently.

"I will need more than your prayers if I am to succeed. Help me don my chain mail."

Father Caddoc accompanied her to a small chamber behind the altar that held a variety of religious articles. He opened a storage chest, pushed the robes aside and removed Vanora's chain mail, chausses, sword and white tabard. The priest left her while she removed her gown and donned the armor and returned after she was dressed.

"Your destrier is still stabled behind the village blacksmith shop," Father Caddoc said. "One of the stable lads caught it and took it away before the gates were secured by Lionheart's forces."

"I know. Mair told me. 'Twas her grandson who took Baron to the village. Drem is taking good care of him for me. I am ready, Father. Open the door."

The priest touched a panel behind the altar, and a door leading to a passageway to the riverbank sprang open. From there it was an easy walk to the village. Vanora planned to bide her time until morning, then show herself to Lionheart's men.

Father Caddoc lifted a torch from a wall

sconce and handed it to Vanora. "You will need a light to see your way. Take the torch and leave it at the entrance of the cave for when you return. I shall pray for our success."

"Thank you, Father. Meet Mair in the hall at Prime tomorrow. I shall show myself to Lionheart's sentries shortly after daylight. You both know what you are to do." She placed her helm on her head and ducked through the opening.

"God go with you," Father Caddoc whispered as Vanora disappeared down the passage.

Lionheart tossed and turned most of the night. He heard the church bells ring Compline and then Matins, but for some reason his mind was troubled and he could not sleep. Warning bells jangled in his brain, and his senses tingled with awareness. Yet he could find naught amiss. The prisoners were secure, and Vanora was safe in her bed where she could do no mischief.

Mayhap that was what was wrong with him. He wanted Vanora in *his* bed. It would not be long now, he thought smugly. His threat to execute her guardsmen would bring her to his bed very soon. He had given her little choice in the matter. When he wanted something, he went after it with a single-mindedness that usually got him what he desired.

He could order Vanora to his bed if he wanted, but using force gave him no pleasure. He liked his women submissive and willing. The thought of Vanora submitting willingly brought a snort of laughter to his lips. The vixen was too proud and independent, but he was confident that once he had her in his bed, he could make her want him. The thought of an eager, warm and passionate Vanora brought a surge of hot blood to his loins. If he did not have the vixen in his bed soon, an erection would become a permanent part of his anatomy.

Lionheart dozed off and on until the sound of the church bells tolling Prime awakened him. Stretching, he rose to begin his day. He had just finished washing himself when Giles burst into the chamber, his excitement palpable.

"He is here! The audacity of the bastard boggles the mind. You must come and see for yourself."

"Take a breath, Giles, and tell me what you are talking about. Who is here?"

"*Him!* The White Knight! He rode up to the gate at first light as bold as you please.

The guards on the parapet saw him first and alerted the garrison."

Lionheart poked his head out the door and yelled for Alan. The lad appeared moments later, out of breath and flushed with excitement.

"I saw him!" Alan crowed. "Him and that great white steed of his."

"Help me with my armor, lad," Lionheart bit out.

Alan hastened to obey. "Is he alone, Giles?" Lionheart asked in a muffled voice as Alan pulled his mail shirt over his head.

"Aye," Giles replied, "but Llewelyn's army could be hiding in the hills, waiting for the White Knight to lure us out."

Lionheart grabbed his sword and strode from the chamber. "I want to see the bastard for myself before I decide what action to take."

Lionheart sprinted up the winding stone staircase to the parapet and peered over the edge. What he saw sent shards of rage racing through him. Clad in his distinctive white and gold tabard, his mail and helm gleaming beneath the rising sun, the knight, mounted on his snowy white steed, was gazing upward. When he saw Lionheart, he raised his sword in a gesture of defiant challenge.

"The bastard!" Lionheart spat.

"What do you suppose he wants?" Giles asked.

" 'Tis obvious. He is challenging me."

"Methinks he will lead us into a trap if we give chase."

"Mayhap he will lead us straight to Llewelyn," Lionheart mused. " 'Tis what we want, is it not? We have been looking for the Black Wolf of Snowdon since we arrived in Wales. A confrontation with him is what we have been training for these long weeks. We shall let the renegade knight lead us to him."

"Aye," Giles agreed. "The men are eager for a good fight."

"Alert the garrison," Lionheart ordered. "Leave two men behind in the gatehouse. Under no circumstance is the portcullis to be raised during our absence. And assign two sentries to guard the prisoners in the tower. The rest are to muster in the courtyard in full battle gear.

"Prepare to die!" Lionheart yelled down to the White Knight. "When we meet in battle, only one of us will walk away!"

A short time later, the portcullis was raised and Lionheart rode through at the head of his impressive army. When the White Knight was absolutely certain of being followed, he raised his sword to his helm in a mocking salute and galloped off toward the distant hills.

Lionheart bit back a curse. The white steed was fast, and the knight seemed to know exactly where he was going. Lionheart kept him in his sights as he galloped steadily upward into the hills. Keeping track of the knight was difficult once they reached the dense woods, but Lionheart's determination did not waver.

"Keep your eyes peeled for an ambush," he warned his lieutenants.

The ambush never materialized. Instead, the knight led the patrol higher and higher, plunging ever deeper into the thick forest. Lionheart had just crested the hill when the knight suddenly disappeared. Assuming that the knave had plunged down the opposite side of the hill, Lionheart led his warriors down the steep incline. When they reached the bottom, Lionheart knew he had been tricked. But to what end?

For what reason had the knight lured them from the keep?

Lionheart's patrol had already ridden off when Mair and Father Caddoc made their way to the tower. Each carried a pail of fresh water.

"What have you there?" asked Sir Osgood, one of the two guards left behind.

"Water for the prisoners," Father Caddoc replied.

"What was all that commotion in the bailey?" inquired the second guard, a mercenary named Fenwood.

"Did you not know?" Mair said in feigned excitement. "The mystery knight Lionheart has been seeking appeared outside the walls shortly after Prime. Lionheart mustered his forces and gave chase."

"God's nightgown, I wish I were with them," Fenwood muttered. "The knight will lead our forces straight to Llewelyn."

"Mayhap you could watch from the battlements," Mair suggested slyly.

The guards exchanged speaking glances. "Leave the water," Sir Osgood ordered. "We will take it in to the prisoners when we return."

As Father Caddoc set down the pail, he accidentally bumped into Fenwood. "God forgive me," he muttered beneath his breath as he handily lifted the key from Fenwood's belt.

Eager to observe the action from the battlements, both guards bounded up the staircase, leaving the priest and Mair behind.

“Do you have it?” Mair hissed.

“Aye,” Father Caddoc said, producing the key from his black cassock.

He fitted the key in the lock and pushed the door open. “Father Caddoc! What are you doing here?” Ren asked when he saw the priest standing in the open doorway. “Where are the guards?”

Mair peered from behind the priest. “Hurry. There is no time to lose. Down the stairs with you and to the chapel.”

The dirty, bearded men poured out of the chamber and clambered down the stairs. Mair held her nose and flinched as they passed but valiantly stood watch until the last man had slipped past her.

Then Father Caddoc locked the door, handed the key to Mair, and fled below with the men. Mair climbed the stairs to the battlements on trembling legs and approached the guards.

“Do you see anything, Sir Osgood?” Mair asked innocently.

“Nay. They must be well into yon woods by now.”

Mair turned to leave, pretended to turn her ankle, and leaned heavily into Fenwood, grasping his tunic for support. With a flick of the wrist she returned the key, wedging it into his belt.

"Here now, are you all right?" Fenwood asked, reaching out to steady her.

"Aye, thank you." Bobbing a curtsey, she hurried off.

" 'Tis done," Mair said when she reached the chapel. "They might suspect but they have no proof. Pray that our lady returns unharmed."

Mair watched anxiously as the last Welshmen fled through the passage behind the altar. Once they reached the riverbank, they would be free to join Llewelyn's forces or return to their homes. Father Caddoc closed the door and breathed a sigh of relief.

"Return to the keep, Mair. I will wait here for Vanora."

Vanora left her steed with Drem and made her way to the river, creeping along the steep bank until she reached the cave. She made sure no one was following, then ducked inside, removed the torch from the sconce, and returned to the chapel. Father Caddoc was waiting for her when she reappeared from behind the altar.

"Thank God," the priest said fervently. "Did all go as planned?"

"Aye, all went well. By the grace of God, your knights escaped through the tunnel,"

Father Caddoc said as he lifted her helm from her head and returned it to the chest.

Together they divested her of her chain mail. While Vanora changed into her gown, the priest put away her armor and sword and arranged the robes to hide them.

"Come, child, we will pray together. Methinks you will need all the help you can get when Lionheart returns."

Vanora was still on her knees in the chapel when Lionheart burst in. His black look did not bode well for her.

"So there you are," he growled. "I have been looking for you. I suppose you know what happened. The White Knight led us on a wild chase into the hills. Then he disappeared. Did you have a hand in this? Was there a reason my men and I were lured from the castle?"

"I have not left the keep; you cannot blame me for something I knew naught about," Vanora said sweetly.

"Did you not?" Lionheart said uncertainly. "Be assured that I will not rest until I have the bastard at my mercy. Pray for his eternal soul, lady, for his days are numbered."

The words had scarcely left Lionheart's mouth when Sir Brandon ran into the chapel and skidded to a halt before him.

"The prisoners are gone, Lionheart! Every last one of them."

His face a mask of fury, Lionheart rounded on Vanora. "What have you done?"

Chapter Four

Vanora took a deep breath to still her racing heart. "What did *I* do? I was nowhere near the tower. Ask the guards if you do not believe me."

"I intend to," Lionheart said with deceptive calm. "Stay where you are. I will deal with you after I get to the bottom of this."

He stormed from the chapel, and for a long time Vanora could do naught but stare at the place where he had stood. Dread created a hollow feeling in the pit of her stomach.

What would Lionheart do to her?

Fear that he would blame Father Caddoc, Mair and ultimately her for releasing the prisoners weighed heavily on her. Lionheart was a harsh man. Had her rash act placed the lives of the two people she loved most in jeopardy? Though she knew Lionheart's mercy would not extend to her, she wanted to . . . had to believe he would not hurt her friends.

"He is angry, child," Father Caddoc warned. "You had best escape now while you have the chance. You may not find another."

"Mayhap you are right, Father. You and Mair must come with me."

"I will stay," the priest maintained. "I am a man of God; he can do naught to me. But you and Mair must go. I will find her and bring her to you."

"Aye, Father, you are wiser than I. My knights are gone and cannot be punished for what I have done. 'Tis time for me to leave. I will find Llewelyn and Daffid."

Father Caddoc hurried off to fetch Mair. Vanora knelt to pray for her safe journey. Unfortunately, Lionheart appeared with Sir Giles at that very moment.

Hands on hips, his face contorted in fury, he roared, "How did you do it?"

"I . . . did naught."

"Do not lie, vixen. You sent the White Knight to lure me from the keep, then released the prisoners while I was gone." He held out his hand, palm up. "The spare key to the tower room — give it to me."

"There is no spare key. I went nowhere near the tower. Did your guards not tell you?"

"Aye, but men do not disappear into thin air. I was told your priest and tiring woman brought water for the prisoners this morn."

Father Caddoc and Mair entered the chapel in time to hear Lionheart's words. "Vanora knows naught," the priest maintained.

Lionheart turned his icy glare on the priest and Vanora's tiring woman. "Explain to me how you released the prisoners," he ordered harshly. "I know Vanora put you up to it, so do not try to tell me otherwise."

" 'Twas a miracle," Father Caddoc said, lifting his eyes heavenward. "Your guards were in the gatehouse. How could anyone leave the castle without their knowledge?"

"That is what I want to know. If my men were remiss in their duty, I will see them punished."

Vanora sent a warning glance to the priest. Apparently, the guards in the tower feared to admit they had left their post, however briefly. Lionheart's justice would be swift and fierce should he find out.

"We know naught," the priest repeated. "We carried water to the tower and left."

"Where was Vanora during this time?"

"In her chamber."

Lionheart's stern gaze found Vanora. Unflinchingly she returned his gaze.

"Did you not see the White Knight at our gate?"

"Nay, my chamber faces the river. I saw naught."

"Am I to believe the prisoners flew out the window?"

" 'Tis as good an explanation as any."

"Giles!" Lionheart roared. "Take Lady Vanora to the solar and lock her inside. We shall see if she can fly out the window." To Vanora, he said, "We will continue this conversation later."

"Do not hurt her, Sir Lionheart," Mair pleaded.

"Unless your mistress tells me the truth," Lionheart bit out, "I can make no promises, for she has sorely tried my patience."

"Come, my lady," Giles said, taking her arm and urging her from the chapel.

"I shall go with Vanora," Mair said.

"Nay, you will not!" Lionheart roared. "Not until I solve this mystery. I do not believe in miracles."

"Perhaps you should," Father Caddoc replied dryly.

When word got out about the prisoners' miraculous escape, Lionheart's men began crossing themselves and muttering about witches and spells. Lionheart was at a loss. Four trusted men had been left behind, two in the gatehouse and two in the tower, and the gatekeepers swore that the portcullis had not been raised during his absence. The prisoners could not have gotten past them without being seen. If he were not a rational man, he might believe it was a miracle.

But since he was a rational man, the only explanation was a tunnel. All castles had them, for they provided an escape route during times of siege. With that thought in mind, he placed Sir Brandon in charge of finding another way in and out of the keep.

'Twas nearly time to sup when Lionheart's anger finally eased enough for him to confront Vanora. He climbed the stairs to the solar, unlocked the door and entered the chamber. His glittering gaze found Vanora sitting in the window seat. She stiffened when she saw him but did not flinch as he stalked toward her.

"Do your worst, sir knight. I fear you not."

His eyes held a wicked gleam. "Perhaps you should. Are you prepared to tell me how the prisoners escaped?"

"I know not." Her gaze flew to his belt. "Will you beat me?"

"I find beatings ineffectual when dealing with women. Does the keep have a secret tunnel?"

Her eyes widened, but her voice held steady. "If there is one, Father neglected to inform me."

Grasping her shoulders, he pulled her to her feet.

The color drained from her face. "What are you going to do?"

There were many things Lionheart wanted to do to her. Press her down onto the bed, cover her with his body and thrust his cock into her warm center. He tried to summon his earlier anger but could not. Though no proof showed that Vanora had released the prisoners, common sense suggested she was guilty.

"Naught, if you tell the truth." He stared at her lips. How could a mouth so lush and inviting spew lies so easily? A jolt of lust stiffened his loins.

His fingers tightened on her shoulders, and against his better judgment he lowered his mouth to hers. He kissed her ravenously, his mouth hot and demanding, his hands sliding down her body to her curvy bottom, pressing her against his hardening loins. He knew by her reaction that she had felt his erection and he deepened the kiss, prodding her mouth open with the bold thrust of his tongue.

What Lionheart had intended to be

punishment soon turned into something totally unexpected: *He enjoyed kissing her too much.* Relished holding her soft body against his. Despite her resistance, he could tell his kisses did not repel her by the way her mouth softened, by the way her body arched. No, this was definitely not punishment. This was pleasure. Pleasure he never expected to find in remote Wales.

Vanora was the essence of the country in which she lived: wild, untamed, savage in her beliefs and strong of body and will. God help him, he wanted her. A low growl escaped his throat as he began tearing off her clothing. He had managed to remove her overtunic before Vanora found the strength to resist.

"What are you doing?"

"Giving us what we both want," Lionheart growled as he dragged her toward the bed.

"Is rape to be my punishment?"

Lionheart went still. "Rape? I am a knight and do not take my vows lightly. I have never resorted to rape to get what I wanted. Women clamor for my attention."

Vanora sniffed. "Not this woman. Release me, sir knight."

"Deny it all you wish, but your body tells me you are not immune to my attentions."

"I am saving myself for Daffid, my betrothed," Vanora said, breaking free and backing away.

"He will never have you!" The vehemence of his words startled him. One day soon he would leave Cragdon and never return. What Vanora did after he left should not concern him. It was up to Edward to decide Cragdon's fate, and ultimately Vanora's, so why was he so adamantly opposed to Vanora's marriage?

"Come to me, and I shall put in a good word for you with Edward."

"Edward is in England," Vanora replied. "Much could happen before your prince arrives. Mayhap Llewelyn will wrest Cragdon from you."

Lionheart laughed. " 'Tis highly unlikely, vixen." He stalked toward her, crowding her against the bed. "I can make you want me with little effort. Shall I show you how easy it would be to coax you into my bed?"

Vanora retreated until the bed was at her back and she could go no farther. She feared this man, not his strength or his temper, but his ability to make her forget he was her enemy. His kisses were a potent drug that rendered her helpless, and his penetrating silver gaze delved too deeply into her soul.

Her chin notched upward. She did not want Lionheart. 'Twas Daffid she wanted. All Englishmen were beasts who raped her homeland as Lionheart would rape her. Her thoughts skidded to a halt when Lionheart pressed her backward onto the bed. She fell in a heap of twisted skirts and bared limbs. Then Lionheart was atop her, his body crushing hers into the furs and his mouth seeking the lush softness of her lips.

His hand slid up the outside of her leg, hot, hard, seeking. She shivered when his hand turned inward, skimming along the inside of her thigh, climbing higher, ever higher, until he reached a place where no man had dared to venture.

"Nay!"

"Why do you tremble?" Lionheart asked. "Has your betrothed never touched you like this?"

"Nay! He would not dare."

"Then I shall be the first," he whispered in a voice taut with desire.

He touched her then, his fingers sifting through the soft curls at the apex of her thighs to reach her moist inner folds. She gasped and tried to slap his hand away, but he merely laughed and slipped a finger inside her cleft, sliding deep on the dewy moisture he found there. She was so sensitive to his touch that she bucked beneath him and bit her bottom lip to keep from crying out.

"Stop!"

"Am I hurting you?"

Vanora felt no pain, just a longing that could easily become pleasure should she give in to it. Lying about her feelings seemed the best course at the moment.

"Aye, you are hurting me."

"Liar."

His finger retreated, then slid deeper, exploring the warm honey of her sheath. Without her volition, a moan slipped past her lips. She felt tender and swollen. The sensation, while foreign, was not unpleasant. The only thing offensive about the caress was the man himself. Willing or nay, if she did not stop his assault now, she would become another victim of Lionheart's lust.

Marshaling her strength, she doubled her fist and rammed it into his stomach. The breath left him in a whoosh and he reared back, his eyes wide with disbelief.

"You struck me!"

She scooted out from beneath him. "You assaulted me."

"You enticed me."

"Now who is the liar?"

Lionheart sat back on his heels, a thoughtful expression on his face. God's wounds, was he mad? When he'd come into this chamber all he had wanted from Vanora was the truth. But from the moment he'd seen her, he'd been driven by lust. The need to make Vanora his had gnawed at him like a mad dog. He felt shaken to the very core. Never had his emotions gotten so out of control.

He straightened his clothing and tried to concentrate, but it was impossible with her scent still upon him. He wanted her so badly he could taste her, but with a shake of his head he cast her from his mind and revisited his reason for this confrontation with Vanora.

"Do you still deny aiding the prisoners in the tower?"

She sent him a wary glance. "Aye."

He gave her a sly smile. "Mayhap I am asking the wrong person. 'Twas the priest and your tiring woman who were in the tower before the escape was discovered. I shall interrogate them immediately."

Vanora blanched. "They are innocent. Do what you will with me but leave them alone. I accept full blame."

"Aha, so now you are admitting guilt. How did you do it?"

Her lips clamped tightly together, Vanora shook her head.

"You are the most stubborn female I have ever met. Because you are unlikely to bend under pressure, I will withhold punishment until I learn how you made it possible for your men to escape. Even as we speak, men are searching for a secret exit. The truth will come out, my lady, and when it does, naught will save you from my wrath."

"There is no secret exit."

"I believe you not. Heed my warning, Vanora. Punishment has many forms." With those cryptic words, he opened the door. "Come, 'tis time to sup. We shall share a trencher and a cup."

When Vanora hesitated, Lionheart placed a hand on her back and firmly guided her out the door. She preceded him along the gallery and down the stairs, pausing when she reached the hall.

"Sit beside me on the dais, lady," Lionheart ordered curtly.

Vanora knew not what to expect from Lionheart, and that confused her. He was being too accommodating, too gentle. She had anticipated a beating at the very least; confinement had also occurred to her as a possible punishment. Yet Lionheart had done the opposite of what she had expected. Caution was called for. She trusted him not.

Before Vanora reached the dais, Mair intercepted her. Her old nursemaid took both Vanora's hands in hers and searched her face. "What did he do to you, lambie? Are you hurt? Has he touched you improperly?"

Vanora squeezed Mair's hands. "I am fine. Do not worry, I can take care of myself."

"Aye, I know your capabilities better than anyone," Mair said. "Does he know?" she whispered, rolling her eyes toward Lionheart.

"Mair, hush!" Vanora warned. No telling what Lionheart would do were he to learn she was the mystery knight he sought. His foe would not receive the same leniency he had afforded Lady Vanora, she guessed.

"Find your seat, Mair," Lionheart said dismissively. "As you can see, your mistress is unhurt. But I am not done with her. Someone must be punished for releasing the prisoners."

"Then you must punish me, master," Mair said. " 'Tis I who unlocked the door."

"What are you saying, Mair?" Father

Caddoc said from behind the old woman. " 'Tis I who unlocked the door."

Dismay widened Vanora's violet eyes. Were they both mad? "Nay! I alone am to blame!"

"Enough!" Lionheart roared. "The one who returns the spare key to me will be held responsible and duly punished."

Vanora realized a spare key would not be forthcoming, because there was none. "Please, say no more," she warned Mair and the priest, her eyes conveying her fear for them. "I will speak with you both later."

Wringing her hands, Mair hurried off, but Father Caddoc lingered, his eyes full of righteous fury. "Touch her and the wrath of God will fall upon you."

"I doubt it not, Father," Lionheart said. "Rest easy. I left your lady's maidenhead intact."

"I will await you in the chapel to hear your confession, child," Father Caddoc said to Vanora in parting.

"How often do you feel the need to confess?" Lionheart asked her with a hint of amusement.

"More often than you, I wager," she retorted. "Do you forbid me to seek absolution from my confessor?"

"Nay, confess to your heart's content. Be sure to tell him you lie on a regular basis." He slanted her an appraising look. "Methinks Cragdon abounds with liars. You, your priest, your tiring woman, all of you are withholding information. But I am a patient man."

Lionheart pulled out a chair and waited until Vanora was seated before seating himself. Immediately his squire filled his cup with wine. Then Lionheart piled food on his trencher and offered Vanora a tender morsel of succulent veal.

"I am perfectly capable of feeding myself," Vanora said, whipping out her eating knife and spearing a piece of meat.

"Aye, you are capable of many things," Lionheart said meaningfully.

Vanora gave him a smug smile. "You have no idea, sir knight."

The church bells were tolling Compline and all was quiet in the keep when Vanora departed her chamber. Wrapped in her cloak, she left the hall and traversed the short distance to the chapel nestled against the curtain wall that rose above the riverbank. Father Caddoc was waiting for her.

"Are you sure you are unharmed?" the priest asked.

"I am fine, Father. Was there something urgent you wished to say to me? Have you news of Llewelyn or Daffid?"

"Aye. I visited the village today and learned that Llewelyn and Daffid are staying at Draymere, Daffid's keep. They are mustering forces to launch an attack upon Cragdon."

"Draymere is but a half day's ride from here," Vanora said excitedly. "When I was a child, I visited often with Father. I shall join them and fight with Llewelyn's army."

"What will I tell Lionheart when he learns you have left the keep?"

"Tell him . . ." Naught came to mind. She thought for a moment, then brightened in sudden inspiration. "I shall pretend to be ill and take to my bed. You and Mair can keep Lionheart away from my chamber until I return with Llewelyn's forces. Tell him I have something deadly and contagious. Most men fear sickness of any kind."

"When will this sudden illness strike?" Father Caddoc asked.

"There will be an abrupt onset of symptoms tomorrow. I shall retire to my chamber and leave at Matins. Wait for me in the chapel."

"I know I advised you to leave, but I

have no good feeling about this, child," the priest said, shaking his head. "Mayhap you should remain here where it is safe until Llewelyn and Daffid begin their siege of Cragdon. You gain naught by placing yourself in danger. What if you are hurt? Even the best of warriors sustain wounds."

"I cannot stay here," Vanora said fiercely. "I fear . . ."

"What do you fear, child?"

I fear for my heart, my soul, my very being. Lionheart threatened everything she stood for, everything she was. His kisses moved her powerfully; just looking at him made her tremble. Enemy or nay, he made her yearn for things that only a husband had the right to offer. His eyes, riveting in their intensity, rested on her far too often for comfort.

"Naught. I fear naught," she lied. "My home is no longer my own. 'Tis impossible to live beneath the thumb of my enemy."

Father Caddoc's probing gaze looked deeper and saw far more than Vanora had wished. "Are you sure that is the reason you wish to leave, child? What is betwixt you and Lionheart that you are not telling me?"

"Naught but enmity, Father. I can do naught here to help Llewelyn. I shall join his army and fight for Cragdon as my father would were he alive. Do not try to dissuade me, for my mind is made up. Will you help me? I have already spoken to Mair, and she has agreed."

After a long pause, the priest sighed and said, "Aye, and may God forgive me if you should suffer an injury."

"Naught will happen to me, Father." Impulsively she kissed his cheek. "Good night."

"A little more flour on my face, Mair," Vanora directed as she prepared to go below for the midday meal.

"Any more and you will look like a ghost," Mair cautioned. "Lionheart is not stupid. He will detect the artifice if you overdo."

"Very well. Just make sure I look pale enough to have an illness that will confine me in my chamber for several days."

Mair stepped back to inspect her work. "I have done all I can to make you look ill. The rest is up to you. Remember to act less than your usual exuberant self."

"Wish me luck," Vanora said as she went out the door.

Lionheart had seen naught of Vanora the entire day and wondered what mischief she was up to. If she did not appear for the midday meal, he intended to go to her chamber and fetch her. Summoning Vanora was not necessary, however, for she walked into the hall a few minutes later.

Frowning, Lionheart watched her dragging steps and knew immediately that something was amiss. A niggling fear assailed him when he noted her pasty complexion. She looked pale and drawn and lacked her usual vitality.

"Are you ill?" Lionheart asked.

Vanora gave him a wan smile. "I fear so. I kept to my bed this morn, hoping it would pass, but I feel little better than I did upon awakening."

She pushed her food around on her trencher, then turned away, her expression filled with repugnance.

"Does the food not please you? Mayhap Cook will fix you something more to your liking."

"I have no appetite," Vanora said with a sigh.

Lionheart stared at Vanora's bent head and felt a helplessness he could not explain. He knew naught of sickness, for he had never been ill. What if she died? The thought sent shivers down his spine. He refused to consider Vanora's death.

"Summon your tiring woman," Lionheart said. "I would speak to her about your malaise."

Lionheart did not see Vanora's smile as with a wave of her hand she summoned Mair to attend her. Mair joined her immediately, grave concern etching her worn features.

"Look at you," Mair clucked. "I told you to remain in bed. What if you are contagious and infect the entire keep?"

Mair's words had the desired effect. An innate fear of illness made most men tremble, and those assembled in the hall were no different.

"Think you Vanora is contagious?" Lionheart asked.

Mair shrugged. "I know not, Sir Lionheart. We must wait for spots to appear to know if 'tis smallpox. It could be the sweating sickness, but symptoms are yet unclear."

"You are the healer. Can you not heal your own mistress?"

"Vanora is stubborn," Mair claimed. "I told her to remain abed, but she refused to listen."

Suddenly Vanora slumped over. Lionheart leapt to his feet and swept her into his arms. "Damn you, woman," he roared, fixing Mair with a frosty glare. "I will take Vanora to her bed, but 'tis up to you to keep her there until she is well. Report daily to me on her condition. Should she die, you will be held responsible and suffer for it."

"I will do my best, master," Mair whined. "But it may be days before I can put a name to my lady's affliction."

Lionheart sprinted up the stairs with Vanora's limp form in his arms. He was loath to put her down when he reached her chamber, but good sense prevailed and he gently placed her on her bed. "Care for her well, Mair," Lionheart ordered gruffly. "If there is a change, I want to know immediately."

Lionheart returned to the hall to finish his meal, but his mind was not on food. Vanora's wan face was imprinted upon his brain. Her expressive eyes had lost their customary sparkle, and her body lacked the spirit that defined her character. The flame within her had been dimmed.

Never in his lifetime had Lionheart thought he would care so much about a woman's health. He had grown up without a mother, and his father had had little use for women after Lionheart's mother had abandoned them. Lionheart did not despise women, but although he loved them for the pleasure they gave him, he trusted them not. From his earliest childhood, Lionheart remembered his father telling him women were a faithless lot, that his own mother had abandoned him for a lover.

Sir Robert led the life of a wastrel, but he had been the injured party in the marriage, and Lionheart had decided early on to love not with the heart but with the body. And since Lionheart had no wealth or lands to leave an heir, he had no reason to wed. Besides, if his own mother had not loved him, what woman would?

Vanora's delicate state of health, however, was worrisome. He wanted to believe he was worried because she could infect his men with disease, but an inner voice whispered otherwise. Pushing these disturbing thoughts aside, Lionheart finished his meal and turned his mind to the hunting party he was planning. 'Twas best he busy himself while awaiting developments in Vanora's condition. Pacing the hall and brooding would do neither him nor Vanora any good.

When Lionheart returned from the hunt later that day, he sent for Mair and was informed that Vanora had become feverish but was resting as comfortably as possible under the circumstances. When he voiced his intention to visit the patient, Mair denied him.

"No one may visit until I know the nature of Vanora's illness," Mair told him.

"Make her well, woman. I command it," Lionheart said.

That night when everyone was abed, Vanora left the keep by way of the chapel. Clad in chain mail and helm, she retrieved her horse from the village and rode through the moonlit night to Draymere, secure in the knowledge that her absence would not be noted for several days. By the time Lionheart discovered her deception, she planned to be on her way back to Cragdon with Llewelyn's army in tow.

A misty dusk had settled over the ground when Vanora finally reached Draymere. She boldly approached the portcullis of the small fortress, hailed the sentry and gave her name. Long moments passed before Llewelyn and Daffid strode from the keep. When they reached the gate, she pulled off her helm and smiled at them. Immediately Llewelyn ordered the portcullis to be raised.

"I recognized your white tabard," Llewelyn said as she rode through the opening.

"What are you doing here?" Daffid

asked. "I like it not when you dress as a warrior and place yourself in danger."

"I can fight as well as you or any man," Vanora retorted. "Besides, did I not clash swords with Lionheart so you and Llewelyn could flee? Even though I knew I could not win the day, I made your escape possible."

"Vanora is right, Daffid," Llewelyn acknowledged. "She placed herself in grave danger for us."

"Nevertheless, I prefer my bride to look like a woman. What are you doing here, Vanora?"

"I heard you were gathering forces to attack Lionheart and came to help."

"Has Lionheart harmed you?" Daffid asked tautly. "I heard he offers no mercy to his prisoners."

"He has done me no harm," Vanora assured him.

"How were you able to leave without being followed?"

"By pretending to be ill and taking to my bed. I wanted to be with you when you storm Cragdon. And I wanted to tell you that presently Lionheart's army outnumbers yours. The barracks was too small to hold them all, and the overflow have bivouacked in the outer bailey."

"We have a plan," Daffid said. "While

half our forces create a diversion at the outer walls, the other half will enter through the tunnel and take the unsuspecting Englishmen by surprise."

" 'Tis a good plan," Vanora allowed, "but you must not kill Lionheart. He is a favorite of Edward's and should be captured and held for ransom."

"I can promise naught," Daffid said. "You should not have left Cragdon. When we lay siege to the fortress, you will remain behind at Draymere where it is safe."

"Nay! I left Cragdon so that I might ride with your army."

The thought of Lionheart's death did not sit easy upon her. She needed to be on hand to prevent unnecessary slaughter. When Llewelyn's forces gained control of Cragdon, she intended to make sure that bloodshed was kept to a minimum. The Englishmen were more valuable to Llewelyn alive than dead, especially Lionheart. The ransom would go a long way to help her people's cause.

"Nay!" Daffid stubbornly maintained.

Vanora turned to Llewelyn. "What say you, Llewelyn?"

"Your determination is as strong as your sword arm, Vanora," Llewelyn said. "I can find no reason to deny your request."

Chapter Five

Three days after Vanora had taken to her bed, Lionheart stood before her chamber door, his anger building as Mair stubbornly refused him entrance. The blasted woman would tell him naught except that Vanora's fever was raging and 'twas likely she was contagious.

"Think you I am afraid of infection?" Lionheart roared. "I would see your mistress for myself."

Mair stood like a rock before the door, arms crossed over her ample bosom. "I cannot allow it. Vanora is sleeping and should not be disturbed."

"Christ's blood, woman!" Lionheart roared. "Think you I would hurt your mistress whilst she is ill?"

He heard not Mair's answer over the commotion below. He turned to see Giles and Brandon bursting forth from the staircase onto the gallery.

"Lionheart!" Brandon cried, panting to catch his breath. "Llewelyn's army is marching toward Cragdon."

"How come you by that information?"
"They were sighted by the patrol."
"Continue."
"The patrol took to high ground and remained unobserved as the army marched past. They returned to Cragdon by a different route to report their sighting."
"How long do we have before they arrive?"
"Several hours. They were moving slowly through the forest to accommodate the foot soldiers."
"Surprise is on our side. Waiting for Llewelyn to attack the castle can only lead to a long siege," Lionheart said after considerable thought.
"What are you going to do?" Giles asked.
"We shall ride out to meet them. Why wait for the attack when we have the element of surprise on our side? We will turn their siege in our favor."
"Our forces are ready to move out at your command," Brandon said.
"We will ride forth as soon as the men are properly armed," Lionheart said. "The sooner the better. Find Alan and send him to fetch my weapons."
Having overheard the exchange, Mair wrung her hands in dismay. If all had gone

as planned, Vanora would be with Llewelyn's advancing army. What was to become of her poor lamb? Briefly she considered divulging Vanora's secret to Lionheart. Were he aware of her secret identity, mayhap he would spare her during the upcoming battle. She decided to confer with Father Caddoc before deciding on a course of action.

As luck would have it, Father Caddoc was in the village on a mission of mercy. During the time it took for Mair to make up her mind, Lionheart and his forces left the keep.

Lionheart's army traveled swiftly and surely toward Lewellyn's advancing forces. Lionheart had the kind of mind that coldly calculated winning strategies in battle. He had the ability to ferret out his opponents' weakness, which made him a dangerous foe. Thus, Lionheart called a halt when his forces approached a long, narrow ravine between two thickly wooded hills.

Sir Brandon rode up to join him. "Is something amiss, Lionheart? Why are we stopping?"

"Do you know of a better place for an ambush?" Lionheart queried.

A smile curved Brandon's lips. "Nay.

'Tis perfect. The forest will hide our men until Llewelyn's army enters the pass."

"Aye," Lionheart said. "Deploy the men at both ends of the ravine. I want the exits closed off after the enemy enters. Their only escape will be through the forest, and there is naught we can do about that but give chase."

Brandon saluted smartly, wheeled his horse and rode down the line, issuing instructions. Immediately the warriors began melting into the forest on either side of the ravine. Brandon and Giles rode back to join Lionheart.

"Brandon, you direct the attack from the left flank. Giles, you take the right. Wait until all of Llewelyn's warriors have entered our trap before closing off the exits," Lionheart said.

The three men rode off in different directions. Lionheart moved up the hill to high ground, where he could watch for Llewelyn's approach, then join the battle where he was most needed.

Three hours later, Lionheart saw the enemy's forces approach the ravine. Mounted warriors were the first to arrive, followed closely by a mélange of foot soldiers dressed in a variety of clothing ranging from chain mail to fur. They looked like a savage horde of Welshmen from legends of old. Lionheart recognized Llewelyn in the forefront and one of the two warriors that rode beside him.

Cursing violently, Lionheart stared at the White Knight, vowing to end his miserable life this day. This time the bastard would not escape him. But before he ran the Welshman through with his broadsword, he wanted to see fear on his face.

His plan was working, Lionheart thought gleefully as he watched Llewelyn lead his forces into the trap he had set for them. When the last of the foot soldiers marched into the narrow ravine, Lionheart's warriors poured down from the hills to close off their means of escape.

Vanora rode proudly beside Llewelyn despite Daffid's objection. Daffid had acted strangely toward her during her stay at Draymere. He had questioned her closely concerning her treatment at Lionheart's hands and was convinced that Lionheart had taken her maidenhead, no matter what she said to convince him otherwise. He was harsher than she remembered, and unappreciative of her attempts to help Llewelyn. Daffid cared for naught but his own glory. She knew he did not approve of her fighting like a man, but 'twas time he realized she was not weak, that she would never depend upon a man for protection. Englishmen had seized her home, and it was her right to defend it. Her father had trained her for just such an occasion, and naught would stop her from fighting alongside Llewelyn's warriors for her birthright.

Vanora was bolstered by the fact that Sir Ren and the men who had escaped from the tower had found their way to Llewelyn and now rode behind her. The only thing that concerned her was the killing that was bound to occur during the heat of battle. Should they engage in hand-to-hand combat, Vanora did not know if she could kill Lionheart, though doubtless he would have no qualms about ending her life.

Sometime during her stay at Draymere Vanora had come to the realization that she did not thirst for Lionheart's death. She could not conceive of a world without his vibrant presence. Though she wanted him driven from her home, she wanted him to live.

Those confusing sentiments were still whirling in her head when she heard Llewelyn yell, " 'Tis a trap!"

Whirling in her saddle, Vanora watched in horror as the surrounding hills came alive with English warriors. They burst forth from the forest mounted and afoot, wielding swords and battle-axes.

"They have sealed the ravine!" Daffid cried, drawing his sword to meet the vanguard of the English forces.

Vanora drew her own sword and braced herself to repel the advancing horde. She clashed with a knight and managed to remain upright as he wielded both sword and battle-ax. She felt the vibrations clear up to her shoulder as her shield took the brunt of the blows. While determination to keep her seat made her oblivious to pain, she wondered how long she could endure. Men stronger than she were being struck down by Lionheart's battle acumen. How had he known Llewelyn's army was advancing toward Cragdon?

Then she saw him, slashing his way toward her, the gleaming silver of his eyes glinting with malice as he rode inexorably in her direction. She awaited him with stoic resignation, not really wanting to die but aware that death was what Lionheart intended for her.

Suddenly Sir Ren appeared before her, his destrier pawing the air as he brought it up short. "Flee, mistress," he cried. "Leave Lionheart to me."

"I will not flee like a coward," Vanora bit out. "See to your own safety."

"Nay!"

The words had no sooner left his mouth than five former Cragdon knights formed a protective circle around her. Five others aligned themselves beside Ren, swords drawn to repel Lionheart's advance. Several of Lionheart's warriors saw what was happening and came to his defense.

When Vanora realized her own knights were preventing her from joining in the battle, she tried to break through their perimeter. Despite her best efforts, she was slowly but surely being forced away from the line of battle, toward high ground.

Over the roar of battle she heard Lionheart's anguished cry. "Coward! Come back and fight!"

Glancing over her shoulder, she saw men falling beneath Lionheart's sword, and fear surged through her. It was she Lionheart wanted. It was not fair that others should die protecting her. But when she tried to return to the battlefield, her warriors refused to give way.

Another quick look over her shoulder made the blood freeze in her veins. Lionheart had slashed past Sir Ren's defenses and was pounding after her. From the corner of her eye she saw Llewelyn and Daffid fighting side by side, but to her dismay, it appeared that the battle was lost, that once again Lionheart's forces had defeated Llewelyn's army.

Even as the thought entered her mind, she saw Llewelyn break away and ride full tilt into the forest. When the Welshmen realized their leader was retreating, they formed a solid line of defense to prevent the Englishmen from giving chase.

"Llewelyn is fleeing!" Giles cried as he rode up beside Lionheart.

Vanora knew Lionheart was torn. He had his own agenda concerning the White Knight, but Llewelyn's capture was more important to England. She felt his disappointment as keenly as if it were hers when he wheeled his destrier and pounded after Llewelyn.

Vanora wanted to remain but knew the battle was lost. Once Llewelyn left, the heart would go out of the fight, and those warriors fortunate enough to be alive would flee.

Was there no stopping that English devil Lionheart? she wondered. What was she to do now? Should she go into hiding until the Black Wolf of Snowdon reformed his army?

Her choices were limited. Darkness was fast approaching, and she had nowhere to go except home. Besides, she would be of most use to her people where she could keep an eye on Lionheart. "Leave me," she told her warriors. "I shall find my own way back to Cragdon. Return to the battlefield and carry the wounded to their homes."

No one thought to disagree as Vanora spurred her mount and was soon lost amid trees and tangled vines. With any luck, she would arrive home before Lionheart returned. In a day or two she would make a miraculous recovery from her illness. And, God willing, Llewelyn would live to fight another day. Meanwhile, she would do her utmost to make Lionheart's life miserable. Mayhap miserable enough to make him leave Wales.

'Twas nearly dawn when Vanora made her way through the passage to the chapel. She was so exhausted she could scarcely walk. Her chain mail weighed heavily upon her shoulders, and her head ached. The acrid stench of battle remained in her nostrils, and the cries of the wounded still rang in her ears. So many deaths . . . too many. Had the English devils not invaded her land, she and her countrymen would be living in peace and she would be wed to Daffid.

The flickering light of a single candle chased away the shadows as Vanora crept from behind the altar. She found Father Caddoc kneeling at the altar railing. She smiled when she saw his head nodding and realized that he was asleep. Gently she shook his shoulder. He awoke with a start.

"You have returned." His eyes roamed over her mail-clad form. "Are you well?"

"I am unharmed, Father."

He glanced behind her. "You are alone."

Wearily Vanora fell to her knees beside him and buried her face in her hands. "Aye. The battle did not go well."

Father Caddoc nodded. "I suspected as much. Llewelyn's forces were sighted by an English patrol. Mair overheard Lionheart planning a surprise attack."

"Lionheart caught us off guard in a narrow ravine, sealed off our escape and attacked from both sides."

"How did you get away?"

"My escape was made possible by Cragdon's warriors. They protected me and saw me to safety when I would have preferred to stay and fight. Llewelyn's forces were in full retreat when I left the battlefield. I am certain those who were not dead or wounded found a safe haven in the hills. Wales is a land of many hiding places with its mountains and forests. It can be a forbidding place to those unfamiliar with the stark face of our landscape."

"You must be exhausted. Find your bed, child," Father Caddoc advised. "Lionheart is sure to inquire about your health upon his return. He has been frantic about you."

Vanora changed into her gown and slowly made her way across the courtyard through the early dawn dampness. Though she heard the banging of pots and the sound of voices coming from the kitchen, she encountered no one as she climbed the stairs to her chamber. She closed the door behind her, locked it and leaned against it, breathing a sigh of relief. Mair awoke at the sound and got to her feet.

Her anxious gaze roamed over Vanora. "Thank God you've returned unharmed. I have been out of my mind with worry since Lionheart's forces rode off to meet Llewelyn's army."

"Naught went as expected," Vanora said wearily. "Lionheart set a trap for us, and we barely escaped with our lives. I rode for hours without rest to reach home before him. There is not a bone in my body that does not ache."

"Did Lionheart see you with Llewelyn?"

"Aye. I was lucky to escape with my life.

Help me undress, Mair, before I fall asleep on my feet."

Mair removed Vanora's clothing, tucked her in bed and tiptoed from the chamber.

Lionheart was in a rage when he returned. Once again Llewelyn had escaped, and with him the White Knight. It galled him to think that the knight and his protectors had made a fool of him again. He wanted Llewelyn, but he wanted the White Knight even more.

Lionheart stormed into the hall, calling for ale and food. His men had scoured the vicinity for the Welsh warriors until darkness made continuing impossible. By then it had become obvious that Llewelyn and his ragtag army had scattered to God only knew where. But Lionheart had taken one prisoner, and an important one at that.

He had captured Daffid ap Deverell, Vanora's betrothed. By a stroke of luck, Daffid's horse had gone lame and he'd been overtaken. Pleased with the capture, Lionheart called off the search and returned to Cragdon with his prisoner.

Giles followed Lionheart into the hall, prodding Daffid before him. "What shall I do with the prisoner, Lionheart?"

Lionheart glared at Daffid, wondering

what Vanora saw in the bearded warrior. Of medium height and stocky like most Welsh warriors, Daffid might be considered handsome if one liked a savage visage, bushy brows and an unruly beard. The thought of Vanora wedding the Welshman was unpalatable. He looked like a man who would demand strict obedience from a woman and employ force to obtain it.

"I will question him," Lionheart said.

Giles shoved Daffid forward. Lionheart sank down onto a bench before the hearth and stretched his hands out to the fire. The night had been damp and chill, and his bones ached from many hours in the saddle. When Daffid stood before him, Lionheart's expression hardened.

"Where is Llewelyn hiding, Daffid ap Deverell?" he asked in Welsh. Since his arrival at Cragdon, he had gained a better understanding of the language and could speak with some fluency now.

Daffid remained stubbornly mute. Giles poked him with the point of his sword. "Speak! Lionheart is not a patient man."

Daffid shot Lionheart a contemptuous look. "Llewelyn does not confide in me. I but follow where he leads."

"Very well. Perhaps you will be more inclined to tell me the name of the white-clad knight who created a diversion at Cragdon's gate after you fled into the castle that day. How did you leave the fortress without being seen?"

"You are mistaken, Englishman. Llewelyn and I never sought refuge at Cragdon. And I know not the knight to whom you refer."

Lionheart's voice was deadly calm, too calm. "Do you not? He was with you and Llewelyn when you entered the ravine."

" 'Twas no one of import," Daffid insisted. His dark gaze left Lionheart and made a sweeping search of the hall. "Where is Vanora? What have you done with her?"

From the corner of his eye, Lionheart spotted Mair and summoned her with a wave of his hand. She approached him warily, wringing her hands, her eyes refusing to meet his.

"How is your mistress? Does her health improve?"

Darting a guarded look at Daffid, Mair said, "Her fever has broken."

"Does that mean you expect a full recovery?" Lionheart probed.

"Aye, though she should remain abed another day or two."

"Has my betrothed been ill?" Daffid asked with mock concern. His contemptuous gaze settled on Lionheart. "Have you made her your whore?"

Naught Daffid had said thus far had riled Lionheart as did the last statement the Welshman had uttered. Would Daffid set his betrothal aside if Lionheart had taken Vanora's virginity? Was Daffid so small a man that he would blame a woman for something that was not her fault?

"Think what you wish, Daffid ap Deverell." He turned to Giles. "Take him to the dungeon and place a guard at the door. I vow this prisoner will not escape like the others."

The hall became a beehive of activity as men wandered in to break their fast after a long day and longer night. Lionheart ate and drank mechanically, tasting little of what went into his mouth. Though exhausted beyond endurance, he could not seek his rest until he had looked in on Vanora. He had not seen her in several days and wanted to reassure himself that she was indeed recovering. He rose and was moving toward the stairs when Father Caddoc intercepted him.

"A moment, Sir Lionheart," Father Caddoc said.

"Hurry, Father, for I am weary unto death."

"Mair told me Daffid ap Deverell is your prisoner."

"Aye, so he is."

"What do you intend for him?"

"Mayhap I will make an example of him and order his execution." Lionheart was so angry with Daffid he would gladly strangle the man himself. Calling Vanora a whore was beyond despicable. Even if Lionheart had taken Vanora's maidenhead, labeling her a whore would be unfair.

"I wish to speak to Daffid. Mayhap I can offer comfort in his darkest hour."

"Nay, I refuse your request. Daffid is to have no visitors. He will not escape like Cragdon's warriors did. I know Vanora aided them, and that they left through a secret tunnel, but I have yet to find it. Do not ask for visiting rights again," he said dismissively.

Lionheart continued up the staircase to Vanora's chamber, opened the door and walked inside without knocking. Surprised to find her unattended, Lionheart approached the bed. She was sleeping, just as Mair had said, but her sleep appeared troubled, for she mumbled incoherently and tossed restlessly.

Extending his hand, he rested it briefly on her forehead, relieved to find it cool to his touch. Bending low, he tried to make out her words, but naught she said made sense. Assured that her health was no longer in jeopardy, Lionheart sought his own bed.

Vanora slept through the rest of the day and night and awoke refreshed the following morning. Ravenous, she asked Mair to fetch food, then quickly devoured the entire contents of the tray.

"Has Lionheart returned?" Vanora asked.

"Aye," Mair answered. "In a mood as black as sin."

"Did Llewelyn escape?"

"Aye."

Before Mair could tell her about Daffid, Vanora said, "We will speak further after I have bathed and dressed."

"Aye, I already ordered your bath."

Resting her head against the rim, Vanora soaked in the hot tub while she considered her next course of action. Torn by indecision, she did not know whether she should leave and find Daffid or remain at Cragdon until Llewelyn reorganized his army. Daffid had been angry with her and had unjustly accused her of bedding Lionheart. Furthermore, he had refused to acknowledge her timely intervention when he and Llewelyn were desperate to escape Edward's army, and he seemed resentful of her warrior skills.

Suddenly aware that the water was growing cold, Vanora reached for the drying cloth Mair had draped over a nearby bench and rose. She had just stepped from the tub when her chamber door opened and Lionheart stepped inside. Vanora froze, the cloth dangling in her fingers as Lionheart's glittering gaze traveled slowly over her nude form. A rosy flush started at her toes and climbed up her body to her hairline.

"Get out!" she cried, wrapping the skimpy cloth around her body. It barely covered her, baring her incredibly long legs and the upper swells of her breasts.

"I think not," Lionheart replied in a voice suddenly taut with desire. "I am pleased to see you have recovered from your illness." He kicked the door shut with his heel and stalked toward her. "I knew you would be exceptionally lovely, but I had no idea how well made you were. Never have I seen such long legs on a woman."

Vanora backed away. "Do not stare at me like that. I am no different from any other woman."

"I beg to differ. I have seen my share of naked women, and without exception they are soft-fleshed and weak-willed. You are neither."

"It pleases me that I am too masculine for your tastes," Vanora retorted. "Turn your head while I don my chamber robe."

Lionheart laughed. "Masculine? Hardly. You are sleek and lithe like a cat but fleshed out in places that proclaim your womanhood." He stared at her bare arms. "Are those muscles I spy, my lady? How come you by muscles?" His gaze slid down her torso. "Have you thigh muscles to match those in your arms?" His eyes darkened from silver to smoky gray. "Or muscles in places that the eye cannot see? I look forward to discovering them for myself."

Vanora was not stupid. She knew precisely what he meant. When she turned to flee, Lionheart grasped the drying cloth and yanked it from her fingers. Caught like a rabbit in a trap, Vanora tried to cover herself with her hands. Laughing, Lionheart pulled her against him, his hands roving freely over the soft skin of her back and buttocks. A slow heat coursed through her veins as Lionheart groaned her name and sought her lips.

Wherever he touched, she burned. Sweet Lord, what was he doing to her? An all-consuming need spiraled through her as his hands sought her breasts and his tongue explored her mouth with slow deliberation. He kissed her until her head was reeling and her knees threatened to buckle beneath her. With an effort born of desperation, she broke free and shoved against his chest.

"Stop! I will not let you dishonor me."

"Methinks you protest too much. You want me, Vanora. I felt your lips quivering beneath mine and tasted your excitement."

"Nay, I want you not."

"Yet I shall have you, my lady."

Seeking to divert Lionheart's attention as well as her own, Vanora said, "Mair said you rode out to meet Llewelyn. Did you capture him?"

"Nay." Her words succeeded in easing the tension as Lionheart moved away and began to pace. Taking advantage of his distraction, Vanora snatched her chamber robe from the bed and pulled it on.

"The man is wily as a fox," Lionheart complained. "His luck cannot hold out forever."

"I pray it does."

Lionheart regarded her through shuttered

eyes. "No matter what you pray, I came away from the battle victorious. Llewelyn has fled and his army scattered to the winds. 'Twill be a long time, if ever, before his ragtag army becomes a viable force again. I doubt he will pose a threat to England in the future."

"You are wrong!" Vanora hotly denied. "Llewelyn will not rest until the English leave us in peace."

Frustrated by her stubbornness and his own lustful need to possess her, Lionheart suddenly thought of a way to punish her and at the same time gain what he desired most . . . her body.

"Aye, Llewelyn escaped but I did return with a prisoner. Someone close to the Black Wolf."

Vanora's heart constricted. "Anyone I know?"

Secretly gloating, Lionheart said, "Daffid ap Deverell."

"Daffid? You captured Daffid?"

"Did I not just say so?"

"Where is he? What . . . what are you going to do with him?"

"He is locked in the dungeon. As for his fate, I considered letting Edward deal with him when he arrives, but I've changed my mind. Llewelyn and his followers need to be taught a lesson. I shall make an example of Daffid and order his execution."

Color drained from Vanora's face as she staggered to a bench and dropped down upon it. " 'Tis inhuman. Say it is not so."

"I will not lie to you, Vanora. I have most definitely decided to execute Daffid."

"English devil! Monster! Have you no mercy, no compassion? Is there aught I can do to save him?"

Lionheart pretended to reconsider. "Mayhap there is a way."

Vanora leapt to her feet. "Tell me! What must I do to save Daffid?"

"Become my leman," Lionheart replied. "Lie with me for as long as I remain at Cragdon, and I will spare Daffid's life."

Vanora recoiled in revulsion. "Why do you want me? You like me not."

"I said no such thing, Vanora. 'Tis you who decided we should be enemies. I like all women, English, Irish, Welsh, Scot or Frank; they all serve a purpose."

"Is that all women are to you? A warm body? Any man that thinks a woman is naught but a vessel for his lust does not deserve a wife. I pity the woman you wed."

"I neither need nor want a wife," Lionheart said. "They are naught but trouble. I seek my pleasure where I will and with whom I please."

"One day some woman will make you eat those words," Vanora predicted.

"Such strong words coming from so sweet a mouth," Lionheart said in a husky purr. "What say you, Vanora? How badly do you want to save Daffid's life? Enough to lie in my arms and take me into your body?"

Indignation stiffened her spine. "I cannot betray Daffid in that way."

"Not even to save his life?"

"Nay . . . Oh, I do not know."

"Mayhap I can convince you."

His arms went around her, forcing her against the heat of his body as his lips devoured hers, draining her very soul from her being. It should not be like this, Vanora thought. Why was her will not strong enough to resist Lionheart's powerful allure? She was not a weak woman; why did she feel as though she were being pulled into the vortex of a raging storm?

Breaking off the kiss, Lionheart stared down into her eyes, his questioning gaze demanding but one answer. "What shall it be, Vanora? Your betrothed's life depends upon your answer."

She returned his gaze, unable to form a

reply. She was saved from committing herself when the door was flung open, admitting a vengeful Father Caddoc.

"For shame, Sir Lionheart!" he challenged. "Remove yourself from Vanora's chamber."

"Nay, Father, I will not. 'Tis my right to take whatever I desire from Cragdon."

"If you want Vanora, you will have to wed her," Father Caddoc declared.

"Father!" Vanora cried.

Lionheart tossed back his head and laughed. "Marriage? Nay, Father, marriage is not for me. Not even Vanora is worth my freedom."

" 'Tis the only way you can have her," the priest vowed. "Be gone, Satan!"

Lionheart slanted Vanora a look ripe with challenge. "Do not take too long to decide, Vanora, for I am not a patient man." Whirling, he strode away, his laughter ringing harshly in her ears.

Chapter Six

"What did Lionheart mean, child?" Father Caddoc asked. "Mair fetched me when she saw him enter your chamber. We both feared that Lionheart would lure you into sinning against God's commandments."

"Worry not, Father," Vanora soothed in an effort to allay his fears. "I can handle Lionheart. You should not have mentioned marriage to him; I am betrothed to Daffid."

"No formal papers were signed. Besides, breaking a betrothal is less a sin than fornication. 'Tis better to marry the devil than be ravaged by one. Do you desire Lionheart, child?"

"Nay! How could you think such a thing?"

"I have lived a long time and see things that others do not. If I am wrong, forgive me. You must love Daffid very much."

Vanora's hesitation spoke volumes about her feelings for her betrothed. "As well you know, the betrothal was verbally agreed upon by Daffid and Father, but I know I will grow to love him."

Father Caddoc looked unconvinced. "I shall pray that God gives you the strength to resist Lionheart's seduction, for I fear that is what he has in mind for you."

If you only knew, Vanora thought, recalling Lionheart's determination to have her in his bed.

"Did you know Daffid had been captured and placed in Cragdon's dungeon? Lionheart intends to execute him."

Father Caddoc paled and quickly made the sign of the cross. "God preserve us all. I shall pray for his immortal soul."

"He is not dead yet, Father. Mayhap you should pray that he escapes the fate Lionheart has planned for him."

"So I shall, child. Take heart, all is not lost yet. I shall be in the chapel should you need me."

Vanora bolted the door after the priest left so she could dress without fear of Lionheart barging into her chamber. Never again would she allow herself to be alone with him. He was too powerful, too masculine, too sexually attractive for her peace of mind. Compared to Daffid, whom she had never even kissed, Lionheart was sin personified.

She must not allow herself to be tempted by him.

Not even to save Daffid's life? a little voice within her asked.

Therein lay her dilemma. Did she have a choice? She would not be able to live with herself if she let Daffid die while the means to save him lay within her grasp. Giving herself to Lionheart was a small price to pay for her betrothed's life. Her maidenhead would be of little use if Daffid died. That thought brought another. Daffid already believed Lionheart had stolen her innocence.

Her decision, however, was not an easy one. Before agreeing to lie with Lionheart, she was determined to explore other means of saving Daffid. She prayed that Lionheart's patience would hold.

A short time later, Vanora tried to visit Daffid and was turned away. Duties kept her occupied until the tables were being set up for the evening meal; then she made another attempt to visit her betrothed.

"Let me take him some food," Vanora pleaded with the guard. "Even prisoners have to eat."

"The prisoner has not been denied food," the guard answered.

"What harm will it do to let me visit him?" Vanora argued.

" 'Tis for Lionheart to decide," the

guard replied, apparently unmoved by Vanora's plea.

Hands on hips, Vanora said, "Very well, I shall take my request to Lionheart."

"Did you wish to speak to me, my lady?"

Hearing Lionheart's voice, Vanora whirled to face him. "I wish to see Daffid. How do I know he is not being mistreated?"

"Because I say he is not."

"I trust you not!"

He grasped her elbow and steered her away from the dungeon. "Come away. 'Tis time to sup."

Vanora dug in her heels. "When may I see Daffid?"

"He is not worthy of you."

"How can you say that? You know him not."

"Do you love him?"

"He is my betrothed."

" 'Tis not what I asked. Do you love him?"

"Of . . . course. 'Tis my duty to love my betrothed."

Her answer seemed to please him. "Have you decided to accept my proposal?"

She shook her head. "I will decide after I have spoken with Daffid and not before."

"Stubborn wench," Lionheart growled, pulling her against him. He would have kissed her had Vanora not turned her face aside.

"The guard," she hissed. "Do not shame me before one of your men."

"Most women would consider it an honor to become my leman. Even the king has his mistresses."

"You are no king," Vanora said with haughty disdain.

Laughter rumbled in Lionheart's chest. Wiping away tears of mirth, he said, "What a merry chase you lead me, vixen. I cannot wait to have you writhing beneath me. Come along, our meal is waiting."

"When will you allow me to visit Daffid?" Vanora persisted.

"Never. Unless," he added in a voice taut with desire, "you come to my bed tonight."

"Then we are at an impasse, sir knight, for I must see Daffid before I make my decision."

"I suggest you reach a decision before Daffid's scheduled execution."

Vanora paled and went still. "You have already set a time?"

"Aye. His head will be removed from his body three days hence. You alone can prevent his death."

"Bastard!" Vanora hissed. "You push me

too far." Whirling away from him, she stomped off.

Lionheart could not prevent the grin that curved his lips. Aye, he was pushing Vanora, pushing her into his bed. The twinge of guilt he felt was quickly banished when he pictured Vanora stretched out beneath him, her glorious sable hair spread out on the pillow, his cock buried deep inside her.

He knew instinctively that she would be passionate, and he fully intended to explore her passion to the fullest. He was not an inconsiderate lover. He would make sure Vanora experienced pleasure, and he would initiate her to sex gently. He was not a ravager of women. Forcing himself on creatures weaker than himself was not his way; he preferred his women submissive and willing. He prided himself on following the knight's code of honor. He had never raped a woman nor forced himself on an unwilling maiden. Seduction, however, was an art he used without guilt or self-recrimination.

Daffid did not deserve Vanora, Lionheart decided. He doubted he would actually execute Daffid even if Vanora remained stubborn. Of one thing he was certain, however: Daffid would not have

Vanora. The man was unappreciative of her special qualities.

After a restless night, Vanora stared out the window at the gray skies and pouring rain, pulling her mantle closer about her to ward off the chill. Cragdon was comfortable most of the time, but the thick stone walls did naught to keep out the dampness. Only today and one other remained before Daffid was beheaded, and she was the only one who could prevent the tragedy. It was a heavy burden to bear.

Even more distressing was the knowledge that she could not stop wondering what it would be like to make love with Lionheart. The attraction between them was intense, though she would deny it vigorously. His kisses made her tremble with longing for something she knew was wicked, and his hands upon her made her think sinful thoughts.

Turning away from the window, Vanora clutched her mantle close about her and left her chamber. She needed to see Daffid before responding to Lionheart's ultimatum. Would Daffid want her to accept Lionheart's indecent proposal? Or would he rather die than see his betrothed dishonored? Vanora hoped to pose those questions to him very soon.

The hall was bustling with activity when Vanora sat down to break her fast after morning Mass. The inclement weather prevented normal outdoor activities, and groups of men huddled around the hearth, engaged in dicing and card games. Lionheart was nowhere in sight.

A servant placed bread, cheese and ale before her, and she ate with good appetite. She saw Mair and called to the tiring woman to join her. "What news is there of Llewelyn?" Vanora asked in a hushed voice.

"I have heard naught," Mair replied. "Mayhap you should ask Father Caddoc. He was in the village yesterday."

"Where is Lionheart?"

"He left with the huntsmen early this morning."

"Doubtless he will return wet and chilled and in a foul mood," Vanora predicted.

Vanora spent the morning supervising candle making, but she had not forgotten Mair's advice about questioning Father Caddoc for news of Llewelyn. Later that day she sought him in the chapel.

"What news have you of Llewelyn?" she asked anxiously.

"Naught, child. No one seems to know where he has taken himself. His army has scattered to the winds."

"How odd. The English will remain in control of Cragdon if Llewelyn gives up the fight, and that does not bode well for Wales and our people. If Llewelyn abandons Cragdon to the English, I will flee."

"Be not hasty, child," Father Caddoc cautioned. "All is not lost yet."

"Has Lionheart given you permission to visit Daffid?"

Father Caddoc sighed. "Nay. He trusts me not. As you well know, no one has ever escaped from the dungeon."

"Aye, Father, I know. Daffid is doomed, and I am the only one who can save him."

"How, child? What can you do that I cannot?"

Vanora deliberately withheld Lionheart's terms from the good Father for fear he would confront Lionheart and earn his wrath. She did not think Lionheart would physically harm a priest, but with Englishmen, one never knew.

"Forgive me, Father, but I must leave. While Lionheart is gone, mayhap I can convince the guard to let me into the dungeon."

If Father Caddoc thought it odd that she did not answer his question, he did not say. "God go with you, child."

Vanora returned to the keep through the drenching rain. The cool breeze signaled the end of summer, and Vanora did not look forward to winter. Were she forced to leave Cragdon, she did not know how she would survive, unless she begged shelter from one of her neighbors.

The guard was no more willing to let Vanora visit Daffid than he had been the previous day. Reluctantly she turned away and returned to the hall. She had just seated herself before the hearth and taken up a piece of embroidery when Lionheart and the huntsmen stormed into the hall.

"Ale!" Lionheart called as he strode to the hearth and stretched his hands out to the fire. " 'Tis a miserable day," he complained to no one in particular.

Vanora said naught as he threw off his mantle and turned his backside to the fire, but she could not help looking her fill. His tunic and hose were soaked through, hugging his muscular body and legs like a second skin. Seeing him like this made it impossible for her to deny that he was a magnificent specimen of masculinity. Tall and broad, thickly muscled about the chest but slim of waist and hips, he possessed the lithe grace of a lion combined with the strength of a bull. He was stubborn, unpredictable and arrogant. When he made up his mind to something, naught could sway him from his course.

"Have I suddenly grown a tail?" Lionheart asked.

Aware that she had been staring, Vanora returned her attention to her embroidery. "All devils have tails, do they not?"

"You sorely try me, vixen. I am cold and hungry and in no mood for your insults. As the lady of the keep, 'tis your duty to see to my comfort."

Vanora set her embroidery aside and rose. "I shall instruct the servants to carry a tub and hot water to your chamber."

"Have you supped yet?"

"Nay."

"Then you will sup with me in my chamber after I have bathed."

Vanora stared at him. "I have no appetite."

"Then you can satisfy mine." He strode toward the stairs, then whipped around and said in a voice that brooked no argument, "Do not keep me waiting."

Vanora dreaded another confrontation with Lionheart. Only tomorrow remained of the three days Lionheart had given her to decide whether or not Daffid lived. She could always flee, but that would be the coward's way out and would solve naught. Fleeing would not help Daffid, nor would it make her own life any easier to bear.

Vanora went to the kitchen to order Lionheart's bath and food, then slowly ascended the stairs to the solar. Alan was with Lionheart, setting out his clean clothing and helping him disrobe. She stopped short of entering the chamber when she noted Lionheart's bare chest and would have fled but that Lionheart had spied her.

"Enter," he ordered. "You may leave, Alan," he told his squire. "We will sup after I have bathed."

Servants arrived with the tub, hot water, soap and drying cloths. They filled the tub and hastened off without looking at Vanora.

"You may scrub my back," Lionheart said as he shucked his chausses without a hint of embarrassment.

Her cheeks flaming, Vanora turned away.

"Well, I am waiting."

Vanora darted a peek over her shoulder, relieved to see Lionheart seated in the tub, his long legs doubled until his knees nearly touched his chin. Gingerly approaching the tub, Vanora picked up the soap and applied it to a cloth. Then she pressed the cloth against his back and moved it in a circular motion. She felt his muscles tense, felt the ripple of awareness that shuddered through him at her touch, and swallowed hard.

"God's toenails," he growled as he grasped her wrist and dragged her around where he could see her. "What are you doing to me, woman?"

"Naught! I am but obeying your orders. Did I hurt you?" she asked sweetly.

He fished in the water, found the washcloth she had dropped, and pressed it into her hand. "Wash my chest."

Vanora's fingers closed over the cloth. "Release my wrist."

The moment the pressure eased, she flung the cloth in Lionheart's face. Then she turned and fled. Precious time was lost when she unsuccessfully attempted to lift the latch with her soap-slick hand. When she tried again, her hand was snatched away.

Whirling, she came face to face with Lionheart in all his nude glory . . . nude and fully aroused. She did not want to stare, but she could look nowhere else. If *that* was what he intended to put inside her, she was certain she would not live to tell the tale.

Her expression must have conveyed her fear, for Lionheart placed a finger beneath her chin and raised her face to his. "I will be gentle with you, Vanora. I swear you will enjoy it."

Vanora shook her head. "You will kill me with your weapon."

"My weapon will give you pleasure." He captured her hand and brought it to his groin. "Touch me."

"I cannot." But even as the words left her mouth, her fingers curled around his staff. " 'Tis soft," she murmured, surprised that she was not repulsed, "yet hard. There is strength beneath the softness."

"Aye, I would show you, Vanora." He removed her hand. "Come lie with me. Let me banish your fears. I swear I will not hurt you."

"You promised me three days in which to decide," Vanora whispered, shaken by a wave of desire that nearly brought her to her knees.

"Tomorrow is the last day. Why prolong the inevitable? When I leave Cragdon you will be free of me. There are worse things in life than submitting to me."

"Name one," Vanora challenged.

"Watching the execution of your betrothed."

"If I agree to your terms, will you free Daffid?"

Lionheart's dark brows shot upward. "Free Daffid?"

"Aye. His execution will serve no purpose. You said yourself that Llewelyn's army has disbanded and is unlikely to pose a threat in the near future."

"I cannot make that promise, but neither will I refuse you out of hand. I will think on it." He stepped closer, crowding her against the door. "I would hear you say the words, Vanora. Tell me you will become my leman."

"Let me speak privately to Daffid and I shall do as you wish."

"Do I have your word?"

She nodded.

"If that is what it will take to bring you to my bed, then you may visit Daffid."

"Now."

"Vanora . . . do not push me."

"Now."

Impatience made his voice harsh. "If that is the only way I can have you, then very well, I will take you to Daffid myself. Give me a moment to dress."

While Vanora waited for Lionheart to don doublet and hose, her thoughts turned inward, to that sinful thing he asked of her. Fornication was a sin, but doing naught while a man died needlessly was a greater sin in her eyes. She glanced sidelong at Lionheart, then squeezed her eyes shut. May God forgive her, but the thought of making love with him sent shivers of anticipation racing down her spine. She could feel her body softening and liquid heat gathering in unmentionable places. If her heart pounded any louder, she feared Lionheart would suspect her wanton thoughts, and she did not want to feed his vanity.

When she confessed her sins, Father Caddoc would surely give her a penance that would keep her on her knees throughout eternity.

"I am ready," Lionheart said, jarring Vanora from her silent ruminations.

As they descended the stairs, Vanora began to regret her promise to Lionheart. What if he had lied about not hurting her? What if he proved to be a brutal lover?

What if she enjoyed his lovemaking? Would that make her a traitor to her people?

"Here we are," Lionheart said when they reached the door leading down to the dungeon. The guard opened the door, and Lionheart took the torch from the wall sconce and preceded her down the winding staircase.

It had been years since Vanora had visited the dungeon, and with good reason. The chambers below the castle were not fit for human occupancy. A succession of small, dark cells lined either wall of a large, well-lit guardroom. The oaken door to each cell was barred from the outside and had but a small barred window. A guard, lounging on a bench, rose to his feet when Lionheart entered the chamber.

"Lady Vanora wishes to speak to the prisoner," Lionheart said brusquely.

"In private," Vanora demanded. Lionheart sent her a warning look. "You promised."

Only then did Lionheart relent and dismiss the guard. "Daffid occupies the last cell," he said before taking his leave. "I will wait for you at the foot of the staircase."

Cautiously Vanora approached the cell. Standing on tiptoe, she peered through the opening. To her surprise, torchlight illuminated the tiny cell, and it was not as bleak as she had feared. A stool and table with the remnants of a meal still upon it were the only pieces of furniture in the cell besides a wide bench with a thin straw mattress that served as a bed.

Daffid was sitting on the cot, his head resting in his cupped hands. She softly called his name so as not to startle him. His head jerked up at the sound of her voice. Leaping from the cot, he ran to the door.

"Vanora! Thank God! Have you come to free me?"

"I tried, Daffid, I truly did, but Lionheart has only agreed to a visit. How are you faring?"

Anger suffused Daffid's face. "You ask that when you can see for yourself how I am forced to live? This place is not fit for an animal, much less a human being. Can you do naught to free me? I was informed that Lionheart plans to separate my head from my shoulders."

"What would you have me do?" Vanora asked.

"Whatever it takes to get me out of this hellhole," Daffid spat. "You are a resourceful wench; surely you can come up with something that will work. You managed to free Cragdon's warriors from the tower, did you not?"

"That was a different situation. There is no escape from the dungeon."

Daffid's eyes narrowed. "Has Lionheart

tired of you already? Does he no longer want you in his bed?"

"Daffid! I am not Lionheart's leman!" *Yet* . . . "Why do you not believe me?"

"Because if I were Lionheart, I would have taken your maidenhead the same day I captured the castle. I am a man, Vanora, and know how men think." His eyes narrowed with sly innuendo. "Mayhap he prefers boys."

"Nay!" Vanora denied, outraged by the suggestion. "Lionheart desires me."

"Enough to listen to your pleas on my behalf?" Daffid asked hopefully. "I do not want to die, Vanora. I want to live to help Llewelyn drive the English from Wales. Do whatever it takes to set me free."

"You want me to fornicate with Lionheart? What of our betrothal?"

"Should you still retain your innocence, which is highly unlikely, the loss of your maidenhead is a small price to pay for my freedom. As to our betrothal, I still want Cragdon and will wed you without your maidenhead."

"You are the worst kind of hypocrite, Daffid," Vanora bit out. " 'Tis my lands you want; you care naught for me. You want me to sacrifice myself for your worthless life."

" 'Tis your duty. A woman's life is naught compared to a man's. Were we wed, you would be required to obey me in all things. I could send you to a nunnery or kill you if it pleased me."

She stared at him coldly. "Mayhap I would kill you first. I have been taught a warrior's skills and will allow no man to abuse me. I hereby set the betrothal aside. Good-bye, Daffid."

"Vanora, wait! Forgive me. I am a man condemned to death and beset by devils. I did not mean what I said. I would honor you as my wife no matter what you were forced to do to save my life. I am merely suggesting that you take advantage of Lionheart's desire for you to gain my freedom. My life is important to the future of Wales. Can you not find it in your heart to help me?"

"I will do what I can," Vanora said, turning away.

With a heavy heart, Vanora slowly made her way to Lionheart. She had always admired Daffid and felt that he would make a good husband, but he had shattered her dreams with a few carelessly spoken words. Mayhap he *was* overwrought with anxiety, but that did not give him the right to speak to her in a disrespectful fashion, or hold her in low regard because she was a woman.

Daffid was not even grateful for her warrior skills. She had sacrificed her own warriors for his and Llewelyn's lives and placed herself in peril. Daffid thought of her as a woman who would become his chattel once they were wed. She had hoped he would see her as being different from other women and respect those differences.

He should appreciate her ability to defend herself and protect her lands, but he did not.

"I heard loud voices. Did your visit with Daffid not go well?"

Vanora gasped in surprise; she had been so deep in thought, she had nearly bumped into Lionheart.

She refused to look at him. "All is well. I found Daffid in surprising good health. Is that your doing?"

"I rarely torture my prisoners."

She turned away and started up the stairs. Lionheart grasped her shoulders and spun her around to face him. "You have not changed your mind, have you? Rest assured that I intend to hold you to your promise."

Vanora no longer felt that Daffid's life was worth any sacrifice on her part, but she had given Lionheart a promise and saw no way to avoid honoring her word. Had she spoken to Daffid first, she would not have been so quick to agree to Lionheart's terms. But deep down she knew she would still have done whatever it took to save the life of a fellow Welshman.

"I have not changed my mind," she assured him.

She preceded him up the stairs. "Shall we get this over with?"

Lionheart's brows flew upward. "Your enthusiasm overwhelms me, my lady. You may not share my excitement, but can you not summon any eagerness for our coupling?"

"You are not the man I pictured when I imagined making love for the first time."

"Daffid is not the man for you," Lionheart said harshly.

Privately, Vanora agreed, but she was not about to admit as much to Lionheart. The man was puffed up enough as it was. "And I suppose you are," she challenged.

His eyes glittered like polished silver. "I will let you decide after I make love to you."

"You offer me naught but fleeting pleasure. What will happen to me when you are gone? Everyone will know I was your whore, and I will spend the rest of my life without a husband. I want a man who will be my partner in life, one who will treat me as an equal, and I want children. All those things will be denied me if you make me your whore."

After giving her words considerable thought, Lionheart said, "I shall ask Edward to find you an appropriate husband."

Although it seemed like a perfectly sound solution, it did not sit well with Lionheart. The thought of Vanora in another man's bed was not something he cared to contemplate.

"Do not bother," Vanora retorted. "Edward would surely choose an Englishman for me to wed, and I cannot bear the thought." Whirling, she stalked off.

Lionheart caught up with her in two long strides. A hush fell over the men gathered in the hall. A stern look from Lionheart was all it took for conversation to resume.

"Pay them no heed," he said when he noted Vanora's flushed face and stiff shoulders. "Should anyone speak ill of you for what we are about to do, he or she will be severely reprimanded. I shall make it clear that you had no choice in the matter."

Her shock was palpable. "You would do that?"

"Aye. Does that surprise you?"

She shrugged. "It does not take much to surprise me where you are concerned."

They ascended the stairs and walked along the gallery. "Are you shocked that I want you? That I would go to extraordinary lengths to get you into my bed?"

"You are an Englishman," she said, as if that explained everything.

"Aye, I am that." Reaching out, he touched the silken sable of her hair, letting his hand fall to her shoulder. "And you are a desirable woman. I could have taken you long ago were I the kind of man who enjoyed forcing a woman, but I am not." His hand slid downward to her breast. "I swear you will find enjoyment in my arms, Vanora, and I promise you will come to me willingly . . . nay, you will beg me to take you."

"Never!" Vanora vowed.

He opened the door to the solar and ushered her inside. "Never is a long time, sweeting. A man as determined as I always gets what he wants, and I want you."

He dragged her into his arms, pressing her against the thick ridge of his desire. Then he kissed her, tracing the outline of her lips as if trying to memorize every curve, every detail of their lush shape. Though she tried to resist him, her will was not as strong as his. He parted her mouth, coaxed it open with his tongue, and seduced her with his urgent need.

Impatiently he undressed her, until she stood before him clad in naught but a thin shift. His eyes darkened with hot hunger as he reached down to pull the garment over her head.

"Stop!"

Lionheart cursed violently as Father Caddoc burst into the chamber.

"God's toenails!" Lionheart roared. "You again! Leave us."

"Nay. I will not allow you to defile Vanora."

"I can do whatever I choose, with or without your permission. Vanora is willing. Ask her yourself if you do not believe me."

Father Caddoc's probing gaze impaled Vanora. "Is that true, child?"

Lionheart held his breath as he waited for Vanora's answer. She wanted him, he knew she did. He recognized all the signs of an aroused woman.

"Aye, Father," she murmured.

Heady relief made Lionheart almost giddy, but he forced himself to hide his elation. "You heard her, Father. Now leave us."

"If you must do this thing, then allow me to marry you. Wedding Vanora will make the act right in God's eyes."

Lionheart gave a shout of laughter. "Surely you jest, Father."

"I do not jest, my son. To bed Vanora, you must wed her."

Lionheart felt like an animal caught in a trap. He was hard and ready to burst, and would agree to almost anything to assuage his need. But marriage . . . ? Ridiculous. He tried to push Father Caddoc out the door, but the priest resisted with surprising strength for one of his advanced years.

"Do not hurt him," Vanora begged.

"I am prepared to perform the rites immediately," Father Caddoc said, bringing out his Bible from somewhere beneath his rusty black cassock.

"Damn you for your interference!" Lionheart shouted. "Think you I need a conscience?"

"I suspect you do," Father Caddoc said calmly.

Lionheart's cock was thick and hard and ready to explode, and he cared not what he had to do to get Vanora in his bed. "Very well, marry us, priest, but it will change naught. There is no room in my life for a wife."

"Do you want Vanora, my son?"

"Aye." His answer, though grudgingly given, sealed his fate.

"Then let us proceed with the ceremony."

Chapter Seven

When Vanora realized the situation was leading to an outcome neither she nor Lionheart wanted, she shook her head in vigorous protest. But before she could voice an objection, Mair bustled into the chamber, clucking over her mistress's state of undress.

"There, there, lambie, I will have you dressed in no time."

It was apparent to Vanora that Mair had been lurking outside the door or she could not have arrived so close on Father Caddoc's heels.

"Nay!" Lionheart shouted, clearly astounded by the unexpected turn of events. "Say the words, Father, then take Mair and leave. You have meddled enough in my affairs."

"Lionheart, this is madness!" Vanora cried, finally finding her voice. "Neither of us wants this."

"Maybe not, but I want *you.*" His steely gaze returned to the priest. "The words, Father. Say them before I change my mind and simply take what I want."

"Nay! There will be no marriage," Vanora cried.

"You have no choice, child," Father Caddoc said. "Think of your immortal soul if naught else. Lionheart is a knight; his code of honor demands that he honor his wife. Become his leman and you earn naught but his disrespect. Either way, he will have you."

"The words, priest," Lionheart bit out.

Father Caddoc opened his prayer book, prompting Mair to fetch Lionheart's chamber robe from a bench and drape it around Vanora's shoulders. Then Father Caddoc began the brief ceremony that would make her Lionheart's wife from now to eternity. When the moment arrived for her to pledge herself to Lionheart, the words stuck in her throat.

"Aye or nay, Vanora," Lionheart warned. "I shall have you whatever your answer."

"Vanora," Father Caddoc repeated, "will you take Lionheart for your husband?"

"Aye, but I like it not."

Lionheart's laughter broke the tension, and moments later Father Caddoc pronounced them husband and wife. Vanora was still reeling from shock when Lionheart pushed the priest and Mair from the room and locked the door behind them.

When he turned back to her, she was stunned by the look of horror etched upon his face.

"Blood of Christ! What have I done?"

"The unthinkable," Vanora charged. "What madness seized you?"

"Lust," Lionheart said, unable to find a better answer. "I thought with my cock and not my head." He stalked toward her. "But you are mine now, Vanora. You cannot say me nay, and your priest cannot appeal to my conscience."

He yanked away the chamber robe, baring her thinly clad body to his raking gaze. She saw his eyes glitter with dark hunger as he grasped the hem of her shift and whipped it over her head. Then his hands were moving on her body, stroking her throat, her breasts, her belly, her thighs. His touch made her flesh burn and her knees tremble. She was shivering all over, shuddering with a volatile combination of anticipation and fear.

It seemed strange that a man who did not love her should touch her with such gentleness. He had married her because he had been badgered into it, and because lust had stolen his mind, not because he had any true feelings for her.

Her own feelings at this moment were

tumultuous. Naught had prepared her for a man like Lionheart. How could an English warrior she had vowed to hate awaken such intense emotions in her?

Lionheart's heart raced as he explored Vanora's body. He marveled at the soft texture of her satiny skin, and was more than a little startled at the strength he felt beneath the softness.

His palms cupped her breasts, tightened possessively around the full, ripe mounds. He brushed the pad of his thumb over her nipples until he felt her respond. His fingers flicked lightly over the rosy crests; he heard her soft cry of protest but ignored it. Seconds before he took one hardened nub into his mouth, he looked into her eyes and saw confusion. His teeth closed about the pink tip. His tongue teased it unmercifully, licking, nipping, tasting and swirling around it in delicate circles. Then his mouth closed over the erect bud and suckled her. He could feel her trembling and increased the pressure.

"What are you doing to me?" she whispered in a voice fraught with panic.

A tormenting ache had started deep inside her and spread through her blood like wildfire. She burned, wanting more of the unthinkable things Lionheart was doing to her while at the same time deploring her wanton nature. Instinctively she arched against him, whimpering a little as she mourned her lost innocence.

"Making love to my wife," Lionheart growled.

His words drove home the knowledge that she now belonged to a man who did not want her. Her dreams of love and fidelity lay shattered at her feet, for surely Lionheart would abandon her once he grew tired of her. However much she regretted her response, nothing could halt the feelings he created inside her. Lust was a powerful force, and lust for her husband rose like a devouring beast within her.

In spite of her reluctance, she found herself waiting breathlessly for Lionheart to quench the heat of urgency within her, to touch her intimately in that place where she ached the most.

As if aware of her need, his hand sought the downy curls and slick folds of the valley betwixt her legs. She trembled uncontrollably at the unfamiliar sensations he was arousing in her. Opening the petals of silky flesh, he caressed her until she was wet and warm and swollen.

"Do you want me inside you, Vanora?"

Lionheart asked in a voice made hoarse by desire.

"Nay." It took all the will she possessed to summon that negative answer.

"Liar."

Sweeping her into his arms, he carried her to the bed. His gaze never left hers as he shed his clothing and lay down beside her. His mouth found a sensitive place on her shoulder and teased it with his teeth and tongue, causing her to writhe beneath him. Lowering his head, he took a nipple between his teeth, flicking it with his tongue as his fingers tormented her feminine flesh below.

Slipping two fingers inside her, he stroked the length of her with small, fluttery movements that made her cry out softly and arch against him. Then his mouth left her breasts and began to travel downward; a cry of dismay ripped from her lips when she realized what he intended. His lips brushed across the flat of her belly, caressing the velvet softness of her thighs, pressing his face into the sable triangle between.

Something dark and primitive surged through her, and she tried to push him away, but he gripped her slender waist and pressed her firmly into the bed furs. When she felt his tongue flick deep inside her hot, slick channel, she gasped in outrage. Then he began to lap her, tasting her with slow, languid strokes, swirling his tongue in and out and over the swollen petals. The little bud of her secret place flowered beneath the heat of his mouth, and Vanora feared the sinful feelings he was arousing in her.

Feared them because she no longer recognized herself in the woman writhing beneath the powerful English knight. Her husband had turned her into a wanton, and she liked it not.

"Stop! 'Tis sinful."

"Naught is sinful between husband and wife," Lionheart said, looking up from the bountiful feast between her thighs. He heaved a regretful sigh. "Mayhap we will save this for another day. Before I leave, I shall teach you all the ways to give and receive pleasure."

"Mayhap you will not be around long enough," Vanora said hopefully.

"I cannot predict the future, but whatever time is left to me will be put to good use teaching my wife how to please me."

Reaching between her thighs, he drew his fingers along her cleft. Honeyed dew seeped over them as he caressed the swollen folds, still slick and wet from his mouth and tongue. Vanora moaned and unconsciously parted her legs wider as he again slipped two fingers inside her and moved them in and out in hard, deliberate thrusts. Liquid fire spilled through her as the deep penetration of his fingers explored her so thoroughly.

Suddenly she was gasping for air. She struggled against the rising tide of passion, but Lionheart was relentless. Then she burst into a brilliant shower of overwhelming sensation. She cried out, a desperate cry that shook her very being.

Lionheart fought for control; his cock was ready to burst and his balls ached with raw need as he guided himself to the entrance of her body. He wanted to thrust his way inside her, to take her quickly and spend himself violently. The only thing that stopped him was the code of honor he had sworn to abide by when he had achieved knighthood. The code demanded that he should honor his wife, and though his hasty marriage was probably the biggest mistake of his life, hurting Vanora was not his intention.

He had aroused her with his mouth and fingers; she was damp and ready. Nevertheless, he proceeded with caution, penetrating her slowly, until he felt the barrier of her maidenhead. He did not go any further, but pulled slowly back, then dipped inside again, and slowly back, over and over, until she grew accustomed to the feeling of being stretched. It was not easy to breach her, despite the dampness that readied her for him. He rocked his hips back and forth, forcing himself a little deeper with each thrust.

Vanora's body resisted the increasing pressure; the pain surprised her. She had known it would hurt but was not prepared for the degree of pain she was suffering.

"Stop! You cannot fit."

If she had expected him to stop, she was mistaken. He merely tightened his arms and held her firmly beneath him, controlling her struggles with his weight and strength, focused now on his own pleasure. He pushed harder, and her tender flesh gave under the pressure, closing around his thick length as he surged full and deep inside her. Finally he was in her to the hilt; she writhed helplessly beneath him, shifting to ease the pain.

"The worst is over, sweeting," he said, soothing her without withdrawing.

The deed was done; she was truly Lionheart's wife now.

Her breathing calmed, became deeper. Now that she was reconciled to the fact that her virginity had been breached, some of the pleasure she had experienced earlier returned. She felt him deep inside her, pulsing strongly within her tightness, and she moved her hips experimentally. It felt . . . good. Nay, better than good. She wanted more. She looked up at him and met his glittering silver gaze.

"Shall I continue?"

She felt his tenseness ease; until then she had not realized how tight his muscles had been. Swallowing hard, she nodded.

"I want to hear you say the words. Do you want me, Vanora?"

Admitting such a thing bit deeply into her pride, but she could no longer deny her need. While her mind utterly denied him, her body wanted him. "Aye, I want you."

He kissed her, deep kisses that shook her to the very core. Grasping his shoulders, she wanted to move more quickly, to finish this and be done with it, but he controlled her; his hands beneath her buttocks rocked her against him. He urged her to accept his pace, sometimes slow, sometimes fast, but always masterful.

He adjusted his weight, leaning into her, pressing her down further into the furs. "I told you we would fit," he whispered into her ear. "Can you feel me inside you?"

She tossed her head back and forth on the pillow, feeling every turgid inch of him filling her. "Aye."

"You are so tight and warm and wet inside."

His words served to heighten her awareness of the motion of his hips, the heat, the pure sexuality of their coupling. She whimpered. He thrust deeper. He overwhelmed her with his passion. The pressure grew, intensified; yet she fought to contain it.

He swore softly. "Do not hold back. Give yourself to me, Vanora. You are mine."

He moved within her, relentlessly, faster and deeper, as if he wanted to touch her soul. She was suddenly frightened of the way she felt, as if she had no control over her body. She pushed aside the inner voice that whispered what she did not wish to hear: that it was Lionheart's right to use her in such a manner, and that she enjoyed what he was doing to her.

Time stood still as she clung to him, their bodies moving as one. She heard her own muffled cries and could not stop them. With each thrust of Lionheart's staff she flew higher, her senses pulsing with soaring ecstasy. Then her body clutched the hard, thick length of him and convulsed in mindless rapture. The pleasurable contractions seemed to go on forever, her cries filling the chamber with sweet music as her body climbed unimaginable peaks.

His hips pounded, his breath grating harshly in her ears. She tightened her muscles on him. He swore loudly, then pushed once more, holding himself inside her, his powerful climax filling her with the vibrant warmth of life.

Breathing deeply, Vanora closed her eyes, aware that something momentous had just taken place. Everything in her world had changed. She was truly and irrevocably a woman now, and to her surprise, she did not regret the loss of her maidenhead. She felt not the pain of ravishment but the joy of being loved. Not loved in the true sense of the word, for Lionheart did not love her with his heart, but loved nonetheless.

Lionheart stared down at her. Her hair was spread in a tangled web of rich sable across the pillow, and her body still gripped him tightly. Reluctantly he left her warm softness and rolled to his side, wrapping his arms around her and bringing her against him.

"That was not so bad, was it?"

His smug expression galled her. "How did you accomplish that?"

He grinned. "Accomplish what?"

"I wanted you not, but you did things to my body that made me . . ." She halted, unable to say the words.

"Made you want me? Admit it, sweeting, I gave you pleasure, just as I promised."

"You hurt me."

"The pain is a woman's burden to bear, but 'tis a small price to pay, is it not? You will experience that same pleasure without the pain many times before I leave Cragdon. I shall see to it."

"Your arrogance appalls me, sir knight." She tried to rise, but his arm tightened around her.

"Where are you going?"

"I am famished. I should go below and see what has become of our meal."

"Nay, I suspect 'tis waiting for us outside the door." He rose and pulled a coverlet over her. "Stay as you are while I fetch it."

Rising naked from the bed, he strode to the door. Vanora's gaze went to the taut mounds of his buttocks, remembering how his muscles had flexed beneath her hands as he drove himself inside her. Her gaze roamed upward, noting the scar near his left shoulder and another on the right, only lower, and another still on his left thigh.

His was a warrior's body, strong and muscular without the sturdy bulk of her own countrymen. No doubt about it, Lionheart was a man without equal. Were he not an Englishman . . . The thought slid away as Lionheart opened the door and found the tray his squire had left for them. He returned with it to the bed. Her appreciative gaze was riveted on his loins.

Even at rest his manhood was impressive. Were all men as magnificently endowed? she wondered. Somehow she doubted it. Her gaze followed the line of hair rising from his groin to his chest, admiring his trim waist and the width of his shoulders. But it was his face to which her attention was drawn: dark, elegant brows, lips that could turn hard at will, and changeable eyes that varied in intensity from glittering silver to smoky gray. The combination was lethal. No wonder women went eagerly to his bed.

Lionheart set the cloth-covered tray on the bed and sat down carefully so as not to upset it. He whisked off the cloth and inspected the contents. The tantalizing aroma of roasted hare and venison pie made Vanora's mouth water. There was also cheese, fresh bread and butter and mugs of ale.

Lionheart retrieved his knife from the nightstand and cut the meat into small chunks. Then he offered the trencher to Vanora. "Help yourself," he said. "It looks delicious."

Vanora pushed a piece of meat onto a hunk of bread and popped it into her mouth, chewing and swallowing with relish. " 'Tis good," she allowed.

They ate quickly, devouring nearly all the food that had been left for them. When they finished, Lionheart set the empty tray on a table and walked to the washstand. He poured water into a bowl, wet a cloth and washed his hands and face; then he carried the water and cloth to the bed. After Vanora washed her hands and face, he took the cloth from her, dipped it into the bowl and pulled aside the coverlet.

"What are you doing?"

"Cleansing my seed and your virgin's blood from your thighs."

She tried to grasp the cloth from his hand, but he would not let her. "I can do it myself. What you intend is not decent."

He sent her a stern look. "I shall decide what is decent and what is not." He spread her thighs, stared at her until she began to squirm in embarrassment, then applied the cloth to her tender flesh.

Mortified, Vanora averted her gaze. When he finished, he used the cloth on himself and returned the bowl to the washstand. Then he lay down beside her. Vanora rolled away and tried to rise, but once again he stopped her.

"Where are you going now?"

"To my chamber."

"This *is* your chamber. We are wed; henceforth you will sleep with me."

Vanora had no intention of continuing this intimacy between them. Lionheart had succeeded in seducing her, but now that she knew how responsive she was to him, she would take steps to protect herself. She would never forgive herself for falling into his arms like a ripe plum.

She gave him a frosty look. "Sharing a bed with you does not appeal to me."

Lionheart's brows lifted. "It has its advantages. I want your things moved into the solar tomorrow. Since your priest badgered me into wedding you, we shall live together as husband and wife for as long as I remain at Cragdon."

He pulled her into the curve of his body, one hand resting possessively on her breast. Panic seized her when she felt his erection prodding her. *Nay, not again!* When he rolled her onto her back, she doubled her fists and pounded his chest.

"Why do you fight me, vixen? You know you cannot win."

"You are an animal," she charged. "No human is capable of mating so soon without a proper resther thating period."

Lionheart laughed. "Obviously, you know naught of these matters, else you would not question my prowess. I am more than capable of making love to you again."

"I would prefer you did not," Vanora persisted.

When his hand moved down her body, she tried not to flinch. She held herself rigid, even when he began to caress her. His hand rose to her breast, his fingers splaying over the sensitive mound, deliberately brushing her tingling nipples until they thrust against his palm.

Vanora drew in a sharp breath, finding it difficult to remain impassive. Glancing up at his face, she saw that his teeth were clenched, his expression hard and utterly determined. Sadness overwhelmed her, for she discerned no warmth, no real tenderness in his caresses this time. But he was arousing her all the same.

"Do not attempt to resist me, sweeting,

for 'twill do you no good. I can make you want me, and well you know it. I can be tender if you allow it, or I can take what I want. 'Tis up to you how our relationship proceeds."

"I am your wife and must submit, but I do not have to like it."

"Ah, sweeting, you are wrong. When we mate, you will most definitely like it."

As if to prove his mastery over her, his hand swept lower. Vanora bit her lip hard as his palm skimmed over her buttocks and slid slowly over her hip to her belly, seeking the warmth of her woman's mound. Despite her clamped lips, she could not stop the moan that slipped past them when his fingers found her wet cleft. She tried to remove his hand, but he merely laughed at her. Urging her thighs apart, he slid his fingers deep into her.

Her breath quickened audibly.

"You drive me to distraction, woman," he growled as he shifted his position and mounted her, then lowered his loins until they met hers.

Squeezing her eyes shut, Vanora averted her face, refusing to let him see how aroused she was. She felt helpless lying beneath him, her body, her very soul exposed to him. She hated it that he could make her want him with so little effort.

He entered her then, thrusting slowly into her with detached control, relentlessly bringing her to the point of no return. Vanora gasped, tremors shooting through her body at the feel of his uncompromising strength inside her. She felt defenseless like this, impaled by his flesh. Yet, when he began to move, a traitorous heat began to blur the edges of her resistance and she flung her arms around his neck and thrust her loins against his in unconscious surrender.

It ended violently, her climax sending her soaring to the highest stars. Lionheart followed close behind, shouting her name as he poured himself into her. When it was over, Vanora lay spent and exhausted, deploring her wanton nature and vowing to be more cautious in her dealings with her husband in the future.

Lionheart's thoughts followed similar lines. Were he not careful, this woman could become more important to him than he wished. It was amazing how lust could lead a man into trouble. He had gotten what he wanted, but at what cost? He was not the kind of man to settle in one place. He was Edward's vassal, sworn to follow him to hell and back if Edward demanded it of him.

Lionheart had no need of an heir, for he had naught to leave to one; marriage was not important to him. Had Edward wanted Lionheart to wed, he would have chosen an heiress for him. Dimly Lionheart wondered how Edward would react to his hasty wedding. Would he find it unacceptable? Would he be angry and invalidate the marriage?

He turned and studied Vanora's sleeping face in the flickering candlelight, surprised to find that he wanted her again. He knew she was not as cold as she pretended, for he had unleashed hidden fires in her that had nearly incinerated him. She could deny it all she wished, but he was experienced enough to know that she wanted him with the same intensity that he wanted her.

There would be no separate chambers, no separate beds. He would accept naught but total surrender from his reluctant bride.

Gathering Vanora in his arms, Lionheart drifted off to sleep, smiling in anticipation of awakening and making love to Vanora in the pale light of dawn.

Vanora was gone when Lionheart awoke fully aroused the following morning.

Cursing, he tossed back the covers and regarded his erection with a sour expression. Vanora had thwarted him again . . . damn her stubborn hide. He had not even heard her leave their bed. After he performed his morning ablutions, he left the chamber in a foul mood.

Sir Giles greeted him with a knowing smile as he strode into the hall. "Your marriage was rather sudden, was it not? You are late in rising. Doubtless you are exhausted, as I would be had I a bride like Vanora in my bed."

"Enough," Lionheart warned. "I admit I thought with the head betwixt my legs and not with the one on my shoulders. The marriage was unplanned, as you well know. 'Twas the priest's doing."

"Seriously, Lionheart," Giles said, "what will Edward say when he learns of your precipitous marriage to a Welshwoman?"

Lionheart shrugged. "My marriage changes naught but my sleeping arrangements at Cragdon."

Giles sent him a skeptical look. "Tell that to Edward."

"Speaking of my bride, have you seen Vanora this morning?"

"I saw her enter the chapel to attend Mass."

His face set in determined lines, Lionheart set out to find Vanora. He found her in the chapel, deep in prayer. He stood in the doorway and watched her until she sensed his presence and looked up.

"Were you looking for me?"

He stalked toward her. "Why did you leave our bed?"

"I always attend morning Mass."

"I wanted to make love to you again," he said in a low voice.

Vanora's violet eyes widened. "Again? 'Tis beyond belief that you would want to do . . . *that* in the light of day."

He shrugged. "Night, day, it matters not. 'Tis called making love, Vanora. Can you not say it?"

"*Do* you love me, Lionheart?" His stunned expression must have answered her question, for she said, "I thought not. What we did was rut like two animals in heat. I remained in the chapel after Mass to pray for forgiveness."

His eyebrows shot upward. "For what do you need forgiveness?"

"I should not have allowed you to expose my wanton nature. I am praying for the strength to resist your next assault."

Dismay crossed Lionheart's features. "Assault? Is that what you call it? Why would you want to resist that which gives us pleasure? 'Tis no sin, what we did, for your priest said the words that made it right in God's eyes."

"Were you not goaded by lust, you would have never wed me."

"True, but 'tis too late for regrets. Get up from your knees, wife. We shall go to the hall to break our fast and receive congratulations on the propitious occasion of our marriage. Both your people and mine need to see us together."

Grasping her arm, he helped her rise. Father Caddoc chose that moment to appear from the sacristy, holding a sheet of parchment in one hand and an inkpot and quill in the other.

"Ah, 'tis good you are both here. I have prepared your marriage document. It but awaits your signatures."

Lionheart looked at the document with scant enthusiasm. Were he to refuse, would the marriage be invalid? He stared at it so long that Father Caddoc cleared his throat and thrust the inkpot beneath his nose.

"Your signature, Sir Lionheart."

Though Lionheart wanted to rip the document to shreds, something inside him would not allow it. His love of freedom warred with the need to possess Vanora, body and soul. Need won out as he dipped the quill in the inkpot and set his signature to the document. When he handed the quill to Vanora, she refused to take it.

"Sign it, child," Father Caddoc encouraged. "You have no choice. The deed was done, was it not?" he asked, alluding to her wedding night.

She turned to Lionheart, her face set in stubborn lines. "Do you keep your word, sir knight? Will Daffid live?"

"Aye, he will live."

"Will you set him free?"

A long pause ensued. "That depends on how well you please me. But never think you can take Daffid as a lover once I am gone. Father Caddoc will make sure you remain faithful to your vows." He fixed the priest with a piercing look. "Will you not, Father?"

Now, why had he said that? Once he left Cragdon, it should not matter to him what Vanora did.

"Fear not, Lionheart," Vanora spat. "I would not have Daffid were he the last man walking the earth."

Grasping the quill, she signed her name on the marriage document, returned it to Father Caddoc and stormed from the chapel.

Chapter Eight

Lionheart caught up with Vanora in the courtyard. He grasped her elbow to keep her from fleeing, then steered her into the hall. He seated her at the high table and left to speak briefly to Sir Giles. He waited until Giles departed, then returned to Vanora's side. 'Twas obvious that everyone knew about their hasty marriage the night before, for Sir Brandon surged to his feet, raised his cup and toasted the couple.

"Felicitations on your marriage," he bellowed.

"And may your marriage prove fruitful," another knight shouted.

One by one, each of Lionheart's knights stood, raised his cup and drank to the couple's health and prosperity.

"Thank you," Lionheart said. "My bride and I would like you to join us tonight at a feast to celebrate our nuptials."

"I do not feel like celebrating," Vanora hissed. "This marriage is a farce, and well you know it."

The warmth left his eyes. " 'Tis a legal

marriage, signed, sealed and consummated. 'Twas contracted in a moment of madness, but now we must live with the consequences. You will not have to put up with me overlong, for soon Edward will have need of me elsewhere."

Vanora broke off a crust of bread and popped it into her mouth. She chewed thoughtfully, swallowed, then asked, "Are you sure you will never return to Cragdon once Edward orders you elsewhere? Do you promise?"

"So far as it is within my power to promise such a thing. I am Edward's vassal. I go where he wills for however long he deems necessary."

"As long as you leave me in peace, I care not where you go."

"Do you not?" Lionheart said, his eyes gleaming mischievously. "You liked me well enough last night."

"Can you not forget what happened last night?" Vanora beseeched. " 'Tis embarrassing to be reminded of my wanton behavior."

"Forget it? Never. I hope to have that wanton in my bed again tonight. Even as we speak, your belongings are being moved into the solar."

Vanora's spoon dropped from her fingers. "You have no right."

"Father Caddoc gave me the right when he married us. You belong to me, Vanora, body and soul. Never doubt it," he said coolly. Then he looked away, as if already distancing himself from her.

"We shall see," Vanora retorted, suppressing a smile.

Though Lionheart's opinion of a woman's role in marriage did not differ from that of other men of his ilk, Vanora liked it not. Daffid had expressed the same sentiments, and she had ended their betrothal because of them. She had hoped to retain an identity of her own after marriage, and mayhap maintain a measure of independence, but men like Lionheart and Daffid expected unconditional obedience from a wife.

"You are smiling. Did I say something to amuse you?" Lionheart asked, regarding her through narrowed lids.

Vanora's gaze refused to meet his. Her thoughts would most definitely *not* amuse him. "Nay. I was merely thinking how peaceful my life was before you came to Cragdon."

Lionheart searched her face, his expression hard and inflexible. "As was mine. I thought you might have been remembering the pleasure I gave you last night. You enjoyed me as much as I enjoyed you."

Vanora withheld a reply. The unexpected pleasure of their coupling was something she preferred to keep private. The brief pain was naught compared to the bliss that had followed. Never had she suspected her body capable of scaling such heights of intense pleasure. Lionheart's touch, his kisses, had driven her mad with wanting. How could a woman hate the man who took her maidenhead with the unexpected gentleness of a caring lover?

Vanora cast a surreptitious glance at her husband and found she did not recognize the uncompromising warrior sitting beside her; where was the enticing lover who had seduced her on their wedding night? She could find no trace of charm or warmth in Lionheart's remote, distracted manner. Which man could she expect tonight when they were alone in their chamber? Would he become the tender lover again? Or would he remain the hard man who sat beside her with a scowl on his face?

She almost preferred the hard, uncompromising warrior, for the tender lover confused her. While the softer side of Lionheart could easily engage her emotions, Vanora preferred the inflexible warrior, for he was a man she could hate.

"I intend to ride to the village today," Lionheart said, interrupting her thoughts. "Since my men have found no trace of Llewelyn, I thought to question your vassals. Think you they can tell me something of value?"

Vanora's attention sharpened. "They are simple people, Lionheart. I trust you will not punish them if they know naught of Llewelyn."

He gave her a patronizing look. "I am not a monster, Vanora. 'Tis not my nature to hurt innocent people."

Vanora's mouth flattened, but she said naught as Lionheart departed. She had much to accomplish today before he returned, and trading barbs would only delay his leaving.

Vanora left the hall and hastened to the dungeon as soon as Lionheart departed. She wanted to be the one to tell Daffid that she and Lionheart were wed. Silently she rehearsed the argument she would use to convince the guard to allow her to pass. To her surprise, there was no guard to stop her. Lifting the torch from the sconce, she slowly descended the stairs to the lower regions of the castle.

The guardroom was empty, and so were

the cells. Daffid was gone. Vanora returned to the hall and hailed Sir Brandon.

"What can I do for you, Lady Vanora?"

"The prisoner. What happened to Daffid ap Deverell?"

"Lionheart had him removed to the tower," Brandon informed her.

Vanora was stunned. She had never expected Lionheart to keep his word. "I should like to see him."

"He is allowed no visitors, my lady. But rest assured he is quite comfortable in his new quarters."

"I merely wished to inform him of my marriage. He was my betrothed. I owe him the courtesy of imparting the news myself."

"If 'tis any comfort, I believe the prisoner has already been informed of your marriage."

"When was Daffid moved?"

"Just this morn. Sir Giles saw to it."

"Thank you, Sir Brandon."

Since Vanora had no further interest in Daffid save preventing his death, she made no more efforts to visit him. Apparently, he was being held until Edward decided his fate.

The stressful days that followed tested Vanora's nerves to the limit. There was naught she could do to escape Lionheart's lovemaking even if she'd wanted to. To her dismay, she was not certain she did want to. Each night, the tender lover returned when he climbed into bed with her. During the day she tried to think of ways to avoid his lovemaking, but when night came he overcame her objections with his tempting kisses and heated caresses.

There was no help for her. She had become a slave to his passion, and it galled her to think how easily he had made her into something she swore she would never become. Each day she prayed for a messenger from Edward, ordering Lionheart's removal to another post, but she waited in vain, for word never arrived.

One afternoon Vanora rode to the village with Mair to attend a woman about to give birth. The birth was a difficult one, and Vanora decided to sit with the woman until her husband returned from the fields. As the day waned, Vanora sent Mair back to the keep for swaddling for the babe and settled down beside the sleeping woman to await Mair's return. She had just started to doze off when a cool breeze from the open door wafted over her.

"Mair, is that you?" Vanora called from the tiny bedroom.

"Nay, Vanora, 'tis I."

Vanora whipped her head around at the sound of Lionheart's voice. "What are you doing here?"

The woman in the bed stirred, and Vanora held her finger to her lips and herded Lionheart from the room, closing the door softly behind her.

"Mair told me where to find you. I bring swaddling for the infant. How fares the mother?"

"I think she will be fine, and the babe is healthy. You need not have bothered. Mair could have brought what was needed."

" 'Tis growing dark. You should not be out alone." His eyes darkened with disapproval. "Furthermore, I did not give you permission to leave the keep."

"Why would I need permission? I have never needed it before. This is my land. No one would dare harm me."

"You are my wife. If danger stalks me, it stalks you. A man like Llewelyn would have no qualms about using you to force my compliance. Do you know what would happen in that instance?"

"Aye," Vanora retorted. "I know exactly what would happen. You would ignore Llewelyn's demands, for you care naught for me."

A growl rumbled from Lionheart's chest. "You sorely try my patience, vixen." He stalked toward her, his eyes suddenly alight with desire. " 'Tis when you are defying me that I want you the most. When your great violet eyes mock me, I want to toss up your skirts and thrust myself inside you."

His admission stunned Vanora. Her defiance should anger him, not arouse him. He was standing so close, she could almost feel the waves of heat emanating from his body. She could almost taste his arousal. What manner of man was he? Did he never tire of rutting?

He dragged her against him, and his mouth claimed hers with a mastery that answered her question more forcefully than words. He kissed her until her head began to spin, prodding her lips apart and thrusting his tongue inside to taste her thoroughly. Vanora suspected he would have taken her on the dirt floor of the cottage if Bretta's husband had not returned.

Flustered, the poor man stopped just inside the door, his face turning a bright shade of red. Stuttering with embarrassment, he said, "Forgive me, master, mistress, but I was told Bretta gave birth today. Are my wife and babe well?"

"They are fine, Gordy," Vanora said, nearly as disconcerted as the villein. "You have a healthy son. Sir Lionheart brought swaddling clothes from the castle."

"Aye, we shall leave you now to greet your new son. Come along, Vanora."

"Let Mair know if Bretta should need further care," Vanora called over her shoulder as Lionheart led her out the door.

"Thank ye, my lady," Gordy called after her.

"How often do you do this?" Lionheart asked as he lifted her into the saddle.

"Do what?"

"Visit the villeins without an escort?"

"Mair was with me."

" 'Tis not good enough. I forbid you to leave the keep without one of my warriors in attendance."

"You cannot bully me," Vanora contended. "I did as I pleased before you arrived and shall continue to do so long after you are gone."

"You will obey me in this, Vanora. Once I am gone, you can do as you please."

"You go too far," Vanora said as she dug her heels into her palfrey's flanks. The horse shot forward, leaving Lionheart behind in her dust.

Cursing, Lionheart caught up with her

and grasped her reins. "What are you trying to do, kill yourself?"

"I am an expert rider," Vanora retorted. "I am merely anxious to return to the keep."

A wicked glint came into Lionheart's eyes. "I am glad, but I doubt you are as anxious as I am."

Fuming, Vanora had no choice but to let Lionheart set the pace back to Cragdon. Surely he did not intend to bed her in the light of day, did he?

He did.

Ignoring her protests, he escorted her through the hall and up the stairs to the solar. "Take off your clothes."

" 'Tis the middle of the day," she sputtered.

"Think you I care? I want you, vixen. Morning, night, it matters not. I crave your fire, your spirit; I want your passion. I do not wish to waste a moment of the time left to me at Cragdon."

Fighting the desire Lionheart roused in her, Vanora shook her head in violent denial. "You confuse my senses and overwhelm my weak body," she cried. "Take what you want and leave me my dignity."

"I shall take what I want but not without wringing a response from you. You are a passionate woman, vixen. Why not admit it and give yourself over to my care?"

"Your care? You care naught for me. Temporary insanity brought us together in marriage. I submit because I have no choice, and because I know you will not be here forever."

"Will you not miss me a little? Am I not a good lover?"

"I hoped for more in a husband. I expected to become a true partner to the man I married, to be respected and loved for myself, not for the worldly goods I bring to the marriage."

"I doubt Daffid ap Deverell would have been the kind of husband you seek."

"For once we are in agreement," Vanora admitted.

He removed his doublet and peeled off his chausses. "Let us cry truce during our private moments," Lionheart said. Grasping her hand, he brought it to his groin. "Take me in your hand, Vanora. See what you do to me? I can think of better things to do than fling insults at one another. When we are in bed, we are lovers, not enemies."

Vanora curled her fingers around his erection, gasping when she felt him harden and expand. Her gaze flew up to meet his. His expression was hard and sensual, his eyes dilated and dark with arousal. Her breath seized; she was stunned by her body's instinctive response to his seduction. She grew so hot she wanted to tear her clothes off and bare her body to him. Only her pride prevented her.

"Shall we get these clothes off you?" he whispered, as if she had given voice to her thoughts.

His hands were swift and sure as he undressed her. Then his gaze swept over her, leaving heat in its wake, and when he raised one hand toward her, Vanora's breath caught and her flesh tingled in anticipation.

A scalding heat flared between her legs, and her nipples hardened into rigid peaks. Lost in the blaze of his eyes, she began to tremble as his hands swept over her body, down her thighs and between, his fingers brushing the bud of her sex. She shuddered, bowing to the inevitable as she melted against him.

When his mouth slanted down over hers, passion flared instantly between them. The turbulence of their clashing wills only added to the heat exploding between them.

Lionheart swept her up into his arms and carried her to their bed. Any lingering anger had turned to burning fever. He no longer wanted to argue with Vanora. When he'd been told that she had left the keep without an escort, his temper had flared. She had deliberately ignored the danger that existed beyond the keep's protective walls. But now all he wanted to do was love her.

Casting all vestiges of anger aside, he lifted her up and set her astride him. Vanora gasped as he slowly impaled her, yet her body accepted him without resistance, sheathing him in silken heat.

Then suddenly they were kissing, mouths hungry and frantic, all the tension of the past weeks erupting in a blaze of animal lust. Her rocking hips met his, driving him deeper inside her as his hands slid up her back to twist in her hair. Her musky scent fired his passion, and he kissed her more fiercely, stoking the fire that flamed between them.

Exultant, Lionheart knew her desire for him was not feigned; he felt it in her kisses, in the way she clung to him, in her hoarse cries of pleasure. He was pure fire, and she was the tinder that set him aflame. She matched the raw force of his passion, moving with him in furious rhythm. Their primitive mating made Lionheart realize that Vanora had been holding back during their previous couplings, that her passion had not been fully engaged. Now that he knew what she was capable of, he would not allow her to hold back any part of herself in the future.

Her eager response crushed Lionheart's restraint, shredded any remnant of self-control. Delving deep, he shattered her with a bold stroke. Breaking off the kiss, she threw back her head and gave a hoarse cry. He watched her face as she flew apart, then followed her to a stunning climax. He held her close as his breath eased and he slowly regained his wits.

"You did it again," Vanora said, glaring at him.

The corners of Lionheart's mouth twitched. "What did I do?"

"You touched me and kissed me and made me want you." She climbed off him and pulled the coverlet up over her breasts. "I have no will where you are concerned. What manner of magic do you use to bring about so wicked a response from me?"

Lionheart chuckled. "Are my kisses not magic?"

"You, sir knight, have an inflated image of yourself. Once you leave Cragdon, I shall forget you ever existed."

"Mayhap I will return from time to time

to remind you. A wife should not forget her lord and master."

Lionheart knew he was deliberately goading her, but her anger had a way of sharpening his senses and bringing them into focus. She stirred his emotions and made him feel alive. War did that to him, too, but the exhilarating emotional impact Vanora had on him was far different from what he felt during the heat of battle.

"God is my lord and master," Vanora retorted.

Her feisty words made Lionheart want to stick around and make her eat them. Everyone knew women had their place, and that place was in the home, raising children and making sure the keep ran smoothly. 'Twas a man's place to protect his family and his lands. Women had little say in matters outside the home.

But Vanora was different. She wanted to be an equal partner with her husband, but such a thing was unheard of. It occurred to him that when he left, Vanora would be making all the decisions concerning her people and lands, unless Edward decided to give Cragdon to one of his faithful followers. That thought brought another . . . a startling one. His marriage to Vanora made Cragdon his. Mayhap he would protest if Edward gave Cragdon to another.

The thought of claiming Cragdon was an intriguing one, for he had never before felt the need for land. He had pledged himself to Edward and had no desire to settle down; furthermore, this remote corner of Wales did not appeal to him. But the thought of Vanora being evicted from her home was not comforting. Obviously, he would have to speak to Edward when he arrived and plead Vanora's cause.

Though he had wed Vanora in a moment of madness, Lionheart held himself responsible for her. The marriage had been consummated and could not be annulled, unless, of course, Edward declared it illegal.

Vanora's taunting words hung in the air between them. "God may be lord and master of all, but you are still answerable to me," Lionheart said.

" 'Tis my fervent hope that one day a woman will be allowed to choose her own husband, and that marriage will be a true partnership. I may not live to see the day, but I vow 'tis coming."

Vanora's prediction gave Lionheart pause. He could not even imagine a world where women's opinions mattered.

"Women have not men's strength," Lionheart maintained.

"Men have not women's fortitude," Vanora retorted. "What would you say if I told you I can wield a sword and ride as well as one of your knights?"

He sent her a hard look. "I would say you are lying. Women have neither the strength to wield a sword nor the courage to use one."

Her secretive smile roused Lionheart's suspicion. What did she know that he did not? Pushing his disquieting thoughts aside, Lionheart rose and walked to the washstand.

" 'Tis time to sup. My stomach is touching my backbone."

"Just like a man to think of his stomach when an argument is not going to his liking," Vanora said.

Lionheart paused with the washcloth in his hands. "Were we arguing? I was not aware of it. Shall I send water up for a bath?"

"Aye, thank you."

After Lionheart had washed and dressed and left the chamber, Vanora donned her chamber robe and waited for the tub and water to arrive. Mair arrived first.

"You seem to enjoy Lionheart's attentions," Mair said. "Have you forgotten that Daffid is still your husband's prisoner?"

"I have forgotten naught, Mair. As I told you before, I broke the betrothal before I was forced to wed Lionheart. Daffid's attitude toward marriage disappointed me. I thought him a better man than he is. I still intend to help him escape if 'tis within my power to do so, for he is a Welshman."

"You have been wed to Lionheart some weeks now. Have you changed your opinion of him? He has made you a tolerable husband. You do not protest his attentions overmuch."

Vanora flushed. "There are certain aspects of this marriage that please me," she admitted. "I have never lied to you, Mair, and do not intend to start now. Wedding Lionheart was not my idea, as you well know, but I am biding my time and making the best of it until he leaves. 'Twould prove disastrous should he learn I am the knight that prevented Llewelyn's capture. No telling what he would do to me."

"I pray he never learns," Mair said fervently. "What do you suppose happened to Llewelyn? No one seems to know where he has hidden himself."

"Have you seen or heard aught of Cragdon's knights, Mair? Do you know if Llewelyn's army has disbanded?"

Mair's voice dropped to a whisper. "Father Caddoc saw Sir Ren in the village yesterday. Sir Ren said that he and those of your knights that have not joined another's service will remain nearby in case you have need of them."

"I look forward to their return after the English leave Cragdon."

"Think you Edward will return Cragdon to you? Lionheart is now lord of the keep. All you once held belongs to him."

"Lionheart cares naught about Cragdon. He is Edward's vassal, sworn to follow his prince."

"What if there is a child?" Mair asked. "Your belly could already be swelling with the Englishman's babe."

Vanora's hands flew to her stomach. "He will not care. Heirs mean naught to him; he admitted as much. He claims loyalty only to his prince and his country. Were I to quicken with his child, the babe would remain mine own."

Mair's eyes widened, but her answer was forestalled when the tub and hot water arrived. After the servants were dismissed, Mair helped Vanora into the tub and laid out her clothing.

"You are making a mistake if you think Lionheart would deny his child, lambie,"

Mair scolded as she bent to scrub Vanora's back.

"The point is a moot one, Mair, for I am not with child." Her voice lowered. "Know you a way to keep Lionheart's seed from taking root inside me?"

Mair stilled. "Is that what you wish?"

Pain darkened Vanora's violet eyes. Nay! She wanted Lionheart's child. It would be something of him to cherish the rest of her lonely days. When Lionheart left, she would be a wife without a husband, abandoned by the man who had married her in haste and left her without regret.

"I can prepare a concoction but it does not always work and can harm the babe should you conceive while taking it," Mair warned.

Vanora sighed. "I do not want to hurt my child should there be one. I do not wish to bear a child whose father would abandon him, but I must obey God's laws."

"You are wise to listen to your heart, child," Mair said. "God will not abandon you."

Lionheart summoned Alan and asked him to see what was keeping Vanora. How long could a bath take? The meal had already begun, and Lionheart wondered if Vanora intended to defy him and eat alone in the solar. He knew she resented him for wringing a response from her when she would have withheld one, but he did not like her capricious moods.

Vanora ran hot and cold. He knew not how her mind worked. His brow lowered, his thoughts turning dark. Mayhap he was better off not knowing. He was becoming obsessed with his bride, something he had vowed would never happen.

He found himself wondering what it would be like to know Vanora's affection instead of her enmity. Would she become a loving wife? Or would she abandon him like his mother? Experience had taught him that love did not exist, that it was a myth, the stuff of storytellers and poets. Yet whenever he thought of Vanora, he wondered. 'Twas lust, he decided. As long as he remembered why he had wed Vanora, his heart was in no danger.

His heart gave an unexpected lurch when Vanora entered the hall and she strode toward him. Clad in a royal purple overtunic trimmed in marten fur and belted with golden links, she looked as regal as a queen. It occurred to him that he had never seen a woman with such a commanding presence. She knew exactly what she wanted from marriage and was not afraid to demand it. Unfortunately, it was not within his power to grant her wish.

He felt himself harden and was not surprised that he wanted to make love to her again.

That startling thought brought Lionheart up short. It was not good to need a woman to the point that she consumed his every thought. Mayhap he needed to separate himself from Vanora for a time. Aye, he decided. 'Twas time to redirect his efforts to finding Llewelyn instead of bedding his wife.

"I am leaving tomorrow," Lionheart said abruptly. " 'Tis time I broadened my search for Llewelyn."

"How long will you be gone?"

"I know not. Do not give the men I am leaving behind too much trouble in my absence. You are not to leave the keep without an escort and can go no further abroad than the village. Nor may you or your cohorts visit Daffid. I have not forgotten what happened the last time I left Cragdon. Prisoners have a way of disappearing from the keep when I am not around. I know there is a secret exit, though I have yet to find it. It would ease things between us if you told me where it is."

Vanora's chin rose defiantly. "There is no secret exit."

He sent her a skeptical glare. "So you say. Rest assured that I shall find it."

Vanora was glad Lionheart was leaving. She did not know how much more she could endure of his lovemaking. The man who bedded her, who knew her intimately, was not this man sitting beside her, issuing orders and expecting them to be obeyed without question. This man was the real Lionheart, she reminded herself. Any softening she felt for Lionheart the lover was instantly obliterated by his arrogant counterpart. Her relief was heartfelt, for despite all her efforts, she had begun to care for him.

"I wish you Godspeed," Vanora said. "I shall manage quite nicely without you."

For some reason, her words appeared to displease Lionheart. He rose abruptly and stormed off. What did he expect? Vanora wondered. He had regretted their marriage seconds after they were wed.

"What did you say to anger your husband?" Father Caddoc asked when he joined her a few minutes later.

"Everything I say or do angers him, except . . ." Her words fell away. "Why oh why did you insist that he wed me?"

Father Caddoc searched her face, then nodded, as if satisfied by what he saw. "Give him time, child. A man like Lionheart must be led gently into love."

Vanora gasped. "Love! Love is the last thing I want from Lionheart. The man does not know the meaning of the word."

"Is he harsh with you? Does he beat you? Mayhap I should have a talk with him."

"Nay, Father, Lionheart has not hurt me." Her shoulders stiffened. "I would not allow it. But I have been thinking," she mused. "With Lionheart away, mayhap I should find Sir Ren and warn him to beware, that Lionheart is on the prowl."

" 'Tis too dangerous," Father Caddoc cautioned. "What if you should encounter Lionheart?"

"I shan't. I will be disguised as a knight and I will have my sword to defend myself. Aye, my mind is made up. I shall leave tomorrow morning after Mass."

Chapter Nine

Lionheart called a halt at the crest of a rocky hill, his gaze traversing the barren land as their horses drank from a bubbling spring. He had seen naught to indicate the presence of the Black Wolf or his army, and that puzzled him.

Lionheart had begun to believe that Llewelyn had fled and was no longer a threat. Lionheart was not yet ready to return to the keep, however. Two days was not nearly long enough to be away from Vanora. His obsession for her still raged. He was beginning to fear that distance was not the answer. Naught would assuage his lust for the passionate vixen he had wed save having her in his bed and making love to her until he was too exhausted to move, much less think.

'Twas Giles who spied the knight riding the path below them and pointed him out. Excitement thrummed through Lionheart when he saw the knight's gold-trimmed white tabard. *The mysterious White Knight!* His fists clenched and he shook with the need to have the knave at the end of his sword.

Were it not for the White Knight, Llewelyn would not have gotten away and he would not be saddled with a wife. He would not have met Vanora, much less wed her.

"Shall we give chase?" Giles asked, jolting Lionheart from his reverie.

"Stay here with the men," Lionheart ordered. "The knave is mine. He has given me much grief, and I intend to put an end to it."

His face set in hard lines, Lionheart mounted his steed and rode off. He trailed the knight for a time, keeping well behind so as not to be seen. Lionheart thought the knight too sure of himself, too cocky. The man seemed oblivious to danger, as if it did not exist for him. Did he go to Llewelyn? Lionheart decided to follow and find out.

Vanora rode blissfully toward Draymere at a comfortable trot, hoping to find Cragdon's knights safely ensconced in Daffid's keep. She needed to warn them to stay put lest Lionheart's patrol find them.

The day was fine, albeit a little on the cool side. Winter would arrive before she knew it, and she recounted all the chores that must be done before cold weather arrived. Her distraction was such that she did not realize she was being followed until she felt the skin crawl on the back of her neck and sensed a menacing presence.

Whirling in the saddle, she saw naught but the forest and its shifting shadows. Just when she was beginning to think that her imagination was playing tricks on her, she saw him.

Lionheart!

Why had she not seen him before? How long had he been following her? Setting her spurs to her palfrey, she raced through the forest and burst into a wide valley that lay between towering mountains. Aware that she could not lead Lionheart to Draymere, she abruptly changed direction, heading for the foothills. She had a better chance of losing Lionheart on rough terrain than on open ground.

Darting a glance over her shoulder, Vanora was dismayed to see Lionheart quickly closing the distance between them. The mountains offered the only means of escape, but she feared she could not reach them in time. Her next option, the one she had hoped to avoid, was to stand and fight.

Wheeling about, sword in one hand and

shield in the other, she waited for Lionheart. He reached her in a cloud of dust and skidded to a halt, his horse prancing in a circle around her. Though his visor was lowered, she would know him anywhere. His powerful warrior's body was as familiar to her as her own. Neither chain mail nor chausses could disguise the strength of his limbs or the width of his shoulders.

"So we meet again," Lionheart growled. He drew his sword and positioned his shield. "Prepare to meet your maker, knave."

Guiding her horse with her knees, Vanora shot forward to meet her foe. She needed the advantage of surprise if she was to survive. She knew Lionheart was stronger than she was and far better at warfare, but she hoped to acquit herself well. If she could unhorse him, she might be able to elude him.

They met in a harsh clash of metal against metal. Vanora ducked beneath the slashing thrust of his sword, using her shield to deflect the brunt of his punishing blow. She brought her own sword down, only to meet his shield. Her horse reared, its front hooves slashing at Lionheart's steed. The steed retaliated, crashing against her smaller palfrey, nearly unseating her.

"Surrender, sir knight, and mayhap I will spare your life," Lionheart roared over her palfrey's scream.

Panic rode Vanora. She feared Lionheart's wrath if he learned her identity. She shook her head and launched another attack. Lionheart met her, remorseless in his fury. She deflected his blow but took the next. The flat of his sword sent her sprawling to the ground. Leaping from his saddle, he stood over her. The diabolical gleam in his eyes, clearly visible through his visor, pinned her to the dirt.

"Remove your helm," Lionheart ordered. "I want to look upon your face before I skewer you."

Her hands were shaking as she raised them to her head. Just as she started to lift her visor, an arrow sang through the air, piercing through a weak link in Lionheart's mail. Clutching the arrow, he staggered and began a slow spiral to the ground.

Crying out in dismay, Vanora searched the hillsides for the archer but saw no one. Rising unsteadily, she knelt beside Lionheart despite the danger of becoming the next target.

The slow rise and fall of Lionheart's chest assured her that he still lived, but the blood pouring from his wound frightened her. She knew what had to be done. Grasping the shaft of the arrow and exerting all her strength, she pulled the barb from his flesh and tossed it aside. She heard Lionheart groan, but no other sound escaped his lips, though she knew the pain must be unbearable. She ripped off a section of his tabard with her knife and searched beneath his mail and hauberk for the wound. When she found it, she made a pad of the cloth and pressed it hard against the lacerated flesh.

He stared up at her through pain-glazed eyes. "You had best kill me while you can, for you will not get another chance."

Vanora recoiled, his words reminding her how much he hated the White Knight. Refusing to speak lest he recognize her voice, she shook her head.

The blood seeping from Lionheart's wound slowed beneath the pressure of Vanora's hand as she contemplated her options. She could not leave Lionheart to bleed to death, nor could she lift him on his horse without help. She pondered the dilemma long and hard but was saved from making a decision when several horsemen rode down from the hills and surrounded her.

Vanora recognized Sir Ren and Cragdon's

warriors immediately. Sir Ren dismounted and knelt beside her.

" 'Twas a lucky shot," he said. "I could not let him hurt you. Come away now; 'tis not safe here. His men cannot be far behind."

Gaining her feet, she pulled Ren aside where Lionheart could not hear them. "I cannot leave him to die."

"You have no choice. You know the consequences."

She did indeed. "He will bleed to death."

Sir Ren stared at her with dawning perception. "I am sorry, my lady, but 'tis for the best."

Vanora glanced back at Lionheart, indecision weighing heavily upon her. If Lionheart died, it would be her fault. "I cannot."

"Hark! Riders approach," he warned.

A cloud of dust appeared in the distance. "Lionheart's men," Vanora said, relieved that help was on the way.

"We must leave," Ren urged, "lest we become prisoners again."

"I cannot leave him," Vanora repeated. She could care for him better than any of his men.

"You are not thinking clearly, my lady," Ren argued. "Your life is in danger as long as he lives."

Vanora inhaled sharply. "What are you going to do?"

"Kill him. 'Tis no more than he planned for you."

"Nay! You will not! Hear me well, Sir Ren. Lionheart will not die by your hand, is that clear?"

"You are too tenderhearted, my lady. Let me slay him for the good of Wales."

"Nay! Help him to mount and return him to his men."

"Are you sure?"

"Very sure."

Vanora returned her gaze to Lionheart. Though he could not hear their conversation, his silver eyes glittered with malice, and no little amount of pain. A shudder passed through her. Knowing that she was the object of his hatred nearly undid her. She took a step toward him but was forcibly restrained by Ren.

Ren snapped a curt order and two warriors went to Lionheart and lifted him upon his steed.

"Be careful!" Vanora cried, struggling to escape Ren's relentless grip. "Release me. I must go to him."

Grasping her about the waist, Ren literally tossed her upon her palfrey. Another knight grasped her reins and galloped off with her horse in tow.

With breaking heart, Vanora knew Lionheart would never forgive her should he learn the identity of the knight he had vowed to slay.

His teeth clenched against the pain, Lionheart watched as the White Knight galloped off. Seen from a distance, the knight had appeared a formidable one, but upon closer inspection, he looked to be a mere lad.

Sweat beaded his forehead. Had not Ren's arrow felled him, he would have slain his opponent. He should feel no guilt for that, he told himself, for the knight had earned his fate, but he could not shake the feeling that he would have been very sorry had he slain the lad. Dimly he wondered why the knight had seemed so reluctant to leave.

Still conscious but quickly fading, Lionheart expected Sir Ren to finish what the arrow had failed to do. He closed his eyes and prepared to meet his maker as two burly knights approached and bent over him. But to his surprise, they lifted him and placed him upon his steed. Clinging to the beast with hands and knees, he concentrated on staying upright as Ren sent the horse off with a slap and a shout.

'Twas then Lionheart became aware of horsemen headed in his direction. More enemy? Shaking his head to clear the haze from his eyes, he recognized Sir Giles and Alan leading the throng. Relief spiraled through him, and he straightened his shoulders as renewed strength surged through him.

By sheer will, Lionheart remained upright in the saddle as Giles thundered up to him and grasped his trailing reins.

"You are wounded!" Giles cried, paling when he saw Lionheart's blood-drenched tabard. "Is that the work of the White Knight?"

"Nay, I had the bastard beneath my blade. The arrow came from one of his compatriots," Lionheart gasped. "I understand him not. He let me live when he could have slain me as I lay helpless on the ground."

The rest of the patrol caught up with Giles, their concern apparent when they saw Lionheart's pale face and bloodstained tabard.

"What are you doing here?" Lionheart asked. "Did I not tell you to wait for me near the stream?"

Giles made an impatient gesture. “Blame me, not the men, Lionheart. After you rode off, I feared you were riding into danger. I tried to ignore the premonition, but the longer you were gone, the stronger it became. I did what I thought was necessary.” He gazed toward the hills. “The enemy is getting away.”

“Let them go. We will never find them in that rough terrain.”

“Can you dismount by yourself? I would see to your wound.”

“ ’Tis naught,” Lionheart said, discounting his loss of blood with a wave of his hand. “Mair can tend me when we return to Cragdon.”

What he meant but did not say was that ’twas Vanora’s healing hand he wanted upon his fevered brow. Strangely, the need to reach his wife was the driving force that had kept him upright in the saddle. Mayhap he was dying, for he could not imagine himself expressing that sentiment unless his time on earth was limited.

Giles regarded him solemnly. “Are you strong enough to ride to Cragdon? Mayhap we should seek help at a nearer keep.”

“Nay,” Lionheart replied. “No one hereabouts would welcome us. Take me to

Cragdon. Tie me to the saddle if I show signs of losing consciousness."

"Where are we going?" Vanora asked when Ren called a halt to rest the horses. They had ridden fast and furiously until they were sure no one followed.

"Since Llewelyn abandoned his army, we have been staying at the holding your father awarded me for my years of faithful service. The keep is in need of repair but it suffices. We feared to leave the area lest you had need of us."

"Llewelyn abandoned you? What makes you say that?"

" 'Tis true, my lady. His army has scattered and he has disappeared. 'Tis rumored he went to England to seek peace with King Henry."

"Nay! Never say 'tis true!"

"I fear so."

Vanora could not believe the Black Wolf of Snowdon had abandoned Wales. What was to become of his people? What was to become of Cragdon?

"Will you accompany me to my keep, Lady Vanora? 'Tis not as grand as Cragdon but 'tis remote and safe."

"Nay, Sir Ren, I cannot. I must return to Cragdon and my people. The only reason I left was to warn you that Lionheart has broadened his search for Llewelyn and his army."

"I will accompany you."

"Thank you, but nay. 'Tis best I ride alone. Lionheart will be traveling at a slow pace because of his wound, and I intend to be on hand when he arrives at Cragdon."

"Cut through the forest, 'tis closer," Sir Ren advised. "Now that you know where to find us, send word if you have need of us. You are not safe at Cragdon. I fear for your life if Lionheart learns who you are. Your father placed you in my charge, and I swore to protect you." He hung his head. "I am doing a poor job of it."

"No one could have foreseen what happened," Vanora said. "My fondest wish is to see you and all those knights who have not pledged their service elsewhere returned to Cragdon."

"Godspeed, my lady. Those faithful to your father remain faithful to you."

Driven by the need to see to Lionheart's wound, Vanora raced back to Cragdon. Dusk was swift approaching when she reached the village. She stabled her palfrey, Baron, in the stall behind the blacksmith's shop and slipped through the encroaching darkness to the river. Following along the riverbank, she found the hidden passage and entered the tunnel. The door behind the altar sprang open at her touch, and she ducked through.

Naught but shadows lingered in the dimly lit chamber as she struggled out of her chain mail and stowed it away. Then she donned her gown and hurried across the courtyard.

She had just reached the staircase when the patrol rode through the gate. Her heart leapt into her mouth when she saw Lionheart weaving back and forth and realized that he had been tied to the saddle to keep him upright. Uttering a cry of dismay, she raced to his side.

"Untie him! Quickly!" She touched his leg, and he stared down at her. "Fetch Mair," she ordered Alan, who had dismounted and hovered nearby. His brow creased with worry, he hurried off.

Giles and Sir Osgood lifted Lionheart from the saddle and would have carried him into the keep had Lionheart not insisted upon walking. With a man on either side to lend support, Lionheart managed to stagger halfway up the stairs before his legs gave way beneath him.

"Do not let him fall!" Vanora cried, rushing to lend a hand. "Take him to the solar."

"The wound is naught but a scratch," Lionheart gasped through bloodless lips. "I have suffered worse in my lifetime."

Both Mair and Father Caddoc were waiting for them in the solar. While Lionheart was being carried to the bed and stripped of his mail and chausses, Father Caddoc pulled Vanora aside. "Is this your doing, child?"

"Nay, Father, 'twas Sir Ren. He wounded Lionheart to save my life. Lionheart ran me to ground a half-day's journey from Cragdon. We clashed swords, and I lost."

Father Caddoc crossed himself.

"I acquitted myself well, Father, but my strength gave out beneath Lionheart's fierce attack."

"You were wrong to leave the keep. Where was Lionheart's patrol while you were engaging in swordplay?"

"I know not, though they arrived not long afterward. I did not want to leave him, Father, but Sir Ren insisted. Once we were sure we were not being followed, I sent Sir Ren on his way and returned to Cragdon. I wanted to be on hand when Lionheart arrived. Excuse me, I must go to my husband."

"I will stay in case I am needed to give last rites."

Blood drained from Vanora's face. "Last rites will not be needed. Lionheart most certainly will not die." Turning abruptly, she fled to Lionheart's bedside.

Mair had already begun probing the wound. His expression wary, Lionheart watched her. "Be careful, woman, I do not intend to die by your hand."

"Mair is a healer; she will not harm you," Vanora said in an effort to calm him.

Lionheart's pain-glazed eyes lifted to Vanora, the glimmer of a smile turning up the corner of his mouth. "It gladdens my heart to hear you say that."

"You have lost a great deal of blood, Sir Lionheart," Mair said after finishing her probing. "But it could have been worse. Who pulled out the arrow and stanched the flow of blood?"

" 'Twas *him*," Lionheart said, his voice lowered to a thin whisper. "The White Knight. I had him at the end of my blade. Know you his name, Mair?"

Mair ducked her head, her eyes veiled. "Nay, I know no such knight. 'Twas a *good* thing he did, however. He may have saved your life."

"Were it not for him, I would still be hale and hearty. 'Tis yet another grievance I hold against the young fool. He is younger than I imagined, and skilled beyond his years."

"Do not talk, Lionheart," Vanora advised. "Conserve your strength."

"Luck was with you," Mair said. "The arrow pierced the flesh beneath your arm but was stopped from doing further damage by your ribs, though they may be cracked. I will bind them after I stitch your wound."

"Make haste," Lionheart said. "Lying abed is a waste of time."

Mair rolled her eyes. "Your wound may not be fatal, but 'tis a painful one. You will not feel like riding or wielding a sword for at least a fortnight."

Lionheart gritted his teeth. "Do what is necessary, woman, and let me decide what I can or cannot do."

Mair carefully cleansed the wound, then threaded a needle with fine silk. "Father Caddoc, hold his arm still," she ordered.

"Nay," Lionheart said. "Vanora shall serve as nurse. Send the priest on his way. He is not needed here. I shall not die this night."

Father Caddoc looked to Vanora for direction, and when she nodded, he left the chamber.

"Proceed, Mair. Do your worst; I am ready."

Vanora gripped his arm and held it away from his body, exposing the wound to Mair's needle. Vanora's efforts were unnecessary, however. Lionheart did not so much as flinch as Mair's needle pierced his flesh.

Vanora marveled at Lionheart's strength. His flesh beneath her hands was warm, his muscles solid. His face was somewhat pale, but his eyes divulged no weakness.

He was a man who carefully guarded his heart. Could she reach it? Did she want to? The answer escaped her. Of one thing she was certain: She did not wish for Lionheart's death.

Lionheart studied Vanora's face as she held his arm steady. She winced each time the needle pierced his flesh, as if the pain were hers. Did she feel something for him? Did he even care? The answer surprised him.

He cared.

" 'Tis done," Mair said as she knotted the thread and broke it off. "Vanora can apply the healing salve and bind your ribs."

"Ask Cook to prepare a rich beef broth," Vanora ordered.

Lionheart tried not to flinch as Vanora bandaged his wound and bound his ribs with strips of cloth. Though light-headed from loss of blood, he did not intend to lie abed. He would not rest easy until the White Knight had been captured and his identity revealed. No matter where the knight and his cohorts were hiding, he intended to run them to ground.

Lionheart had heard naught from Edward and wondered what was happening in England. Had Simon de Montfort prevailed over King Henry? Had Henry signed the Provisions of Oxford that provided for a council of barons to advise the king? Was Edward still wavering between de Montfort and his father?

Lionheart's thoughts skittered when Vanora rose to leave.

"Wait, I would have a word with you, wife."

Vanora halted, regarding him warily. "You really should rest."

"I will, after we have spoken. I think you know more than you pretend about the White Knight. Give me his name and tell me where he is hiding."

"I know naught," Vanora replied.

"So you said. Did you know 'twas Sir Ren, your own captain of the guard, who came to the White Knight's aid when I had the knave beneath my sword."

"You call him the White Knight?"

"Aye, 'tis the name I gave him, for I know no other. He is younger than I expected, and not as brawny as he looked from afar, but deadly nonetheless. I want him, Vanora. I will not rest until my sword tastes his blood, this I vow."

His silver eyes bored into her. "Tell me what I want to know. Were it not for the White Knight, I would not be lying in this bed."

Stunned by the fierceness of Lionheart's words, Vanora fled from the chamber. His vendetta against the White Knight frightened her. For her own well-being, she had best retire her knight persona. Lionheart was too close to discovering the truth.

Both Mair and Father Caddoc were waiting for her when she returned to the hall.

"Is he sleeping?" Mair asked.

"Nay, he will be out of bed before he heals properly. Inflexible man," she muttered.

"Tell us what happened," the priest urged.

"Lionheart had me beneath his sword. Were not Sir Ren's aim so true, I would be dead," Vanora said, shuddering. "Thank God he was nearby when Lionheart caught me alone."

"You should not have left the keep while Lionheart and his patrol were abroad," Mair scolded.

"Had Lionheart slain you, he would have been devastated when he learned he had killed his own wife," Father Caddoc chided.

"Mayhap," Vanora replied uncertainly. "His vendetta against me is frightening. 'Tis as if his purpose in life is slaying the one he has named the White Knight."

"Nevertheless, you must not ride again as a knight, child. If you value your life, you must take steps to protect it. I have prayed mightily on this and am convinced the Lord will not let us down. The English may not leave Wales in our lifetime, but I am confident we shall persevere. Lionheart is not a bad man, and I believe he cares for you as much as a man like him can care for a woman."

If Lionheart truly cared for her, Vanora thought, she would be content.

"Forget my problems for a while," she said. "How fares Daffid?"

"I spoke with his guard just this morn," Father Caddoc replied. "Daffid is not suffering. He is being fed and allowed to bathe. I suspect boredom is his worst enemy right now."

"Do you still have strong feelings for Daffid?" Mair asked.

"Nay. I have no feelings for him but compassion for his plight."

"Come to the chapel with me, Vanora," Father Caddoc urged. "We will pray together for our country's survival."

Though Vanora would rather pray for her own deliverance from a certain Englishman, she went willingly enough with the priest. She had almost reached the door when she heard Mair say, "Sir Lionheart! What are you doing out of bed?"

Spinning on her heel, Vanora was shocked to see Lionheart staggering into the hall. Uttering a cry of dismay, she rushed to his side.

"Are you mad!" she gasped. "You should be in bed."

He attempted an unconvincing smile. "Do not coddle me. Where is Sir Giles?"

"I am here, Lionheart," Giles said, rising from one of the trestle tables set up for the evening meal. "Have you need of me?"

Lionheart lowered himself onto the nearest bench. "Aye. I want you to take a patrol out at dawn and continue the search for the White Knight and his cohorts. I will join you if I am able —"

"You shall not," Vanora said.

He ignored her. “I want the White Knight more than I have ever wanted anything in my life. He is nearby; I can feel it in my bones. Bring him to me, Giles, and I shall present his head to Edward on a platter.”

Sir Giles snapped a salute and strode off. Lionheart felt Vanora’s stillness and glanced up at her. Her face had gone as white as the White Knight’s tabard.

Chapter Ten

Lionheart healed quickly, due to the daily applications of salve Mair spread on his wound. And to Vanora's excellent care of him and his own determination to regain his strength so he could run the White Knight to ground. Being bested by a mere slip of a lad who doubtless had just won his spurs made him look like a fool.

A sennight after he had been wounded, Lionheart returned to the training field, not actually participating but directing his knights and their squires. When he had voiced his intention to resume his duties after breaking his fast that morning, Mair threw up her hands and rolled her eyes. Vanora was more vocal.

"Are you mad? 'Tis too soon to participate in strenuous activity," Vanora chided.

"My warriors must train to retain their skills," Lionheart argued. "They are seasoned warriors, unaccustomed to inactivity." He sent her a heated look, his voice low and seductive. "My body craves stimulation after lying abed so long. Too much time has passed since I made love to my wife."

A rosy flush colored Vanora's cheeks. " 'Tis too soon for that, too."

"You do not know me well if you think a small wound can stop me from bedding you. Tonight, vixen, you and I will do more than sleep in our bed. Have you not missed my attention?"

"Nay, not at all. Excuse me," she said, rising abruptly. "I have duties to attend."

A grin lifted Lionheart's sensual lips as he watched Vanora flee. Her lie did not fool him. When he took her into his arms tonight and sheathed himself inside her, she would be as eager as he to make love. No amount of denial would convince him that she did not want him. Aye, tonight he would have her, and she would beg him to take her before the night was spent.

His body began to harden at the thought of a naked, writhing Vanora beneath him, her eyes glazed with passion and his name on her lips. A man could die happy with such an arousing image imprinted upon his mind.

That image remained with Lionheart throughout the day. When he began to tire and his ribs reminded him that he was not yet fully healed, he had but to think of his cock inside Vanora's soft body and his exhaustion melted away.

When Lionheart returned to the keep for the midday meal, Vanora was nowhere about. When he inquired after her, he was told she had accompanied Father Caddoc to the village to visit a sick child. A frisson of fear slammed through him, until he learned that a man-at-arms had accompanied her and the priest.

'Twas while he was still enjoying his meal that a messenger arrived from Prince Edward. Lionheart welcomed him and eagerly perused the missive he carried. 'Twas the first he had received from Edward in all the weeks he had been at Cragdon. Giles and Brandon crowded around Lionheart, as eager as he for news of Edward.

"What does the prince say?" Giles asked. "Is Simon de Montfort causing trouble for Henry?"

"Edward says that Henry wriggled out of his promises to the barons by appealing to the Pope to absolve him," Lionheart revealed. "Civil war is inevitable."

"Does he mention Llewelyn?" Brandon asked.

"He says he brings news of Llewelyn and will tell us when he arrives. We are to expect him at Cragdon within a fortnight."

"Is that all?" Giles asked.

"Nay, he writes that he has personal news to impart, and that he is bringing a surprise visitor with him."

"Interesting," Giles mused. "Have you any idea what he is talking about?"

"Nay. Edward loves surprises. It could mean anything."

The news that Edward was on his way cheered his army of discontented men. With civil war in the offing, they were eager to join the conflict. But whose side would Edward take? Lionheart wondered. On one hand there was de Montfort, Edward's uncle by marriage and one of the men in line to rule England after Edward, Henry's rightful heir. There were many who thought Simon de Montfort would make a better ruler than Henry.

On the other hand, Henry, weak though he might be, was still England's king, and Lionheart doubted that Edward would abandon his father, for to do so meant that Edward would lose the throne after Henry's death. Edward was born to rule and would not willingly relinquish that which was his by divine right.

Lionheart did not doubt that Edward would defend the throne and his own ascendancy, rallying to his father's side with his army. Edward might make de Montfort think he was wavering, but the prince was loyal to his country and his father.

As for Edward's personal news, Lionheart was willing to wager it involved his wife, Eleanor of Castile, whom he had wed as a young lad and then left behind when he had returned to England. Had the young princess arrived in England?

It occurred to Lionheart that Edward's arrival would mean an end to his days at Cragdon. He was pledged to Edward and would follow whichever course the prince chose in the conflict between de Montfort and Henry. And, he thought with more than a little regret, he would have to leave Vanora behind.

The thought left a curious void he was hard put to describe. He had never missed a woman once an affair ended and he moved on. What was there about Vanora that made him reluctant to leave her?

Vanora returned to the keep late that day in a melancholy mood and went directly to the solar to clean up before the evening meal. The child she had attended with Father Caddoc had died. She had been ill since birth with a lung ailment and her death had been expected, but Vanora still grieved along with the parents.

Lionheart was waiting for her in the solar. "I hoped I would not have to fetch you home," he said in greeting. " 'Tis late. Is the child well?"

"She died," Vanora said.

"I am sorry for it. Have the parents other children?"

"Aye, but they still mourn her."

"News arrived from Edward that might cheer you," Lionheart said. "He is on his way to Cragdon."

Vanora frowned. "Why should that cheer me?"

"Mayhap because I will be leaving with the prince when he returns to England."

Vanora went still. 'Twas what she wanted, what she had prayed for, was it not? Why, then, did she feel empty, as if a void had opened in her heart?

"That is indeed good news," she choked out. "I cannot wait until Wales is free of all Englishmen."

"Do not count on regaining control of your keep," Lionheart warned. "Edward does not easily give up what he has won. Cragdon is a prize he will want to add to his Welsh holdings. 'Tis possible he will leave a seneschal and a company of knights to manage the estate in his absence."

"What will become of me and those who depend upon me?" Vanora asked.

Lionheart shrugged. "I know not. I shall ask Edward to allow you to remain, if that is your wish."

"My wish is to be left in peace."

"Is that your only wish, Vanora? Do you not care that once we part we may never meet again?"

I care but dare not admit it. "Nay, why should I?"

"We are wed and have shared a bed, vixen."

"Will you miss me, Lionheart?" she challenged.

Vanora was shocked when his face expressed a myriad of emotions. Was it possible he cared for her? What nonsense, she chided herself. Lionheart possessed, he did not love.

"I will miss having you in my bed," Lionheart admitted. He tipped her face up to his. "And I will miss our spirited conversations. Few women challenge me as you do, and I shall regret having to leave before taming you."

Vanora blew out an angry breath. "I am not an animal in need of taming. I am a woman with a mind of her own and the courage to express it."

"Indeed," Lionheart agreed. "My stay at Cragdon has been a most interesting experience. There are many things I shall miss and some I will not. You are a beautiful woman; my lust and your priest made you my wife, but I cannot regret our wedding for you have made my time at Cragdon . . . entertaining, to say the least. One thing I do regret, however, is my unfinished business with the White Knight."

"Why can you not forget him?" Vanora implored. "Doubtless he is someone unimportant."

"You may be right, but nevertheless the knave has embarrassed me." His voice hardened. "Mayhap I will return one day, seek him out and slay him."

Vanora shuddered. She prayed that day never came. The day Lionheart learned the truth would be the last day of her life.

"Are you ready to sup? My stomach is voicing its hunger."

"Not yet. I will join you after I wash and change."

Lionheart departed, leaving Vanora much to think about. His admission that he would miss certain things had surprised her. Was he referring to her? Though he had not actually admitted he cared for her, she would savor his words long after he was gone, when loneliness plagued her.

She would miss Lionheart more than she cared to admit. He had managed to touch her heart even though her mind utterly rejected him. He was a man like no other. He was hard when it counted, yet his tenderness when he made love to her belied that hardness. He was strong of mind and body, yet fair when it came to dispensing justice. Daffid was proof of Lionheart's fairness, for he had been neither tortured nor starved. He was, in fact, quite comfortable in the tower.

Vanora took her time washing and dressing, her thoughts dwelling on Lionheart's imminent departure. 'Twas good that he was leaving, for she was becoming too involved in his life. *Liar.* She realized she was not being honest with herself. Though his departure was what she had prayed for, she did not want Lionheart to leave.

Sighing with regret for what could have been and what would never be, Vanora completed her toilette and left her chamber.

Throughout the long meal, Lionheart's intent gaze rested on Vanora so often she found his scrutiny unnerving. His eyes were the color of smoke, and the harsh planes of his face were stark with barely suppressed desire. His heavy hand rested on her thigh, teasing her flesh as she tried to concentrate on her food.

"Finish your meal," he whispered into her ear. "Tonight you will find me an eager lover."

When had she ever found him less than eager? "Do not embarrass me, Lionheart. Your men are watching us."

"Let them. They know what I want." He sent her a wolfish grin. "What we both want."

"You are far too sure of yourself, sir knight. I do not want you."

He rose and held out his hand. "Come, wife, I intend to prove you wrong. We have but a fortnight to indulge ourselves."

Her heart pounding with excitement, Vanora placed her hand in his, mesmerized by the husky tone of his voice and his smoky gaze. She neither heard the buzz of voices as they left the hall nor saw the exchange of knowing looks.

The moment Lionheart closed the door behind them, he whispered her name. "Vanora."

She looked up at him. There was something intensely, dangerously sexual in his gaze, and it aroused a matching response in her.

"Do you want me, Vanora?"

Want him? She wanted him like a wild animal yearned for her mate. But doubtless he knew that. She opened her mouth to deny her body's needs, but words failed her.

He gave an ironic smile, then captured her mouth, kissing her endlessly, his passion stunning. She made a small choked sound deep in her throat and responded with swift intensity, painfully aware that when he left her she would never see him again. Their tongues met and clung, their breath mingled, their arms unerringly finding each other. There was a vivid immediacy in his kisses, as if he too realized their time together was limited and wanted to use it to the best advantage.

Lionheart tore off her clothing with indecent haste, then removed his own, tossing everything aside with careless disregard. Chances were he would never know Vanora's passion again after he left. Never feel the warm pressure of her skin. Or feel the pebbled texture of her nipples with his tongue. Or hear her moans of pleasure when he caressed her wet, intimate flesh.

Sweeping her into his arms, he carried her to their bed and lay down beside her.

Though he ached with the need to thrust inside her, he deliberately paced himself, wanting to prolong her pleasure as well as his. He kissed her, her mouth, her chin, the throbbing pulse at the base of her throat. His left hand drifted beneath her buttock, steadying her as the fingers of his right hand teased through her dark curls, between her silky folds to fondle the sensitive petals of her sex.

Waves of heat surged through her. She was on the verge of splintering when his hand suddenly left her. A choked sound of protest escaped her lips and she caught his hand, trying to return it.

"Not yet, sweetheart, 'tis too soon," Lionheart murmured.

Her labored breathing slowed as he regarded her through slumberous eyes. Tentatively she lifted herself against him; words were superfluous as she silently begged for more. He kissed her shoulder; she arched her neck. Dropping his head, he caught her breast in his mouth, drawing strongly upon her nipple. She gasped, suspended on the pinnacle of burgeoning passion. Her nipples tightened, her breath grew harsh, and she writhed beneath him.

Dazed by passion, she could scarcely breathe, much less think as his fingers returned to her weeping center. Then those talented fingers entered her, sliding in and out at the same time his thumb brushed her sensitive nub. A scream rose in her throat. He caught it in his mouth, smothering it with a kiss.

"Please," Vanora murmured brokenly.

"Please what?"

"M-make love to me."

"Soon, very soon."

Then suddenly his fingers were gone, replaced by his mouth, his breath hot against her as he teased and taunted the swollen folds with his tongue and mouth.

Lionheart felt her limbs tremble, heard her catch her breath as she splintered. When she had quieted, he rose up and reversed their positions, bringing her atop him. Then he thrust hard and deep inside her. Her blissful look set him aflame. Her breasts, ripe and firm, swayed before him in wanton abandon. Lifting his head, he caught a nipple and suckled, savoring the heat of her silken sheath as she began to move on him.

She was killing him. She arched her neck and he kissed her there. His heartbeat thundered as they moved toward completion. He wanted to grasp her hips and hasten the pace, but he gritted his teeth and persevered. Instead he moved as she commanded, so near to bursting he groaned with each stroke. He was going to die a happy man . . . a victim of sexual excess.

At last she cried out, her body convulsing with each contraction. He watched her through narrowed lids, enjoying the sensation of her sheath clamping around his cock. Not until she collapsed on his chest did he allow himself to plunge deep and fill her with his seed.

Vanora sighed and relaxed against him, waiting for him to stir. He made no move to leave her, remained inside her still, a part of her. After a time, she could feel him growing hard again. Her eyes, still glazed from his lovemaking, flew open, surprised to see him gazing up at her curiously, as if puzzled by his response to her.

A tiny hope bloomed in her bosom, a flickering flame of yearning that he might care for her, that he would miss her, though he would never love her, she was sure. Then suddenly she found herself on her back, with Lionheart looming over her, his expression fiercely possessive and his eyes aglow with renewed desire.

"Surely you cannot . . ." Vanora gasped. "You just . . ."

"You continually misjudge my prowess,"

Lionheart hissed as he began to move strongly inside her.

Wantonly she locked her legs around his back and arched her hips to take him deeper, to meet his thrusts again and again, until her loins quickened and her breath seized. Shock waves rippled through her entire body, sending her reeling toward completion. How could she respond so quickly after her strong climax just moments ago? she wondered before her thoughts scattered. What magical hold did Lionheart have over her senses?

Then the earth dropped out from beneath her. Sensation burst through her like a volcanic explosion. It was only dimly that she felt the shudders undulating through Lionheart's body before he collapsed atop her in a boneless heap.

She heard him groan when he pulled out and rolled over to lie beside her. She rose up on her elbow, her eyes filled with concern.

"You hurt yourself," she chided.

" 'Tis naught."

"You have not given your ribs enough time to heal. Men," she snorted. "They are as randy as goats and ever ready to rut."

" 'Twas well worth it," Lionheart said, wincing as he shifted positions.

"Let me check your bandage. You may have opened your wound."

Hopping out of bed, Vanora lifted the candlestick and held it above his bandaged chest. "No blood," she said with a sigh of relief. "Cracked ribs take time to heal. You did not wait long enough before" — she blushed — "engaging in strenuous exercise."

"Did I not tell you I intend to make the most of the fortnight left to us?" He sent her a mocking grin. "You did beg me to make love to you, did you not?"

"Your conceit is boundless," Vanora charged. "As you well know, I had no choice in the matter. You have the experience and knowledge to make me want you. My body is not my own, but yours to command."

" 'Tis as it should be," Lionheart said with the arrogance of one aware of his own appeal and proud of it.

Vanora knew better than to argue the point, for she knew it would do little good. Instead, she changed the subject.

"Think you Edward will accept our marriage?"

She felt him stiffen. "Is that what you want?"

Vanora grappled long and hard with his

question. Nay, 'twas not what she wanted, she decided. She opened her mouth to reply when a sudden thought occurred to her. What if Lionheart left her with child? His seed had not found fertile ground yet, but the possibility still existed. If their brief union produced a child, she wanted Lionheart to acknowledge him or her.

Swallowing hard, Vanora said, "Mayhap 'twould be best if the marriage stood."

He gave her a blank look. "You want to remain married to me, even though 'tis inevitable that we will part?"

She nodded. "If we create a child during our brief marriage, I want him or her to be legitimate."

Lionheart did not respond. He could not. Speech had deserted him. He had never considered children, for he'd never intended to wed. Marrying Vanora had been a spur-of-the-moment decision. Admittedly, he enjoyed bedding her, even liked their verbal sparring. But children had never been a priority with him. He had naught to leave a wife and child but his name. His father had seen to that.

True, he would inherit his father's title upon his death, but he never intended to use it, for he preferred to be recognized for his deeds as a knight and not for an empty earldom. 'Twas not that he was penniless, for knighthood had its own rewards, but he was landless.

"Lionheart, did you not hear me?" Vanora prodded. "Do you agree with me?"

"A child never crossed my mind. Are you . . . have I given you a babe, Vanora?"

"Not that I am aware of." Her chin tilted upward. "I care not what you think of me, but I would have you acknowledge our child should there be one. I cannot bear the thought of our child being branded a bastard. I think 'tis best that we let our marriage stand."

"Mayhap you will not conceive," he ventured.

"Mayhap you are right, but only God has control over that. You may have already planted your seed inside me."

His gaze slid down to her stomach. "I suppose having a child would not be the worst thing to happen to me."

"How kind of you to say so." The hard edge to her voice should have warned him. "But since a child is merely speculation at this point, mayhap you should forget I mentioned it. Once you leave Cragdon, you need never look back. Forget I ever existed."

Never look back? Forget Vanora? Somehow that thought produced a hollow feeling in the pit of his stomach. He wished it were a simple matter of erasing these weeks at Cragdon from his mind. Unfortunately, that was impossible. Vanora had given him something no other woman had. He had no idea what it was, could not even describe it, but he knew it existed.

Suddenly it came to him. No one had ever cared what happened to him. Whether she acknowledged it or not, Vanora cared. Lionheart was astute enough to know when a woman's feelings were engaged.

What about his own feelings? He could not afford to have feelings, he decided. He was Edward's man and would follow him to the ends of the earth if need be. He had no room in his life for a wife and even less for a child.

"Regardless of what you think, Vanora, I am not completely devoid of feeling. I will acknowledge any child we make during our brief marriage. And I will entreat Edward to allow you to remain at Cragdon. I own no land or keep where you may live, so taking you to England is out of the question."

"I refuse to live in England, so it matters not. If I am forced to leave Cragdon, I shall find my own way, but it will be in my own country."

"You must do what is best for you. Know, however, that I will return to learn whether I have a child. No matter where you go, I shall find you."

It surprised Lionheart to realize he spoke the truth. He wanted, nay, needed to know if a child resulted from their coupling. He would not abandon his son or daughter. He had no idea how he intended to keep track of Vanora and his offspring while campaigning with Edward, but it never occurred to him to shirk his duty.

The following days sped by with impossible haste. Vanora tried to keep her hands busy and her mind occupied with thoughts other than those of her future. She and Lionheart had not had another serious discussion, and she supposed that was the way he wanted it. Unfortunately, it was not so easy for her. She had come to the painful realization that Lionheart had engaged her emotions, though she had desperately tried to avoid that kind of entanglement. When had it happened? How had her enemy managed to make her care for him?

What would he do to her if he learned she was the White Knight?

She shuddered. The thought was a

frightening one, and she prayed that Lionheart would never learn her secret.

A vanguard from Edward's party arrived to announce the prince's imminent arrival. The progression from London had taken less time than expected, and the prince was but two days' journey from Cragdon. Lionheart decided to ride out the next morning to meet him and advised Sir Giles to have a dozen men ready to ride with him at dawn.

That night he made love to Vanora until exhaustion claimed them both. Then he awakened her in the middle of the night, teasing another response from her. Then, as the church bells tolled Prime, she turned into his arms and he made love to her again, as if it might be the last time. And it might be. Edward could leave the day after he arrived, taking Lionheart with him.

He left Vanora sleeping soundly, worn out from vigorous lovemaking. He found Alan waiting in the hall for him. After he broke his fast with bread, cheese and ale, he and Alan descended the stairs to the armory, where his squire helped him don his chain mail. Sir Giles arrived a few minutes later.

"The men are ready to ride," Giles said.

Lionheart turned to Alan. "Have you seen to my provisions?"

"Aye, Lionheart. All is in readiness."

Lionheart nodded approval. "I am anxious to see Edward. Doubtless much has happened in England in our absence."

"Think you we will leave Cragdon?" Giles asked.

"Aye, 'tis inevitable."

"I, for one, am glad," Giles admitted. "And I am sure I speak for all the men. We are growing bored with inactivity. The Welshmen are no threat to England without Llewelyn. We are warriors, eager to go where Edward leads."

The cadre of knights and their squires rode out from Cragdon just as the sun poked out from a bank of clouds, promising a fair day. They camped that night on a rocky hillside, dined from their rations and bedded down. They rolled out of their blankets before dawn and continued on their way. The sun had just risen when Lionheart spied Edward's party, with Edward himself in the lead, sitting proud and tall in the saddle.

Spurring his steed, Lionheart rode out to meet his prince. Edward saw him and waved.

" 'Tis about time you returned, Lord Edward," Lionheart said as he reined in beside Edward. "We are moldering at Cragdon."

Edward removed his helm; the sun reflected off his golden hair, creating a halo around his head. Lionheart thought he had never looked more kingly.

" 'Tis good to see you looking fit and healthy," Edward replied.

"What news of Simon de Montfort? Have you decided to cast your lot with him?"

"Nay. I have changed my allegiance from de Montfort to Henry. Should de Montfort prove victorious, he will name himself king and deny me my birthright. I cannot let him do that. The crown is mine by divine right. No one shall take it from me."

"Have you news of Llewelyn?"

"Aye. He has fled to London and signed a peace treaty between England and Wales. There is talk of a betrothal between him and Simon de Montfort's daughter."

"God's nightgown! So we are at peace with Wales now."

"Aye, but once I am king I am determined to bring both Wales and Scotland under English rule. We will speak of that and my plans for the future later. I have yet to impart the most exciting, the most wondrous news."

"You had best tell me before you burst," Lionheart laughed.

"I am in love!" Edward crowed.

"That is no news. I cannot count the times you have been in love."

"Eleanor has arrived from Castile."

"Your wife? You are in love with your wife?"

"You should see her, Lionheart. She is sweet and shy and lovely beyond words. I have truly lost my heart to her."

Lionheart wanted to laugh at the tall, golden youth but dared not. Apparently, love was a serious business to the boy who would one day be king. "Does she return your feelings?"

"Aye, I think so. I am ready to commit myself wholly to my wife. If Eleanor is willing, we will consummate our marriage upon my return to London."

Silently Lionheart wished Edward luck with his bride. More luck than Lionheart had had with his own wife. That thought brought on another. He had yet to apprise Edward of his marriage to Vanora.

He was still thinking about how to break the news when Edward said, "Enough of me and serious matters. Are you not curious about the surprise I brought you?"

"I can think of naught that would surprise me."

Grinning, Edward turned in his saddle and raised a hand.

Lionheart paid scant heed to Edward's words, for he was still considering the nature of Edward's surprise.

"Lionheart, behold your surprise," Edward said gleefully.

Chapter Eleven

Certain that nothing Edward had planned for him would surprise him, Lionheart swiveled in the saddle. His grin faded when the last person in the world he expected to see emerged from within the ranks of warriors and knights. His mouth dropped open and he turned to glare at Edward.

"God's blood! What have you done?"

"I hoped you would be pleased," Edward said, apparently puzzled at Lionheart's lack of enthusiasm. "Dunsford was but a few hours out of the way, so 'twas no trouble to fetch your leman."

Lionheart stared at the buxom blonde riding toward him with a coy smile fixed on her ruby lips. Althea! He had left her at Dunsford months ago. Why had Edward brought her? Young though he was, Edward had a reason for everything he did. There was no time to question him, however, as Althea reined in beside Lionheart.

"Lionheart!" she said effusively. " 'Twas so lonely at Dunsford without you. I was beside myself with happiness when Prince

Edward came to fetch me."

"Welcome to Wales, Althea," Lionheart returned, trying not to show his annoyance. Just what he needed, a leman *and* a wife under the same roof.

"I feared you would be lonely without a woman's comfort," Edward began, "and sought to please you."

"What other surprises have you brought?" Lionheart asked in a tone ripe with annoyance.

Edward sent him a sharp look. "I have other news, but it will keep. I wish to reach Cragdon tonight."

"Then we must ride hard," Lionheart said, spurring his steed.

Lionheart took the lead, riding hard and fast to clear his head. How would Vanora react to Althea? he wondered. Knowing Vanora as he did, he wouldn't be surprised if the vixen challenged Althea to a duel. That image made him smile. Soft as a down pillow and feminine to a fault, Althea would probably swoon if Vanora challenged her. Althea was made to pleasure men, and he had spent many delightful hours rutting between her thighs. On the other hand, Vanora's lithe, supple body pleased him so well that he could not recall what it was he had admired about Althea.

Why had Edward brought Althea to Wales if he did not intend to remain? Lionheart wondered. With a civil war in the offing, Edward would probably take his army back to England, and if he did, Lionheart would leave with him. Or would he?

Edward's party stopped briefly at noon to eat from their rations, but Lionheart found no opportunity to tell the prince about Vanora. Edward was full of plans for the inevitable war between de Montfort and his father and wanted Lionheart's opinion. Althea hovered nearby, apparently anxious to speak privately with him, but Lionheart adroitly avoided her.

Once they resumed their journey, there was no time for talk. After several days in the saddle, Edward was anxious to reach Cragdon. The church bells were tolling Vespers when they rode through the portcullis. The warriors bivouacked in the outer bailey welcomed their prince effusively. Edward returned their greeting warmly and dismissed his own men to find places among their comrades; then Edward, Lionheart and Althea rode on to the keep.

The tables were already in place for the evening meal when Lionheart entered the hall. His eager gaze found Vanora standing near the hearth, conversing with Father Caddoc.

"The keep pleases me," Edward said as his assessing gaze swept over the large, well-kept hall.

Lionheart knew precisely when Edward's gaze found Vanora. "God's blood, who is that beauty?" Edward hissed beneath his breath. "I did not think the Welsh were capable of producing one such as her. You sly dog. Now I understand why my surprise displeased you. If I did not have sweet Eleanor waiting for me, I would be tempted to try her myself."

"Send the Welshwoman away," Althea demanded. "Lionheart no longer has need of her."

Lionheart sent Althea a dismissive look. " 'Tis not so easy, Althea. You see, Vanora and I —"

"I shall tell her myself," Althea said. "Prince Edward brought me here for you, and I will tolerate no other woman vying for your attention."

"We will settle this later," Edward said. "I am famished."

Lionheart ushered him to the high table. From the corner of his eye he saw Vanora hurrying over to join them. He stifled a groan and prepared himself for Vanora's reaction to Edward.

"What is this?" Edward asked when Vanora planted herself before the prince.

"How soon can I expect you and your army to leave Cragdon, my lord?" Vanora asked sweetly.

"Vanora," Lionheart warned. "Not now."

"Why not now? I want my home and lands returned to me."

"Your home? Your lands?" Edward replied. "Who are you?"

"I am Vanora of Cragdon. Cragdon belongs to me."

"I was under the impression that Cragdon belonged to me," Edward replied. "Were not your knights routed by Lionheart? Is not the castle occupied by Englishmen?"

"But you will leave and take your English warriors with you, will you not?"

"Aye, my visit will not be an extended one, but Lionheart —"

"Turn her out of the keep, Lord Edward," Althea interrupted. "The Welsh bitch deserves no mercy."

Vanora's gaze found Althea. "Who is she? Have you recruited women in your army?"

Edward laughed. "This is highly entertaining. Vanora has the tongue of an asp and a spirit to match. Methinks Lionheart has not been bored during my absence. I brought Lionheart's leman because I thought he would be desperate for amusement, but I see now I was wrong."

"His leman?" Vanora gasped.

"Aye. I made a special effort to bring Althea to Cragdon."

Vanora sent Althea a disdainful look, then directed her glare to Lionheart, one elegant brow raised. "Have you not told him?"

"Told me what?" Edward asked.

Lionheart shrugged. "There was no time."

Edward raised his hand. "Cease. Tell me later. I wish to sup before listening to news I may or may not like. Sit you down beside me, Lady Vanora, and regale me with tales of Lionheart's misconduct whilst I eat. Lionheart, amuse yourself with your leman whilst I converse with Vanora; I fear Althea has sorely missed your companionship."

Looking extremely uncomfortable, Lionheart flashed Vanora a silent warning before taking his place beside Althea.

"I had hoped for a better welcome than this," Althea whined. She touched his thigh beneath the table and smiled up at him. "Are you not happy to see me,

Lionheart? I have missed you dreadfully."

Somehow Lionheart doubted that. Althea was not a woman content with long spells of celibacy. She had doubtless opened her thighs to another love less than a sennight after he'd left her.

"Your presence complicates matters," Lionheart returned. "I cannot understand why Edward brought you here when we are to leave soon."

Althea's blue eyes widened in disbelief. "Has he not told you?"

"Told me what?"

"Mayhap he wants to tell you himself. Forgive me for speaking out of turn."

Lionheart could not wait for the meal to end to learn Edward's plans for him. For all his meager years, the prince was a man who did not make decisions lightly, or without good reason.

Vanora could not help liking the young prince. Longshanks, as he was fondly called, looked every bit the future king: a golden man with a golden future. But he also appeared to be the kind of man who knew what he wanted and was not afraid to seize it. She feared Wales was doomed should Edward decide to bring her country under English rule.

"Are you Lord Rhys's heir?" Edward asked, chewing thoughtfully on a piece of succulent braised veal in cream sauce.

"Aye, I have no brothers." Her chin tilted upward. "Cragdon is mine."

Edward chose not to reply as he returned his attention to his trencher. Vanora picked at her food, her gaze straying to Lionheart and his leman. Althea was a beauty — she could not blame Lionheart for claiming her — but why had Edward brought her? Surely he did not intend to leave the woman at Cragdon, did he? Althea's presence did not make sense.

Ever forthright, Vanora swallowed hard and asked, "Why did you bring Lionheart's leman to Cragdon? I thought you intended to fetch Lionheart and your army and return to England."

Edward sent her an appraising look. "Have you grown fond of Lionheart?"

Vanora flushed and looked away. "I am merely curious."

"So is Lionheart, I'll wager." He arose. "Shall we retire to my chamber, Lionheart? We have much to discuss."

"The north tower has been made ready for you," Vanora said. "I will show you the way."

"Nay, stay and entertain Althea," Edward commanded. "Lionheart can show me the way."

Vanora glanced at Althea, her ire rising when she saw the woman staring adoringly at Lionheart. She turned away and would have left the hall but Althea stopped her.

"I am weary, mistress. Show me to Lionheart's chamber so that I may ready myself for him. We have been apart many months."

"I will show you to a chamber, but it will not be Lionheart's," Vanora retorted.

Althea sent Vanora a venomous glare. "How dare you! I have traveled a long distance to be with Lionheart and will not be denied by a woman who has played the whore for him."

"How, pray tell, does that make you better than me?" Vanora charged.

She wanted desperately to tell Althea she was Lionheart's wife but decided to wait until Edward had been informed.

"You have a sharp tongue for a woman in your position," Althea said.

"What position is that?"

"A woman whose home is no longer hers, and will soon be evicted."

"Are you so sure of that?"

Althea sent her a smug smile. "Aye. I

know why Edward brought me here and you do not."

"Nor do I care. Excuse me, I will have a servant show you to your chamber. Rest well, Althea," she threw over her shoulder as she stomped off.

"I am well pleased with Cragdon," Edward said as he sprawled on a bench before the hearth, a flagon of ale in his hand.

Lionheart stood before him, legs spread, arms folded across his chest. "Do you want to tell me why you brought Althea to Cragdon? Her presence here troubles me."

Edward sighed. "You are not going to like this, Lionheart, but I have plans for Cragdon that include you."

Dread lanced through him. "How so?"

"First, let me be the first to inform you of your father's death. As his sole heir, you will inherit his title."

"Title to what?" Lionheart scoffed. "My father and I have been estranged for many years. He sold his lands and everything of value he owned and became one of Henry's courtiers, a man dependent upon the king's largess. His death does not affect me one way or the other."

"Mayhap it should. Apparently, your mother learned of your father's death and has returned to England. She is living in London."

Pain flashed in Lionheart's eyes. "I care not. She abandoned me years ago. She has her life and I have mine. What has my father's death to do with Cragdon?"

Edward sighed and thrust his fingers through his blond locks. " 'Tis not right that a man of your character and rank should be landless. Therefore, I am gifting you with Cragdon and all it entails. You are now Lord Lionheart, Earl of Cragdon."

"You are giving me a title and Welsh lands?" Lionheart asked in disbelief.

"Aye. Cragdon is a jewel, Lionheart, and important in the scheme of things. The estate sits in the midst of Llewelyn's kingdom. I need someone strong to protect my Welsh holdings. When I am king, I intend to rule all of Britain, and that includes Wales and Scotland. When the time comes, I shall wage war against both countries and surround them with great fortresses to bring them to heel."

Lionheart searched for the meaning behind Edward's gift and suddenly knew that his fears had been realized. "God's blood! You intend for me to remain in Wales!"

"Aye. I need you here, Lionheart, to be my eyes and ears."

"You need me to lead your army," Lionheart shot back.

"I have men aplenty, but only one I trust enough to act as guardian of my property. When I begin my campaign against Wales, you and Cragdon will be here to support me."

"Nay, I refuse!"

"Are you not my vassal, Lionheart? You have been my mentor and my friend for as long as I can remember."

"Aye, I have followed wherever you led. I have pledged myself to you, but ask me not to sit idly by while you go to war."

"I *am* asking you, Lionheart. I need you at Cragdon. Your loyalty shall not go unrewarded. When I am king, you will have the greatest estate England has to offer. 'Tis not within my power to grant you that estate now so Cragdon will have to do."

"And, you brought Althea to cozen me into doing what you wanted."

"Althea is a boon I grant to keep you content at Cragdon. Should you desire a wife, I shall endeavor to find one worthy of you. Althea, of course, would never do as a wife. You deserve a young heiress who has never known a man's touch. You have my vow on this."

Lionheart realized there would be no

better time to tell Edward about Vanora. "You are not the only bearer of surprises; I have something of import to tell you."

Edward smiled. "I know. You took the lady Vanora as your leman. How you will divide your time between Althea and Vanora should be interesting. Unfortunately, I cannot linger to watch you handle the sticky situation."

"I am married," Lionheart said without preamble.

Edward dropped the flagon of ale he was holding and looked at Lionheart as if he had just grown horns. "You are what? When? How? Who? God's blood, I cannot believe it! You, a man who has avoided marriage like the plague, have suddenly wed. What jest is this?"

"I wish it were a jest." Lionheart began to pace. "I married Lady Vanora some weeks ago."

"My God, man, why?"

Lionheart shrugged. " 'Twas a simple matter of lust, Lord Edward."

"Why did you not rut with the wench and be done with it?"

"Her priest would not allow it. He stood within the chamber and refused to budge until I wed the woman. My cock was so eager for her, I would have agreed to anything. You are young, you do not know what it is like to want a woman the way I wanted Vanora."

"And now that you have had her, do you wish me to invalidate the marriage?"

At one time, it had been precisely what Lionheart wanted, but now he was not so sure. He had also thought he would be leaving Vanora and Cragdon behind, but it appeared that Edward had other ideas. If he were to be Cragdon's new lord, it would not hurt to keep Vanora as his wife. Besides, he had not yet tired of her and had much to gain and naught to lose by being wed to a Welshwoman.

"I believe I shall keep Vanora, Edward. The marriage is legal in all respects. She had a prior verbal agreement with another but broke the betrothal before we wed."

"Methinks you are smitten," Edward said, grinning. "Now you know how I feel about my Eleanor. She is the moon and stars, and I am the luckiest of men."

Lionheart shifted uncomfortably. He did not like speaking openly of feelings. It was one thing to admit he desired Vanora but another to reveal tender feelings when he was not certain they existed.

For years Lionheart had protected his heart against emotional involvement. 'Twas far better to remain detached than to suffer the fate of his parents. All he knew of love was that it hurt.

"I did not know you were a poet, Edward."

"You do not know everything about me."

"I have known you since you were a youth of seven sent to foster with your uncle."

"Ah, well, I suppose you do know me better than anyone. Just as I know you. 'Tis obvious you care for Vanora. And your marriage does settle many things. You married Cragdon's heiress and became its owner and lord without my intervention. No one can dispute your legal right to Cragdon. I am pleased with this marriage, Lord Lionheart, well pleased."

"Pleased enough to let me return to England with you?"

"Nay, I am sorry, Lionheart, but I have need of you in Wales. 'Tis possible Llewelyn will break the peace treaty and rally his countrymen around him. That could place England in jeopardy, for our army cannot fight effectively on two fronts. Should that happen, de Montfort would win and name himself king."

"I like it not, but as your vassal I will do as you wish," Lionheart groused.

"I grow weary. It has been a long day. Is there aught else I should know?"

"There is a Welsh prisoner in the south tower."

"You took prisoners?"

"Just one, Daffid ap Deverell. He was taken during our last skirmish with Llewelyn's forces. I left his fate for you to decide."

"Release him," Edward said. "There is no reason to hold him now."

When Lionheart seemed reluctant, Edward asked, "Is there something I should know about Daffid?"

"He was Vanora's betrothed."

"Think you he will cause trouble?"

"Possibly."

" 'Tis best to avoid trouble while the peace treaty is in effect. Placate Daffid as best you can and send him on his way."

"And Althea? Will you take her back with you?"

"Ah, Althea. She will have to remain until you can make arrangements to return her to her father, for I cannot take her with me."

Lionheart bit out a curse. "My life is complicated enough without Althea underfoot. I will make arrangements as soon as possible. How many men-at-arms can you leave me?"

"Twenty is all I can spare. The rest will return to England with me. I need every man at my disposal to defeat de Montfort's army."

" 'Tis not nearly enough if I am to send Althea home with an escort."

"I am sure you will find a way," Edward said, stifling a yawn.

Lionheart took Edward's yawn as dismissal and withdrew; his disappointment was so keen he could barely contain it. He needed to be with Edward when he rode into battle. How could Edward leave him behind in this godforsaken land? He was a knight and a warrior, not a steward or keeper of Edward's property. Anyone could be a steward, but not everyone had his skills as a warrior.

Sir Giles was waiting in the hall for Lionheart. Lionheart saw him and swerved in his direction.

" 'Tis a fine kettle of fish Edward has delivered," Giles teased, referring to Althea. "Will your leman accompany us when we leave?"

"Nay," Lionheart said sourly.

"Is that why you are upset?"

" 'Tis more than that, Giles, much more. Althea is but one piece of bad news Edward brought with him."

"There is more?"

"Aye. Edward has ordered me to remain at Cragdon and hold the keep for England. He has made me Earl of Cragdon."

"An earl? Edward made you an earl?"

"In a manner of speaking. I learned from Edward that my father has died, and that I have inherited his title. Since the title is an empty one, I care not about it, but Edward has gifted me with Cragdon, and now, it seems, I am a man of property and income."

"Congratulations, Lord Lionheart."

"I like it not. 'Tis not my decision to remain at Cragdon while Edward leads his army against de Montfort. He is leaving but twenty men behind to defend the castle." He searched Giles's face. "Can I count on you, Giles? I have need of you at Cragdon."

"Like you, I prefer a good battle to inactivity. But if Edward thinks 'tis necessary to hold Cragdon, then I shall not desert you, my lord."

"I pray Sir Brandon agrees with you, for I will have need of him too. Edward will choose which warriors are to stay at Cragdon, but I will feel better if my two principal knights remain in my service."

"Think you Althea will cause trouble between you and Vanora?" Giles asked.

"More trouble than either of us knows," Lionheart surmised. "Althea is not an easy woman to placate. Once she learns that Vanora and I are wed, she will make all kinds of mischief until she can be returned to England."

Giles's eyes sparkled. "Althea is a beautiful woman. I would not mind taking her off your hands."

"Be my guest, Giles. Vanora is more than I can handle at the present time. Excuse me, I had best find my wife now and tell her I am to remain at Cragdon."

"Good luck, Lord Lionheart." Giles's grin told Lionheart that he did not envy him his task.

Giles strode off to find his own bed, but Lionheart lingered, his mind still reeling. How could this have happened to him? Of all the men Edward could have chosen as Cragdon's new lord, why him?

"May I have a word with you, Lionheart?"

Lionheart whirled to find Father Caddoc standing behind him. "You will have your say whether I wish it or not," he grumbled.

"I like not this situation with your leman," the priest chided. "Think you Vanora will allow her to remain at Cragdon after you leave?"

"Things have changed, Father," Lionheart explained. "Edward has gifted me with Cragdon. I am to remain as its new lord."

"You became Cragdon's lord when you wed Vanora," Father Caddoc informed him. "Did you not know that?"

"I had not thought much about it since I did not intend to remain at Cragdon. My place is with Edward, but he has other plans for me."

"Does Vanora know?"

"Not yet. She will not be pleased."

"Mayhap you will be surprised."

"What is that supposed to mean?"

The priest sent him an exasperated look. " 'Tis not for me to say. You still have not explained what you intend to do with your leman. I seriously doubt Vanora will allow you to bed another woman."

Lionheart frowned. " 'Tis not for Vanora to allow or disallow." Lionheart had no intention of bedding Althea but he would never admit as much to Vanora. The woman already had too much power over his senses.

The priest stifled a smile. "You have much to learn about Vanora."

How true, Lionheart mused. "Worry not about Althea, Father. I intend to send her back to England."

The priest nodded and bade Lionheart good night. Lionheart glanced toward the solar and resolutely started up the winding staircase. He was striding down the gallery when a figure detached itself from the shadows and stood in Lionheart's path. His hand flew to the hilt of his sword, then relaxed when he recognized Althea. A sigh hissed past his lips. His life was becoming more complicated by the minute.

"What are you doing here, Althea? Does your chamber not please you?"

"That bitch refused to take me to your chamber. A servant told me you slept in the solar, so I waited here for you."

She threw back her cloak, baring her nearly nude body to him. Her thin shift concealed naught. Her coral nipples glowed as if rouged, and the thatch betwixt her legs glittered like pure gold. Compared to Vanora's lean length and firm breasts, Althea's legs were too short and her body too soft, almost flabby.

"The woman you just called a bitch is my wife, Althea," Lionheart said.

Althea recoiled as if struck. "You are wed? When did this happen? Does Edward approve?"

" 'Tis not for Edward to approve or disapprove. What is done is done."

She sidled close and pushed her pillowy breasts against him. The musky smell of her arousal, combined with an exotic perfume she wore, teased his senses. He inured himself to her seduction and tried to back away, but she clung to him like a vine, pushing her soft mound against him.

He retreated. She followed. "I have a wife, Althea, and no need of a leman," Lionheart maintained.

She cupped his cock and smiled up at him. "You are growing hard in my hand, Lionheart."

She squeezed; he groaned. "You take unfair advantage of me." He slapped her hand away and set her apart from him. "Go find your bed, Althea. I have no need of a leman tonight or any night."

"I will change your mind," Althea purred as he pushed past her.

"I doubt it," Lionheart said.

Taking a deep breath, he opened the door and entered the solar. His gaze found Vanora and he nearly lost the ability to speak. She was sitting on a bench, running a comb through her long hair and gazing absently into the flames. Her shift had slipped off one creamy shoulder, exposing a firm, round breast.

She turned toward him, her face composed but her eyes as turbulent as a storm-tossed sea. "Have you finished with your leman already?"

"I was with Edward."

Disbelief darkened her violet eyes. "So you say."

He crossed the room and lowered himself to the bench beside her. " 'Tis the truth. Why do I need a leman when I have you?"

Vanora sniffed the air, then leapt to her feet and backed away. "Liar! You reek of sex and *her*." She glanced downward, her gaze lingering on his loins. "Did she not satisfy you?"

Lionheart cursed. " 'Tis not what you think. Althea accosted me on the gallery and . . . and . . ."

". . . made you hard," she finished.

Lionheart cursed. "I want her not, Vanora. I was with Edward for a time, then stopped to speak with Giles and Father Caddoc. I will hear no more about it."

"It matters not to me whom you bed, Lionheart," Vanora stated. "Just make sure you take your leman with you when you leave."

"Vanora . . ."

She sent him a hard look. "How much longer must I put up with you? Will you leave tomorrow, or the next day, or the next? I hope 'tis soon."

"As much as you wish it, sweeting, 'tis not to be. I shall remain at Cragdon indefinitely. Edward wants me to become lord of Cragdon, though I never aspired to the title."

"Nay, it cannot be true! How am I to bear it?"

Chapter Twelve

Vanora grappled with Lionheart's words, struggling to make sense of them. She could not imagine Lionheart remaining at Cragdon under any circumstances. Why did Edward want him to remain? The one thing Vanora did understand now, however, was Edward's reason for bringing Althea to Wales. She was here for Lionheart's pleasure. Obviously, it was Edward's way of indulging Lionheart for leaving him behind at Cragdon.

"Why is Edward leaving you behind?" Vanora asked, her voice quivering with an unexplained emotion.

"He wants me here to protect his property," Lionheart answered. "Not just Cragdon, but all his property in Wales. Think you I like it? I prefer to fight alongside Edward."

"Fight? Is England at war?"

"Civil war. King Henry is at odds with his barons. Simon de Montfort leads the opposing forces."

Vanora digested that, then asked, "Did Edward bring news of Llewelyn?"

"Aye. He is in England. It appears that our countries are at peace now. He and Henry signed a treaty. There are rumors that Llewelyn will wed Simon de Montfort's daughter."

"If there is peace between our countries, why must you remain at Cragdon?"

"Because Edward asked it of me, and because I am a Welsh landowner by virtue of our marriage."

That was not what Vanora wanted to hear. But then, she seriously doubted the words she craved were in Lionheart's vocabulary. "What about Althea? Just say the word and I will relinquish my place in your bed to her."

"God's blood, think you I want Althea? 'Twas not my idea to bring her to Cragdon. Edward acted on his own because he thought it would please me. He knew he needed to placate me after ordering me to remain at Cragdon."

"Will Edward take her back to England when he leaves?"

"He says he cannot. I intend to send her home to her village as soon as I am able."

"I shall move into another chamber until your leman is gone," Vanora said. "Mayhap you will change your mind about bedding her, since she is so eager."

She grabbed her chamber robe from the bench and moved toward the door. Lionheart grasped her arm in passing and hauled her against him. "We spoke vows. You cannot leave my bed unless I approve, and I do not approve."

"I obey my God and no one else," Vanora retorted.

"Shall we summon Father Caddoc to settle the dispute? You *know* what he will say. A woman must cleave to her husband and obey him in all things. Even if I took Althea as my leman, you would have no say in the matter."

"Try it and see," Vanora challenged.

Lionheart laughed. "If I did not know better, I would think you were jealous."

Vanora snorted. "Do not delude yourself, my lord. Would you not protest if I took a lover?"

His eyes darkened to stormy gray. "You are mine, Vanora. I do not share what is mine. Do not even consider it."

"If I did not know better, I would think *you* were jealous," she tossed back at him.

"Mayhap I am," he admitted. His arms tightened around her. "Kiss me, wife."

"Are you sure 'tis me you want to kiss and not Althea?"

"Very sure." He cupped her chin and

raised it, waiting for her to obey him.

Temptation overwhelmed her. 'Twas not much of a stretch to reach his lips. Tilting her head back, she touched her lips to his. 'Twas all the encouragement Lionheart needed. His mouth opened on hers, their tongues tangled and breaths mingled. He kissed her endlessly, until her heart pounded and her knees began to buckle.

Placing his hands beneath her buttocks, he lifted her and carried her to their bed. Then he stripped off her shift, tore away his tunic and hose and joined her.

"Wait," Vanora said as he bent to take a pert breast into his mouth. "You did not tell me what Edward said about our marriage."

He lifted his head. "Later," he growled, returning to his succulent feast.

"Now."

He sighed. "Very well. He is pleased."

"Obviously not pleased enough to take Althea with him when he leaves."

"Enough! I will deal with Althea in my own way."

"I've changed my mind about wanting to remain married to you," Vanora declared. "Our marriage was not supposed to be a permanent arrangement. You were forced to wed me."

A growl of exasperation emerged from Lionheart's throat. "Most marriages are arranged. 'Tis the way of things."

Vanora took a deep breath and asked, "Do you truly wish to remain wed to me?"

Lionheart shrugged. "If I am to remain at Cragdon, the arrangement suits me well enough. I never wanted a wife and family, but now that I have lands of my own, the idea of children has appeal."

"You want children with me?"

"Unless you are barren, 'tis likely to happen whether we wish it or not."

Anger surged through Vanora. Gathering her strength, she pushed him away and rolled off the bed. " 'Tis not good enough, Lord Lionheart! I want my husband to be passionate about marriage and children."

A glint appeared in Lionheart's eyes. "You want passion, my lady? Then I shall give you passion."

She turned to flee, remembered she was naked and stopped at the door. Lionheart caught her and carried her back to the bed. "Aye, passion I have in abundance."

His lips found hers unerringly. She wanted to fight, to prove she was not vulnerable to his kisses, but it was she who rose into the kiss, her hands digging into his shoulders. Marshaling her resistance, she braced her hands against him to push him away, but when his fingers traveled down her stomach to delve into her weeping center, she dragged him closer.

With his tongue he traced a feathery circle around one peaked nipple. The rosy crest sprang taut into his mouth. She stifled a groan and let her fingers wander where they would, learning him by touch as well as by sight.

He lifted his head, gazed down at her. A soft laugh betrayed his victory. "Am I passionate enough for you, sweeting? 'Tis what you want, is it not?"

"I want . . . I want . . ."

"I *know* what you want, and you shall have it . . . when I am good and ready."

Vanora closed her eyes tightly, suddenly frightened of the way she felt. She no longer had control over herself; she was Lionheart's, to do with as he pleased.

"Stop! I do not want this," she cried.

If he heard, he ignored her. His mouth took hers once more as he spread her thighs and fondled her, his drugging kisses turning her to putty in his arms. His kisses were starkly sensual, bold, his tongue a probing sword that pricked her senses. When his mouth left hers and latched onto a nipple, she arched against him and surrendered to his passion . . . and hers.

Abruptly she pressed her hands against his chest and pushed. Startled, he reared up. She scrambled to her knees and shoved him down onto the furs. When she crouched over him, he blinked, as if suddenly aware of her intention.

He opened his mouth to protest, but the word lodged in his suddenly dry mouth. Her lashes lowered. She leaned closer. The silken caress of her hair, swinging forward to brush his thighs, created a firestorm inside him that was tantamount to torture. Distracted, he held his breath as her head bent toward him.

He felt the touch of hot breath first, like a brand against the most sensitive part of his body. Then her lips touched, kissed, caressed him lingeringly; they parted and took him into the hot cavern of her mouth. Every muscle locked. He struggled to breathe, struggled to deny the feelings assailing him. Vanora was the only woman who had breached the walls guarding his heart.

"God's blood, woman, you are killing me!"

She smiled up at him. "Good."

He fought to maintain a modicum of control, but the task was a daunting one with Vanora's warm mouth upon him and her tongue driving him out of his mind. He was close to the breaking point when, muscles bunching, flexing, he lifted her away and pulled her up over him. Instantly she wrapped her long legs about his hips and positioned herself over him.

He nearly exploded when she captured the throbbing head of his sex in the slick flesh between her thighs, leaving him poised at her entrance, desperate and aching. Then she took him into her hand and sank down, impaling herself on his rigid hardness. Lowering her head, she covered his lips with hers, brushing them, tantalizing them, her sizzling passion driving him wild.

His arms closed like a steel vise about her. His hands found the creamy globes of her buttocks, lifting her to meet his long, deep thrusts. Their bodies shifted, then locked tight. With a groan of surrender, he unleashed the tension coiled inside him.

The power, the force, the dominance of his male ego took over. Vanora sensed it in the taut sinews that held her. Tightening her arms around his neck, she held him closer, reveling in the towering passion the two of them had unleashed.

"Love me, Lionheart," she whispered

against his lips. "Please love me."

"I am," he answered.

Vanora knew immediately that he did not understand what she was asking. He thought in physical terms, not emotional ones. While she knew without a doubt that she loved him, he had not the slightest notion what it meant to love with the heart as well as the body.

His teeth gritted, his body drawn taut as a bowstring, Lionheart drove into her, letting instinct take over. He hung on by sheer will, watching her face tighten with passion, then ease as he felt her hot sheath soften to receive his seed. Shudders wracked him; closing his eyes, he gave himself up to pleasure so intense he felt as if his soul had left his body.

An eternity later, Lionheart rolled away. Lying on his back, one hand flung over his eyes, he tried to make sense of what had just happened and the way he felt.

He had never known love. After his mother left his father gave him less attention than he did his horse. Lionheart had never allowed a woman to get close enough to him to discover his flawed heart. The heart his mother had destroyed.

"What are you thinking?" Vanora asked.

He glanced over at her. She was lying on

her side, staring at him. He shrugged, unwilling to share his private thoughts, especially now, when his thoughts were of her. "We should get some sleep. Edward is an early riser, so I thought to take him hunting in the morning."

She placed a hand on his chest. He flinched and swore under his breath. The compulsive need to love her again surged like a tidal wave over him. What was wrong with him? He was thoroughly, remarkably sated, and yet he wanted her again. Would he ever tire of her? He seriously doubted it. Looking at her, seeing the quizzical expression on her face, Lionheart felt something in his chest shift. The feelings and emotions that poured through him were confusing. They rattled him and left him feeling vulnerable. It was not a comfortable feeling.

"Go to sleep," he growled, and was instantly sorry that he had spoken so harshly. The sudden intake of her breath told him that he had hurt her. She deserved better from him.

"Go to sleep," he repeated, gentling his voice.

Lionheart was gone when Vanora awoke the following morning. Rising, she washed, dressed and hurried down to chapel just as the bells tolled Prime. Kneeling quietly in a pew, she lowered her head to pray as Father Caddac began the Mass. Chapel was lightly attended this morning, and Vanora supposed that everyone had gone hunting with Lionheart and Edward.

Though the Mass had ended and Father Caddoc had left the altar, Vanora remained on her knees to pray. She was rudely interrupted when someone behind her spoke her name. She recognized the voice immediately and turned to confront Daffid ap Deverell.

"Daffid! You are free."

"Aye. Your *husband*," he said, spitting the word out like a curse, "released me from the tower. He said Wales and England are at peace, and that Llewelyn is to wed Simon de Montfort's daughter. I do not put much faith in this peace Llewelyn has wrought, but it served to free me."

"Think you Llewelyn will break the peace treaty?"

"War is inevitable. When Edward becomes king, he will not be satisfied until both Wales and Scotland are under his rule. He has ambitions beyond his years."

"What are you going to do now?"

"Return to Draymere, I suppose. I

wanted to see you before I left. Come with me, Vanora. Your marriage to Lionheart is a sham. You were betrothed to me."

"I ended the betrothal, if you recall. You are not the man I thought you were. I liked not what you asked of me. Nor do I like being treated like chattel."

He grasped her wrist in a bruising grip. "You are an Englishman's chattel now. How can you bear the shame?"

Vanora recalled the delicious pleasure Lionheart had given her last night and did not regret for a minute casting Daffid aside. Nor was she shamed. She had not wanted to wed Lionheart, but her heart now recognized him as the only man for her.

"Release me," Vanora hissed.

"Nay, you are mine. Cragdon is mine. Think you I like living at Draymere? 'Tis naught compared to Cragdon. Your father promised me your lands and your hand in marriage. When Lionheart leaves, I shall take back that which is rightfully mine."

He grasped her other wrist and pulled her against him, his thick chest pressing against her breasts. Then his mouth slammed down on hers, hard, ruthless, defiant. Vanora choked back the bile rising in her throat and tore her mouth free.

"I am wed. You have no right to kiss me."

"What do you think Lionheart will do when he learns the identity of the White Knight he is so eager to find?" he taunted.

"You would not dare!"

"Would I not?"

"My, my, who is this?" a feminine voice said from behind them. "Does your husband know what is going on behind his back?"

Moving away from Daffid, Vanora glared at Althea. "You know not what you are saying. Naught is going on behind Lionheart's back. Daffid was merely bidding me good-bye."

"Daffid," Althea repeated. "The name is Welsh, is it not? Introduce us, Lady Vanora."

Sighing resignedly, Vanora introduced Althea to Daffid.

"What brings you to Cragdon, Althea?" Daffid asked.

"I came with Prince Edward. I am Lionheart's leman."

Daffid's brows shot upward, but before he could comment on that startling bit of news, Vanora said, "Unless you wish to return to the tower, you had best leave, Daffid."

Daffid glared at her. "I will leave, but do not forget what I said. Cragdon is mine." Whirling on his heel, he stormed off.

Althea regarded Vanora with suspicion. "What did he mean? Why does he think Cragdon belongs to him?"

Vanora saw no help for it. If she did not tell Althea, someone else would. "Daffid was my betrothed. I decided we did not suit and broke the betrothal before I wed Lionheart."

"You looked like you suited well enough from where I was standing," Althea snorted. "How long have you been whoring behind Lionheart's back?"

"I do not have to answer to you," Vanora returned. "There is but one whore here, and 'tis not I. Excuse me, there is much to be done today, and exchanging barbs with you is a waste of my time."

So saying, she raised her chin and swept past Althea.

Lionheart returned to the keep later that day in a cheerful mood. The weather had been brisk, just right for the hunt, and they had bagged a variety of small game. Edward enjoyed the hunt as much as Lionheart did, and they had planned a sennight of hunting before Edward returned to England.

Mugs of mulled wine were passed around as Lionheart settled into a chair before the hearth. Edward stood nearby, staring pensively into the flames.

"This brief sojourn is just what I needed, Lionheart," Edward said. "Soon I will be involved in a battle to defend my birthright. If Father were stronger and less enamored of harboring foreigners at his court, civil war would not be necessary."

"You shall persevere, Edward, I know you will. I am here should you need me. Just send for me, and I will hie myself to your side."

"I have never doubted your loyalty, Lionheart. I regret having to leave you behind, but 'tis necessary. Should a messenger arrive bearing my colors, you will know I am in trouble. I pray it will not come to that. Excuse me, I wish to change before the evening meal."

Lionheart watched Edward walk away, his golden head held high and proud. Despite his youth, he was a splendid warrior and would make a wise king. Lionheart was proud of the young man he had befriended.

From the corner of his eye Lionheart saw Althea approaching and heaved a weary sigh. The look on her face did not bode well for him. What now? he wondered.

"Lionheart, may I have a word with you?"

"What is it, Althea?"

"Not here. In private."

"I have no time for this."

"Please, Lionheart, 'tis important. I promise you will not be sorry."

"If this is some trick, Althea —"

"Nay, no trick. Come to my chamber. 'Tis about your wife."

The word "wife" startled him. What did Althea know about Vanora? "Very well, but do not try your seductive wiles on me. I did not ask you to come here and am sorry that Edward took it upon himself to bring you. When you leave, you will be amply compensated for any inconvenience. Consider it your dowry."

Disregarding his words, she grasped his hand and pulled him toward the winding staircase that led to her chamber. Only one person noticed. Giles's disapproving gaze followed them until they were lost to sight.

"You are acting strangely, Althea. Are you unwell?" Lionheart asked when they reached the top landing.

"I am very well." She flung open the

door and strode inside, waiting for him to follow. Once he was inside, she closed the door.

"All right, I am here. Why the secrecy?"

"I did not want others to hear something that would cause you embarrassment. I truly care for you, Lionheart."

He heaved another sigh. "I know that and regret the way things turned out. I am fond of you, too. Now tell me what it is that I should know."

"I met Daffid ap Deverell today. What was Vanora's former betrothed doing at Cragdon?"

"Is that what this is about? Daffid was being held prisoner in the tower. When Edward arrived, he advised me to release Daffid. I did so this morn." A frown creased his brow. "Where did you see him? I assumed he had left Cragdon."

"You assumed wrong," Althea said with a smirk. "I saw him kissing your wife in the chapel."

Lionheart inhaled sharply. Vanora had denied having feelings for Daffid, and he had believed her. Had she lied? Had she been planning mischief even as they made love last night?

"There is more," Althea said.

Lionheart's lips thinned. "Tell me."

"They were discussing the White Knight. Do you know who that is?"

Lionheart's attention sharpened. "Are you certain?"

"Aye."

"What did they say?"

"Daffid threatened to divulge the identity of the White Knight, and Vanora became angry."

"What else?"

" 'Tis all I heard. But their kiss spoke louder than words. 'Twas a passionate kiss, Lionheart. 'Twas obvious they had been lovers and were eager to resume their relationship.

Lionheart knew for a fact that Daffid and Vanora had never been lovers, for he had taken her maidenhead on their wedding night. His eyes narrowed. Mayhap Vanora wanted them to become lovers.

Lionheart had always suspected that Vanora knew the White Knight's identity. Was it Daffid? Nay, he thought not. The knight had neither Daffid's stocky build nor his years. Who was he? Lionheart was certain he had not seen the knight at Cragdon. He would recognize him were he to show himself. Not his face, but his carriage and build. Strange as it might seem, the mysterious knight seemed as familiar to him as his own body.

"Are you going to punish Vanora, Lionheart?" Althea asked. "You should beat her for betraying you. I would never betray you."

"Stay out of this, Althea. I will take care of my wife. If you speak of this to anyone, I shall turn you out of Cragdon to make your own way home."

Althea threw herself into his arms. "I will say naught. I do not want to leave you, Lionheart. Ever."

Catching him off guard, Althea shoved him backward. He had not expected her to be so strong. He tumbled onto the bed, and she fell atop him in a tangle of arms and legs.

"What are you doing, woman?"

"Relax, Lionheart. I want us to enjoy what we once had together."

Vanora entered the hall, her gaze searching for Lionheart. She knew Edward had returned and wondered where her husband had disappeared. He was not in the solar and obviously not in the hall. She spied Sir Giles and summoned him with a look.

"How may I help you, Lady Vanora?"

"Have you seen Lionheart? I was told

he had returned from the hunt."

Shuffling his feet, Giles avoided Vanora's eyes. "I cannot say, my lady."

"What can you not say? Has Lionheart returned or has he not?"

"He has returned."

"Is something amiss, Sir Giles? Is there some reason you do not want me to know where Lionheart has gone?"

Giles cleared his throat. "I . . . I . . ." he looked anywhere but at Vanora.

Vanora felt the beginnings of a headache behind her eyes. For some reason, Giles did not want to reveal Lionheart's whereabouts. But that was not acceptable to her.

"Speak, Sir Giles. Tell me what it is you do not want me to know. Has aught happened to my husband?"

"He is well, my lady."

"Then kindly tell me where I might find him."

"W-with Edward," Giles lied.

As if to mock his words, Edward strode into the hall. "Have either of you seen Lionheart?"

Both Giles and Vanora shook their heads.

"Tell him he can find me with my warriors should he ask for me," Edward said, striding out the door.

"Where is he?" Vanora hissed. "Do not lie to me, Sir Giles."

Giles swallowed hard. "The last I saw of him he was accompanying Althea to her bedchamber. I am sure his intentions were honorable," he quickly added.

"Have a man's intentions ever been honorable?" Vanora retorted as she stormed off toward Althea's chamber. If Lionheart had been bedding his leman, she would make him very sorry.

Vanora paused at the top landing and held her ear to the door. Thick oak prevented her from hearing what was going on inside. She thought she heard creaking bed ropes but could not be certain. Inhaling a steadying breath, she lifted the latch and pushed open the door.

Her gaze was drawn to the bed, where a man and a woman sported in obvious enjoyment. She tried to stifle the cry of outrage that gathered in her throat but could not. How could he? Only a depraved man or an unfeeling one could make love to his wife and then seek out his leman the next day. Apparently, Lionheart was both.

Vanora's cry resounded loudly in the stillness of the chamber. Lionheart managed to free himself from Althea's clinging arms and legs in time to see Vanora fleeing through the open door. He tried to follow, but Althea clung to his neck and refused to let go.

"Let her go, Lionheart," Althea pleaded. "Everyone knows you wed Vanora for her land, and because her priest demanded it of you. Had you been able to bed her without wedding her, you would have done so. Cragdon is yours now; you need no longer pretend you are satisfied with the marriage."

"You are wrong, Althea," Lionheart bit out, unwinding her arms from his neck and flinging her away. "I could have taken Vanora without wedding her if I had wanted to force her. Or I could have found another woman to satisfy my lust, but only Vanora would do. I wanted her, Althea. 'Tis as simple as that," he said with a jolt of insight.

"Are you saying you love her?" Althea gasped. "Not you, Lionheart. You take but do not love. You were ready to leave Vanora behind and follow Edward before he commanded you to remain."

"Aye," he admitted. "But that does not mean I would not have returned at some point in time." That truth startled him. He would indeed have returned, because there was a connection between him and Vanora that defied distance and time.

He strode toward the door.

"Where are you going?"

"To find my wife."

"Daffid and your wife were kissing. What are you going to do about it? And what about the White Knight?"

Lionheart did not answer, but his mind would not let the matter rest as he beat a hasty retreat. If Althea had seen Daffid and Vanora kissing, he wanted to know the details before he decided on his own course of action. It was unacceptable behavior, and he would not stand for it. As for the White Knight, he would force Vanora to reveal his identity and have the man's guts for garters.

Lionheart stormed into the solar. Vanora was not there. He strode along the gallery, opening doors until he found her. She was putting fresh linens on a bed in an unoccupied chamber.

He paused in the doorway. "What are you doing?"

Her glare told him it was none of his business.

"Vanora —"

"Oh, very well. I refuse to sleep in the same bed with you. I am moving out of the solar to make room for your leman."

"What you saw was not what it seemed."

"My eyes did not deceive me, my lord."

"Things are not always the way they look."

"You were engaged in intimate relations with Althea, were you not?"

"Nay, I was not." His eyes narrowed. "You were observed kissing Daffid in the chapel."

"I see Althea wasted no time in telling you. What else did she say?"

"We will get to that later. Why were you kissing Daffid? Do you regret breaking your betrothal to him?"

"Did Althea not tell you I was an unwilling participant in the kiss? Daffid sought me out in the chapel to say goodbye. The kiss was unexpected and unwelcome."

"Was it? Very well, I know appearances can be deceiving, even if you do not. Shall we go on to another subject? Althea heard you discussing the White Knight. She said you spoke as if you knew his identity. Who is he, Vanora?"

Vanora blanched. "I know not. Forget him, Lionheart. There is peace between our countries, and the reason to seek him out no longer exists."

"How can I forget someone who made a fool of me? Nay, I shall hunt him until I find him. I am your husband; you owe me your fealty. Give me the name of the knave, and I shall forgive you for kissing Daffid."

"You forgive me? How dare you! Daffid's kiss was forced on me, but you went willingly to Althea's bed. You should ask *my* forgiveness."

"I have done naught to warrant forgiveness, while you, on the other hand, have many secrets." He pinned her with a hard look. "You will sleep in my bed until I decide otherwise, is that clear?"

"Have I no say in the matter?" she shot back.

"None whatsoever. Know this. I accept that Daffid forced his kiss on you, but I will not tolerate your secrecy concerning the White Knight. When I find him, and I will, he shall not escape my wrath."

Turning abruptly, he stormed off.

Vanora was torn. Had she jumped to conclusions about Lionheart's involvement with Althea? Nay, her eyes had not deceived her, and Giles did say that Lionheart had gone willingly with Althea. Had Althea somehow contrived to make it look as if she and Lionheart had become lovers again?

That thought brought a more perplexing one. What was she going to do about the

White Knight? Discovery was threatening her peace of mind as well as her relationship with Lionheart. The longer Lionheart remained at Cragdon, the greater the danger. Her future stretched uncertainly before her. Should Lionheart discover her identity as the knight upon whom he had sworn vengeance, her life would be forfeit.

Chapter Thirteen

A message arrived for Edward that evening. Exhausted from several days of hard riding, the messenger handed the rolled parchment bearing the king's seal to Edward and went immediately to find a meal and a bed. Edward unrolled the parchment, read the contents and cursed beneath his breath.

"Bad news?" Lionheart asked.

"Aye. The king has need of me. Civil war has begun. Simon de Montfort has announced his intention to march to Westminster if Father does not sign the Provisions of Oxford. I must return to England immediately." He rose. "Excuse me, I must inform my troops of the change in plans. I had hoped to tarry at Cragdon another few days but 'tis no longer possible."

Lionheart stared moodily into his ale after Edward left. The idea of Edward riding into battle without him did not sit well with him. Even more distressing was the niggling suspicion that he did not really want to leave Vanora despite his eagerness to follow Edward. He glanced at Vanora, wondering what she was thinking.

As if reading his thoughts, Vanora said, "I am not unhappy that Edward is leaving. It will be good to be rid of the English warriors camped in the outer bailey. 'Tis too bad you cannot go with him."

"And leave you to Daffid?" Lionheart said. "Should there be a child, I want to be sure it is mine."

If looks could kill, Lionheart would be dead. She rose abruptly. "Excuse me, I should inform Cook of the imminent departure of our guests. I am sure their leaving will please her, for they have been a huge drain on our stores."

Lionheart's fingers curled around her wrist. "Are you trying to avoid further conversation with me?"

She gave him a mocking smile. "How perceptive of you. Since you enjoy Althea's company so much, I give you leave to entertain her tonight."

"You try my patience, Vanora. I need to speak to Edward and will deal with you later. We have unfinished business, you and I."

Vanora went still. "Unfinished business?"

"Aye, the White Knight. If you do not

tell me what you know about him, I shall offer a reward for the information I seek. I will question every man, woman and child until I find someone willing to accept my coin in return for the knight's identity."

"Good luck, my lord." Wresting her arm free, she hurried off.

"Your wife is a sharp-tongued shrew," Althea sniffed, moving closer to Lionheart. "What is it you see in her? She is not as beautiful as I am, nor as even-tempered. And I wager she is cold in bed."

Lionheart grinned. "You would lose that wager, Althea. How can you not think Vanora beautiful?"

"I am not as enamored of her as you are," Althea observed.

Lionheart had naught to say to that sally. Enamored? Was he enamored of Vanora? 'Twas not acceptable. There were many things he admired about her: her beauty, her spirit and her strength. He even enjoyed their verbal sparring, but he did not like being lied to. Vanora's refusal to divulge information about the White Knight angered him.

"I have business with Edward, Althea. I will send Giles to entertain you."

Giles was happy to oblige. After a word from Lionheart, he hurried to Althea's side and led her off to a private alcove where they could converse in private. Stifling a grin, Lionheart wished his friend luck in finding his way into Althea's bed, though he doubted the handsome knight would need it. Althea was ripe for bedding.

Dismissing Althea from his mind, Lionheart went in search of Edward. He found the prince conversing with his squire in the courtyard.

"We were just discussing preparations for our departure," Edward said when Lionheart joined him. "We march at dawn."

"Do you go directly to Westminster?" Lionheart asked.

"Nay. I will join the rest of my army near Lewes to await de Montfort's next move."

"You will be careful, will you not?"

Edward clapped Lionheart's back. "Aye. I learned well from you, my friend. Shall we return to the keep and drink to England?"

One drink led to another, and by the time Lionheart dragged himself up to the solar, he was well into his cups. Using the dim light of a single candle to guide him, Lionheart staggered up to the solar. Closing the door quietly behind him, he shuffled toward the bed. Vanora was curled on her side, apparently sound asleep as he cast off his clothing and slid into bed beside her. She gave no indication that she was aware of his presence, and Lionheart scooted closer, molding her body into the curve of his.

He hardened instantly, pushing his loins against the creamy mounds of her buttocks. She stirred but did not awaken. His hands slid around to her breasts, cupping them, toying with her nipples. When his hand slid down her stomach to explore the moist folds of her sex, Vanora awoke with a start.

"What are you doing?"

"Fondling my wife."

"I am not interested, Lionheart."

He slid a finger inside her, chuckling when he felt her muscles clench and moisture flood his hand. "Are you sure?"

Gritting her teeth in frustration, Vanora cursed her body's response. She wanted Lionheart, and he knew it. But she could not afford to love him. All her people knew she was the White Knight. Though she did not think they would betray her, she could not be certain. If Lionheart offered coin for information, the temptation might be too great to resist.

The worst of it was her uncertainty of Lionheart's reaction once he learned the truth about her. Would he order her death? Or had he grown fond enough of her to allow her to live?

Lionheart turned her on her back and hovered over her. "Kiss me, Vanora."

His slurred words brought her to a startling realization. "You are drunk!"

"Not too drunk to make love to my wife."

The steely arms that held her, the hard body behind her, were insistent. She knew their coupling would be heated. The rough eagerness of his voice, the tension of his muscles, sent excitement racing through her.

Then he proceeded to show her that he was capable of making love under any condition. He did not ask, he simply took. He kissed and caressed her until she was a mass of sharp sensation; he left no part of her body untouched. When he finally entered her, she nearly swooned with ecstasy. What mortal woman could resist a virile man like Lionheart, drunk or not?

He moved in her, thrusting, withdrawing, his strokes becoming frenzied as he neared completion. She made a soft sound deep in her throat and responded with swift intensity, lost in the all-encompassing desire he kindled in her. She heard him call her name. The feeling inside her grew tighter and tighter until she felt as if she would snap from the strain. Poised on the brink for a breathless eon, she exploded into a thousand tiny pieces, tumbling into a void of raw sensation.

Clinging to him, half sobbing, she held him as his own shattering orgasm released his seed into her. With a groan, he rested his forehead against her cheek, breathing raggedly. Then he raised his head and gazed down at her with a troubled look.

"How did this happen? When did it happen?"

"How did what happen?"

Immediately a veil slid down over his eyes. "Pay me no heed. I am too drunk to think clearly."

He rolled away but kept his hand on her hip as if loath to release her. "Go to sleep. We will talk tomorrow about the secrets you are harboring."

Her heart nearly stopped. "Secrets? I have no secrets."

No answer was forthcoming. When Vanora raised her head to look at him, his face was composed in sleep.

Edward left the following morning after Mass. Vanora, Lionheart and Althea were on hand to bid him farewell.

"Ride a ways with me, Lionheart," Edward invited. "We can discuss battle strategy while we ride." He turned to Vanora. "Fear not, my lady, your husband will return to you ere the day is out."

Lionheart placed Sir Giles in charge and accepted Edward's invitation to join him. Vanora's relief at seeing the bulk of Edward's army leaving was enormous, despite the fact that twenty Englishmen would remain at Cragdon. She could deal with twenty men, but an army was daunting. It would be good to have her home back to normal, or as normal as it could be with an Englishman for a husband.

"Lord Lionheart does not like being left behind," Althea said. "A warrior needs to fight."

"Lionheart may be disappointed but he will not disobey Edward."

"With only twenty men at his disposal, Lionheart will find it difficult to return me to England. In the fullness of time, he may decide my bed holds more appeal than yours."

Vanora thought the same thing but withheld her opinion. Her eyes narrowed as she considered the ramifications of Althea's presence at Cragdon. If Althea remained, mayhap she would divert Lionheart's attention from the White Knight. Vanora seriously debated leaving Cragdon through the hidden exit and finding Sir Ren. She wanted to ask him to plead with the crofters to keep her secret should Lionheart question them. Since England and Wales were at peace, Sir Ren was free now to come out of hiding. Would Lionheart allow her knights to return to Cragdon? she wondered.

That thought heartened her. It would be good to have people she trusted around her. Aye, she decided, she would broach the subject when Lionheart returned. But first she needed to find out if Sir Ren was willing to return.

Vanora was so engrossed in her own thoughts, she was unaware that Sir Giles had pulled Althea aside for a private conversation. Taking advantage of their absence, Vanora beat a hasty retreat. Instead of returning to the keep, however, she went directly to the chapel. She found the priest puttering about in the sacristy.

"Father, might I have a word with you?"

"Of course, child. How may I help you?"

"Lionheart intends to question the crofters about the White Knight and is going to offer a reward for information."

Father Caddoc paled and crossed himself. "That could prove disastrous. While there is a tenuous peace between England and Wales, there is none between Lionheart and the knight upon whom he has sworn vengeance. I fear for you, child. A greedy crofter willing to exchange information for coin could be your undoing. One does not goad a man like Lionheart."

"So I have learned. I am thinking of finding Sir Ren and asking him to speak to the villeins on my behalf. My palfrey is still stabled behind the forge. What if Lionheart were to recognize Baron? I shall ask Sir Ren's advice about hiding Baron elsewhere."

"You cannot ride out alone," Father Caddoc warned. " 'Tis too dangerous."

"I must."

"Nay, 'tis not acceptable. The peril increases each time you don the trappings of a knight. You are a woman, Vanora, and not meant to don armor and fight."

"I can fight as well as any man," Vanora said. "Have I not proven myself?"

"You can hold your own against most men, but not Lionheart. There is no one, man or woman, more skillful or deadly. He would cut you down without mercy."

"Nevertheless, I must go. I believe Lionheart is beginning to care for me, and

I cannot risk his learning the truth."

"Do you love him, child?"

"I tried not to, Father, but I could not help myself. We both know why Lionheart wed me, and 'twas not because he cared for me. I thought that once he left Cragdon, I would never see him again. I could have accepted that, embraced it even, for then my feelings for him would not get out of hand and I could forget him. But his remaining changes everything. I yearn for him to return my love."

"What you ask is not impossible, Vanora. I believe Lionheart cares for you more than he wants to admit."

"I had begun to hope it was so, but everything would be ruined if one of Cragdon's people tells him the truth about me."

"I shall speak to them myself."

"Forgive me, Father, but Sir Ren would be more effective. You are a kindly soul and have not the heart to speak with the firmness Sir Ren could command."

"Is there aught I can say to turn you away from your foolish course?"

"Nay, Father. I am determined."

"I see that your mind is made up, so I shall offer prayers for your safety. Is there aught else I can do for you?"

"Aye. Keep an eye on Althea. I shall ask

Mair to do the same. I know not when Lionheart will return her to England and I trust her not. She will do whatever it takes to get Lionheart in her bed."

"Aye. Between Mair and me, Althea will find it difficult to seduce your husband."

"Thank you, Father. I want a chance to make Lionheart love me without Althea's interference."

Vanora left the chapel in a pensive mood. She had admitted to Father Caddoc that she loved her husband, but it had not been easy. Unrequited love hurt.

The hall was unusually quiet as Vanora crossed the empty space on her way to the storeroom. The situation at Cragdon had been hectic too long and she savored the quiet. When she saw Althea enter the hall and move in her direction, her peaceful mood was shattered.

"What do you do for entertainment around here?" Althea asked. "I am dying of boredom."

"You may mend linens if you want something to do. I can always use another pair of hands. Mair will be happy to provide you with thread and needle."

" 'Tis beneath me," Althea said with a toss of her head. "When will Lionheart return?"

"He did not say, and I would advise you to stop using your wiles on him. He has stated more than once that he does not want you."

"Is that a warning?"

"Take it however you want."

"Lionheart does not love you. He knows not the meaning of the word. Trust me, for I know Lionheart far better than you do."

"You are wasting my time, Althea," Vanora said. "If you do not wish to help, then see to your own entertainment."

"Perhaps I shall find Sir Giles. Mayhap *he* is not too busy to entertain me."

Vanora was more than happy to be rid of Althea and wondered how long she would have to put up with the waspish woman. There was room for but one woman in Lionheart's life, and it was definitely not Althea.

Lionheart and his small entourage rode with Edward to Cragdon's eastern border. Before they parted, Lionheart extracted Edward's promise to send for him should he encounter difficulties. But Edward was adamant about keeping Lionheart at Cragdon.

"An English presence so close to the border can prevent raids on Marcher lands. The Marcher lords complain, but Henry is too consumed with his own needs and pouring money into fruitless wars to heed their cries for help. That will change when I am king."

Lionheart knew the earnest young man would rule justly and prayed that Edward lived to fulfil his destiny. Lionheart worried a great deal about the pending battle with Simon de Montfort's forces and wished there were a way to convince Edward to release him from his duties at Cragdon.

"Let me continue on to England with you," Lionheart said hopefully. "I can send word to Cragdon that I am not returning. Sir Giles will make an admirable administrator for Cragdon during my absence."

"Nay, Lionheart. 'Tis you I want at Cragdon. Sir Giles does not have your ability. Did I not promise I will send for you should I have need of you?"

Lionheart supposed that would have to suffice, though he liked it not.

"I am sorry about Althea," Edward apologized. "I foresee trouble but doubt not your ability to handle it. I like Vanora. Her mind is sharp and her wit keen; she will keep you on your toes. She is not as sweet-tempered or as biddable as my Eleanor, but a woman like that would not suit you."

Lionheart bade Edward farewell and turned back toward Cragdon, his mind grappling with his problems. First and foremost, he had to return Althea to England as soon as possible, even if he must escort her himself.

Second, he must make some sense of his relationship with Vanora. He had never suspected that his heart would become involved.

Last but not least, he had unfinished business with the White Knight. Now that Edward was gone, he could concentrate on finding the vexing knave.

Lionheart considered stopping at the village to question the crofters but decided against it. He had already been away from the keep too long and could well imagine the fireworks erupting between Vanora and Althea. He smiled wryly. Althea did not have a chance. His Vanora was strong and clever and capable of handling Althea's machinations.

All was quiet when Lionheart rode through the portcullis. It seemed strange to find the outer bailey empty of tents and men and only a handful of men-at-arms about in the inner bailey. The hall was unusually quiet, except for servants setting up tables for the evening meal. Lionheart's stomach growled at the thought of food. He had not had a decent meal all day.

Glancing across the hall, he saw a woman standing in the shadows near the hearth. Her back was to him, and she seemed to be staring into the dancing flames. Assuming it was Vanora, he crept silently up to her and placed his arms around her, nuzzling her neck. He knew immediately that something was wrong when the woman in his arms giggled. Vanora did not giggle. Nor was her body so full and voluptuous.

His arms fell away instantly and he hastily retreated.

Althea whirled to face him. "Lionheart!" she cried in gleeful welcome. "I knew you would come to your senses. You wanted me, but you were being stubborn about it. Fear not, I forgive you."

"I thought you were Vanora," Lionheart replied. "Where is my wife?"

Althea pulled a face. "You have a drudge for a wife. She has been working alongside the servants most of the day. Were I an earl's wife, I would have servants waiting on me hand and foot."

"Mayhap 'tis good you are not an earl's wife." Turning, he strode away.

Aye, Lionheart thought, he would have to do something about Althea soon, very soon.

He found Vanora in the solar, mending one of his tunics. She spared him but a brief glance when he entered the chamber.

"I am home," Lionheart said. His words gave him pause. When had he begun to think of Cragdon as home?

"So I see. Did all go well?"

"Edward is well on his way to meet de Montfort."

"You will be bored at Cragdon without an army to command."

"Mayhap. 'Tis the first time in my memory that I have had a place to settle. Except when I was fostered, I have spent my life following Edward. My brief sojourns at Dunsford were but respites from battle, a place to heal from my wounds."

Vanora gasped. "How many times were you wounded?"

His eyebrows shot upward. "Too many to count. Warriors are wounded in battle, 'tis unavoidable. The scars have faded since."

He removed his cloak and tunic, poured water into a basin and began to wash. Vanora regarded him for a long moment, then said, "I see a scar on your left arm."

"A sword slash. I let my shield slip."

She walked over to him and traced the wound with her fingertip. Lionheart stiffened, then let out a groan. "Behave, wife, lest you find yourself on your back."

Vanora's hand stilled. His skin felt hot. She wanted to stroke the hair-roughened surface, to feel his muscles tauten and ripple beneath her touch, to find his scars and place her mouth upon them.

She wanted him to love her.

Lionheart covered her hand with his. "Though I am famished, I will happily oblige you, for I, too, am eager for loving."

Blushing, Vanora whirled away from him. "Nay, feed your stomach; the other can wait."

Lionheart entered the hall and seated himself beside Vanora. Alan immediately poured ale into his cup. Sensing Lionheart's gaze on her, Vanora glanced at him, flushing when she saw that his eyes were dark with desire and that his need for her still raged. Their gazes met and locked, the invitation in his eyes blatantly sensual. Her heart pounded, and heat poured through her veins. Never had she felt so consumed by a mere look. Then Althea sauntered into the hall and seated herself beside Lionheart, shattering the tension between them.

Food was set on the table and passed around. Vanora made a pretense of eating from the trencher she shared with Lionheart, but Althea's presence spoiled her appetite. Sharing a meal and home with Lionheart's leman was intolerable. She was Lionheart's wife, and should not have to vie for his attention.

"How soon will you send Althea back to England?" she blurted out. "The woman does not belong here."

Althea heard and bristled angrily. " 'Tis not for you to say, Vanora. 'Tis up to Lord Lionheart, and he does not appear anxious to part with me."

" 'Tis best for everyone that you leave as soon as possible," Lionheart said. "You will return to your village well dowered, ensuring your choice of husbands."

"Will I have an earl?" Althea asked defiantly.

"You know better than that. I am sure you will choose wisely, but do not expect to land a title."

"Sir Giles will wed me," she said, sending Vanora a triumphant smile. "He is enamored of me."

"I pity Sir Giles," Vanora muttered beneath her breath.

"I cannot tell Sir Giles whom to wed," Lionheart replied.

"If I wed Sir Giles, I can remain at Cragdon," Althea theorized.

"Why would you want to? You said Cragdon bored you."

"I could be happy with Giles."

"I will not allow it," Vanora said.

"I will speak to Giles," Lionheart said. "I cannot say him nay if he wants to wed Althea."

Vanora sent him a blistering look. "I cannot believe you would consider letting Althea remain at Cragdon. We both know what she is up to. Why would you wish her on poor Giles?" Her eyes narrowed. "Unless, of course, you intend her for yourself under the guise of wedding her to your friend."

Lionheart sighed. "You are jumping to conclusions, vixen. I know not if Giles wants to wed Althea. I will speak to him as soon as he returns from guard duty."

Vanora fumed with impotent rage. Althea's ploy would serve only herself. Rising abruptly, she excused herself and strode purposefully from the hall. Althea left soon afterward.

Lionheart remained seated, waiting for Giles. When the knight appeared, Lionheart beckoned to him. Giles sat down beside Lionheart and helped himself to food.

Lionheart sipped ale while Giles ate. As if aware of Lionheart's pensive mood, Giles set down his eating knife and asked, "What is on your mind, Lionheart? I can always tell when something is bothering you."

"I do indeed have something on my mind, Giles, and it concerns you."

Giles took a healthy swallow of ale, then set down his mug. "I am all ears."

"Althea thinks you are enamored of her."

Giles laughed. "In a way, 'tis true. I want to bed her. Do you object?"

"Nay, not at all, but Althea has something more permanent in mind."

Giles choked on the bite of cheese he was chewing. "Marriage? You know me better than that, my friend. My parents would disown me if I wed a woman of Althea's ilk. Besides," he added somewhat sheepishly, "I am betrothed. I was going to ask your permission to return home long enough to wed and bed my bride. She is seventeen now and ready to become a wife. Althea is merely a diversion. I plan to bring Deirdre back to Cragdon with me after we are wed."

"I had forgotten you were betrothed. Once you are wed, your wife is welcome to join you at Cragdon," Lionheart said, "and doubtless Vanora will agree. As for dallying with Althea, I suggest you tread carefully. She is angling for a proposal. I am inclined to believe she will do anything to remain at Cragdon."

"Send her back to England as soon as possible," Giles advised.

"I intend to but wanted to make sure you had no tender feeling for her. I feel somewhat guilty for my shabby treatment of her. I wish Edward had not brought her to Cragdon."

"Edward had no idea you were wed." Giles paused, a smile hovering on his lips. "I suspect Vanora is eager to be rid of Althea."

"You have no idea," Lionheart replied, rolling his eyes. He rose. "I am off to find my wife and tell her the good news."

Lionheart trudged up the stairs to the solar, imagining Vanora's relief when she learned Giles had no intention of wedding Althea. Smiling, he opened the door and ducked just in time to avoid the pitcher that came flying at him. He was not so lucky avoiding the next missile aimed at him. He saw stars when a leather boot clipped the side of his head.

"God's blood, what are you doing!" he roared.

Ducking the second boot, Lionheart reached Vanora just as she hefted his sword which had been resting against the wall. He wrested it from her hand and tossed it aside.

"A sword is a dangerous weapon," he growled. "You could hurt yourself with it."

" 'Tis not me I wish to hurt," Vanora snarled.

His lips thinned. "Nevertheless, never raise a sword against me again. Do you want to tell me what this is all about?"

"Gladly! I refuse to have your leman in my home. If Sir Giles wants her, he must leave Cragdon and take Althea with him. I cannot believe you would countenance wedding her to Sir Giles and letting her remain under my roof."

"Must you raise a sword against me to make your point? 'Tis not a woman's weapon."

To Lionheart, Vanora had never looked more appealing. Anger became her. Flames shot from her violet eyes, and her whole body seemed to glow from within. With her hair swirling around her shoulders in wild abandon, she was incredibly, sensually arousing. His loins hardened, and he felt a strong urge to sweep her into his arms and make love to her until they were both exhausted.

Vanora wanted to laugh in Lionheart's face. It was not the first time she had taken up a sword against him, and she prayed it would remain her secret.

"If you settle down for a moment and let me explain, I am sure you will be pleased with what I have to say."

"Does it concern Althea?"

"Aye. Are you jealous, sweeting?"

"What if I am?"

"You have naught to be jealous about."

She did not believe him. "Tell me about Althea and I shall decide for myself."

"Very well. Giles does not want her. He is already betrothed. I plan to return Althea to England as soon as arrangements can be made."

Vanora searched his face for the truth, realized he meant what he had said, and flung herself into his arms. Laughing, Lionheart swept her up and carried her to their bed.

Chapter Fourteen

Lionheart took long, blissful minutes undressing Vanora and himself, then made slow, tender love to her. Inserting his right hand between her knees, he began drawing teasing patterns on the inside of her thigh, his caress drifting upward by gradual increments. Her legs opened in blatant invitation as his fingers teased through dark curls and silky folds to the moist flesh beneath.

She traced the edge of his ear with her tongue, then nibbled down the length of his throat to the hollow at the base. He groaned.

His mouth found that sensitive place on her shoulder and tormented the spot with teeth and tongue. He could feel her pulse beating crazily, jerkily, at the hollow of her throat and her nipples growing hard and rigid as his fingers played with them and his thumbs brushed the turgid peaks.

He lowered his head, blew upon a wet crest, then took it into his mouth. He suckled the ripe bud, took it between his teeth, hot tongue flicking the sensitive tip until it tautened. Then he plied his mouth on her other nipple. He could feel her body vibrating with desperate need as she took his head in her hands and stroked his hair. His tongue moved from one breast to the other, his fingers slipping inside her to stroke her slick cleft.

Suddenly his mouth left her breasts, meandering down to the swollen folds of her womanhood, where, as she writhed beneath him, his lips kissed her and his tongue tasted her. She felt something unfurl inside her, then blossom wildly, making her arch her hips frantically against his marauding mouth. Over and over, she cried out as tremors shook her, until she lay quiescent and sated beneath him.

"Come inside me," she begged, pulling Lionheart over her. Lifting her head, she kissed him, tasting her own musky scent on his lips. She caught his moan in her mouth, raised her hips and met his thrust as he entered her. His hips began to move quickly, and she lost herself to the motion of the moment, to the thrusting that seemed to sweep her away to a higher plane.

"God help me, I cannot get enough of you," he said on a swift intake of breath.

He quickened the motion of his hips and grasped her legs, raising them over his shoulders for better leverage. He rode upward, moving harder and faster, until she felt herself drifting away to a place where naught but pleasure ruled. As if from a great distance she heard him shout her name and go still inside her as his warm seed flooded her.

She lay still under the weight of his damp body, sated and content, her body vibrating with ecstasy.

He drew back and stared down at her. The look on his face was one of surprise and wonder. He gazed at her as if she were someone he did not know, as if he had just learned something of great import.

"Is aught wrong?"

He traced his thumb along her bottom lip. "Naught is wrong."

"Why are you looking at me like that?"

"Like what?"

"Like . . . I know not . . . as if you are seeing me for the first time."

"You are imagining things," he said gruffly. He slid off of her and onto his side.

"I am not imagining things."

"I was just thinking how beautiful you are. Your skin has a translucent glow, like shimmering pearls."

"I have never seen a pearl," Vanora said wistfully.

His brows shot upward. "Pity." His finger traced over her collarbone, down her arm and over her ribs.

"Forget about pearls," Vanora said, removing his roving hand from her body. "Tell me how soon I can expect Althea to leave Cragdon."

Lionheart sighed as he gathered his straying wits. "You are amazingly persistent when it comes to Althea. She will be gone within a sennight. I am thinking of sending Sir Giles and two men-at-arms to escort her to her village. Sir Giles wants to return home to wed his betrothed, so I thought I would kill two birds with one stone. Giles can act as escort and continue on to his home.

"Giles has asked to bring his bride to Cragdon after he is wed, and I have granted permission," Lionheart continued. "I hope you approve. Deirdre is but seventeen and will doubtless need the support of another woman."

"I shall be pleased to have Deirdre at Cragdon. I hope she can adjust to living away from England."

"I am sure any help you give her will be appreciated by both Giles and his bride."

"I plan to accompany the party to the

border myself to make sure they reach English soil safely."

"Must you go?" Vanora asked.

"Aye. Edward misled Althea about her welcome at Cragdon, and the least I can do is make sure she reaches England without mishap."

Vanora digested his words and wondered if now was a good time to broach the subject of bringing Sir Ren and her own men-at-arms back to Cragdon.

"I have been thinking," Vanora began somewhat hesitantly, "that Cragdon lacks sufficient men-at-arms to defend it. Since our countries are at peace, what say you about allowing Sir Ren and Cragdon's warriors to return?"

Lionheart's frown did not bode well for her idea. "You want me to welcome back a man who put an arrow into me? I would not be safe in my bed with Sir Ren in the keep."

"We are at peace with England," Vanora reminded him.

"Let it rest, Vanora," Lionheart said tiredly. "I will not have men in my keep I cannot trust. Sir Ren is loyal to the White Knight. Once I return from escorting Althea to the border, I can concentrate on finding the knave and those who shield him."

He sent her a sharp look. "You can save me a lot of trouble if you tell me what you know about him."

Vanora shook her head and turned away. Her greatest fear had come to pass. Once Lionheart returned, he would search out and destroy her friends. 'Twas imperative that she find Sir Ren and tell him to remain out of her husband's reach.

"What will you do if you find Sir Ren and the White Knight?"

"The White Knight I will challenge and personally fight in hand-to-hand combat. If I do not kill him, he will be consigned to Cragdon's dungeon. As for the others, mayhap I will consider leniency and free them if they swear fealty to me. But my goodwill does not extend to the White Knight," he added harshly.

Vanora had naught to say to that. Squeezing her eyes shut, she prayed for her own safety as well as that of her faithful defenders. At least, she thought, Lionheart would not kill Cragdon's warriors. 'Twas only the White Knight he intended to slay. Pray God he never found the one he sought.

The weather turned cold and blustery the next day. Lionheart feared that if he did not send Althea back soon, she would be stuck at Cragdon for the winter. With that thought in mind, he spoke to Sir Giles the following morning.

"You mentioned your desire to return to England to wed your betrothed, Giles. To that end, I have decided to place you in charge of Althea's escort."

"Think you it is wise to leave Cragdon with so few defenders?" Giles asked.

"If I do not send Althea on her way now, she could be here the entire winter. Once Althea is returned to her village, you can continue on to your home. I can spare but two men-at-arms to accompany you, but I shall see you safely to the border myself. Once you are on English soil, you should encounter no trouble."

"My parents will be happy to finally see me wed," Giles said. "My only fear is leaving you shorthanded. 'Twill be at least a month before I can return to Cragdon."

"No danger to Cragdon presently exists, Giles. 'Tis a good time for you to fetch your bride. And your home is not far from Althea's village."

"How soon do we leave?" Giles asked.

"In two days. Choose two men to accompany you, and take enough food to last your journey. You will also need a tent for Althea's comfort."

"I will take care of everything, Lord Lionheart."

Everything except Althea, Lionheart thought as he spied the object of his thoughts crossing the hall. Girding himself for the confrontation, he waited for her to reach him.

"All the arrangements have been made, Althea," Lionheart said.

"What arrangements?" Althea asked warily.

"You are to leave Cragdon two days hence. Sir Giles and two men-at-arms will act as escort."

Althea's expression turned mutinous. "Nay! You cannot send me away now. The weather is too uncertain. You could be sending me to my death."

"I doubt that. I shall accompany you to the border to make sure naught goes wrong."

"Why can I not remain at Cragdon? Did you speak to Sir Giles about wedding me?"

"Aye, but he declined."

"He declined? Mayhap I should speak to him myself."

"He is already betrothed, Althea. All the wiles at your disposal will have little impact on either Giles or myself. I am sorry things turned out the way they did, but you were brought here with expectations I could not honor."

While Lionheart was speaking with Althea, Mair and Vanora were making plans in the solar.

"Lionheart intends to accompany Sir Giles and Althea to the English border," Vanora confided. "While he is away, I shall find Sir Ren and tell him to make sure he does not cross paths with Lionheart."

"I thought Father Caddoc talked you out of that foolish idea."

"He tried to, but I would not be dissuaded. I swear, Mair, this is the last time I shall don armor and leave the keep unaccompanied."

Mair's eyebrows shot up. "Are you content, then, as Lionheart's wife?"

"I could be," Vanora said wistfully.

Crossing her arms over her ample bosom, Mair sent Vanora a smug smile. "I knew Father Caddoc was right to insist that Lionheart wed you. Your husband is not a bad man, despite his English heritage. Though you have sorely vexed him, he has not raised a hand to you. Most husbands are not so indulgent. Do you love him, lambie?"

"Loving Lionheart was never my intention, but the heart does not always obey the mind. I know not when I fell in love with him, or how; I just know I want him, to love me as much as I love him, and that it will never happen."

"What makes you so sure?" Mair challenged. "Lionheart is his own man. He would not have wed you if he had no feelings for you. He could have ordered his men to escort Father Caddoc from the solar and had his way with you without benefit of marriage."

"I suppose," Vanora said doubtfully.

"I have not noticed Lionheart making use of his leman," Mair contended. "He is sending her back to England, is he not? I predict a long and happy life for you, lambie. I cannot wait to bounce your children on my knee."

"You may be right, but there is still one thing that stands between us."

Mair nodded sagely. "Aye, the knight you become when you don armor. 'Tis time that knight disappeared forever. Out of sight, out of mind," Mair reminded her. "Once the knight vanishes, Lionheart will turn his mind to other matters."

"I agree, Mair, but I cannot retire the knight until I confer with Sir Ren. One more time, and then I will end it. Lionheart is leaving. I will find no better time to accomplish my task. When I return, I shall bury my armor and sword with no regrets. Wales is at peace, and so shall I be."

Two days later, Lionheart lingered behind to bid Vanora good-bye as the rest of the party rode ahead.

"I shall not be gone long . . . four days at the most. Two to reach the border and two to return. Sir Brandon can handle whatever trouble arises, but I expect none."

Grasping her about the waist, he pulled her against him and kissed her soundly. "Take care of yourself, vixen. Try not to miss me too much."

"Why would I miss an Englishman with little to commend him save for the length of his sword arm?" Vanora teased.

Lionheart laughed. "Is that the only length you appreciate?" he asked archly. "The length of my —"

She clapped a hand over his mouth. "Enough."

His silver eyes twinkling mischievously, he kissed her again and bounded into the saddle. When he reached the gate, he turned back to wave. She returned his salute, then hurried to the chapel, where

Mair and Father Caddoc awaited her.

"Do not try to talk me out of this," Vanora said by way of greeting.

"We can but try," Father Caddoc replied.

"You cannot leave now," Mair cautioned.

"I know. 'Tis too soon. I will not leave until Lionheart and his party are out of sight."

Mair wrung her hands. "Promise this will be the last time, lambie. My heart cannot stand it."

"Aye, the very last."

"Do you know where to find Sir Ren?" Father Caddoc asked.

"Aye. Father deeded him land and a manor not far from here. 'Tis where I shall find him."

"What is that I hear?" Mair asked, turning toward the altar. Vanora heard it too, the familiar scraping sound of a door opening.

She lurched forward, then stopped in her tracks when Daffid stepped out from the shadows of the altar.

"I saw the Englishman and his leman leaving the fortress with a small escort," Daffid said. "I came as quickly as I could, Vanora."

Vanora could not think, much less speak.

Tense silence lay as thick as the dust beneath their feet until Mair shattered it. "What are you doing here, Daffid?"

Daffid smiled smugly. "Claiming what is mine. Lionheart has returned to England, has he not?" He turned to address Father Caddoc, his expression unyielding. "Declare Vanora's marriage to Lionheart invalid due to a previous betrothal and marry us immediately, Father."

"No betrothal agreement was drawn up or signed," the priest reminded him.

"It matters not. 'Twas what Vanora's father wanted. We all know she was forced to wed Lionheart against her will. The English bastard is gone now, and only a handful of Englishmen have been left behind to defend Cragdon against attack. Very soon I shall have sufficient men and arms at my disposal to enter the castle from the hidden entrance, kill all the guards and claim Cragdon for my own."

"You are mistaken, Daffid," Vanora said. "Lionheart is the new lord of Cragdon. He is not leaving Wales."

"I saw him leave with my own eyes," Daffid insisted.

"He goes no further than the border. I expect him to return long before you can muster men and gather arms. Should you try to enter through the hidden entrance, you will find it sealed."

"Lionheart is remaining in Wales?" Daffid said incredulously. "I cannot believe he would let Edward leave without him. I have heard rumors that civil war looms large on England's horizon, and that Edward will lead his father's army. Lionheart is Edward's right arm. 'Tis unlikely he would remain behind while his prince goes to war."

" 'Twas Edward's wish that Lionheart remain in Wales. The prince charged Lionheart with the protection of his lands in Wales."

"Does Lionheart know about the secret entrance into the castle?" Daffid asked.

"Nay." Her eyes narrowed. "Why?"

"I refuse to give up what should be mine."

"Vanora is wed to Lord Lionheart," Father Caddoc maintained. "The union is legal and binding and cannot be put asunder."

Daffid sent the priest a disparaging look. "Have you turned traitor? I will never forgive you for forcing my betrothed to wed an Englishman. The least you can do to make amends is support my effort to regain Cragdon."

"England is at peace with Wales, Daffid," Father Caddoc said. "Lionheart has become Cragdon's lord by right of marriage. Forget vengeance and return home. Find another woman to wed."

"Heed Father Caddoc," Vanora advised. "I am content with Lionheart. Please leave before you are discovered."

"You are both traitors to your people," Daffid charged. "I will leave for now, but when I return, it will be with an army behind me. There are still men willing to follow where I lead. The castle is undermanned, and I will be victorious."

"Do not try it," Vanora warned.

"I will allow no woman to dictate to me," Daffid said ominously. Moving back into the shadows, he disappeared behind the altar.

"The entrance has to be sealed," Vanora said after a long silence.

"Aye," the priest agreed. "I shall see to it immediately."

"Nay, not immediately," Vanora replied. "Leave it until after I return."

Mair hesitated. "But Daffid —"

"I promise to be back before Vespers. 'Tis imperative that I speak with Sir Ren before Daffid gets to him. I need to warn him against joining Daffid's army. I shall explain that I am content with Lionheart and ask him to ignore Daffid's call to arms."

"Let me go in your stead," Father Caddoc offered.

Vanora contemplated the priest's suggestion and promptly discarded it when she considered his frailty and advanced age. "Nay, I must do this myself."

Her lips pressed into a thin line, Mair helped Vanora don her chain mail and helm. "God go with you," Mair said as Vanora disappeared through the opening behind the altar.

The small party escorting Althea to England had made good time. They stopped briefly at mid-morning to allow their horses to drink from a stream and then continued on their way. Thus far the journey had been uneventful, and Lionheart could not wait to reach the border and return to Vanora.

But no sooner had they set out again than Althea's horse stepped into a foxhole and went down, his screech of pain echoing through the frosty air. Althea went flying, her scream nearly as loud as that of her injured mount. Lionheart's heart nearly stopped when he saw Althea lying motionless on the ground. Leaping from his steed, he ran to her side.

Relief rushed through him when he saw that Althea was conscious and stirring. "Where are you hurt?" Lionheart asked, helping her to sit up.

"My ankle. I fear 'tis broken," Althea gasped, clutching her leg and rocking back and forth. "It pains me something fierce."

Lionheart lifted her skirts and carefully inspected her ankle. His expression turned grim when he noted the swelling. Carefully he probed her flesh. "I can feel no break," he said with heartfelt relief. " 'Tis naught but a bad sprain."

Giles dismounted and strode over to join them. "Althea's mount will have to be put down, Lionheart."

"Aye, see to it."

Lionheart regarded Althea with growing apprehension. He could not expect Althea to continue in her condition, even if she were to ride pillion behind him. Forcing her to continue the journey in her condition would be cruel. There was no help for it; they would have to return to Cragdon.

"I am in pain, Lionheart," Althea wailed. "Help me."

"We will return immediately to Cragdon,"

Lionheart replied. "Mair can treat your injury better than I."

He did not see Althea's smile through her tears, for Giles's return distracted him. "I put an arrow through the animal's heart," Giles reported. "Think you we can purchase another horse at the next village?"

"Probably, but Althea is injured and cannot ride. I must return her to Cragdon immediately. But you and your squire will continue on to your home so you can wed your betrothed." He mounted his steed. "Althea can ride pillion behind me. Lift her carefully, Giles."

Althea's arms circled Lionheart's waist as Giles placed her behind him and arranged her skirts decently about her legs. Once she was settled, Lionheart set his steed on a path toward Cragdon.

"Godspeed," Lionheart called to Giles as they parted ways.

'Twas late afternoon when Lionheart and his party reached Cragdon. Reining in before the keep, Lionheart lifted Althea from his steed and carried her inside, shouting for Vanora and Mair. Mair appeared almost immediately. When she saw Lionheart with Althea in his arms, her hand flew to her heart and the color drained from her face.

"My lord, we . . . we did not expect you to return so soon. Is aught amiss? What has happened to Althea?"

"Althea's horse broke a leg and had to be put down. Althea was injured, forcing us to return to Cragdon." He mounted the stairs to Althea's chamber. Mair hurried after him. "Where is Vanora?" he called over his shoulder.

"She . . . is about somewhere, my lord. She may have gone to the village."

Lionheart reached Althea's chamber and placed her on the bed. "She is all yours, Mair. I trust you to treat her injury."

"Stay with me, Lionheart," Althea begged. "What if I am hurt worse than you think?"

"Mair will keep me informed," Lionheart replied. "I need to find Vanora."

"God help us all," Mair muttered as Lionheart strode off.

Vanora was not in the solar, and none of the servants or men-at-arms had seen her since early that morning. The guards at the portcullis had not opened the gate to her, nor had she been spotted from the parapets. The horse she usually rode to the village was still in the mews, and no other horse was missing. Lionheart sent men in every direction in search of his errant wife, but Vanora was nowhere to be found.

The only place he had not yet looked was the chapel. Since he knew she often sought the priest's counsel, he expected to find her with the holy man. He found no one but Father Caddoc bent over the altar rail, praying fervently for Lionheart knew not what.

Lionheart spoke the priest's name softly and waited to be acknowledged. Father Caddoc raised his head and stared at Lionheart as if he were the last man on earth he expected or wanted to see. He crossed himself and rose with difficulty.

"You have returned sooner than expected," he said.

Warning bells went off in Lionheart's brain. What was going on? Both the priest and Mair were acting strangely. What mischief had Vanora gotten herself into now?

"Althea's horse stepped in a hole and had to be put down," he explained. "Althea was injured, so we returned to Cragdon. Mair is with her now. Have you seen Vanora? She seems to have disappeared."

Father Caddoc's gaze darted toward the altar before returning to Lionheart. "Not since this morning, Lord Lionheart."

"Do you know where she is now?"

Father Caddoc swallowed hard and asked God to forgive his lie. "Nay, I do not. Shall I help you look?"

"Nay, I will find her myself."

After Lionheart strode off, Father Caddoc fell to his knees and buried his face in his hands, offering prayers for their guidance. If Lionheart discovered Vanora's secret, the priest held scant hope for the survival of their marriage.

Lionheart could find Vanora nowhere. 'Twas as if she had disappeared from the face of the earth. It was growing dark, and Lionheart feared for her safety. He had long since decided there was a secret exit from the keep, though he had not yet found it. But he was convinced now that Vanora had used it to leave Cragdon.

Lionheart sent Alan to fetch a fresh horse from the mews and left the keep. Alan followed on his own mount. "Have you heard the servants discussing anything I should know about?" Lionheart asked the lad.

"Nay, my lord. These Welshmen are a secretive lot. They discuss naught while I am around. Think you something has happened to your lady?"

"Nay, lad. I am probably worrying unnecessarily. I am sure we will find her in the village. She must have slipped unnoticed from the keep."

Though Lionheart wanted to believe his own words, he could not. His men were not lax in their duty. They would have seen Vanora if she had left the keep. She had left secretly, that much was clear, and with Father Caddoc's blessing. Where had she gone? Lionheart's fears escalated when he failed to find Vanora in the village. What mischief was she up to?

"Mayhap she went walking along the cliff behind the keep and fell," Alan offered.

Lionheart considered Alan's words. He had stood on the cliff behind the castle a time or two and knew the incline to be steep and dangerous. Beneath the cliff the river ran swift and deep. If Vanora had fallen, she could be hurt, or dead, or swept away by the current. But what reason would Vanora have to walk along the cliff?

" 'Tis worth a look," Lionheart said, reining his horse toward the cliff. Though he found it difficult to believe Vanora had tumbled down the incline, he was desperate enough to search in unlikely places.

He dismounted, tossed his horse's reins to Alan and approached the edge of the precipice. His anxious gaze searched the area below and saw naught. He was about to turn away when a movement caught his eye. At first he thought 'twas merely shifting shadows caught in the moonlight, or his imagination, but a premonition kept him from turning away. Then the shadows parted, and he was certain the figure he saw was not a figment of his imagination.

As the figure stepped from the shadows, the shimmer of gold on white and the glint of chain mail caught his eye, and he knew 'twas the White Knight.

"Take my horse to the mews," Lionheart instructed Alan.

"What are you going to do?" Alan asked. "Did you see Lady Vanora? Shall I fetch help?"

"Nay, lad, 'twas not my lady I saw. And nay, I need no help. This is something I must do on my own."

Reluctantly Alan led the horses off while Lionheart sought an easy way down the cliff. He found a little-used path overgrown with weeds and scrambled down while keeping his eye on the knight. By the time he reached the riverbank, the knight had disappeared.

" 'Tis not possible," Lionheart muttered darkly. Where had the bastard gone?

Glancing upward along the cliff, he knew it was impossible for the knight to have climbed to the top without his knowledge. Nay, the knave had to be hiding in the weeds and shrubs that grew along the riverbank beneath the cliff.

Lionheart began his search at the spot he had last seen the knight. Drawing his sword, he slashed through the undergrowth, sending weeds hither and yon. When his efforts failed to produce the knight, he turned his attention to the large boulders at the foot of the cliff. He sliced his way through thorny bushes and peered around rocks, cursing the knight's uncanny ability to appear and disappear at will.

Was the knight an unnatural spirit? Nay, he scoffed, he did not believe in ghosts. He had crossed swords with the knight; there was naught unworldly about the way the knight had fought.

Rage guided his sword as he slashed at the tangle of weeds and shrubs, but it was intuition combined with desperation that finally prevailed. His wild slashing had revealed a gaping opening that lay concealed behind thick foliage.

A light went on inside his head. He did not need a seer to tell him that he had stumbled upon the long-sought secret entrance into the keep. The tunnel explained a great deal, but left much more unexplained.

There was no time like the present to learn where the passage led, Lionheart decided as he ducked inside. He had no torch to guide him, so he felt his way through absolute blackness by clinging to the wall and placing one foot before the other. The path was relatively dry and seemed to lead steadily upward. At length he bumped into a blank wall and stopped in his tracks. Was this the end, then?

Thin shards of light seeped from around the edges, and Lionheart realized he was facing a door. Feeling blindly, he found a latch and released it. Inhaling sharply, he stepped from the tunnel, wondering where he would find himself.

Chapter Fifteen

Lionheart stepped from behind the altar into the empty chapel, his mind whirling with confusion. He knew not what to make of this astonishing development. The secret entrance came as no surprise, but the knowledge that the White Knight was able to come and go at will stunned him.

Racking his brain, Lionheart began a mental evaluation of every servant within the keep. The majority were women, the only males being a potboy, a spit turner, and two elderly men. None of the four fit the White Knight's description. He dismissed Father Caddoc out of hand.

Had the knight been residing within his keep without his knowledge? Impossible! Yet indisputable evidence led him to believe that he would find the knave within Cragdon's walls. Rage surged through him. Everything became crystal clear. Vanora not only knew the knight's identity but she sheltered him beneath her roof. And the priest and her tiring woman were coconspirators.

Lionheart strode out the door and was in the courtyard when the truth hit him . . . hard. He felt his heart thud. He took a deep breath, but there was still a cold lump in his throat. He did not want to believe it, but the facts were irrefutable. He had always admired his wife's taut, sleekly muscled body. She was like no other woman he had ever known. Her strength, he realized, came from wielding a sword. What a fool he had been! His nemesis had been beneath his nose all the time, and he had been too consumed with lust to notice.

Lust . . .

Aye, 'twas the only explanation, for there had been countless clues to lead him to the truth. Clues he had ignored in order to satisfy his raging hunger for his bride. No more, he vowed. He had given Vanora sufficient time to confess, but she had defied him time after time, refusing to name the knight. He could not abide liars.

Lionheart saw Sir Brandon crossing the courtyard and summoned him with a wave of his hand.

"Is aught amiss, Lionheart?" Brandon asked.

"Follow me," Lionheart said without preamble. Turning on his heel, he retraced his steps to the chapel.

"Take a look behind the altar," Lionheart directed. He had left the door ajar purposely, and it did not take Brandon long to discover the opening.

"God's blood! What is this?"

"The entrance into the castle we have been searching for. I want it sealed immediately. Is that clear?"

"Aye, perfectly."

His face carved in harsh lines, Lionheart left the chapel, marched across the courtyard and stormed into the hall. He looked neither right nor left as his angry steps carried him up the winding staircase to the solar. Servants scurried out of his way, crossing themselves when they saw the rigid set of his shoulders and his forbidding expression.

He burst into the chamber and slammed the door behind him. Legs spread in a confrontational manner, arms akimbo, he glared at Vanora.

Vanora had been expecting Lionheart, for Mair had told her of his unexpected return. Vanora had retired immediately to the solar to make up a story explaining her absence, one she hoped would satisfy her husband. One look at his face, however, told her all was lost.

He knew!

Somehow, some way, Lionheart had learned she was the White Knight. She had never seen him in such a rage. The blood vessels in his neck stood out, and his hands were clenching and unclenching at his sides. His lips had thinned, and his eyes . . . heaven help her, the look in his eyes chilled her to the bone. She shivered and waited for the heavy hand of his anger to fall upon her.

"You!" he raged, pointing a finger at her. "You played me for a fool! Did you think I would never find out?"

"I have no idea what you are talking about," Vanora said, pretending innocence.

He stalked forward until they stood nose to nose. His rage was so stunning she could not move, much less speak.

"Do you not?" He removed his sword and thrust it at her. "Take it. Show me your skill."

She shook her head and backed away. He followed.

"I know you can use it. Go ahead, take it."

Hoping to appease his anger, she took the sword but let it hang limply in her hand. "I cannot raise a sword against you."

He laughed, the harsh sound grating in her ears. "You had no such problem in the past."

She refused to admit to anything until she knew exactly how much he knew. "What are you implying?"

"I am not implying, wife. I know who you are."

The color drained from Vanora's face. "How could you know such a thing? I can explain why you could not find me when you arrived. I was in the wine cellar."

Lionheart was not impressed. "Good try but not good enough. I watched you from the top of the cliff. I saw you walk along the riverbank and disappear into the hidden passage."

"What makes you think 'twas me?"

"A simple process of elimination. You, wife, are the White Knight." His voice was deadly calm, too calm. "There is no one else it could be, unless you wish to tell me 'tis Father Caddoc, or mayhap one of the young kitchen lads."

She inhaled sharply. She could incriminate no one but herself. Lionheart knew it and so did she.

Stiffening her slender shoulders, she faced him squarely, her expression resigned. "Do with me what you will, my lord, for I alone bear the guilt. I do not regret helping Llewelyn, for peace with England came as a result, and I am not sorry for aiding my warriors. The only thing I can say in my defense is that I did not know you when we clashed swords as I do now."

She could not bear to look into his eyes; his contempt for her shone in them like a beacon.

"Why did you not tell me? I could have killed you!" he roared. "I *wanted* to kill you." He shook his head. "I am not a killer of women, but you would have made me one. 'Tis unforgivable."

"I wanted to tell you, but I feared your reaction, and rightly so."

"You fear naught," he scoffed. "Who taught you to wield a sword?"

"My father. I was all he had, and he encouraged me to train with his men."

"He did you no favor."

"What are you going to do?"

"The door behind the altar is being sealed as we speak. Who knows about the entrance besides yourself, your priest and your tiring woman?" His eyes narrowed. "Nay, never mind," he said before she could answer. "Obviously, Daffid, Llewelyn and Cragdon's warriors knew of the entrance, for they have all used it. I am surprised I was not slain in my sleep by one of your countrymen."

"I warned Daffid against it," Vanora said unthinkingly. "He wanted to, but . . ." Her eyes widened and her lips clamped tightly together when she realized what she had just divulged.

Lionheart glared at her. "When did you see Daffid? Today, when you left the keep?" He grasped her shoulders, his fingers digging into her flesh. "Lie not to me, Vanora. Did you go to Daffid today? Has he made you his whore?"

"Nay! You accuse me unjustly. I admit I left the keep through the secret passage, but I did not go to Daffid. He came here. My intention when I left was to contact Sir Ren. I wanted to tell him to refuse Daffid's plea to join a rebellion he is planning."

Vanora knew by Lionheart's hardened expression that she had said too much.

"So you did see Daffid. Think you I am stupid?"

"I told you, I did not go to Daffid. He came here," Vanora repeated. "I advised him to go home and forget about me and Cragdon, that I am content with you. I planned to have the entrance sealed after I returned today so Daffid could not use it to hurt you. He wants Cragdon and refuses to give up his dream of possessing it."

"So he plans to kill me, wed you and

claim Cragdon," Lionheart guessed.

"Aye, but I would not have allowed it. I told you, I am content with you."

Lionheart gave a snort of disgust. "Tell that to someone who might believe you. You played me for a fool and conspired behind my back with your countrymen. I should beat you and turn you out, but you are not worth the trouble."

Turning his back to her, he stormed toward the door.

"Lionheart! Wait! Do not go. Beat me, confine me, but do not turn away from me. I can bear punishment but not indifference."

He whirled to confront her. "From this day forward you are naught to me. You may go where you will, do as you please, for I care not."

Spinning on his heel, he stomped off. Vanora could not let him go like this. There had to be something she could do to appease his anger. Was there nothing she could say to convince him she had done naught but fight for her country, the same as any man would have done? That she was a woman should not matter. If the White Knight were a man Lionheart would have slain him and felt no guilt, but being made a fool of by a woman had wounded his pride.

If she did not reach out to him now, the breach between them would never be healed.

"Lionheart! I love you!"

He did not turn, but she could tell by the stiffening of his shoulders that he had heard her. He reached for the door latch.

"Lionheart! Please believe me."

He dropped his hand from the latch but said naught. His only reaction was an outburst of bitter laughter as he opened the door and walked out on her.

Vanora stared at the door. She would not cry, nor would she beg. No man, no matter how much she loved him, was worth the anguish she was feeling. Keeping her secret identity from Lionheart had been wrong, but his callous treatment of her now was despicable.

The door opened and Mair slipped inside. "My poor lambie," she wailed, rushing to Vanora's side. Taking Vanora's face between her hands, she searched it for bruises. "Where did he hurt you?"

"Where it does not show," Vanora choked out.

"Never say he punched you! Did he crack a rib? Mayhap I should take a look."

"Nay, Mair, he did not lay a hand on me." She placed a hand on her chest.

" 'Tis my heart that is broken. He will never forgive me."

"He is a man, lambie. When you, a woman, crossed swords with him, you pricked his pride and compromised his honor. Say what you will about Lionheart, he takes knighthood seriously. He would never knowingly injure a woman. Had he slain you, he would never have forgiven himself. Give him time to come to grips with the notion that a woman can wield a sword and defend her country as well as a man."

" 'Tis too late, Mair. Lionheart will never forgive me, and even if he does, I know not if I can forgive him for his harsh stand against me. He broke my heart, Mair. When I told him I loved him, he laughed at me."

Mair held out her arms and Vanora rushed into them. Though tears threatened, she did not cry. She had known the consequences when she donned armor and raised her sword against Lionheart, and now she must accept them. But oh, it hurt, hurt terribly to be spurned by the man she loved.

"Show Lionheart your mettle, lambie," Mair advised. "Put on your best gown and come down to the hall to sup. Father Caddoc and I will be there to support you."

Vanora swallowed her refusal and nodded her head instead. She would not let Lionheart know how badly he had wounded her. His refusal to acknowledge her love had almost been too much for her to bear. But Mair was right. She was not going to hide in her chamber and give Lionheart the satisfaction of knowing how deeply he had hurt her.

"None of this would have happened if Lionheart had not returned to Cragdon before he was expected," Vanora said. "Was Althea really injured, or was it merely an excuse to return to Cragdon?"

"Althea took a nasty fall," Mair replied. "But aside from a few bruises and a sprained ankle, she is fine. I did what I could for her, but she should remain off her feet for another few days."

"Pity," Vanora murmured. "I shall be ready in a moment, Mair. We can go below together."

Head held high, chin tilted, Vanora entered the hall and walked to her usual place at the head table. Her steps faltered, then stopped completely when she saw Lionheart enter the hall carrying a simpering Althea in his arms. He strode directly to the dais and settled Althea in the chair on his right. Sir Brandon sat on

Lionheart's left. The remaining chairs had been removed, probably on Lionheart's orders.

Mair tugged her arm. "Come, lambie, there are two empty places beside Father Caddoc."

Her cheeks flaming, Vanora slid onto the bench beside the priest. He patted her hand. "Are you all right, child?"

"I am fine, Father. I see Lionheart wasted no time in replacing me."

"I will speak to him about keeping his marriage vows."

"Save your breath. Does everyone know about me? About who I am, I mean?"

"Nay, and I am sure everyone is wondering what happened between you and Lionheart."

"Has the entrance behind the altar been sealed?"

"Aye. Lionheart saw to it."

" 'Tis just as well."

Vanora had no appetite. And seeing Althea and Lionheart together, conversing intimately, made her stomach roil with nausea. She wanted to flee but would not give Lionheart the satisfaction.

Lionheart did his best to keep his gaze from straying to Vanora. He had thought he would feel pleasure when Vanora saw Althea occupying her chair, but her hurt expression tugged at a place inside him he thought he had closed off to her.

"I am glad you finally came to your senses," Althea purred. "I knew your infatuation with Vanora would not last. 'Tis not your nature to remain faithful to a wife." She leaned close. "What happened? Did you find her with another man?"

"Forget Vanora," Lionheart said. "How is your ankle? Does it pain you?"

"Mair said I should not put weight on it." She gave him a coy smile. "I hope you do not mind carrying me about."

"It will be my pleasure," Lionheart said, placing his hand over hers.

Though he smiled and gave the impression he was enamored with his leman, his thoughts were with Vanora and the way she had deceived him and lied to him and made a fool of him. Were he inclined toward violence against women, Vanora would be black and blue. Never had he been so angry at another human being.

He could not forgive Vanora. He would prove to her that she meant naught to him. What made it difficult, however, was the fact that he had finally acknowledged to himself his feelings for Vanora. It would be a stretch to imagine himself in love, but he had begun to care.

"What are you thinking, Lionheart?" Althea asked. "You seem so distant."

"It has been a long day and you must be exhausted. If you are finished eating, I will carry you to your chamber."

She held out her arms and smiled up at him. "I am ready. I have been waiting for this night since I arrived at Cragdon."

Lionheart's answering smile turned grim as he swept Althea into his arms and carried her from the hall.

Vanora's lower lip trembled as Lionheart left the hall with Althea in his arms, but she remained amazingly calm despite the gloating smile Althea directed at her over Lionheart's shoulder. Rising on unsteady legs, she excused herself and ascended the stairs to the solar. After Lionheart's open attentiveness to his leman, everyone in the keep probably knew that Lionheart had turned from his wife. His public display of affection for Althea was humiliating. How could she bear it?

When Vanora reached the solar, she found Alan collecting Lionheart's belongings. He flushed a deep red when he saw her and stammered an apology.

"I . . . I am sorry, my lady, but Lord Lionheart directed me to fetch his belongings."

" 'Tis all right, Alan, do what you must. I will not interfere." She walked to the window and stared out until Alan finished and quietly left.

Lionheart had truly turned away from her, she thought despondently. With a heavy heart she prepared for bed. Before she crawled beneath the furs, she spied Lionheart's sword lying where she had dropped it. With almost loving care, she picked it up and rested it against the hearth, refusing to cry over the man who had disdained her love. She climbed into bed and closed her eyes, but sleep was an elusive goal that dangled just out of reach.

Lionheart settled Althea on her bed and would have left had she not grasped his arm and pulled him down beside her.

"Where are you going?"

"To find my bed. I am as tired as you are. It has been an eventful day."

"But I thought . . . You led me to believe . . ."

"You are injured. It would be cruel of me to impose upon you tonight. I will send a servant to help you prepare for bed. Sleep well, Althea."

What in the hell was wrong with him? Lionheart wondered. Althea was willing; why did he walk away from her? Cursing himself for a fool, Lionheart stomped off to the chamber that had been prepared for him. It was not as comfortable as the solar, but at least Vanora would not be there to tempt him with her provocative smile and seductive body. How could she have made sweet love with him while living a lie?

What bothered him was not so much the fact that Vanora was the White Knight, but the knowledge that she had kept the truth from him. The realization that he had come close to killing her nearly brought him to his knees. Killing his own wife would have destroyed him, and for her deception he could not forgive her.

Without volition, Lionheart's steps took him to the solar. It was not where he wanted to be, but something stronger than his own will had led him there. His hand worked independently of his mind as he opened the door and stepped inside. The fire in the hearth had burned low, casting the room in shadows. His gaze went immediately to the bed.

Vanora must have sensed his presence, for she raised herself on her elbow and peered at him through the dancing shadows.

"Did Alan forget something?"

Lionheart went still. What was he doing here? As he searched his mind for an answer to Vanora's question, his wandering gaze found his sword propped up beside the hearth.

"Aye. I came for my sword."

"Do you expect an attack in the night?"

He strode to the bed and glared down at her. "I know not. You tell me."

"Fear not. You are safe, Lionheart. Should you need assistance, I willingly offer my sword arm in your defense."

"You go too far, Vanora," Lionheart warned. "One day that sharp, unruly tongue will land you in trouble."

Now that he had calmed down, he recalled Vanora telling him she loved him. Though he put no faith in her words, he could not help saying, "You claimed you loved me. Were that true, you would not have deceived me."

Firelight flickered across her pale face. She was a study in brazen grace and white-hot defiance. For a brief moment he thought he saw a glimmer of pain pass over her features, but her words quickly disabused him of that notion.

"Love died when you turned away from me and sought comfort from Althea. I feel naught for you but contempt, Lionheart. What I did was what any man would do for his country."

"You are most definitely not a man. Had I slain you, I never would have forgiven myself."

"Is that what your anger is about? I knew the risk when I donned armor and fought to defend my home. Had my father been fortunate enough to have had sons, they would have done the same as I."

"My anger lies deeper than that, Vanora. You had every opportunity to tell me you were the knight I sought yet you lied each time I questioned you. I am your husband. You should have trusted me enough to tell me the truth."

"You were an unwilling husband and an Englishman besides. I feared . . . I feared . . ."

"What did you fear?"

"That you would hate me," she blurted out. "Or hurt my friends for keeping my secret." Her next words were low and raw with anguish. "I did not know I would love you."

There it was! That word again. Lionheart felt the strain of maintaining his anger but refused to let his guard down.

"But you no longer love me," he probed. *Was he insane? Why did he care?* He did not easily forgive and forget, but the demon inside him would not be hushed.

"You are correct, my lord. I no longer love you; you are free to return to Althea. And do not forget your sword."

Lionheart knew he should leave, but the demon that plagued him gave him no peace. "If you feel naught for me, kiss me and prove it." *Was he utterly mad?*

Her expression mutinous, Vanora reared up, pulling the covers up to her neck to shield her bare breasts. "Did Althea's kisses not satisfy you?"

"Forget Althea. I dare you to kiss me, vixen."

She glared at him. "Is this some new form of punishment you have devised?"

Aye, punishment for myself, he thought miserably. He had no idea why he was torturing himself like this. Nevertheless, he had to know if Vanora was lying about loving him. He could think of many reasons why she would lie and needed to know the truth for his own peace of mind.

"What are you afraid of?" Lionheart taunted. "I want to know how far you will go with your lies."

"What will kissing you prove?"

"That you invented your love to appease my anger. Or," he said, his voice low and harsh, "that you love me still."

Vanora looked away. "Unrequited love hurts, Lionheart. You told me I no longer exist for you, so I banished you from my heart."

Would that I could do the same. The bed sagged beneath his weight. "I am justifiably bitter and naturally distrustful of you after discovering your deceit." He caressed her cheek with the back of his finger, continuing downward over her collarbone, stopping at the pulsing hollow at the base of her throat.

She pushed his hand away. "Stop it! You cannot take, and give naught in return. Go away, Lionheart. I cannot bear this kind of punishment. 'Tis cruel of you to demand that which you are not willing to return in full measure."

"What, pray tell, is that?"

"Your love."

He rose abruptly, his expression stony. "You have not earned my love. In fact, I know not what I am doing here."

"Your sword, Lionheart, remember? You came for your sword."

"Since you are so fond of swords, you

may keep it," he returned coolly. "Forgive my intrusion. It will not happen again."

Vanora was torn. Her good sense applauded Lionheart's departure, but her heart wanted him to stay. The thought of him returning to Althea's bed made her sick to her stomach. Besides, she refused to accept that he hated her. He had come to her chamber tonight on a flimsy excuse. Whether he realized it or not, his intention had been to make love to her. How could she let him go to Althea when her heart told her she could win Lionheart's love if she really tried?

That thought brought another. Did she want a man who had washed his hands of her and held her in contempt? Was love worth the anguish of letting a man use her body merely because he desired her?

The answer stunned her. One could not put a price on love. Mayhap her love was strong enough for both of them. How long could his anger hold out against the awesome power of love? Was she willing to let him take comfort in Althea's arms?

"Nay!"

Lionheart was halfway to the door when Vanora's outburst stopped him. He spun around. "What did you say?"

She swallowed hard and prayed she was

not making a mistake. "I am willing to kiss you if you still wish me to."

He sent her a mocking smile. "I have changed my mind. Althea would be more welcoming."

Deliberately she let the covers fall to her waist, baring her breasts. "Then go to her. I but wanted to prove how little your kisses affect me."

She had definitely pricked his interest, for his eyebrows rose a fraction of an inch and he returned to the bed. His gaze dropped to her breasts. "What is going on, vixen?"

"You tell me. You came to my chamber after you swore I meant naught to you."

"My sword —"

"It could have waited until morning. Tell me you hate me. Tell me you want naught to do with me. Tell me 'tis Althea you want, and I will believe you."

"Aye, all of those," Lionheart said gruffly. He sat down on the edge of the bed. "Learning you were the White Knight turned me inside out." He grasped her shoulder. "Damn you! Why are you doing this to me?"

She tilted her head up. "Because I refuse to believe you hate me."

His lips hovered scant inches from hers.

"I despise what you did," he whispered.

"But you do not hate me."

"I cannot abide liars."

"You want me."

His breath was hot upon her cheek. "My body feels but does not think."

She moved closer, brushing her breasts against his chest. He did not move away. "What is that supposed to mean?"

He took her hand and placed it on the hard ridge of his sex. "It means I cannot stop my body from wanting you, though my mind rejects everything you stand for. You are a woman, not a man. When you donned armor and led men into battle, you risked your life unnecessarily."

Her brows shot upward. "Why should that bother you?"

He met her gaze with a puzzled look. "If I knew the answer to that, I would not be here. I would be with Althea, giving her what she wants."

His reply left her breathless and giddy. Mayhap there was hope for them. If there was a small unguarded place in his heart where she could plant herself and grow, she vowed to find it. Testing the depth of his resolve, she closed the space between them and pressed her lips to his.

He exploded. There was no other word

for it. She looked into his face; the angular planes were burnished a dark gold by the fire's glow. His eyes, stormy gray and intense, searched hers. Her breath seized. She raised her hands to his chest; the fire within him scalded her. Then his mouth covered hers. Their lips met and fused. Hungrily. His kiss was ravishing, nearly brutal as he tore the bed coverings away and closed his arms about her.

She felt his hands lock around her waist, then shift her beneath him, his body hot and ready. She was stunned but undaunted when he broke off the kiss and said, "Mistake this not for love; 'tis merely rutting."

His words did not please her, but she had set her course and would not be swayed from it. Instead, she offered him her mouth anew. He did not hesitate but claimed it rapaciously, his hands gliding down her back, molding her to him, cupping the firm curves of her bottom and urging her hips nearer.

Warning bells rang in his head; his demons whispered a litany of reasons why he should not be making love to Vanora. But he banished them, heeding instead the dictates of his body. He could not wait. Removing his chausses took but a moment; his tunic could wait, but he could not.

Then he spread her legs, positioned himself between them and shoved inside.

Panting, sweating, aching with raw need, he pounded into her hot center. Again and again. She cried out, shuddered, but he barely heard above the thumping of his heart. He gritted his teeth, thrust hard and deep. Erupted. The relief that filled his body was blinding, the heat gut-wrenching. He had known many women in his lifetime. None like her. Was it his fate to spend the rest of his life with a woman who satisfied him like none other?

A woman he could not trust?

A woman who wielded a sword like a man?

Chapter Sixteen

Vanora snuggled against Lionheart, waiting for him to speak. When he said naught, she touched his chest. "You would be more comfortable if you took off your tunic."

Her words must have awakened his demons, for he jumped out of bed and glared down at her. "Damn you! You must be feeling smug right now. I know not what you did to me, but it will not happen again." He groped for his chausses and yanked them on.

Vanora felt as if her world had just exploded. "Why did you make love to me?"

"We rutted, Vanora. There was no love involved. I but followed the dictates of my cock. You wanted me, and I obliged."

"Get out! Get out and never come back. I cannot bear the sight of you."

Lionheart stared at her a long, silent moment, then stormed off.

He could not believe what had just happened, what he had allowed to happen. 'Twas as if he had no will where Vanora was concerned. This could not go on, he told himself. He needed to get away for a time, to clear his mind and heart of his wife's influence. Aye, 'twas what he would do. He would escort Althea back to England himself and . . .

Nay, that would never do. He could not risk losing Cragdon. Daffid and his cohorts were still a threat to his holdings; he could trust no one but himself to defend the keep. Sir Brandon was a good man but he had not Lionheart's experience. With only twenty men at his disposal, Lionheart knew it was not going to be easy to defend the fortress against Daffid and an army of Welsh savages.

His dilemma loomed large before him. Vanora pulled him to her on an invisible string, and he liked it not. But Lionheart could do naught to control his unruly body where Vanora was concerned. When she fluttered her sooty eyelashes at him, his heart did flip-flops and his loins tightened. What was he to do? The answer, he decided, was to avoid her and spend more time with Althea. Mayhap with time he would be able to summon enough desire for his former leman to bed her.

Vanora went about her normal duties with a heavy heart during the following days. True to his word, Lionheart made a point of ignoring her. It was as if she did not exist. Even worse, he and Althea were growing closer. Vanora knew not if he was bedding his leman, but all the signs said he was. She had too much pride to ask Mair or one of the servants about Lionheart's sleeping arrangements.

During those trying days, Vanora made an effort to avoid Althea, but when their paths happened to cross, Althea was quick to boast about Lionheart's attendance upon her. Though Althea's ankle had healed, Lionheart had made no attempt to return her to England.

One day Father Caddoc was called to the village on a mission of mercy, and Vanora decided to go with him. Bundling up in her warmest woolen tunic and fur-lined mantle, she rode through the outer bailey where Lionheart was training his men.

Despite the cold, he had stripped to the waist, the exposed parts of his body glistening with sweat. Her gaze lingered on his bronzed torso, admiring his bulging biceps and the muscles rippling across his back. Magnificent was too tame a word to describe him. How she missed him: their verbal sparring, the darkening of his silver eyes when he made love to her, his hard body covering hers.

She wanted to hate him for his blatant disregard for her but could not. He allowed her no opportunity to get close to him, to try to make things right between them. She understood his pride; why could he not understand hers? The man was impossible.

Dragging her gaze away from his impressive form, Vanora tried to concentrate on her mission in the village. A villein's wife was dying, and she was bringing warm blankets and food to the family. Mair had already used all her knowledge of healing to treat Bretta, but she had not improved and death was near.

Vanora's mind was still on the sick woman when she heard Lionheart roar for her to stop. She reined in and waited for him. This would be the first time he had spoken directly to her in a fortnight, and she wondered why he deigned to speak to her now.

"Go on ahead, Father," she instructed. "I shall follow after I have spoken with Lionheart."

"Are you certain?" the priest asked worriedly.

"Aye. Gordy's wife needs you more than I do."

Lionheart loped easily up to her and grasped the reins. "Where do you go?"

"To bring food and warm clothing to a villein's family. The wife lies near death, and I would offer what comfort I can to the family. May I go now?"

His eyes narrowed. "Aye, as long as you do not go to Daffid."

"I am naught to you, Lionheart. You said I could go where I pleased."

"Does it please you to go to Daffid?"

"Not unless you drive me to him," she taunted. "I would have been content as your wife if you had not cast me from your life."

"You are still my wife."

"Am I?" Would he accept her challenge? "You want me not."

"You are wrong, wife. I want you with every breath I take. I cannot look at you without wanting you. But I am too strong to become a victim of your lies. My own mother found naught in me to love, so why should I believe you would be different?"

"Your mother? What has she got to do with us?"

"I misspoke. I do not wish to talk about that woman. I merely wanted to warn you that I will banish you to a convent should you betray me with another man."

"I thought you had no care for what I did," she goaded.

"Challenge me not, Vanora, for you cannot win. I will not be humiliated by your indiscretions."

Indignation stiffened her shoulders. "What about your indiscretions?"

"What about them?"

She jerked the reins from his hand. "Go to the devil, Lionheart, and take your leman with you!"

Lionheart lifted his head, inhaled sharply of the cold, exhilarating air, and laughed. He had not felt so alive since he had last made love, nay, rutted with Vanora. How he missed her! Her keen wit and acid tongue, her sleekly muscled body . . . God's blood, why did his life have to be so complicated?

Invigorated, he returned to the training field, ready to take on all twenty of his men and their squires.

Vanora entered the village and reined her mount toward Gordy's wattle-and-daub hut. She knew she was too late when she saw a group of weeping women gathered outside the hut. Her heart sank. She dismounted and pushed her way through to the door.

"Is she gone?" Vanora asked a bent old woman hovering in the doorway.

"Aye, Bretta is in peace now." She wiped away a tear. "What will become of her little ones?"

Vanora had no answer as she entered the hut and knelt beside Father Caddoc to offer prayers for the dead woman. Three small children huddled around their father, tears streaming down their pale little faces.

"Whatever will I do without my Bretta?" Gordy sobbed. "I cannot care for the children myself, my lady."

"Do you have relatives?"

"Aye, a sister."

"Would she be willing to help out?"

"Aye, she is a widow with no children, but I have no means to get her here. She lives a half day's journey from Cragdon."

"After Bretta is buried, I shall lend you a horse so you can fetch her," Vanora offered.

"I will care for the children until Gordy returns," a woman said from the doorway. "Take the children outside so we can prepare your wife's body for burial."

"I will help," Vanora offered.

"Nay, my lady, 'tis not right."

"Go home, Vanora," Father Caddoc urged. "Leave the food and blankets with me. I will pray over Bretta and see that the children are warm and fed."

Vanora gave reluctant agreement. "When you are ready, Gordy, come to the keep, and I will see that you are given a horse for your journey."

Too grief-stricken to speak, Gordy nodded. Then the women who had come to prepare the body edged Vanora out of the cramped hut. After handing Father Caddoc the food and blankets she had brought, Vanora left. She was approaching the outskirts of the village when she heard someone call out to her. Glancing over her shoulder, she saw Sir Ren behind her.

"Lady Vanora, I have been waiting daily for you or Father Caddoc to come to the village."

"What has happened, Sir Ren?"

"Daffid approached me and Cragdon's knights about joining his army. He plans to attack Cragdon when he has enough men behind him."

"I hope you heeded my warning and refused him."

"Aye. I do not like the English any better than the next man, but as long as we are at peace with England, I will not join a rebellion. Naught will bring Edward's wrath down upon our heads like an uprising."

"You are wise, Sir Ren. I shall apprise Lord Lionheart of Daffid's plans."

"Daffid believes the castle is weak, that it lacks warriors to defend it."

" 'Tis true, I fear."

"We want to return to Cragdon. We remain faithful to you and wish to defend your lands against aggression, be it English or Welsh. I told the others I would speak to you about it. Will your husband allow us to return if we swear fealty to him? Does he wish to kill me for shooting an arrow into him?"

"Lionheart has unmasked me, and he knows that you wounded him in order to save my life. He would have slain me had you not prevented it. I know not what is in Lionheart's heart and cannot predict his reaction to your appearance at Cragdon. Will you still want to swear fealty if it means imprisonment?"

He nodded. "I would risk it for you and Cragdon, aye."

"And for Lionheart?"

"He is your husband and our new liege lord. Giving our loyalty to you would be the same as offering it to him."

"Where are the others? Did they come with you?"

"Aye. Ten knights and their squires await your answer."

Glancing past Sir Ren, Vanora saw Cragdon's warriors fanned out behind him. For a moment she was too close to tears to speak.

"What say you, my lady?" Sir Ren asked.

"Aye, come with me and I will entreat Lionheart on your behalf," Vanora said, praying she was not making a mistake. If she led these good men to imprisonment or worse, she would never forgive herself. But Lionheart *had* said he would be lenient if they swore fealty to him. And they *did* carry word of Daffid's plans. That should prove their worth to Lionheart.

Lionheart heard the sentry's warning before the riders reached the outer portcullis and hurried out to meet them, his fear escalating when he saw Vanora surrounded by Cragdon's former defenders. What did they want? Had they taken Vanora hostage? He should have known better than to let her go to the village without an escort. If they had hurt her . . .

Sir Brandon caught up with him. "The archers are positioned on the battlements and await your orders."

"I do not want Vanora hurt. The archers are to hold until I hear Sir Ren's demands."

Vanora approached the portcullis alone. Lionheart was there to meet her.

"Raise the portcullis," Vanora said.

"Are you hurt?" Lionheart asked, peering at her through the iron bars.

Vanora sent him a startled look. "Why would my own men hurt me? Nay, Lionheart. Sir Ren sought me in the village to warn me about Daffid. Daffid is gathering the remnants of Llewelyn's disbanded army and intends to attack the castle."

"You lied to me again," Lionheart charged. "You went to the village to meet with Ren. What are they doing here? My archers are in place and awaiting my signal."

"Nay, I did not lie! I did not know Ren was in the village. He and Cragdon's former defenders come in peace. They wish to swear fealty to you. They want to defend Cragdon against Daffid's attack."

Lionheart found that difficult to believe. "I still bear the scar from Sir Ren's arrow."

"Had he not wounded you, you would have slain me. Is that what you wish?"

"I wish our paths had never crossed," Lionheart gritted from between clenched teeth.

In truth, he would have been devastated

had he slain Vanora; he ought to thank Sir Ren for preventing such a catastrophe. "How do I know they will not slay me in my sleep?"

"They are knights. Their word is their honor. Once they swear fealty, they will not betray you."

He glanced past Vanora at the waiting men. "Very well, I will speak to them. Raise the portcullis," he called to the sentry.

Sword in hand, Lionheart stood aside as the men rode through the portcullis. When they were all inside, Lionheart bellowed, "Stop right there! Dismount."

The knights and their squires dismounted and stood facing Lionheart. Lionheart paused before each man, judging his trustworthiness by looking into his eyes. After a lengthy inspection, he asked, "Do you accept me as your liege lord? Do you pledge fealty to me?"

"And to your lady," Sir Ren added.

As one, the knights and their squires knelt before Lionheart and pledged their fealty.

"You will be kept under surveillance until you prove yourselves," Lionheart maintained. "Any suspicious activity will be reported to me immediately. Sir Brandon is the new captain of the guards, Sir Ren. Are you willing to serve under him?"

"Aye. I vow to serve you and your lady with the same loyalty I gave to the previous lord of Cragdon."

"So be it," Lionheart said. "Sir Brandon!" The knight stepped forward. "See to the men's billeting and assign them duties."

"You will not regret it, my lord," Sir Ren vowed.

Vanora turned her mount toward the keep. "Wait," Lionheart ordered. She reined in sharply.

"What now? I am tired. Bretta's death has saddened me. Her family is bereft. She left three small children and a grieving husband."

Lionheart's expression softened. "I will see what I can do to ease their lot."

"I already offered Gordy the use of a horse to fetch his widowed sister to care for his motherless children. Friends offered to care for the children in his absence."

Though loath to let her go, Lionheart stood aside. "Go, but heed my warning, wife. I allowed your knights to return against my better judgment. Do not conspire with them against Edward or me. Cragdon is mine, and I hold what is mine."

"Do you, Lionheart? Do you hold what is yours? I think not."

Her challenge rang in his head long after she galloped off. What was she implying? It had taken all his willpower to remain aloof from her this past fortnight. Though Althea had tried to revive the passion he had once felt for her, he remained unmoved. 'Twas Vanora he wanted and Vanora he could not allow himself to trust . . . to love.

Vanora said she loved him. He wanted to believe her, he truly did, but a perverse demon inside told him he was unlovable.

Althea did not love him. He only served a purpose in her life. Nor did Vanora love him. How could she when he had forced her into a distasteful marriage?

Then how to explain Vanora's passion? he wondered. He did not know. Nor could he explain her need to don armor and wield a sword. Women's minds were convoluted and beyond understanding. If he did not hold firm against Vanora's wiles, he could lose his soul to her.

Despite his reservations, he was proud of the way Vanora had defended her former knights and turned the hard edge of his anger into acceptance. If not for Vanora, her knights would be occupying Cragdon's dungeon. He had forgiven Sir Ren for wounding him, for he knew he would have done the same if an enemy threatened Vanora.

Lionheart firmly believed that the situation between him and Vanora had to be resolved. Just being in the same room with his enticing wife drove him mad with wanting. Ignoring her had not worked. Nor had dancing attendance upon another woman. Perhaps, he thought, smiling, he should do as his body demanded and make love, nay, rut with Vanora and appease the hunger raging inside him. She *was* his wife. Why should he not take advantage of his God-given right?

Lionheart returned to the training field, but his mind was not on his sword. After a time he gave up and returned to the keep. He saw Vanora speaking with Sir Penryn and joined them.

"Is there a problem?"

"Nay, my lord," Penryn replied. "Lady Vanora and I were discussing whether or not we had ample supplies to see us through the winter. I told her I would check the storerooms and granary."

"Inform me of your findings, Sir Penryn. If need be, we can purchase what we need from neighboring estates or the closest town."

Sir Penryn took his leave. Vanora turned away, but Lionheart stopped her. "I would have a word with you, Vanora."

"And I with you."

Their conversation was forestalled by Althea's arrival.

"Who are those strange men in the keep, Lionheart? They look like Welshmen."

"They are Welshmen," Lionheart answered. "They are Cragdon's former defenders."

"What are they doing here?"

"They have sworn fealty and are joining my garrison."

"Are you mad? We will all be slain in our sleep." Her spiteful gaze fell on Vanora. "I suppose we can thank *her* for this."

"My knights are honorable men," Vanora asserted. "They would never break their pledge."

"I have been thinking, Althea," Lionheart began. "Now that we have extra men to defend Cragdon, I can spare two warriors to escort you to your village."

Vanora sent Lionheart a startled look. "You would do that?"

"Aye. Althea has overstayed her welcome. The weather is still mild and there is no snow as yet. If she does not return now, she will be forced to remain the winter."

"You have been so attentive of late, I thought you wanted me to stay," Althea whined.

Vanora snorted. "Attentive? Is that a new name for rutting?" She spun on her heel. "If you wish to continue our conversation, my lord, you will find me in the solar."

Lionheart started to follow, but Althea clutched his arm, holding him in check. "You did not mean what you said, did you? We were becoming close again. I do not want to leave you, Lionheart."

Lionheart shrugged free. "We will speak of this later, Althea."

"Why must you pant after her like an obedient puppy? Vanora has but to pull a string and you follow. You are not the man I once knew."

"I agree, I am not the same man," Lionheart said as he strode off.

Vanora wanted to believe Lionheart meant what he said about sending Althea away, but the leman's words had sorely tried her temper. Vanora did not need to be reminded how attentive her husband had been to Althea. His open display of affection for his leman was the talk of the keep.

When Lionheart had allowed her knights to return, Vanora had begun to hope that he had softened toward her, and that he was ready to forgive her lies. What did he want to discuss with her? Did he want to mend the rift between them?

Vanora spun around toward the door when she heard it open and shut. Her heartbeat accelerated when she saw Lionheart standing before her, his expression unreadable.

"What do you want?"

"We have not finished our conversation." He removed his sword and placed it on a bench.

"What is it you wish to discuss? Before you begin, I thank you for allowing my knights to return to Cragdon."

"I thought we might discuss Althea."

Her chin tilted upward. "That subject does not interest me. Choose another."

"Nay, we will discuss Althea. I was serious about returning her to England. She does not belong here."

Vanora's mouth dropped open in disbelief. "I hardly thought you meant it when you told Althea you were sending her home."

"I rarely say things I do not mean."

"I assumed you were enjoying your leman's attentions."

"You assumed wrong. If you recall, I tried once before to send her home, but fate intervened."

"What are you *really* trying to say to me, Lionheart? Have you forgiven me?"

"Trust must be earned, Vanora, but I am willing to give you a chance to redeem yourself. I do not know that I can ever forgive you for recklessly endangering your life, but I can ignore your presence no longer. I tried to pretend you did not exist, and I failed."

"You seemed content enough rutting with Althea. And for that I can never forgive *you*." Deliberately she turned her back on him.

Grasping her shoulders, he swung her around to face him. "Do not turn your back on me. Listen very carefully to what I am about to say. I did not rut with Althea. Not once in all the time she was here."

"Am I supposed to believe you?"

"*I* am not a liar, Vanora."

Vanora flushed and looked away; his insinuation stung. But could she believe him? "Are you really going to send Althea away?"

"I just said so, did I not? 'Tis not Althea I want."

Joy swelled Vanora's heart. She wanted

to hear him say he needed her, and that he cared for her and no other. Swallowing her pride, she asked, "Do you intend for us to share a bed again?"

"I thought I made that clear. Aye, I want you in my bed. You are my wife; 'tis your duty to lie with me."

That was hardly what Vanora wanted to hear. Duty had naught to do with a loving relationship. "Do you love me?"

A long silence ensued. "If you are referring to sentimental love, it does not exist. I enjoy your body. I admire your intelligence, your courage, your pride. Is that not enough upon which to build a life?"

Nay. "I had hoped for more. When I said I loved you, what did you think I meant?"

Another long silence stretched between them. Finally he said, "Women are sentimental creatures. You probably meant that you enjoy my body as much as I enjoy yours. Somewhere in our relationship we found common ground, and you interpreted that as love."

"Who hardened your heart?" Vanora asked. " 'Tis obvious you have no perception of how women feel or how they think. Did you not love your mother? Love for one's mother is a child's first experience of tenderness. 'Tis the best and truest form of love one can know."

His stony expression and stiff shoulders were the first indication that she was treading in dangerous waters.

"Do not mention my mother to me. She has been banished from my memory and does not exist."

Vanora stared at him. " 'Tis always difficult to lose a dear one. I lost my beloved mother five years ago and miss her every minute of every day."

"You are wrong if you think I miss my mother," Lionheart said with cool disdain. "To my knowledge she is very much alive, but I have had no contact with her since I was too young to recall I even had a mother. She abandoned me."

"I do not understand."

"Nor do I. The very mention of her offends me. I do not wish to discuss her."

Lionheart's startling admission gave Vanora insight into his dealings with women. He could not love because no one had taught him how. He had barricaded his heart and refused to allow tender sentiments inside because his mother had disappointed him. His own mother had abandoned him. Did the woman have no feelings? 'Twas no wonder Lionheart put no faith in marriage.

"I will not leave you like your mother

did," Vanora said quietly. "Though you would have walked away from me and our marriage if Edward had not ordered you to remain at Cragdon, I would have honored our vows. Why did your mother leave you?"

He shrugged. "Father said she took a lover and left me behind when she fled. He may have lied, but it no longer matters. He was not much of a father anyway. I have made my own way in life."

" 'Twas a life without love," Vanora whispered.

"There has been no shortage of women in my life."

Vanora winced. "Did any of them love you?"

"All of them loved me for what I could give them."

"All women are not the same. The kind of women you have known love with their bodies, not their hearts."

" 'Tis simpler that way. There is no room for disappointment when the heart is not engaged."

"I love you with my heart, Lionheart. But even if you neither want my love nor return it, I shall take what you offer."

Lionheart frowned. "And what is that, wife?"

She tossed her head, sending her burnished curls swirling around her shoulders. "A warm body. You are very good at giving pleasure, husband. Though I have had no one to compare you with, I am certain you are the best."

Vanora's words gave Lionheart an uncomfortable feeling in the pit of his stomach. Did he want to be remembered as a warm body and naught else? Did he really want Vanora to stop loving him? Suddenly the idea of being loved piqued his curiosity. He had never felt loved before.

Nay, he thought, shaking his head to clear it of stupid notions. He refused to fall into the trap Vanora had set for him. If he let his guard down and allowed himself to love Vanora, 'twas inevitable that she would disappoint him as his mother had. Vanora had already proven herself untrustworthy.

"Perhaps 'tis best that we enjoy what we have together and forget maudlin sentiments. I am comfortable with the physical relationship that exists between us."

She sent him an exasperated look. "What of children, Lionheart? Will you love them should God in His mercy grant us offspring?"

Lionheart's expression grew pensive.

"My children will not lack a father's . . ." His sentence ended abruptly.

"A father's love? Is that what you were going to say?"

"God's blood! You confuse me with your words. I will not neglect our children as my parents did me."

"Will you love them?" Vanora persisted.

His expression gave ample insight into his confused mind, but his answer did not disappoint her.

"Aye, damn you, I will love them!"

Vanora sent him a blinding smile. "You *do* know how to love. Mayhap there is hope for us after all, husband."

Chapter Seventeen

Vanora's words rendered Lionheart speechless. She was still hoping for love after he had told her it did not exist for him. Since she seemed to be waiting for a reply, he sought a glib answer.

"I will love you, wife, with my body, whenever you wish, be it night or day. My cock is always willing."

His arms circled her and dragged her close, the rigid proof of his desire prodding ruthlessly against her softness. It had been so long since he'd made love to Vanora, his body throbbed with need. He wanted her, desperately. Watching her from afar had been torturous. He belonged in her bed, in her arms, inside her. Deep inside her.

He kissed her neck. Desire thickened as she melted into him, her body molding itself to his. His caressing hands unerringly removed her tunic. He slid the fabric off her shoulders and peeled away her shift. He dipped to kiss her nipples, his hands skimming down her back and cupping her bottom. Still holding her against him, he walked with her to the bed and lowered her down upon the furs. His smoldering gaze did not leave her as he shucked off his clothing.

"It has been a lonely fortnight," he growled. "My cold bed offered no comfort. I want to make love to you."

Her great purple eyes glittered as her gaze dropped to his loins. Reaching out a hand, she enclosed the pulsing staff, feeling it throb against her palm. She smiled impishly, seductively, as her fingers circled and squeezed him. Anticipation pounded through him when she pulled him to her and touched the tip of her tongue to the glistening head of his cock. The sensation of her flicking tongue undid his control. Roaring, he pushed her down and lowered himself on top of her.

His mouth covered hers, forestalling any protest Vanora might have made. The desperate need for total consummation instantly pounded though him. She clutched his shoulders and kissed him back more aggressively than she ever had before.

Her hungry response sent desire rampaging through him. He returned his mouth to her neck, and then to her swelling, beckoning breasts. He teased her with his tongue, her sounds of pleasure spurring his ardor. Removing her hands from his shoulders, he slid down her body. Spreading her legs, he looked at her with smoldering eyes. Kneeling between her thighs, he kissed her stomach, around her navel. Lower still. Reaching down for her ankles, he lifted first one leg and then the other onto his shoulders.

Cradling her hips in his hands, he kissed up her thigh to his goal and planted his mouth there. Her frantic cries and pulsing flesh sent waves of desire spiraling through him. *This* was what he had missed. *This* was what he needed. She rocked slowly, rhythmically as he explored deeper, his hunger turning primal as his tongue lashed into her. He kept her on the edge, frenzied, mad with a need that aroused him even more than her taste, before he sent her screaming into a dazzling climax.

He rose up and moved over her; the sound of her gasping breaths sent his own tautly leashed passion out of control. Her feminine softness yielded to him. Desire scorched him, making him aware that he was still hard and throbbing, still unfulfilled. Flexing his hips, he plunged inside her so hard, the bed ropes rocked beneath them.

He tilted her bottom and sank deeper.

Setting the rhythm, he moved her to afford them the greatest pleasure, going as deep as he could, building her passion to match his own. She lifted her hips higher, moaning and twisting her head from side to side as he pumped in and out, harder, faster. He felt her quiver, felt violent little tremors pulsing against him. One more thrust and she came hard, crying out his name.

Waiting for her climax was the hardest thing he had ever done. But wait he did, his body taut with raw need until she stilled. Only then did he give his passion full rein, gripping her hips in his hands and pounding inside her, driving himself closer and closer to completion. A shudder ran through him and he spilled violently, coming hard and fast, filling her with his essence.

They lay there for what seemed like an eternity, until his breathing slowed. Then he lifted his head and looked down at her. When he saw her smiling at him, he realized he was lost, that he never had a chance.

"What are you thinking?" she asked.

That love is a fearsome thing. But he held his tongue. He was not ready to commit himself. Giving a woman that kind of power over him was daunting.

"I am thinking that you will never leave my bed again."

"You left mine, remember?"

"I must have been mad. In this we are very well matched, sweeting; I shall not make the mistake of leaving your bed again."

It was a start, Vanora thought. She could make him love her; she knew she could.

During the following days Lionheart made all the necessary preparations for Daffid's expected attack. He strengthened the walls where they were weak and posted lookouts on the wall walk. He trained his men relentlessly, preparing them both mentally and physically for battle.

A tenuous harmony existed between Lionheart and Vanora during those days. Passion brought them together and kept them returning to the beckoning bed in the solar. Though Lionheart drove himself until he was too tired to draw a breath, he still found the energy to make love to Vanora.

"How soon will Sir Giles return?" Vanora asked one night as they lay in languorous contentment after a satisfying bout of lovemaking.

"Soon. Within the next few days, surely."

"You miss him," Vanora stated.

"Aye, he is my right arm just as I am Edward's."

As you are mine, Vanora thought but did not say.

The day Althea left was a happy one for Vanora. She stood beside Lionheart as he placed a heavy purse in Althea's hand and bade her Godspeed.

"Spend this wisely, Althea," Lionheart advised, "and you shall not want for the rest of your days. Find a husband who will love you and give you children."

Althea hefted the purse and sneered. "I will take your gold, Lionheart, but you are making a mistake. Mark my words, one day your wife will betray you."

White lines bracketed Lionheart's mouth as he sent Althea and her escort on their way.

"Good riddance," Vanora muttered. "You were more than generous with her."

Threading her arm in his, she turned him toward the keep, more at peace now than she had been in a very long time. With Althea gone, there was naught to distract Lionheart, naught to keep him from giving her his undivided attention. Her days as the White Knight were behind her, and she need never lie to Lionheart again.

But Vanora's happiness was short-lived. Three days later a rider appeared at the portcullis. He was admitted immediately and brought directly to Lionheart. Vanora hurried over to join him, anxious to learn what the commotion was about. She recognized the young man immediately. It was Peter, Sir Giles's squire. A frisson of fear slid down her spine. She knew intuitively that something unforeseen had happened to Sir Giles, and that the consequences were going to destroy her chances to win Lionheart's love.

Peter was wild-eyed and disheveled, his chest heaving from his exertions and a yet unnamed fear. His tunic was rent, and a stream of blood ran down his arm.

"Speak, lad," Lionheart said. "Where are Sir Giles and his bride?"

His voice was coiled taut as a spring, and Vanora moved close, offering the comfort of her presence.

"We were outnumbered," Peter said, gasping for breath. "We acquitted ourselves well, but defeat was inevitable."

Grasping the lad's tunic, Lionheart yanked him forward until they were nose to nose. "What happened?"

" 'Twas Daffid ap Deverell. He holds Sir Giles and his lady hostage."

"Release him, Lionheart," Vanora said. "The lad is wounded and in need of attention."

He released Peter's tunic; the lad nearly fell to his knees but caught himself. "Aye, fetch Mair," Lionheart ordered. A man-at-arms hurried off to find the tiring woman.

"Help is on the way, lad. Meanwhile, tell me everything. How did you escape?"

"I did not escape. Daffid let me go to bring you a message."

Lionheart's lips flattened. "Proceed."

Peter's gaze lingered briefly on Vanora, then returned to Lionheart. "Daffid said he will not harm Sir Giles and his lady if you send Lady Vanora to him."

Lionheart's expression turned grim. "What else?"

"You have a sennight to comply with his request. If your lady does not arrive within the allotted time, he will" — he swallowed convulsively — "kill Sir Giles and his bride."

"I will go to him," Vanora said firmly.

"Nay!" Lionheart roared. "You will not!"

"I must if we are to save Giles and his bride. Daffid will listen to me. Mayhap I can talk some sense into him."

"I will think of something that does not involve you," Lionheart said. "How defendable is Daffid's keep?"

" 'Twould not be difficult to scale the walls, but I fear his army would overwhelm yours ere you breached the keep. Besides, Daffid would kill Sir Giles and Deirdre before you could get to them."

"I know what you are thinking, Vanora, and I will not allow it. Stay with young Peter until Mair arrives." Turning on his heel, Lionheart strode off, motioning for Sir Brandon and Sir Ren to follow.

Mair arrived moments later with her chest of herbs, ointments and simples. She clucked over Peter's wound and led him to the kitchen in search of hot water. Vanora hurried up to the solar, where she could think without being disturbed.

She knew that any action Lionheart took to rescue Giles and his lady was bound to fail. Even if he fought his way past a force twice, nay, three times the size of his own, which was highly unlikely, he would not find Giles and Deirdre alive. Daffid would slay them in retribution.

Vanora racked her brain for an answer. She knew she could not allow Daffid to kill two innocent people. And the thought of Lionheart dying was too painful to contemplate. Nay, it was up to her to find a way to save Giles and his bride . . . and Lionheart. But to do so meant breaking her word. She had promised Lionheart she would never don armor again, but desperate times called for desperate measures.

Lionheart was distracted when they retired to the solar later that evening. As he prowled the chamber, she felt his anguish as if it were her own. She said naught as she waited for him to speak, her gaze running over his broad, strong body, a smooth-muscled fighting machine that could give pleasure as well as exact punishment.

Finally he stopped in front of her, his hands clenched into fists, his silver eyes hard with purpose. "You know Daffid better than I. Think you he will kill them?"

"I wish I could give you assurances, but I cannot. What I know of Daffid I cannot like."

"He was your betrothed," Lionheart charged.

"He was my father's choice. I did not object to a verbal betrothal, for I thought Daffid would make a good husband."

He sent her a sharp look. "Do you still feel that way?"

"Nay. Daffid is not the man I thought he

was. There is an ugly streak in him that disgusts me."

" 'Tis as I feared. A man such as Daffid will not hesitate to kill if he is thwarted. He is mad with jealousy. I have what he wants."

"Daffid wants Cragdon."

"Daffid wants *you,* but as long as there is a breath in me he shall not have you."

"Daffid will kill if forced to it," Vanora said softly. "Let me go to him, Lionheart. I am willing to trade myself for Giles and his wife. I am clever. Once they are free, I know I can find a way to return to Cragdon."

"Are you mad? You are a woman. I am perfectly capable of rescuing my vassals. If there is no other way, I shall storm the castle."

" 'Tis what Daffid wants, Lionheart. You cannot win. Daffid's forces outnumber yours. Granted, his men are ill trained, but they have might on their side. Once Daffid lures you to Draymere, your small army will be cut down, leaving him free to claim Cragdon."

"And you," Lionheart added.

Ignoring his last remark, Vanora tried one last time to convince Lionheart of the logic of her plan. " 'Tis suicide, Lionheart, and will not save Giles and Deirdre."

"At least we shall die with honor, Vanora." He held out his hand. "Come to bed."

Realizing there was naught she could say to change Lionheart's mind, Vanora placed her hand in his and allowed him to undress her. He loved her roughly, frantically, their coupling taking her beyond herself, beyond mere pleasure. She knew his ardor was partly due to battle lust, but hers was fueled by the love she bore him.

When it was over, they rested, and then he loved her again, this time with sweet languor and tenderness. Later, after Lionheart had fallen asleep, Vanora shed tears of remorse for what she had to do to save the lives of those she cared about.

Lightly she touched her stomach, where she had reason to believe Lionheart's child grew. She was glad she had not yet told him.

A shiver of fear for that fragile life within her slid down her spine, but she quickly banished it. Deep down she knew she and her babe would return to Lionheart unharmed.

The following morning Lionheart met with his chief knights to formulate a plan of action. Seeking help from neighboring landholders was out of the question. Englishmen were interlopers in Wales, and no help would be forthcoming. Suggestions were offered, but Lionheart knew that naught could change the fact that the lack of men would probably spell their doom. Everyone agreed, however, that an attempt must be made to save Sir Giles and his lady wife.

"Sir Ren, you know Draymere best. Is there a way to gain entrance to the castle without storming the portcullis or scaling the walls?"

His lips pursed in thought, Sir Ren shook his head. "Nay, my lord. Draymere is an old keep and in sad repair. I am aware of no secret entrances or postern gates. 'Tis a well-known fact that all castles have tunnels and secret exits. Only thus could supplies be brought in during siege and couriers escape unseen, but I am not privy to Draymere's secrets."

"Can you give me a rough estimate of the number of men Daffid has at his command?"

"Over one hundred, Lord Lionheart. Every one may not have bows or swords, but staves and cudgels can be deadly weapons when wielded by men who hate Englishmen."

"Why not attempt a night attack?" Sir Brandon suggested. "We could scale the walls, silence the guards and make our way into the keep."

"I was thinking along those same lines," Lionheart mused. "We have less than a sennight to plan our siege. A cloudy, moonless night would be best. Sir Brandon, prepare the men. I want them ready to move at a moment's notice. Pray for at least one cloudy night during the sennight Daffid has allowed us."

That evening, in the privacy of the solar, Lionheart shared his plans with Vanora.

"All your men-at-arms will be needed to storm Daffid's keep, and that will leave Cragdon undefended," Vanora warned.

Lionheart shrugged. "It cannot be helped. I am counting on our surprise attack to confuse Daffid's forces. If all goes as planned, the Welshmen guarding the portcullis will be replaced with my own men, thus preventing anyone from leaving Draymere to attack Cragdon."

Vanora feared that Lionheart's plan would fail and that he would die alongside Giles, Deirdre and the rest of Cragdon's defenders. With Lionheart dead she would be at Daffid's mercy. Nay, she could not let that happen . . . would not let it happen.

She knew what she had to do to prevent needless deaths and was willing to take the risk.

"When will you attack?"

"Soon. The moon is on the wane, and even as we speak clouds are gathering over the mountains. Tomorrow night, or at the very latest, the night after that."

"Let me go with you."

"Nay, 'tis impossible. Stay here and await my return."

"And if you do not return? What then?"

"Then you are free to wed Daffid as your father wanted."

There was an untamed wildness in Vanora that night. She could not get enough of Lionheart. Her mouth and hands tasted him, explored his body until he was mad for her. But she would not be appeased until he had completely exhausted himself and fallen asleep. It was well after Matins when Vanora kissed Lionheart lightly upon the lips, arose without waking him and dressed. After making sure he still slept, she opened his clothes chest, removed his distinctive red tabard with a rampant lion emblazoned in gold on the front, and hid it beneath her mantle.

Silent as a wraith, Vanora left the solar

and descended the stairs to the hall. Her footsteps whispered through the rushes as she made her way to the front door. A sentry stepped out from the shadows.

"Where go you, my lady?"

Vanora started violently, then relaxed when she recognized one of her own knights. "You startled me, Sir Eldin. I could not sleep so I decided to go to the chapel and pray."

" 'Tis late, my lady."

"Aye, but 'tis never too late to pray."

Sir Eldin must have agreed, for he let her pass.

Hugging the shadows, Vanora slipped inside the chapel and went directly to the chest in the anteroom that contained her armor, helm and sword. She quickly shed her gown and with great difficulty donned her chain mail. Then she pulled on Lionheart's red tabard and stuffed her own white and gold tabard inside her mail shirt. She shoved her helm over her head, sheathed her sword and lowered her visor.

Assuming a masculine gait, Vanora strode to the mews wearing Lionheart's colors, saddled a steed from among the horses and mounted with the help of a mounting block.

So far, so good, she thought, but the

hardest was yet to come. While posing as a man-at-arms, she had to convince the sentry to raise the portcullis. Inhaling sharply, Vanora squared her shoulders and boldly reined her horse toward the gate, thanking God that she was tall enough to pass for a man.

"Who goes there?" the sentry challenged as she approached.

Lowering her voice an octave, Vanora said, "Raise the portcullis."

"State your name and your mission."

Thinking quickly, Vanora gave the name of one of her own knights who would not be well known to Lionheart's man. "Sir Morse. Lord Lionheart has sent me forth to spy on Daffid's fortress."

The sentry looked not at all convinced. "Mayhap I should check with Lionheart before I raise the portcullis."

"Think you Lionheart will be pleased to have his sleep disturbed and his orders questioned in the middle of the night?"

Vanora's words must have given the sentry second thoughts, for he turned away and cranked up the portcullis. "Go with God, Sir Morse."

Vanora certainly hoped God would guide her, for she needed all her wits about her if she was to manage Giles's and

Deirdre's release and see to her own rescue before Lionheart placed his life in jeopardy.

The sun was high overhead when Vanora caught sight of Draymere's turrets. Reining her steed to a halt, she shed Lionheart's colors and donned her own white tabard, letting Lionheart's red and gold flutter away in the wind.

Vanora knew the moment she was spotted, for she heard the shouts echoing down from the battlements. Draymere had no outer bailey; the portcullis opened directly into an inner courtyard surrounded by high walls. Vanora halted at the portcullis, raised her visor and stared upward, waiting for Daffid to appear.

"Is that you, Vanora?" Daffid shouted down at her.

Vanora removed her helm, letting her long hair fly free. " 'Tis I, Daffid. Raise the portcullis and let me pass through."

Daffid disappeared, then reappeared a few minutes later in the courtyard. Vanora waited with growing apprehension as he strode toward her. She had much to lose if her plan failed, but a great deal to gain should she succeed.

Vanora's thoughts scattered when Daffid appeared at the portcullis. "Where is your cowardly husband? Is he the kind to hide behind a woman's skirts?"

"I came alone and of my own free will, Daffid. 'Tis what you wanted, is it not? You no longer have need of hostages. I demand that you release Sir Giles and his lady."

Daffid signaled the sentry to raise the portcullis. When it was of sufficient height, Vanora rode through. She winced when she heard the gate clang down behind her. Her fate and that of Sir Giles and his lady were now in her hands.

Daffid frowned. "Is this a trick?"

"No trick, Daffid. I came as you instructed. Those were your terms, were they not?"

"Aye, but I did not think Lionheart would let you go."

"I offer myself in exchange for the hostages."

"Come inside. 'Tis cold out here, and you have come a long way," Daffid hedged. "We will drink a cup of mulled wine while we talk."

A young lad ran up to take her reins. Vanora dismounted and followed Daffid, making note of the large number of men milling about the courtyard. Daffid had not been idle these past weeks.

Draymere was naught compared to Cragdon, Vanora thought as she entered the drafty keep. 'Twas no wonder Daffid was eager to seize her lands and home. The rushes on the floor smelled sour, and dusty webs hung over them like lacy curtains. She allowed Daffid to seat her before the hearth and sipped the wine a servant thrust into her hand.

She watched Daffid closely, trying to decipher his thoughts. Daffid was sly but not overly intelligent. Vanora felt confident that she could outwit him. But first she had to make sure Giles and Deirdre were released and sent on their way.

"Think you Lionheart will come after you?" Daffid asked.

"He will not," Vanora said with a conviction she hoped was true. She prayed Lionheart would have more sense than to storm a castle he could not possibly take. "He cares more for Sir Giles than he does for me. Most likely he will be glad to be rid of me."

"You cannot save him, you know. He will come, and I will be waiting."

"I know not what you mean."

" 'Tis simple, my dear. I have considerable manpower at my disposal. I know how many men Lionheart has, and he cannot possibly hope to defeat me with his paltry force of twenty-odd. In fact, I *want* him to attack Draymere. I welcome an attack. Naught would please me more than to send the bastard to hell. Then both you and Cragdon will be mine."

"England and Wales are at peace, Daffid," Vanora warned. "Killing Lionheart could renew hostilities. Is that what you want?"

" 'Tis bound to happen sooner or later. Think you Edward will leave Wales in peace once he becomes king?"

"Edward is not yet king, Daffid. He is still a young man, and his father is in good health. Many things could happen before Edward ascends to the throne. Attacking an English fortress will only hasten a war that could be years off."

"Cragdon is not an English fortress. It should be mine, and I intend to make it so."

"Cragdon belongs to Lionheart by right of marriage."

"Bah, the marriage is illegal. I had prior claim." The smile he gave her was not reassuring. "But you are here now, and soon Lionheart will come for you. When he does, I will be waiting."

Vanora bit her lip to keep from telling

Daffid what she thought of him. "I am here. I met your terms. Lionheart will not come. If you account yourself a man of honor, you will release the hostages."

Daffid puffed out his chest. "No one questions my honor."

"Then prove it. Release Sir Giles and his lady."

"You try me sorely, Vanora. When we are wed, you will show me respect. Beating down your spirit will give me great pleasure."

He summoned a guardsman with a wave of his hand and ordered him to fetch the hostages. Vanora waited with growing apprehension for them to appear. Had they been mistreated? She hoped not, for otherwise Lionheart would seek revenge.

The guardsman returned, prodding Sir Giles along with the point of his sword. Blond, petite and deathly pale, Lady Deirdre clung to Giles, obviously frightened out of her wits. Vanora's heart went out to the young girl. Newly married and traveling in a strange land, her welcome had not been an auspicious one.

Vanora leapt to her feet. "Sir Giles! Are you and your lady unharmed?"

Giles came to an abrupt halt. "Lady Vanora? Is that you? Whatever are you doing dressed like that?"

" 'Tis of no account, Sir Giles. Introduce me to your wife before you leave."

Giles looked more than a little confused. "Forgive me, my lady. I am pleased to present to you my wife, Deirdre. Deirdre, greet Lady Vanora, Lord Lionheart's lady."

Sobbing, Deirdre grasped Vanora's hand and clung to it. "How can I ever thank you, my lady? I so feared we would not reach Cragdon alive."

Giles's eyes narrowed. "Where is Lionheart?"

"At Cragdon."

"I do not understand. What are you doing here without him? Are you certain we are free to go?" He stared at her chain mail and sword and frowned, as if suddenly aware of where he had seen that particular white tabard before.

"Nay, it cannot be! Tell me you are not the White Knight."

" 'Tis true, Sir Giles."

"How is that possible? Does Lionheart know?"

Daffid laughed, apparently enjoying Sir Giles's shock.

" 'Tis a long story. One I am sure Lionheart will tell you upon your return to Cragdon." She turned to Daffid. "Let them go now."

He pulled her aside. "In a moment. I would have a private word with you first."

"What is it now?" Vanora hissed.

"I want you to give Sir Giles a message to carry to Lionheart."

A chill ran down Vanora's spine. "What message?"

"Tell him to explain to Lionheart that you came to me because I am the man you want. Make your explanation creditable. Lionheart must believe that you would rather become my leman than remain his wife. Naught will bring him here faster than the knowledge that another man is bedding his wife."

"You want me to lead Lionheart to his death?"

"Aye. Lionheart's death is what I have always wanted."

"I cannot."

"I will slay the knight and his lady where they stand if you refuse."

Vanora closed her eyes and asked for God's help. What terrible thing had she wrought? 'Twas bad enough that she'd left without Lionheart's knowledge, but now she must also deny her love for him. She had not counted on that.

"If that message is delivered, Lionheart will never come for me. He will hate me and leave me to my fate."

Daffid laughed. "If you think that, you underestimate Lionheart's pride. I am a man. I saw the way Lionheart looks at you."

" 'Tis you who underestimates Lionheart's pride."

"Mayhap, but I will risk it. After you give Sir Giles the message, he and his lady may leave. I will be listening, so make very certain you tell Giles exactly what I have instructed you to say."

Vanora prayed that Lionheart would be so disgusted with her once her message was delivered, he would forget about storming Draymere. Once Giles and his wife were free, Lionheart would have no reason to attack. Vanora would have accomplished what she had set out to do without bloodshed.

Daffid gave her a shove toward Giles. She stiffened her shoulders and composed words of betrayal in her mind.

"My lady, are you all right?" Giles asked. "Are we free to leave now?"

"You and Deirdre may go," Vanora said, "but I am staying with Daffid."

Giles shook his head. "Nay. If you cannot leave, then neither shall we."

"I do not wish to return to Cragdon,"

Vanora said, stumbling over the lie. "Will you carry a message to Lionheart?"

"Of course, my lady," Giles said, "though I understand naught of this. Is Daffid forcing you to remain against your will?"

"I thought I made myself clear, Sir Giles. I was forced to wed Lionheart, but my heart has always been with my betrothed. 'Tis Daffid I want. Tell Lionheart to heed well my words, for I am not in need of rescue."

"If that is your wish, my lady." Giles's voice dripped with contempt. "I shall deliver your message word for word."

"Guard!" Daffid shouted. "My guests are free to go. Return their horses to them and escort them from my lands."

Her throat clogged with tears, Vanora watched them leave, and with them her future with Lionheart. She had just given Lionheart another reason to distrust her.

Chapter Eighteen

"Where is she!"

Lionheart's roar shot up through the rafters and vibrated through the hall. He had awakened that morning to find Vanora gone. At first he had thought naught about it, but as the day progressed without a sign of Vanora, he knew with certainty what she had done.

Hoping he was wrong, he had dispatched a man to the village and instigated a thorough search of the keep and outbuildings. His anger mounted when he realized that only one explanation was possible. Vanora had deliberately disobeyed him and gone to Daffid. He felt it in his bones, knew it with every breath he took. Damn her to perdition!

"Who was the sentry last night?"

" 'Twas I, Lord Lionheart," Sir Eldin said, stepping forward.

"Did my wife leave the hall while you were on duty?"

"Aye, my lord. She said she could not sleep and was going to the chapel to pray.

I saw no reason to stop her."

Lionheart's gaze searched for and found Father Caddoc. "What do you know of this, priest?"

"Naught, my lord. Vanora did not confide in me."

"The secret door behind the altar . . ."

". . . is still sealed, my lord, just as you ordered."

"Where is Mair?"

"Here, my lord," Mair said, shuffling toward him, head bowed, shoulders slumped.

"Did your mistress confide in you? Do you know where she went?"

Clearly distraught, Mair wiped away a tear and shook her head.

Lionheart dismissed her with a glance, and the woman shrank away, her shoulders quaking.

"Who was on duty in the gatehouse last night?"

"That would be me, my lord," Sir Osgood said.

Lionheart speared the man with a piercing look and asked, "Did you raise the portcullis for my wife last night?"

"Nay, Lord Lionheart. I raised the portcullis but once the entire night, and that was for Sir Morse."

Sir Morse pushed through the crowd.

"Nay! I did not leave the keep last night."

Rage swept through Lionheart. Of course Sir Morse had not left the keep. 'Twas his wife who'd left under the guise of Sir Morse.

"I wish to speak in private to Father Caddoc," Lionheart said. "The rest of you are dismissed. Arm yourselves and be ready to ride within the hour."

Lionheart waited until the hall cleared before addressing the priest.

"Where does Vanora keep her armor?"

"In a small anteroom at the rear of the church. Think you she left Cragdon disguised as Sir Morse?"

" 'Tis exactly what I think," Lionheart growled. "Come, we will go to the chapel together and see for ourselves what folly my wife has wrought."

The chest in the anteroom yielded naught but dusty robes. Too angry to speak, Lionheart slammed the lid down and stormed off. Vanora had gone to Daffid. What in God's holy name did she expect to accomplish? Her reckless act had only handed Daffid another hostage. Lionheart had no recourse now but to storm the fortress and pray that the prisoners survived.

Squinting up at the sun, Lionheart realized there was not a moment to lose. If his forces were to make a surprise night attack, they would have to leave immediately. Foolish, foolish Vanora. Her sacrifice on his behalf had done naught but endanger her own life.

Lionheart was striding across the inner courtyard when a warning blast from the battlements stopped him in his tracks.

"Two riders are approaching!" a sentry called out.

Lionheart climbed the outside stairs to the parapet and, shading his eyes against the glare of the sun, spotted the riders. They were approaching slowly, heads bowed.

"One of them is a woman," someone shouted.

"Raise the portcullis!" Lionheart ordered. Racing down the stairs, he arrived at the inner gate as the new arrivals passed through.

He recognized Sir Giles but not the lady with him.

Lionheart grasped Deirdre's reins and swung her from the saddle. But for Lionheart's support, her legs would have crumpled beneath her.

Giles dismounted and swept Deirdre into his arms. "My lady is exhausted," he said. "She has been through a harrowing experience."

"Take her up to your chamber," Lionheart instructed. There was a great deal he wanted to learn from Giles, but his wife's health came first. "I will send Mair to attend her and await you in the solar."

"Aye, Lionheart. I will not be long."

Lionheart sent for Mair and directed her to Giles's chamber. Then he climbed up to the solar, prowling restlessly. His relief was palpable when Giles presented himself a short time later.

"How fares your lady?"

"Mair gave her something to soothe her nerves and put her to sleep. Deirdre has a delicate constitution, and I feared she would fall apart before we reached Cragdon."

"Tell me what happened."

"Peter probably told you most of it. We were attacked upon the road and taken to Draymere. Peter was released to carry Daffid's message to you."

The question burning on the tip of Lionheart's tongue came tumbling forth. "Where is Vanora? Is she with Daffid?"

Giles's expression grew wary. "Aye. Did you send her?"

"Nay, I did not. She crept from our bed in the middle of the night and rode forth from Cragdon garbed as a knight. Sir Osgood raised the portcullis, but I blame him not, for she tricked him."

Giles hesitated a moment, then said, "She was wearing chain mail and a white tabard trimmed in gold."

"Aye. I have known that my wife was the White Knight for some time. When I confronted her, she promised she would never don armor and ride as the knight again. Through some misguided notion, she thought she could save you and Deirdre without my help."

"She said . . ." Giles's words fell off and his gaze slid away from Lionheart's.

"What is it, Giles? Did Daffid do my wife harm? Did she give you a message to carry to me?"

"I was given a message to deliver, but I hesitate to do so. I hate to be the bearer of unwelcome news."

"Spare not my feelings, Giles. I would know the truth."

He sent Lionheart a pitying look. "I spoke with Vanora before leaving Draymere."

Lionheart's shoulders tensed. "Go on."

"She said to tell you she does not need rescuing, for her heart belongs to Daffid."

A nerve ticked along Lionheart's jaw. "Is that all?"

"I think so . . . except . . ."

"What is it?"

"She said she was forced into a marriage she did not want and wished to remain with Daffid."

It was a lie. It had to be a lie. But deep in his heart Lionheart knew Vanora could not love him. No one had ever loved him, not his mother, not his father, and not Vanora. He had been a fool to believe her lies.

"Leave me. See to your wife's comfort and seek your own rest. I will meet Deirdre tomorrow, when she is recovered from her ordeal."

"I pray you are not planning to storm Draymere," Giles said. " 'Tis what Daffid wants, you know. He has gathered a small army within Draymere's walls. They will cut our forces down without mercy."

"My course of action is yet unclear."

"Then I will leave, for I can see you wish to be alone."

Giles took his leave and strode toward the door, hesitating as he reached for the latch. "Lionheart, about Vanora —"

Lionheart shook his head. "Nay, Giles, I do not wish to discuss my wife."

"I understand," Giles said.

Once Giles had left, Lionheart dropped down upon a bench and buried his head in his hands. *What have you done, Vanora?* He had thought she'd gone to Daffid to negotiate Giles's and Deirdre's release. But after listening to Giles, he realized just how wrong he had been. The pain of betrayal made him realize what a dunce he had been to believe that Vanora cared for him. Thank God he had not declared his growing emotional attachment to her. He would have felt twice a fool for admitting his feelings to a woman who cared naught for him.

He rose and crossed the room to the bed. The warm, womanly scent of her skin and her hair still clung to the bedding. In his mind he pictured her lying there, sprawled in wanton abandon while he feasted on the creamy curves of her body. She was a woman to drive a man to distraction, and he had allowed himself to be beguiled by her feminine wiles. He recognized within himself the inability to withstand the power she held over him, but no longer, he silently vowed.

Wanting a woman who did not want him was a waste of time and energy. Wife or no, he washed his hands of her.

What if you are wrong? an inner voice asked. What if Vanora had deliberately lied about her feelings to save Giles and

Deirdre? What if Daffid had forced her to say those hateful things?

Not likely, Lionheart's demon replied.

So what in the hell was he going to do? Should he lead his men into a battle they could not win to rescue a woman who by her own words neither needed nor wanted rescuing?

Lionheart was still undecided when he sought out Sir Brandon a short time later and told him that, although the men were to remain on alert, they would stay within the keep this night. He needed time to mull over Vanora's words.

In a sparsely furnished chamber that overlooked the courtyard, Vanora slept poorly that night. She had awakened early and had just pulled on her chausses when a knock sounded on the door. It opened scant seconds later, admitting a swaggering Daffid carrying a drab garment over his arm.

"Daffid, I am not dressed!" Vanora said, diving for a coverlet to wrap around her bare torso.

"I am your betrothed. There is no shame between us."

"I still have a husband," Vanora reminded him.

Daffid gave her a smug smile. "Not for long. Preparations are being made for Lionheart's expected attack even as we speak."

Vanora's chin angled upward. "He will not come."

"I say he will."

He walked toward her, a stalking beast with a lustful gleam in his eyes. "In the meantime, there is no reason why we cannot satisfy our desire for one another."

Vanora recoiled. "There is every reason in the world. First, I do not desire you, and second, I am still wed. You cannot touch me without fear of going straight to hell when you die."

He laughed. "I do not fear hell, and you are not strong enough to keep me from taking what I want." He forced her backward against the bed with the strength of his stocky body.

Vanora bared her teeth. "Touch me before I am willing and I swear you will regret it the rest of your life. You know I am not a fragile damsel, and I am more than capable of defending myself. You have seen my strength, Daffid. You know I have a strong sword arm. Take me against my will and I swear I will sever your manhood from your body."

The fierceness of her words and the determination behind them brought Daffid up short. "I do not fear you, Vanora."

Vanora stifled a smile. The indecision in his voice belied his words. "You should fear me. Respect my position as a married woman and we shall get along for as long as I choose to remain at Draymere."

" 'Tis not your decision to make," Daffid responded. "You will remain here until I slay Lionheart. Once he is dead, we will wed and live out our days at Cragdon. I can wait. The reward will be all the sweeter when you come to me willingly."

"Lionheart will not come, and Cragdon is impenetrable."

"There is still the secret entrance."

"It has been permanently sealed."

Daffid shrugged. "No matter. If Lionheart plays the coward and does not come, we will surround the keep and wait until starvation drives him out. Once he leaves Cragdon, he is a dead man."

Vanora turned her back on him, unable to deny his words. The sheer number of men at Daffid's command would most assuredly prevail if Lionheart left Cragdon and attempted an attack upon Draymere.

"Here," Daffid said, tossing the garment he had been carrying onto the bed. "Put this on. Your armor offends me. I will not have you wearing it at Draymere."

Vanora turned her head and stared at the rough garment. "I prefer my armor."

"A servant's garment was all I could find. 'Twill have to do until you have access to your own clothing. It will not be long, Vanora, this I vow. Come down to the hall when you are dressed and we will break our fast together."

"I would attend Mass first."

"There has been no priest at Draymere since my father's death many years ago. My estate is poor compared to the size and wealth of your lands. There is no village and but a few villeins who dwell within the keep. The nearest priest is Father Caddoc, and he is at Cragdon, a half-day's journey away."

"Nevertheless, I shall go to the chapel to pray before I break my fast," Vanora persisted.

Daffid frowned. "Very well, but do not linger overlong."

Vanora found the chapel in sad disrepair, like all of Draymere. Daffid was a careless landholder. She remembered coming to Draymere with her father when she was a child and playing in the well-tended garden behind the keep while her father and Daffid's talked. Daffid was rarely home, for he had been fostered during those years. But after Daffid's father died, the son had allowed the keep to fall into ruin.

Vanora knelt before the altar, recalling those days she had wandered Draymere's grounds with a child's freedom and innocence. She had spent many pleasurable hours exploring the small keep. She smiled, recalling how she pretended to be a damsel in distress waiting to be rescued by a brave knight who would risk all for her. Funny, she reflected, but the knight never had Daffid's face.

One day she had discovered a small postern gate overgrown with weeds and had tried to open it, but her child's strength would not budge it.

Vanora went still. *There was a postern gate!* She had forgotten about it. That childhood memory had come unbidden when she had begun to reminisce. Since Draymere had never been under siege, Daffid would have had no reason to use the gate in recent years, and even less reason to believe she knew about it. The knowledge would bear exploring, Vanora decided. After offering a prayer of thanks, she left the chapel and joined Daffid in the hall.

* * *

Lionheart felt the onerous weight of indecision bearing down on him. There was still a raw place in his heart that did not want to believe Vanora had betrayed him with Daffid. Three days had passed since Giles and Deirdre had returned to Cragdon. His temperament during those days was such that no one dared to approach him about his plans. He was like a beast with a thorn in its paw.

After the meal that evening, Father Caddoc found the courage to approach Lionheart. "My lord Lionheart, may we speak in private?"

"I am in no mood for conversation," Lionheart growled. "Can it not wait?"

"Nay, my son, it cannot."

Lionheart hissed out an impatient sigh. "Very well, Father, what is on your mind?"

"I am worried about Vanora, my lord. I do not believe she stayed with Daffid willingly."

"You have no proof of that," Lionheart said gruffly. "My wife's message was quite clear. She does not want rescuing. Why should I risk the lives of my men for a woman who cares naught for me?"

"Something is amiss," Father Caddoc warned. " 'Tis you Vanora loves."

Lionheart gave a snort of disbelief. "She has a damn strange way of showing it."

"I do not blame you for your reluctance to pit your twenty-odd men against a hundred or more."

"Think you I would hesitate if I thought Vanora wanted rescuing? I have no proof that Daffid forced her to deny our marriage, to deny us."

"Let me go to Draymere," Father Caddoc said. "I will learn the truth and bring it back to you."

"Nay, I will not allow it. I am responsible for your life and will not let you risk it."

"What risk, my lord? I am a frail old man who but wishes to visit the woman who is like a daughter to me. I shall go alone, unarmed and in peace. Daffid will not refuse me entrance, nor will he keep me from leaving."

"What do you hope to gain?"

"The truth, my lord. Mayhap I will find a way to resolve this intolerable situation."

"That would take a miracle, Father."

The priest raised his eyes heavenward. "Did you not know? God is a miracle worker, my son."

Lionheart knew that God worked in mysterious ways but he was positive it would take more than a miracle to turn him into a man that someone could love.

"What say you, my lord?" the priest prodded. "Will you order your sentries to stop me if I attempt to leave?"

"Do as you please, priest. I do not own you. You are free to come and go as you like."

Lionheart stood on the parapet beside Giles shortly after the hour of Prime the following morning as Father Caddoc rode forth from Cragdon mounted on a mule.

"Where does the priest go?" Giles asked.

"To Draymere. He has some foolish notion that Vanora is being held against her will." He turned away. "How is Deirdre? I have had little chance to talk with her. Does she miss England?"

"Deirdre is young enough to miss her family, but I hope to give her a family of her own one day."

"Methinks you care a great deal for your little bride," Lionheart teased.

"Deirdre is sweet and biddable, Lionheart, and she claims to love me. How can I not love her in return?"

"How indeed?" Lionheart said, turning his head to hide his bitterness, for he knew love did not exist.

"I know you have been unwilling to discuss Vanora with anyone, but it does not help to keep your feelings within yourself. I believe you care for Vanora more than you are willing to admit and her rejection has caused you pain."

"Vanora's rejection is but another in a long line of rejections I have known over the years," Lionheart said.

"Nay, this is different, more hurtful. You love her. Deny it not, Lionheart, for I am a man in love myself and can see how highly you value your wife."

"Have you no duties, Giles?" Lionheart bit out.

Giles stared at Lionheart a moment, then shrugged and strode away. Lionheart returned his attention to the priest, who was now but a small dot in the distance.

"Go with God," Lionheart whispered. His words were snatched away and carried off by the wind.

'Twas near dusk when Father Caddoc, bowed with fatigue and shivering from cold, reached Draymere. He gave his name when challenged by the sentry and waited in silent prayerfulness to be admitted or turned away.

'Twas Daffid himself who appeared at

the portcullis a few minutes later. "What do you here, Father?"

"I come in peace, my son. It occurred to me that Draymere has no priest, and that some of your men might be in need of confessing and receiving absolution."

"If you have come to take Vanora back to Cragdon, you are not welcome here. Furthermore, Vanora has no wish to return."

"I am an old man, Daffid. You have naught to fear from me. Open the portcullis. I am cold and in need of rest and sustenance. Aftcr I am rested, I will hear confessions. In the morning I will say Mass and take my leave."

"You are right, Father," Daffid confirmed. "I have naught to fear from you. Very well, you may enter and shrive those who feel in need of it."

Vanora was in the garden behind the keep and had no idea the priest had arrived. She had waited until dusk, when shadows and dim light would prevent discovery, to search for the postern gate she remembered from her childhood. She had managed to sneak out twice to explore but had failed to find the gate. The walls were overgrown with weeds and ivy, making the search extremely difficult. There was always the possibility, of course, that her childhood memories had failed her, that imagination had become reality in her mind.

"Vanora, where are you?"

Vanora started violently as Daffid's voice rolled through the keep like a winter storm. Lifting her skirts, she hurried inside. He met her at the door.

"What were you doing out there?"

"I enjoy walking in the garden. It soothes my soul."

"There is naught in the garden but weeds and brambles. Hardly a soothing combination. Come with me, I have a surprise for you."

A frisson of apprehension slid down Vanora's spine. She could well imagine the kind of surprise Daffid was capable of providing. Girding herself for the worst, Vanora followed him to the hall. Just inside the door, she stopped short, certain her eyes were deceiving her. But when she saw Father Caddoc smiling at her, she knew she was not imagining him. He was here, really here.

"Father Caddoc," she cried, rushing forth to greet him.

Though weary in body, the priest's sharp gaze searched her face. "You are well, child?"

"Of course she is well," Daffid answered. "Why would I harm my intended bride?"

"You are mistaken, Daffid. Vanora is already wed. I performed the ceremony myself."

"I have prior claim," Daffid said. "Her marriage is invalid. Vanora was forced to wed Lionheart."

"No papers were signed between you, and Vanora agreed to the marriage to Lionheart."

"Father!" Vanora interrupted, fearing that Daffid would harm him if he did not hold his tongue. Hoping to distract the priest, she sat down beside him and asked, "How long can you stay?"

"He is leaving after morning Mass," Daffid said. "He said he came to hear confessions, but methinks he lies. Think you I am stupid? Father Caddoc wanted to see for himself that you have not been harmed. 'Tis obvious Lionheart sent him. Tell the good priest you are well, and that you wish to remain with me, so he can carry your words back to Lionheart."

"Is that true, child?" Father Caddoc asked. "I want to hear in your own words that you are not being mistreated or held against your will."

Daffid leaned over and hissed into

Vanora's ear, "Tell him you want to be with me, else the priest is a dead man."

Father Caddoc, who was hard of hearing, pulled Vanora's sleeve and asked, "What did Daffid say?"

"Naught that matters, Father. To answer your question, I wish to remain with Daffid. I never wanted to wed Lionheart."

"I thought you and Lionheart had come to an understanding, that you were content with your marriage."

"Finish your meal, Father," Daffid growled. " 'Tis late, and there are many men in need of confessing."

Vanora searched frantically for a way to speak privately with the priest.

"Will you hear my confession before you leave, Father?"

"Aye, 'tis why I am here."

"Nay, Vanora, 'tis not necessary," Daffid said. "You have naught to confess. You may return to your chamber after you have eaten."

Father Caddoc started to protest, but Vanora's eyes flashed a message that the priest understood and heeded, albeit reluctantly. Vanora finished her meal in silence and excused herself. But instead of returning to her chamber, she slipped through a rear door into the garden. Scrambling among the ivy and weeds, she ran her hands along the wall, looking for the opening she remembered from her childhood. Shivering in the bone-chilling cold, she despaired when her hands encountered naught but rough stone and thorns. A rustling behind her caught her attention, and she spun around.

"Looking for something?"

Daffid!

"I . . . I was just enjoying the fresh air," Vanora stammered.

"I know what you are up to, Vanora."

"You do?"

"Aye. My sentries have kept an eye on you and reported your comings and goings. Since there is naught in the garden but thorns and weeds, I realized you had remembered the postern gate and were looking for it."

"You made no move to stop me," Vanora charged. Caution fled when Daffid appeared amused instead of angry. "Surely you must know I have no intention of staying with you."

"I figured that out long ago, but it matters not. I want Lionheart dead, and you shall help me accomplish his death. As for the gate you are looking for, it no longer exists. I had it removed and the wall repaired after Father's death."

"Why?"

"It was not needed. There is another way out of the keep. No one but myself knows about it because Draymere has never been under siege."

"I will find it," Vanora declared.

"You will not. Lionheart will be dead long before you find it."

"He will not come," Vanora retorted.

Daffid glared at her through the encroaching darkness. "I have changed my mind about waiting until Lionheart is dead to bed you."

Vanora opened her mouth to protest, but he stopped her words with a forceful kiss that made her want to vomit. She bit down hard on his tongue. He cursed and lashed out at her with the back of his hand. Her head snapped back beneath the force of his blow, and stars whirled in her head. Pushing the pain aside, she spat out the taste of him and wiped her mouth with the back of her hand. "I despise you!"

"It matters not. I will still have you. I wanted to be gentle with you, but it seems you would have it otherwise."

She turned to run, but he snagged her around the waist and dragged her into the keep.

"Father Caddoc will stop you!" Vanora cried.

"He is hearing confessions in the chapel. Stop struggling. You may be strong, but I am stronger. Once I plant my child in you, you will change your mind."

"Your plan is doomed," Vanora charged. "I am already carrying Lionheart's child."

Vanora prayed her calculations were correct, that missing her last woman's time meant Lionheart's seed was growing inside her. She had told no one, for she wanted to be certain before informing Lionheart. She had no idea how Daffid would react, or if the news would even make a difference in what he intended. The words had come unbidden from her mouth.

Daffid's response was immediate and violent. He shoved her to the floor and stood over her, rage contorting his face.

"Bitch! Whore! You disgust me. Your babe will not live to see the light of day. I will kill it ere it gushes forth from your body."

Vanora tried not to cringe but could not help it. The cruel, sadistic smile stretching his lips frightened her. She would not have thought Daffid capable of slaying an innocent child.

* * *

Vanora was on hand when Father Caddoc left the following morning.

"Godspeed, Father," Daffid said. "Convey to Lionheart my felicitations and tell him that if he does not leave Cragdon two days hence, I shall kill Vanora."

The priest blanched. "You cannot mean that, Daffid!"

"Every word," Daffid replied. "Tell Lionheart I will bring Vanora to Cragdon. When he sees us, he and his men are to ride forth, unarmed and wearing no armor. Only then will I release Vanora into his care and allow him and his men to leave in peace."

"Nay! Do not believe him," Vanora cried. "Daffid will kill Lionheart. Tell him not to leave Cragdon no matter what Daffid promises."

Daffid's blow sent Vanora flying. Father Caddoc started to dismount and go to her aid, but Daffid applied the flat of his sword to the mule's rump, sending the priest on his way.

"Father," Daffid called after him. "Be sure to tell Lionheart to do as I say if he wishes the child that Vanora carries to see the light of day."

Chapter Nineteen

His legs braced against the wind-driven snow, Lionheart pulled his mantle close about him and stared out over the battlements with growing apprehension. He had been standing on the parapet since early this morn, waiting for the priest, his imagination running rampant. The suspense of not knowing what was taking place at Draymere was unnerving. Would Father Caddoc become another hostage? Would Vanora consent to return to Cragdon with the priest? Would Daffid let her?

Lionheart blinked once, then again as a small figure emerged through the swirling snow. He heard the sentry's warning blast, his heart sinking when he saw that Father Caddoc had returned alone.

Lionheart descended the outside staircase, arriving in the courtyard as priest and mule plodded through the gate. Father Caddoc dismounted with difficulty, his face etched with fatigue and his shoulders bowed beneath the weight of his age. Then the priest raised his head, giving

Lionheart a glimpse of hell in his eyes.

"Come inside the keep to warm and refresh yourself," Lionheart said. Though he was eager to have his questions answered, he could not in good conscience do so until the priest was made comfortable.

"Nay, Lord Lionheart, I must go to the chapel and pray. I can rest and eat after I have asked God for help in your time of need. Come pray with me, my son."

Lionheart's breath seized. Something dreadful had happened at Draymere. The chapel was as cold as the chill in his heart, and a deep foreboding stirred deep within him. Shivering, he fell on his knees beside the priest.

The profound silence was eerie; the soft, whispering sounds of the priest's prayers barely stirred the air. Though he did not know what Father Caddoc was praying for, Lionheart added his own silent petitions to those of the priest.

Just when Lionheart thought he would go insane with waiting, Father Caddoc sighed and rose on creaking joints.

"Now I am ready to warm myself by your fire and appease my appetite."

Lionheart accompanied the priest into the keep and settled him in a chair before the hearth. Though the tables were being set for the evening meal, Lionheart ordered mulled wine and food to be brought immediately. Father Caddoc took a healthy swallow of wine and regarded Lionheart with a sadness that made his heart plummet.

He knew without being told that the news from Draymere was the worst possible. His knees suddenly went weak, and he dropped onto a bench.

"Speak freely, Father. What did you learn at Draymere? Did Vanora refuse to return home with you?"

"Vanora was not given the choice. She is Daffid's unwilling prisoner."

"Nay, Father, you misunderstand the situation," Lionheart argued. He knew Vanora had gone to Draymere willingly; according to Giles, she had placed herself into Daffid's keeping.

"You understand naught," Father Caddoc said. "Although Vanora went to Draymere willingly, she had no intention of remaining."

Lionheart gave a snort of derision. "Did she tell you this?"

"She was not allowed to speak with me in private, not even to confess."

"Then how can you possibly know what is in Vanora's mind?"

"I baptized her. I watched her grow and guided her through childhood to become the kind of woman she is today. Her mind is an open book to me. She expressed through silent communication what she could not say in words. Unfortunately, she had misjudged the extent of Daffid's greed. She thought she could convince Daffid to release Sir Giles and his lady without risking her own freedom. She was wrong."

"Vanora's parting words to Giles indicated otherwise. Do you expect me to believe that Vanora's motive for surrendering herself to Daffid was purely selfless? 'Tis too much to ask, Father."

"Vanora loves you, Lionheart. And I believe you love her. She did not expect to love an Englishman, nor did she intend for this matter with Daffid to get out of hand."

A chill of foreboding snaked down Lionheart's spine. "What are you keeping from me, Father?"

"I bear a message from Daffid. In two days hence he intends to bring Vanora to Cragdon. He said he would kill her before your eyes if you and your men do not ride forth from Cragdon when he arrives. You are to carry no arms, nor wear armor."

"He wants me to abandon Cragdon?"

"Aye. Once you and your men have ridden through the portcullis, he will release Vanora and let you leave in peace."

"And you believe him?"

The priest shrugged. "Daffid has turned from God. I do not trust his word."

"Was it also Vanora's wish that I leave Cragdon?"

"Nay. Vanora was unhappy with Daffid's demands. Her parting words were a warning to you. She said you should not leave Cragdon, that if you obey Daffid, you and your men will be slain."

"She told you this at the risk of her own life?" Lionheart asked in a voice laden with disbelief.

"Aye. She cares naught for Daffid."

"I cannot do as she wishes, Father. Daffid may kill her if I fail to comply with his wishes. I wonder," he mused thoughtfully, "if Daffid realizes he is breaking a peace treaty his own prince has wrought. Mayhap he is bluffing."

The priest's guileless gaze probed deep into Lionheart's soul. "There is more."

"Go on."

"Daffid knows Vanora is carrying your child. He said the babe will never see the light of day if you fail to comply with his wishes."

Lionheart leapt to his feet. "What! That cannot be true."

" 'Tis not impossible, is it?"

Lionheart could not deny it. He and Vanora had lain together often enough to make a babe. Fear for Vanora and the child she carried was so great, he began to tremble. Then he swore. Once she was returned safely to him, he would beat her for placing two lives in danger . . . or make endless love to her.

"Aye, Father, 'tis entirely possible. Where is Mair? Mayhap Vanora confided in her."

"I am here, Lord Lionheart," Mair said, appearing from behind him. Her face was pale and drawn, and it was obvious from her swift arrival that she had been hovering nearby.

"Where is Vanora, my lord? I am frantic with worry. Why did she not return home with Father Caddoc?"

"I will tell you everything I know, but I would ask a question of you first."

Mair gave him a wary look. "What is it you wish to know?"

"Is Vanora expecting my child? Has she spoken to you about it?"

Mair blanched. "Vanora did not confide in me, but I have reason to believe it is so. She has not had her woman's time since the day she was wed. 'Tis one of the reasons I am so worried about her."

Lionheart's lips thinned. If Mair suspected that Vanora carried his babe, then it must be true. Without mincing words, he told Mair everything Father Caddoc had said.

The news that Daffid intended to kill Vanora if Lionheart did not leave Cragdon sent Mair staggering onto a bench. "Say it is not so," Mair begged. "I cannot believe it of Daffid. Vanora's father would never have arranged the marriage if he were aware of Daffid's cruel nature."

"Think you Daffid is bluffing?" Lionheart asked in a voice taut with fear.

"Greed and frustration with one's lot can turn men against God," Father Caddoc interjected. "When Daffid lost his claim to Cragdon, he abandoned his values and repudiated his honor. In his present frame of mind, I believe him capable of . . . anything."

Mair burst into tears. "My lambie is lost," she wailed.

"I need to think," Lionheart said. Spinning on his heel, he strode off.

He could not think, much less carry on a conversation in his present state. His hands clenched at his sides in frustrated fury. He wanted to kill, and would have if Daffid were within his grasp. Needing to be alone, he climbed the winding staircase to the battlements and walked to the edge.

Avoiding contact with the sentries, he looked out over the frozen ground, the wind whipping his cloak and hair, feeling neither the biting cold nor the snow that stung his face. Vanora was carrying his child, and both would likely die if he did not abandon Cragdon to Daffid. He had sworn to defend Cragdon and hold it for England, and Lionheart's word was his honor. But honor was naught if it meant sacrificing his wife and unborn child for a pile of stone.

Did Daffid actually intend to let him and Vanora leave in peace? Lionheart wondered. He could not imagine such a thing. Daffid intended for him to die. But Lionheart was not the obliging kind. He would find a way to foil Daffid. His own life mattered not; 'twas Vanora and the babe she carried that must live.

Clearly, he had to abandon Cragdon as Daffid had directed. Lionheart left the parapet in a grim mood. His men deserved to know what they would face when they rode forth from Cragdon.

* * *

"You have chosen the only course open to you," Giles said after listening to Lionheart's explanation. "If not for Lady Vanora, Deirdre and I would still be Daffid's hostages. As long as we are alive, we have a fighting chance to escape Daffid's plans for us."

"I agree," Sir Brandon approved. "Any one of your men would ride to his death before abandoning you, Lionheart."

Lionheart returned his regard to Giles. "Not you, Giles. You and Deirdre must leave and return to England immediately."

Giles gave him a startled look. "Nay. Do not ask it of me, Lionheart."

"For Deirdre's sake, you will obey me. Go and inform your bride."

"I like it not," Giles said, stomping off.

Lionheart turned to Sir Ren. "You and your men may remain safely within the keep if you so choose. Daffid will spare your lives because you are his countrymen."

Sir Ren looked offended. "We swore fealty to you and Lady Vanora, my lord, and will honor our pledge. If you ride into the face of danger, so shall we."

Such loyalty humbled Lionheart. He expected as much from Englishmen, but the

Welshmen had a choice. That they remained loyal to him was a testimonial to their high regard for Vanora.

"So be it. Daffid wants us to abandon Cragdon when he arrives or he will kill Vanora. We are to ride forth without armor or weapons. But I have a plan that will not leave us defenseless. Listen carefully while I explain."

Vanora had slept very little after Father Caddoc left Draymere. She tried to picture Lionheart's reaction when he learned she was carrying his child but gave up after imagining the extent of his anger. She prayed his fury would keep him from leaving Cragdon and riding to his death, for she knew Daffid did not intend for him to live. And if Lionheart died, so would their child. Daffid would make sure of that.

After Father Caddoc's departure, Daffid had locked her in her chamber. She had languished there until she was released just prior to their departure for Cragdon. She had wanted to don her armor, but Daffid had forbidden it. Instead, she was given a drab woolen cloak to cover her coarse brown tunic, escorted to the courtyard and hoisted upon her horse.

Surrounded by members of Daffid's ragtag army, Vanora had no choice but to follow as they rode from Draymere. She was so closely watched, she could not have escaped if she had wanted to. Snow dusted her cloak with white, and her feet felt like two chunks of ice, but the cold was the least of her worries. She prayed desperately for a miracle.

Despite her fervent prayers, Vanora knew that Lionheart would do exactly as Daffid ordered . . . and lose his life in the bargain. She racked her brain for a solution, anything that would save Lionheart and his men, but could think of naught. So she went back to praying for a miracle.

An eerie silence hung over Cragdon's snow-shrouded walls as Daffid's army approached the fortress. Naught was stirring but a chill wind that blew swirls of snow up from the ground and engulfed them in a cloud of white. Vanora could barely make out the shapes of the castle's towers as she peered through the churning storm.

Daffid signaled for a halt just beyond the reach of archers stationed on the battlements and their deadly arrows. Vanora knew Daffid was taking no chances, but his caution proved unnecessary. With growing horror she saw Lionheart lead his small cadre of men through the raised portcullis. They wore no armor and carried no weapons.

"Nay!" she cried, urging her horse through the ranks to Daffid's side. She would have ridden to Lionheart, but Daffid jerked the reins from her hands as she rode past and stopped her.

If Lionheart heard her warning cry, he did not heed it as he led his men fearlessly toward Daffid's waiting army. Terror-stricken, Vanora began to tremble. The man she loved was going to die, and she could do naught about it.

"Spare him, Daffid," Vanora pleaded. "Cragdon is yours. Let that be enough."

"Lionheart cannot live if we are to wed," Daffid said. "If I spare him, we both know he will return with an army behind him."

"Think you Edward will not retaliate once he learns of Lionheart's death?"

"That might not be for a very long time. England is fighting a civil war. Edward cannot be spared to return to Wales."

Vanora's attention returned to Lionheart. His men were now fanned out behind him in a wide arc. Lionheart reined in several horse lengths from Daffid, yet still close enough to be heard.

He glanced briefly at Vanora, then returned his gaze to Daffid. "Cragdon is yours to claim, Daffid. Release Vanora."

"Fool," Daffid rasped. "I am not stupid. Where are the rest of your men? I count but twenty."

"Cragdon's Welsh knights await you within."

"They were wise not to ally themselves with Englishmen. You do know, however, that I cannot allow you to live."

"I know you are a man without honor," Lionheart replied.

"I cannot afford to let honor get in the way of what I want," Daffid stated.

He raised his hand, and immediately archers stepped forward, their bows raised and ready to loose their arrows at the unarmed Englishmen.

"Before you meet your Maker, know you that your child will die ere it draws its first breath," Daffid said. "The child will be taken from Vanora at the moment of birth and drowned."

A cry of outrage left Vanora's lips. "You are a monster, Daffid! God will punish you."

Daffid only laughed. He seemed to derive great pleasure from taunting Lionheart. At that moment, Vanora's frantic gaze fell upon Daffid's dagger. Her horse and Daffid's were very close, and no one saw her lean over and slip the dagger from its sheath. Not even Daffid suspected until Vanora grasped his neck in the crook of her arm and held the sharp edge of the dagger against his jugular.

When he started to struggle, she pressed the blade into his flesh.

"Bitch! Whore! What are you doing?"

"Order your archers to back off and lower their bows," Vanora hissed.

"You are a woman," Daffid jeered. "You will not kill me."

"You are mistaken, Daffid. I would kill to protect my husband and child. You know I am strong. If you do not do as I say, I vow I will slit your throat."

"I am your betrothed," Daffid claimed. "You owe me your loyalty."

"Lionheart is my husband, I owe *him* my loyalty."

Lionheart could not believe what was happening. What had seemed like a hopeless situation had suddenly taken an unexpected turn. He watched in growing amazement as Vanora held her advantage. God's blood, did the woman have no fear?

He started forward but reined in sharply when Daffid cried, "Come any closer and I will order my archers to loose their arrows."

"Methinks you are in no position to issue orders," Lionheart replied.

"I will take my chances with Vanora," Daffid answered.

"Obey Lionheart," Vanora advised, pressing the blade deeper into his flesh.

Daffid swallowed hard. "I would rather die than let Lionheart have you and Cragdon. There are a hundred men behind me. Think you they will let Lionheart live if you slay me?"

"Look behind you!" Lionheart shouted loud enough to be heard above the howling wind. "You are surrounded! Lay down your arms."

"You lie!" Daffid cried.

Suddenly an arrow came whizzing from behind, felling one of the archers. Confusion reigned and men scattered as more arrows hit their targets.

"Let him go, Vanora, and come to me," Lionheart called.

"Who is out there?" Daffid yelled when he saw his men break ranks and run.

"Vanora's Welsh knights and villeins armed with bows and swords," Lionheart answered.

"Stay and fight!" Daffid called to his men. "Do not run away like cowards."

Another volley of arrows emerged from

the dense veil of snow, and Vanora could now make out shapes through the thick blanket of white. Lionheart's claim seemed to be true, but Vanora could scarcely believe her villeins had taken her husband's side against their own countrymen. She could see Sir Ren's hand in this and blessed his loyalty.

"Vanora! Come to me!" Lionheart yelled as he rode forward to meet her.

Vanora was torn. If she removed the dagger from Daffid's throat, he and Lionheart would attack one another. She also knew that Lionheart's pride would suffer if she defied him. It rankled that he would not let her fight at his side, for he was well aware of her skill with a sword. Then she remembered the babe she carried, and her anger deflated. Lionheart was right. She had already endangered the precious life she carried and could not continue on this reckless bent.

At the same time that she removed the blade from Daffid's throat, she dug her heels into her horse's sides. Cursing, Daffid lunged for her reins as she flew past.

"I will kill you both for this!" Daffid screamed.

Vanora reached Lionheart safely. There

was so much she wanted to say to him, but she swallowed her words when she looked into his face. His features were set and inflexible, and his silver eyes were as dark and forbidding as the storm swirling around them.

His words were brusque, clipped. "Return to the keep, Vanora. Once you are inside, lower the portcullis. You will be safe there."

"What are you going to do?"

"Daffid cannot go unpunished."

Suddenly she became aware that Giles, who always protected Lionheart's back, was missing. "Where is Sir Giles?"

"Gone. I sent him and his lady to England, where they would be safe. No more talk, love. Do as I say. Wait for me in the keep."

Suddenly she became aware of the resounding clash of swords and realized that Lionheart's men were now engaging the remnants of Daffid's army in battle. "How did your men come by their weapons?"

"They were hidden beneath their cloaks." He withdrew his own sword and rode with grim purpose toward Daffid. "Go, love. Take care of our child," he called over his shoulder.

Her heart leapt into her mouth when she

saw Daffid riding forth to meet Lionheart. Aside from the fact that Giles was not there to protect Lionheart's back, Daffid wore armor while Lionheart did not, and the lack could be Lionheart's undoing.

Vanora could not leave. Not when Lionheart might need her. She watched in dismay as Lionheart and Daffid met amidst the pandemonium around them.

Both men had dismounted and were squaring off on the ground, their feet unsteady on the wet snow as their swords flashed silver in the receding light of the lowering sky. Vanora stifled a scream when Lionheart slid and fell, but he was up within seconds, driving Daffid back with his powerful sword arm.

A thick curtain of snow prevented Vanora from following the combatants with any degree of accuracy. Lionheart had more height than Daffid, so she kept her gaze trained on the taller of the two heads as they circled and lunged, then retreated. Her heart leapt into her mouth when Lionheart's feet again slid out from beneath him, but he quickly regained his footing and drove Daffid back with skill and dexterity.

Then Daffid fell and Lionheart pounced, pinning the Welshman to the frozen ground with the tip of his sword. What Lionheart did not see was one of Daffid's men stealthily approaching him with a dagger in his hand.

"Nay!" Vanora cried. But of course no one heard her over the din of battle. She gave her palfrey a vicious kick and tightened her hold on the reins. The animal pawed the air, then shot forward.

She reached the assailant just as he raised the dagger to drive it into Lionheart's back. She rode into him at full tilt, the impact sending him flying through the air to land with a dull thud. The ruckus brought Lionheart's head around. His expression was fierce when he saw Vanora, but he said naught. There was no need; his glowering features said it all. Ignoring his silent warning, Vanora held her ground, fully prepared to defend Lionheart's unprotected back.

"Vanora, do not let him kill me!" Daffid pleaded.

Dispassionately Vanora looked down at Daffid. "You intended to kill me, Daffid. You deserve no mercy."

"Nay. I lied," Daffid pleaded.

"You would have slain my child," Lionheart accused.

Vanora was torn. She hated Daffid for

what he'd intended to do to Lionheart and her unborn child, but did she want his death? She was so involved in the unfolding drama of life and death that she was unaware of the profound silence around them. Swords were stilled, the atmosphere was no longer charged, and men's voices were silenced.

Then she heard the thud of hooves upon the snow-packed ground and looked past Lionheart to find the source. Men on horseback, two score or more, heads bent against the wind, rode across the battlefield toward them.

" 'Tis Edward!" Vanora cried, recognizing the banner flying in the wind.

"It seems I have arrived just in time," Edward said when he reached them. "England is at peace with Wales, yet it appears a war is in progress." He glanced at Daffid, lying motionless beneath Lionheart's sword, then returned his gaze to Lionheart, one eyebrow raised.

Lionheart had just begun his explanation when Sir Giles reined in beside him. Lionheart's mouth dropped open. "Giles! I thought you were on your way to England."

"I was, until I met Lord Edward and his escort. I explained what happened, and he suggested that Deirdre and I return to Cragdon with him. That's not all, Edward brought —"

"Is that Daffid ap Deverell?" a man asked as he stepped from behind Giles.

Lionheart's surprise was profound when he saw Llewelyn, and it took a moment to find his tongue. "It is indeed," he answered. "Your countryman threatened to kill my wife. I am going to end his miserable life for his crime."

"Do not let him slay me, Llewelyn," Daffid begged. "I but wanted what should have been mine. Lionheart claimed my betrothed and left me with naught. Cragdon should be mine."

"What say you, Llewelyn? Shall Lionheart kill your countryman?" Edward asked.

Llewelyn appeared thoughtful. "My betrothal has tempered my warlike humor. I allow you have good reason, Lord Lionheart, but I beg you to spare Daffid. Since I am on my way to my home to prepare it for my bride, I will take Daffid with me. I vow he will not bother you or yours again, for I will wed him to my widowed sister."

"Nay!" Daffid protested. "I will not wed Caron. She is older than I by ten years."

Llewelyn shrugged. "If you prefer death, I am sure Lionheart will oblige."

"I like not my choices," Daffid spat. Lionheart's grin must have changed his mind, for he quickly added, "Very well, I will wed your sister, but only under protest."

Nevertheless, Lionheart was reluctant to let Daffid go. "He does not deserve to live."

Edward intervened. "Let Llewelyn deal with his countryman however he deems best," Edward advised.

With remarkable forbearance, Lionheart removed his sword from Daffid's throat.

Daffid sent Lionheart a fulminating look, then rose and picked up his sword.

"Listen well," Llewelyn roared to the remnants of Daffid's army. "Return to your wives and children. I have no argument with England at the present time." His gaze found Daffid. "Forget Cragdon, Daffid. It belongs to Lionheart through his marriage to Vanora. I will not dispute his claim to her lands."

"Wise of you," Edward said dryly. "I would invite you to spend the night at Cragdon, but it belongs to Lionheart and 'tis his place to extend the invitation."

When Lionheart remained mute, Llewelyn squinted up at the sky. "The snow seems to be thinning; my party will continue on to Draymere. Thank you for the escort, Lord Edward."

"I should have killed him," Lionheart muttered after Daffid and Llewelyn departed.

"I know you have just cause," Edward said, "but England is not ready to undertake a war with Wales. Rest assured, however, that when I am king, Wales will be brought to heel."

"What is happening in England? Was the civil war put down? What of Simon de Montfort?"

"My uncle is home, licking his wounds," Edward said, "but I am sure we have not heard the last of him. Father is too weak to hold him down for long."

Lionheart looked past Edward, his narrow-eyed gaze following the progress of Daffid's rapidly scattering army. "What brings you to Cragdon?"

"Father asked me to provide escort to Llewelyn. And," he added, "to bring someone who is most anxious to see you."

Lionheart groaned. "Not another surprise. I just rid myself of your last surprise."

"This one is —"

"Nay! It can wait until later. I will see to my wife first. My keep is open to you and your men. Accept my welcome and make yourselves comfortable."

Vanora gave a squeak of surprise when Lionheart reached out, grasped her about the waist and lifted her from her horse onto his.

"Little fool!" Lionheart raged. "Did I not tell you to return to the keep?"

"A 'thank you very much for saving my life' would suffice," Vanora replied dryly.

"You could have been hurt . . . or worse. You do not use the sense God gave you."

His jaw was clenched so hard, she feared his teeth would break. "Why are you angry? You were about to be stabbed in the back. I did not think, I simply reacted."

Lionheart withheld his reply as they rode through the portcullis. He did not stop until they reached the courtyard. Lionheart dismounted, handed the reins to a lad and hauled Vanora into his arms. He remained ominously silent as he strode with her into the keep. Mair and Father Caddoc hurried over to greet them, but Lionheart's grim expression stopped their words. He brushed past them and continued on to the solar.

Once inside their chamber, Lionheart set Vanora on her feet and slammed the door. His expression was so fierce that she backed away, fearing his anger was directed at her. She had done so many things to turn him away from her, she had expected him to abandon her to Daffid. On the other hand, he had not hurt her when he'd learned she was the White Knight, and he had been willing to give up Cragdon in exchange for her life, even if it meant losing his own in the bargain.

No man would risk so much for a woman unless . . .

He loved her.

"Little fool," he repeated. Then he hauled her into his arms and kissed her.

Chapter Twenty

"Damn you," Lionheart growled against her lips. "I thought I had lost you. I wanted to kill Daffid when Giles told me you preferred that bastard to me."

Vanora regarded him through a veil of tears. "I said that to save your life. I . . . I admit I was wrong to think I could influence Daffid. I thought I could talk him into releasing Giles and his bride, and that he would let me leave after I accomplished what I had set out to do. If I left the matter to you, I feared you would launch an attack upon Draymere and die in the attempt. Most of all, Daffid wanted you dead."

His arms tightened around her. "Think you I did not know that? I have never been so frightened in my life, or so angry when I learned what you had done. I thought you cared not for me. I was stunned and then enraged when Father Caddoc told me you were expecting my child. Why did you not tell me?"

"I was going to, but circumstances intervened." She sent him an aggrieved look.

"How could you believe I cared not for you when I told you I loved you?"

"I did not believe it possible. How could you love me? No woman has ever loved me. I am unlovable."

"Nay, Lionheart, you are everything a woman could want in a man. You are courageous, selfless, strong, honorable —"

"Cease, woman! Tell me no lies."

She stamped her foot. "Think you I would lie about something as important as love? Can you not return a small portion of my love?"

"Love does not exist. Love is . . ."

"Aye, Lionheart, I am most interested in hearing your description of love."

His expression softened as his thoughts turned inward. When he spoke, it was as if the words spilled forth from a place long dammed up inside him.

"Love is wanting — aye, a terrible wanting that churns the innards and confuses the mind. Love can hurt, especially when it is not returned."

Held in thrall by his words, Vanora said, "Go on."

"Love can unman a warrior and make him weak. Love can make a man want to protect his woman. It can drive all thought from his mind but the need to hold her close and pleasure her. Love can blind a man to what is important in life."

"What is that, Lionheart? Tell me what is more important than love?"

He sent her a wary look. "Everything is more important than love. Country, king, honor, duty."

"Aye, I understand. You love your country, your king, your honor and your duty."

"Of course. 'Tis the only kind of love that exists."

Vanora refused to accept his view. "Tell me how you feel about me. Spare not my feelings, for I would know the truth."

Reaching out, he caressed her cheek; his touch was so tender she squeezed her eyes shut to stop the tears. "Are you sure you want to know?"

She swallowed hard. "Aye."

"Very well. I want to protect you," he said solemnly. "I cannot look at you without wanting to lay you down and thrust myself inside you. I admire your courage, your strength, your honor and your loyalty. Your beauty inspires me, and despite your sharp tongue, I enjoy your company."

He paused thoughtfully before continuing. "My life would be dull without you. I was desperately unhappy when I thought you wanted Daffid." He frowned, then brightened. "I love making love to you."

Incredible joy suffused her features. "You love me, Lionheart. How can you doubt it? What you just described is exactly how I feel about you. 'Tis love, Lionheart. You are most definitely *not* unlovable, and I would challenge any woman, including your mother, who said otherwise."

The heat of his gaze slid over her with burning intensity. "I want to make love to you, my fierce vixen. My arms ache to hold you; I want to see your pleasure when I drive myself inside you and bring you to climax. I have been too long without you."

"Aye, my love. If you cannot say the words, then show me."

Sweeping her into his arms, he carried her to the bed. As he began to undress her, he scowled, as if suddenly aware of the rough clothing she wore. "What is this? Why are you dressed like a servant?"

"Daffid would not let me wear my armor. This was the best he could provide for me."

"It offends me," he said, and promptly removed the coarse tunic and shift, kissing the places where the rough wool had abraded her skin.

He loved her body, all sleek curves and smooth, feminine flesh. He ran his fingers through her hair. He loved her hair, the color of dark sable, loved the way the silky strands curled around his fingers. He loved the way she responded to him, the way she looked at him, her purple eyes dark with undisguised passion. There was naught coquettish or shy about her need for him.

He loved her courage, the way she stood up to him and refused to bend beneath his will. He loved . . .

Vanora.

His thumb moved along her jaw, and she leaned her cheek into his palm. "What are you thinking?" Vanora asked.

He did not reply. His emotions were too raw to reveal. Instead, he tilted her face up for his kiss and settled his mouth very gently over hers. He could feel her pulse beating beneath his fingers as he deepened the kiss. His own heartbeat accelerated. What if he had lost her?

He was desperate to love her, to show her how much she meant to him. He wanted her to forget whatever unpleasantness she had experienced at Daffid's hands . . . and his own.

He kissed her shoulders, lowered his head and took one of her full breasts into his mouth. The tip crested quickly, a pebbled little bud that tasted sweet against his tongue. He licked the peak and felt a little shudder go through her. Her fingers moved to his tunic, working frantically to rid him of his clothing.

Reluctantly leaving his succulent feast, Lionheart shed his mantle, tunic, chausses and boots. Then he returned to the bed, his face stark with need.

He kissed his way from her breasts to her belly, moved lower, parted her legs and tasted the tender skin on the inside of her thighs.

His hand found the soft nest of sable curls and spread her with his fingers. Then he kissed her there, his tongue parting her soft, slick folds, stroking her, devoting all his attention to the tiny feminine bud that seemed to swell beneath his probing caress. Settling his mouth over her warm, wet center, he took her with his tongue.

"Lionheart!"

Her cry spurred him as he used his mouth and tongue with consummate skill. Her body quivered, tightened. He felt the tension building within her, and the struggle to control his burgeoning passion was fierce. He did not stop. Not until she cried out in pleasure. Her release was swift and shattering, jolting her with the force of it.

Cupping her bottom, he brought her tight against his devouring mouth, holding her captive while his tongue ravished her again and again. She climaxed a second time, shaking and trembling and crying out his name.

His pulse surged. Tension coiled in his gut as he raised himself above her, his body slick and glistening with sweat. His gaze held hers as he slowly filled her with himself, slid deep inside, slid out again, then drove into her, heightening both their pleasure.

He throbbed, every part of him, from the roots of his hair to his toes. Heat flared between them as their gazes held and clung. Still he held himself back, gauging every penetration, bringing her slowly but surely back to the peak of passion, until he had her moaning beneath him, digging her nails into his shoulders, his name like a litany on her lips.

He cursed, so close to the edge he feared he would expire. "Again, sweeting," he groaned. "Come with me."

She whispered his name, then came apart. He drove into her one last time and lost himself to an all-consuming heat that scorched him from the inside out. His body clenched and convulsed as pleasure spilled through him.

"I love you, Vanora."

Vanora went still. "What did you say?"

"Aye, I love you. Only a fool could doubt it, and I am no fool."

Little by little his breathing slowed. Easing himself down beside her, he brought her into his arms and listened to the pounding of her heart, smiling when he realized his own heartbeat matched hers.

"Are you all right? I did not hurt the babe, did I?"

"Nay, we are both fine." A thoughtful pause ensued. "Tell me more about the love you just discovered. Then we will discuss the babe."

He sighed, a deep soulful sound that warmed her heart. "You were right," he admitted. "All those things I admire about you are part of something greater. 'Tis love, sweeting, I realize that now. Sometimes love cannot be explained; it can only be felt. I do love you, Vanora. You refused to give up on me, even when I decried love and declared myself unlovable."

Her eyes grew misty. "If I could teach you to love yourself, I would be the happiest of women."

"As long as you love me, 'tis all I need."
"Our child will love you."
His expression grew fierce. "And I shall love him, or her. I vow that no child of mine will ever feel unloved. My parents taught me too well how distrustful of his own worth an unloved child can become. Think you we will have a son?"
Vanora's eyes crinkled with mirth. "If not the first, then the second, or third, or . . ."
His hand flattened on her stomach. "Let us concentrate on this one before we plan others." He removed his hand and sat up. "I suppose we should go below and greet Edward properly."
"And do not forget the guest he brought with him. I wonder who it is."
"I am almost afraid to ask."
They took their time washing and dressing, then descended the stairs and entered the hall arm in arm. Servants were waiting to serve the evening meal when they reached the high table. Edward occupied the place of honor, and a handsome woman of middle years sat on his right.
"Who is the woman beside Edward?" Vanora asked quietly. "She looks vaguely familiar, but I know her not."
When Lionheart failed to reply, Vanora

glanced at him, her curiosity piqued by his perplexed expression. "Do you know her?"

"Nay," Lionheart bit out. There was an edgy wariness to his voice when he greeted Edward. "Welcome to my home, Lord Edward."

" 'Tis about time you left your bower," Edward teased. "Your lady wife's cheeks are exceedingly rosy. Am I to assume you are both happy with this marriage?"

"I am content," Lionheart said, giving Vanora's hand a squeeze.

"As I am," Vanora added.

"I hope your ordeal at Daffid's hands was not overly distressing, my lady," Edward remarked.

Lionheart answered for Vanora. " 'Twas agony, for me as well as my wife. Vanora carries my child."

The woman beside Edward clapped her hands. "Oh, how wonderful! 'Twas what I always wanted for you, Lionel."

Lionheart turned his attention to the woman. "Do I know you, madam?" he asked bluntly.

The woman choked out a sob, her expressive silver eyes bright with longing. "I had hoped . . . but it has been so long and you were just a babe."

Lionheart's fists clenched until his

knuckles turned white. "Who are you, madam?"

The woman turned away, too overcome with emotion to reply. Edward stepped into the void. "Greet your mother, Lord Lionheart. The Lady Barbara begged me to escort her to Cragdon so that she might renew your acquaintance."

Rage contorted Lionheart's face. "You are not welcome in my home, madam. Tomorrow I will provide escort back to wherever it is you came from."

He turned away, but Vanora placed herself in front of him, refusing to give way.

"Sit down, Vanora."

"Nay. Lady Barbara is your mother and you are being discourteous. Can you not see how much you have hurt her?"

"What about *my* feelings? Can you not see that it pains me to have her here?"

Lady Barbara reached out a beseeching hand. "Lionel, my son, please allow me to explain. If you still wish me to leave after you hear me out, I will gladly remove myself from your home and your life."

"I received no explanation when you abandoned me, madam. You knew what my life would be like with my father, but you cared not."

"I have heard her story, Lionheart," Edward said, "and implore you to listen. Think you I would have brought her here if I did not think reconciliation was possible?"

Lionheart gave an impatient wave of his hand. "Naught that woman has to say interests me."

"Please, Lionheart, hear her out for my sake," Vanora pleaded. "For our child's sake."

"Think you words can redeem her in my eyes?"

"Redemption is not what I seek," Lady Barbara said softly. "I but want you to know the truth."

"Why? When I was young, I yearned for a mother to love me. I was only a babe when you abandoned me."

"Lionheart, please," Vanora pleaded.

Lionheart did not want to hear anything his mother had to say, but he could not deny Vanora's request. For her sake he would listen before he sent the woman on her way.

"Very well. I will hear you out after I have supped, but do not expect sympathy, for I have none to give you."

The meal progressed amidst desultory conversation between Lionheart and Edward. Lady Barbara ate sparingly while casting surreptitious glances at her son. When Lionheart finished his meal, he rose abruptly and asked Edward's leave to retire. Once it was granted, Lionheart invited Vanora and Lady Barbara to join him and stormed from the hall without looking back to see if the women were following.

Lionheart entered the solar and strode to the hearth, staring into the dancing flames. When he heard the ladies enter behind him, his fists clenched at his sides, his white knuckles the only sign of his anguish. Taking a calming breath, he turned to confront his mother.

"Sit down," he bit out. Both ladies obeyed instantly.

He turned back to stare into the fire, seeing naught but the blood red of the flames. The silence in the chamber was profound, broken only by the crackle of a splitting log in the hearth and the breathing of the women seated before it.

He turned abruptly, staring directly at his mother, startled to see his silver eyes reflected in hers.

"How do I know you are my mother?" he barked.

A wave of pain passed over Lady Barbara's features, and Lionheart hardened his heart, refusing to feel any filial sympathy.

"Friends in London will vouch for my identity should you demand it."

Lionheart knew he would not demand it, for he could see himself in her.

"Lionheart, you said you would listen to what Lady Barbara has to say," Vanora reminded him.

He returned his gaze to his mother, who sat rigid and motionless, her hands folded in her lap. "Very well, Lady Barbara, for my wife's sake, I will hear you out. Please proceed."

Lady Barbara sent Vanora a tremulous smile. "Thank you." When she returned her gaze to Lionheart, her eyes were shimmering with unshed tears.

"I never wanted to leave you, my son. Your father cast me from your life and told me if I tried to see you, he would slay both of us. I believed him. I feared for your life; my own was unimportant. Robert was a vicious man. But a day did not go by that I did not yearn for you. 'Twas only after Robert's death that I was able to return to London without fear of reprisal. My first thought was of you and my desperate need to see you again. I sought out Lord Edward and begged him to bring me to you."

Lionheart's disbelief was etched on his

glowering features. "If what you say is the truth, 'tis likely my father had good reason to cast you from our lives."

"Was he a good father to you, Lionel? I cannot imagine it, for he was the worst kind of husband to me, though he doubtless turned you against me before you could walk. Before he cast me out, he beat me so badly the nuns at the convent I joined feared I would die of my injuries."

The first stirrings of doubt assailed him. "Father said you took a lover and abandoned us."

Lady Barbara gave him a sad smile. "There was no lover. Your father said what he wished everyone to believe."

"Why did Father cast you out? He must have had good reason."

"It shames me to tell you what really happened."

Vanora clutched Lady Barbara's hand, giving it a squeeze of encouragement.

"Speak freely," Lionheart said. "I can think no less of you than I do now."

"Your father was as deeply in debt back then as he was when he died. He sold everything, leaving you naught but your name. He turned to King Henry for support, becoming one of his courtiers, accepting whatever crumbs the king doled out. But it was not enough to support his extravagant way of life."

Vanora must have noted how hoarse her voice had become, for she poured a goblet of wine and handed it to the older woman. Lady Barbara took a sip, then continued.

"You may find this hard to believe, son, but I swear 'tis the truth. You were but a year old when your father sought to . . . sell my services to his friends. He thought it a perfect solution to his lack of funds."

Somehow Lionheart could believe it of his father. "Continue."

"I refused, of course, but your father was adamant. One night he locked me in my chamber and sent up a man who had paid him to . . . to use me."

She began to weep softly, without making a sound. The silent tears coursing down her cheeks affected Lionheart more deeply than her words.

"What happened?"

"I fought when he tried to force me. I fought for my honor, my pride, for my very life. I . . . hit the man with a poker, and at first I thought I had killed him."

The tears kept falling. She dug into her sleeve for a handkerchief and fought for control. "When your father learned what I had done, he realized I would not be so easily managed and beat me senseless. I awakened in a convent without any memory of what had transpired. The first years were easy, for I knew not who I was and prayer seemed to bring me solace.

"But as the days and weeks passed, I felt as if something was missing from my life. Two years later my memory returned, and I tried to leave to find you. Apparently, the abbess informed your father of my recovery, for he visited me at the convent and threatened to kill you should I attempt to see you or report what had been done to me. You see," she whispered, "he had already spread the story that I had fled with a lover."

"How tragic," Vanora whispered.

"Since I had nowhere to go, I remained at the convent until the abbess informed me that Sir Robert de Couer was dead. Free at last, I contacted friends I had not seen in years. They gave me funds to travel to England to find you. Naught in my life was more important than finding my son and making amends."

Lionheart said naught as he regarded his mother through shuttered lids. "You must have feared Father greatly."

"Have I disillusioned you, my son? Did you love your father?"

"I hated him," Lionheart said darkly. "He was no father to me. I saw him infrequently after I was fostered, and not at all after I earned my spurs."

Lady Barbara seemed to breathe easier after Lionheart's admission, but she appeared small and fragile and pathetic beneath the weight of her sad memories.

She arose with effort, seeming older than her years. Her eyes were riveted on Lionheart's face, as if memorizing his features. "You are more handsome than I imagined, everything a mother could want in a son. Thank you for hearing me out."

"Where are you going?" Lionheart asked.

"To the chapel. I want to thank God for giving me a son who rose above his father's cruelty to become the man you are today." She smiled at Vanora. "You are just the kind of woman I always wished for my son. Tell my grandchildren I shall love them just as I have loved their father all these years."

"You may tell them yourself . . . Mother," Lionheart said.

"Thank you, Lionheart," Vanora said quietly.

Incredible joy suffused Lady Barbara's face. "Oh, my son, I have been praying for this day. Not one moment passed during the last twenty-five years that I did not yearn for your love, wondering what kind of man you had become under your father's tutelage. I thank God for guiding you over the years, and for giving you Vanora to love." She sent him a shy smile. "May I hug you?"

Lionheart opened his arms, and his mother walked into them. They remained thus for a long time, until they regained their composure.

"You are welcome to stay as long as you like, Mother," Lionheart said. "I am sure Vanora will be glad for your company."

"It will please me to have you on hand to welcome your first grandchild into the world," Vanora said.

"Aye, I will stay, but only until your child arrives. After that, I will make do with occasional visits. I do not want to interfere in your lives. 'Tis enough to know that my son has accepted me into his life again. Now if you will excuse me, I still intend to visit the chapel. Nearly a lifetime of prayer is a difficult habit to break."

After Lady Barbara took her leave, Vanora flew into Lionheart's arms. "You have made two women very, very happy. I am so proud of you, Lionheart. It took courage to admit you were mistaken about the woman who birthed you. Your mother was an innocent victim of your father's cruelty, but you suffered as well."

"The suffering was naught compared to how I felt when I thought I had lost you to Daffid, or when I realized you were the White Knight and how close I came to killing you. That was true suffering. I love you with my whole heart, vixen."

Vanora gave him a blissful smile. "Like your name, you possess the heart of a lion, but even lions love. Take me to bed, Lionheart. Hold me and never let me go."

Epilogue

The day Vanora and Lionheart's son was baptized was as fine a summer morning as anyone had ever seen. The beaming parents stood before the baptismal font in the chapel, Vanora tenderly cradling the babe in her arms as Father Caddoc poured water over the tiny infant's head. A misty-eyed Lady Barbara stood behind the proud couple, her happiness reflected in her glistening silver eyes.

Prince Edward and his bride, Eleanor, flanked the new parents, standing as godparents to the four-week-old Edward Lionel de Couer. The servants and crofters craned their necks for their first view of the future Lord of Cragdon, magnificently garbed in white satin robes that covered his tiny form from neck to toe.

Little Lord Edward protested loudly as water spilled over his forehead but settled down when his adoring father took him from his mother and rocked him gently in his arms. After the brief ceremony, the celebration spilled outside into the warm summer sunshine, where tables of food and drink had been set up in the courtyard to accommodate the guests.

Lady Barbara followed Vanora to a bench in a shady nook and sat down beside her. "I cannot recall ever being this happy," Barbara said, "unless it was the day Lionel was born." She sighed. "But alas, we were too soon parted. The months I spent with you and my son have made up for all those years of separation."

Vanora glanced over at Lionheart, who was showing off his son to Edward and Eleanor. "You sound as if you intend to leave us."

"Aye, 'tis time I returned to England. You and Lionheart must live your own lives, with no interference from a doting mother and grandmother. I asked for Edward's escort back to England when he returns."

"I will be sad to see you leave," Vanora said, meaning every word. "Can I not persuade you to stay a little longer?"

"Are you planning to leave us, Mother?"

Lady Barbara smiled up at Lionheart. "I did not hear you approach."

Lionheart handed the babe to Vanora. "The babe was beginning to fuss. I think he is hungry. I heard you say you were leaving, Mother. Where will you go? Do you have sufficient funds to provide for yourself?"

Barbara flushed and looked away. "I intend to appeal to the king. He was always generous with your father. Mayhap his generosity will extend to me."

"I cannot allow it," Lionheart said. "If you insist on returning to England, I will see to your support. But both Vanora and I want you to remain at Cragdon. Your grandson has need of a grandmother to spoil him."

A tear leaked from Barbara's eye. "You truly want me to remain?"

"Aye. 'Tis lonely here for Vanora. Except for Sir Giles, none of my knights are wed, and I'm sure Lady Deirdre can use your wise counsel, for she is expecting her first child."

"If you really want me —"

"We do," Vanora said, quick to echo Lionheart's words. She handed the babe to his grandmother. "Would you take him inside and ask Mair to put him in dry swaddling? Tell her I shall be up directly to feed him."

"I shall change his swaddling myself," Barbara said.

"That was kind of you," Vanora said

once Barbara had left. "Have you forgiven your mother?"

"How could I not? She was as much a victim as I. If I ever become like my father, don your armor and take your sword to me."

She sent him a cocky grin. "I doubt that will ever happen, but I shall keep my sword handy just in case."

"It could have happened had you not showed me how to love. Without you to point out the error of my ways, I would have condemned my mother out of hand when she arrived and lost the opportunity to learn the truth and get to know her."

"Have you learned to love her?"

"Aye, I have."

Vanora beamed happily. "I am pleased you asked Lady Barbara to stay. I want her on hand to greet each and every one of our children when he or she comes into this world."

Lionheart's eyes darkened. "I feared the pain of birthing our son was so great you would not want another."

"Mair said the birth was easier than most she has attended. Birthing pains, no matter how severe, are quickly forgotten. If God so wills, we will have other children to love, Lionheart."

"As we will love each other. There may be times I will have to go off to fight, but I will always return to you."

Lionheart's promise was tested when Edward summoned him to help defeat Simon de Montfort in 1265 at Evesham in a battle that led to Simon's death. Lionheart returned home in time to welcome his fourth and last child and only daughter into the world.

The employees of Thorndike Press hope you have enjoyed this Large Print book. All our Thorndike and Wheeler Large Print titles are designed for easy reading, and all our books are made to last. Other Thorndike Press Large Print books are available at your library, through selected bookstores, or directly from us.

For information about titles, please call:

(800) 223-1244

or visit our Web site at:

www.gale.com/thorndike
www.gale.com/wheeler

To share your comments, please write:

Publisher
Thorndike Press
295 Kennedy Memorial Drive
Waterville, ME 04901